I0772334

THE GAP YEAR

THE GAP YEAR

WADE WALKER

First edition: July 2023
Hardcover ISBN: 979-8-9885654-0-6
Paperback ISBN: 979-8-9885654-1-3
eBook ISBN: 979-8-9885654-2-0

Cover illustration by Fernanda Suarez

Book cover and layout design by *the*BookDesigners

To my moms, who taught me to love these books

And to my wife, who always believed

1

Anna was reasonably sure her father wasn't going to kill her before lunch. *But we'll just have to see how things go.*

It was a summer Tuesday morning, two weeks after her high school graduation, and Anna Reyes was staring at the email that could wreck her whole future. The words "Entrance examination results…" were all that fit in the little popup on her phone's lock screen. But that was enough to set her hand shaking as she fumbled her phone up from the bathroom counter and touched the interface ring around its edge. She set her still-running hair dryer down with the other hand as the phone linked up with her tiny neural implant.

Alixa? Can you summarize it, please? Anna's stomach was plummeting in sick premonition, and she couldn't bear the long seconds it would take to read through the email herself.

Your weighted score was eighty-seven percent. Her phone's neural net spoke the crushing words soundlessly into her mind. *Your raw score was sixty-three out of one hundred.*

Her hair dryer whirred to itself on the counter, forgotten, as her mind raced back over what Alixa had told her, trying to undo what she'd heard.

She was leaving in less than fifteen minutes to meet her celebrity-physicist father Mateo Reyes in Austin. She was starting her own physics degree at the University of Texas in the fall, as an incoming fellowship student in her father's research group. Expectations were always high for fellowship students, and her being named Reyes sent them higher still. So she and her father were going to plan out her summer self-study program, to make sure she'd crush it. And then they'd have a nice lunch.

Only now, none of that's going to happen.

Anna set down her phone, stunned. Her hands picked the hair dryer and brush back up, distractedly resuming the routine of taming her dark, unruly hair. Her fellowship required a weighted score of at least ninety percent, no exceptions. And without that fellowship, there was no way her father was going to try to shoehorn his very-smart-but-apparently-not-quite-brilliant daughter in among his award-winning graduate students and famous colleagues.

Alixa, what was the breakdown? As if it mattered.

You scored very well on the computational and visualization portions of the test, her phone said to her over their mental link. *Your only lagging score was in manual symbolic manipulation.*

Of course it was. Anna closed her eyes with a groan. Symbolic had always been her weakest area, but she'd thought she had finally brought it up to scratch. *How much longer until the car gets here?*

Your pickup time is in thirteen minutes. Alixa paused. *Do you wish to cancel?*

For a long moment, Anna thought about it. It would be so easy to just bail, for once. Make her apologies to her dad. Pick something easier to do with her life?

No. She met her own eyes in the mirror. *No way.*

It seemed like she'd spent her whole life studying, doubling and tripling down at every setback. Skipping parties, hangouts, friendships. If she gave up now, all that sacrifice would be wasted.

I'm doing this. I just don't know how yet.

She turned off the hair dryer and put it away, her decision solidifying. Getting to Austin would take the better part of an hour. So she'd have to figure out some kind of plan before she got there.

Back in her bedroom, she quickly pulled on a plain gray T-shirt from a monochrome row of similar shirts in her closet, then added shorts and sneakers, practical choices for the late-May Texas sun. She paused halfway out the door, frowning as damp hair brushed her neck.

Ugh. There was a wet patch in the back that she must have missed. Anna raked at it with her fingers, then gave up. *It'll have to dry on the way.*

She hustled down the half-flight of stairs to the kitchen. Her mother Helena sat on a stool at the counter, sipping her coffee as she pored over dense legal text on her tablet.

"Morning, sweetie!" Her mother's smile faded into concern. "Aren't you cutting things a little close for your meeting with your father today?"

Anna tried to plaster a carefree expression over her inner turmoil. "Eh, I've still got…" She checked her phone. "Eight whole minutes!" She thumbed the screen as she looked up, hiding the email about her exam results. She could discuss those with her mother if she survived the morning.

"You know how your father packs his schedule." Her mother's expression was as neutral as her tone. "If you miss it, you might not get another chance for a month."

"No worries, Mom." Anna tapped her usual breakfast order on her phone's screen, the gestures so quick that she'd already finished and dropped the phone on the counter before she could've asked for it mentally. "I've got this."

Almost immediately, the kitchen fab above the stove went *ding!* and a bagel appeared behind the window in the fab's front door. Anna pulled the door open, grabbed the warm, newly made bagel, split it expertly with a table knife, and popped it into her dad's old antique toaster.

Her mother rolled her eyes in amusement. "You know fabs can make those pre-toasted, right? Pre-buttered, even?"

Anna smiled back, their well-worn shared joke making her forget her dire situation for a moment. "Admit it. They smell way better when you toast them by hand." She nodded toward her mother's tablet. "How're the votes looking on your bill?" She grinned. "Any last-minute blackmail letters you need me to drop off in Austin?"

"Not today, at least." Her mother's smile turned wry. "It's all over the news this morning. Every state's legislative calendar is on hold. They're waiting for some closed-door special session in Washington, D.C., to finish so they can all take some kind of emergency vote. They're being *very* secretive about the reason, but I'm sure it's not to fast-track one environmental lobbyist's boring amphibian diversity bill."

Anna snatched her bagel out of the toaster just before it began to char, buttered it with a few swipes of the knife, and began wolfing it down, alternating bagel bites with swigs of iced tea from a bottle she'd fabbed while the bagel was toasting. Her mother raised an eyebrow.

"Ahm layh, emembuh?" Anna said with her mouth full.

Her phone buzzed on the countertop. *Pickup in two minutes,* the screen said. *Destination, the University of Texas at Austin, Archibald Wheeler Hall.*

Anna's appetite shriveled, her stress about the upcoming meeting with her father closing back in. Wheeler Hall was the building where her father had worked for as long as she could remember. Ever since middle school, she'd daydreamed about all the great scientific discoveries they'd make together once she finally joined him there. Now that dream was coming apart right in front of her, and she had less than an hour to figure out how to pull it back together. She chewed the last of her bagel glumly as she stood up and pocketed her phone.

"Say hello to your father for me." Her mother's smile was a fraction less than full. Her parents' divorce had been sticky, though they had tried not to let it affect their only child.

"I will, Mom." Anna hugged her mother briefly, but hard. Then her phone vibrated in her pocket just as she saw the car through the front windows, coming down to land gently in the yard. She squeezed her mother one last time, then broke the hug and ran out the front door, waving as she closed it behind her.

The car waited in the front yard, its bulbous yellow body hovering low on four glowing blue repellers, hemmed in amid spiky juniper bushes and paddle-shaped prickly pear cacti. Anna rushed down the porch steps and reached for the car's door handle, anxious to be away.

Then she paused, looking behind her at a brown beetle trapped on its back on the smooth path, six legs waving helplessly in the air. It was a common sight this time of year, one that she normally didn't just walk past.

This time she wavered. *Less than an hour! And what's one beetle, more or less?*

But finally, she dropped her hand with a sigh. She walked back to the struggling insect, then nudged it carefully out into the yard with one foot.

We've gotta put out there what we want to get back. She gave the beetle an ironic wave after it righted itself and crawled away into the grass. *At least* somebody *gets a lucky break today.*

She ran back to the waiting car and jumped in, settling uneasily into its deep single seat as it rose smoothly into the sky above the El Paso suburbs. The narrow Rio Grande glinted off in the distance, and the dry olive-green and brown landscape flashed by below as the car climbed, leveled off, and surged east.

In this part of west Texas, you could still see the scars of long-gone oil fields, small white squares connected by long straight lines etched into the rocky soil. In her grandparents' time they'd still been recognizable as old-fashioned ground roads, but now they were just whitish streaks cutting through the grass and scrub. Even the mighty roadbed where the old Interstate 10 had run was little more than a long hump that notched the limestone hills here and there.

Okay, let's work through this. Anna struggled to guide her circling thoughts into some coherent plan. *I missed the ninety percent cutoff on the entrance exam. So my application for the fellowship that dad's sponsoring me for will be denied. Which means I probably won't be accepted into the honors physics program, either.* She bounced one leg on the car seat as she thought. *I guess I could apply for normal admission. That'd put me in the right college, at least.* Her heart sank at the idea. *Then I could spend my first six months really sweating my symbolic manipulation, then re-take the exam and place into honors the hard way. Yay?*

But even if that worked, would she fit in afterward? She'd met some of her father's students. None of them seemed like they even knew what a remedial course was. They were curve wreckers, not test re-takers. *And would Dad even be able to sponsor me a second time? Isn't that nepotism or something?* She wasn't sure what the university's rules were, but handing out second chances to your own children sounded pretty questionable.

Then a horrible thought struck her. *Dad probably doesn't even know that the exam results came back later than usual this year. What if he thinks I've known about my score for weeks, and I've been trying to hide it somehow?*

She groaned, frustrated, and unthinkingly opened her social media feed to distract herself, flicking through it using her phone's mental link and touchscreen at the same time. She skimmed a story about that congressional emergency thing her mom had mentioned at breakfast, but it was all just speculation. Her mom would be itching to dish the inside story for her later, anyway. She skipped over a few more posts before her eyes caught on a headline that screamed, "Shocking rumors from Hawaiian telescope facility!"

Must be something from Dad's feed. She made an amused face. *I thought scientists didn't do clickbait. How shocking could a telescope possibly—*

She yanked herself back to the present, slapping the phone face-down onto the seat beside her to hide the screen. *Get it together, Anna. You've got less than...* She flipped the phone back over to check, then put it face-down again. *Forty minutes now, to think of how—*

Her phone vibrated under her palm, the sound dull against the seat. She flipped it warily, thinking it might be some social media notification come to suck her back in, but it was her mom calling.

Crap. Her mom's profile picture looked up at her from the screen, surrounded by a whimsical border of tree frogs and horned lizards. *I don't have time for this!* The phone buzzed in her hand, insistent.

Anna squeezed her eyes shut briefly. Then she took the call, transferring it to the car's big screen as she dragged her happy face on again. Her mother's face appeared, life-sized but from an odd angle since she was calling from her reading tablet in the kitchen.

"One more thing, sweetie." Her mother's face was kind. "You were in such a hurry, I didn't get the chance to ask about it before you left." She raised her tablet to look into the camera squarely. "Did you ever get your entrance exam results back?"

Anna froze, trying to hide her panic, heart thudding in her chest.

Her mom was still talking. "I remember you saying that the results were late." She looked at Anna through the camera, concern plain on her face. "And you've been so worried about them."

"Yeah, um." Anna managed to get her voice working. "Yeah, they're really late this year but..." She groped for something true but misleading. "There's no point in me freaking out until after they come in."

"You know I'll love you just the same, no matter what." Her mom smiled. "But I'm not worried. You studied your heart out for that exam. You're going to show your father more than he ever expected."

Anna felt that one in her gut. "But…" She hesitated, wondering how far she could go without confessing everything. "What if I don't make the cut?" She spoke quickly to cut off her mother's interjection. "I know I'm not going to fail or anything. But what if I… fall a little short?"

"I know what kind of daughter I have." Anna's mother laughed, and the confidence in that sound filled Anna with gratitude. "You're not the kind that falls short. And even if you did…" Her mother shrugged, smiling. "It's not like your father would kill you or anything. You two would work it through somehow."

Anna winced as her mother unknowingly echoed her own morbid thoughts of earlier that morning. "Any ideas on how to do that?" She pushed it as far as she dared. "Just in case?"

"Play to his ego." Her mother's face took on a shrewd edge as she turned her voice cartoonishly girlish. "'I'm so sorry, Daddy. I didn't realize how hard your career really is. I should've taken your advice more seriously.' Get him to help you plan a gap year of studying, then shoot for next year." She smirked. "And you can study just as easily in Rome or Tokyo as you could here, so it doesn't have to be all work and no play. What he doesn't know won't hurt him."

Anna's mouth hung slack, and her mother laughed again. "You're welcome. I did learn a few things from being married to the man for thirteen years."

That would *be a lot nicer than piling exam study on top of all my freshman weed-out classes.* But every scrap of Anna's pride rebelled at the thought of taking her failure and turning it into an excuse for a year abroad. *It wouldn't feel right. I need to* deserve *it!*

"Thanks, Mom." She gave an appreciative smile before she remembered this was all supposed to be hypothetical. "Hopefully it won't come to that, though." She checked the time. *Crap, only ten minutes left until I land!*

"Hey, let me let you go." She tried not to look as hurried as she felt. "I still need to go over some of the stuff Dad and I are talking about, and I'm almost there."

"Sure honey, take care." Her mom gave her a significant look. "And don't worry. If you focus on what your heart really wants, the rest will sort itself out."

Her mother cut the connection, and Anna slumped back in her seat. She checked the time again: eight more minutes. *Well, there's probably not that much more to think about anyway, except—*

Her phone buzzed with a text. Her eyes flicked over the details: her friend Susan, pool-side cookout next week, barbeque ribs, don't dress like a nerd because that guy you like will be there... She jerked herself away, dismissing the notification. *I'll text back later. I've still got a few more minutes left to—*

Anna's phone buzzed yet again, and she felt her throat tighten as her father's icon popped up on the screen. *No!* She quashed a resurgence of panic. *I'm not ready yet!* But then she felt a new resolve forming. Things would work out, or they wouldn't, but it was time to get this over with.

She took a deep breath and accepted the call, this time on her phone's display instead of the car's. For a conversation like this, she needed every advantage she could get.

"Anna?" her father said. "I'm sorry, but there's been a change of plan."

"Wait. A change?" Anna was off-balance already. "What kind of change?"

"I got called out to Washington, D.C., on short notice yesterday. I can't get back to Austin until early this evening." Her dad's normally handsome face looked puffy and shiny on her phone's small screen. "Some military VIPs tapped me as a subject-matter expert for a closed-door congressional hearing that started this morning. I was up all last night preparing."

Weird, Anna thought. *That's gotta be the same thing Mom was talking about. What are the chances?*

Her father rubbed his forehead and frowned distractedly. "A disturbing topic, too. I was so caught up I didn't even think to message you. But I should be done here in an hour, so I'll still be there in time for dinner. In the meantime, I asked Indy to show you around the new lab and take you to lunch since I can't make it. You remember her, right? From when you came down last December?"

Indiana Fuller was one of her father's postdoctoral students, and co-author of several of his more recent scientific papers. Anna had talked to her once or twice, most recently at a Christmas party at her father's house out in the hill country west of Austin. Indiana had come across as intimidatingly smart and sophisticated, even though she'd probably been trying to reach out and put Anna at ease. But honestly Anna had spent more time that night raiding the buffet and talking to Susan, who she'd brought along for company, than she had socializing with her dad's students and colleagues.

"Yeah, I remember her," Anna said. "She seemed nice. Really knew how to punish a roast turkey." Anna paused, her guilty secret forgotten for a moment. "Is everything okay, Dad? You look a little *weird*, somehow." She looked more closely at her father's face on the phone screen, but couldn't tell if he was just tired, or something else.

"I'm fine." Her father frowned down at something out of view of his phone's camera. "We had some unexpected data come in from the new instrument at the Mauna Kea observatory."

"Oh hey, I think I saw that story in your feed earlier," Anna said. "What's *that* about?"

"I can't go into the details." He ran a hand through his short, dark hair. "Some congressman's aide heard something he shouldn't have through a back channel. Then instead of asking an expert to explain it, he repeated some garbled version to his boss, who called an emergency session to yammer about possible government responses. I'm not sure how much has been leaked to the media at this point, but your mother could probably tell you. A lot of state legislatures are standing by to put in their two cents afterward." He looked down, annoyed. "Politicians. Those idiots are always getting worked up about things they don't understand. I'll try to talk some sense into them face to face when I go on in a few minutes."

Anna settled herself mentally, then launched into her confession. "So, Dad, there was something I wanted to—"

"I'm sorry Anna, but I really need to run." He smiled, distracted but reassuring. "We'll talk at dinner, and get everything planned out."

"But, it'll just—"

The mute icon lit as her father said something to somebody offscreen, then disappeared again. "Sorry Anna, but this time it's really urgent. See you soon?"

Anna nodded, biting down on her disappointment. "Sounds good, Dad. See you in a little while."

She hung up on an already blank screen, then exhaled heavily. *Hooray, now I can keep worrying about this until dinnertime!* Her heart sank as she slapped her phone down on the seat beside her.

Anna felt the car begin to descend into Austin and leaned closer to the window to watch. She'd always loved how the land folded up into forested limestone hills, thickly covered with live oak, mesquite, and mountain laurel. The scrubby treescape extended great wedges into the very center of Austin, where hundred-story skyscrapers shared space with gnarled centuries-old oak trees and the winding Colorado River.

The University of Texas campus was a rare island of twentieth-century style in the midst of modern buildings and wildlife preserve, still occupying its original forty acres north of the ancient gold-domed capitol building. Its only concessions to modern urban planning were the occasional block of greenery where old infrastructure like cooling towers had been demolished and replanted as parkland, and the fact that the old ground roads had been ripped up and replaced with tree-lined malls.

As the car set down gracefully beside Wheeler Hall, Anna collected her phone and quickly scanned the cabin to make sure she hadn't left anything. Then she stepped out into the humid Austin air, dismissed the car with a wave, and tried to put on a brave face for anyone who might be watching for her.

Keep it together, Anna. Just wait a few more hours, make your apologies, and your life will be back on track.

3

Anna looked around, squinting against the glare, then shielded her eyes and walked over into the shade of one of the campus's ancient live oak trees while she waited for her vision to adjust. The Austin sun was already fierce, and it was still an hour before noon.

After a tense minute or so, she still didn't see anyone waiting for her outside Wheeler Hall or on the sidewalk nearby. Which was a good sign. *At least I'm not late!* A few students dotted the walkways, but the campus was quiet during the summer, and Anna had the tree to herself except for a fat brown squirrel on the thick branch above her.

She left the shade of her tree and walked through the tinted glass doors of the white limestone physics building, then up a short flight of stairs to the elevator lobby. She'd been here before and was apparently still cleared for entry, since the doors had recognized her and opened at her approach.

Just as Anna realized that she had forgotten to ask her dad where his new lab was, an elevator dinged open nearby, and a huge black-and-white border collie hybrid trotted out.

"Anna! Welcome back to Austin. Your dad's so sorry he couldn't make it." Indiana's voice came from a speaker in her matte silver collar instead of from her grinning doggy jaws, but it sounded exactly like you'd expect a twenty-something female human post-doctoral student to sound.

"Hey, Indiana. Nice to see you again." Anna was a little self-conscious, since she'd only said a few words to Indiana around the edges of mostly-adult conversations that didn't really include her. Plus, even here in the state capital, students like Indiana were a rare sight. *Poker face, Anna. Don't gawk like you've never been to the big city before.*

As a genetically engineered hybrid canine, Indiana was considerably bigger than a normal dog, maybe 170 pounds of sleek muscle and fur. Her coat was shiny black, with a white blaze on her muzzle and forehead, and white socks running up her forelegs and onto her deep chest. Her heavy toenails clicked on the pink granite floor of Wheeler Hall's lobby. Anna noticed that those toenails were painted a bright, sparkly pink, and she raised a mental eyebrow.

"Please, call me Indy." The big canine spoke with a glint in her light-brown eyes. "I'm sorry Professor Reyes couldn't be here. He just called me ten minutes ago. Lucky for him, I'm always in the lab! Life of a postdoc, you know."

Anna nodded as if she understood completely. *Yep, life of a postdoc! We all know how* that *goes.* Anna had always loved science, but the idea of graduating from college, and then college again *two more times* to get a Ph.D., and then *staying* at college to work for your professor afterward, probably seemed pretty insane to any normal person.

Anna fell into step as Indy led the way back into the elevator. On the short ride up, she resisted the urge to ruffle the glossy black fur of Indy's neck, then resisted the subsequent urge to ask if she could. *You wouldn't ask to pet another human's hair, would you?* Her family had always had dogs—the normal, smaller kind—but now didn't seem like a good time to mention it. *Don't make things weird, Anna.*

The elevator doors slid open, and Anna and Indy stepped out onto the tenth floor.

"Ooo, this is new." Anna looked down the hallway, which glowed with natural light from large windows in the elevator lobbies at either end. The last time she'd visited her dad's lab, back before Christmas, it had been in the second sub-basement or something. It was still a science building though, so everything smelled faintly of burnt plastic, dust, and desperate studying.

At regular intervals along the right side of the hallway, thick metal conduits snaked up out of the floor and disappeared into ports cut low into the wall. Indy stopped halfway down at a solid-looking metal door and smiled back at Anna, casually flashing a set of teeth big enough to frighten a buffalo.

Cool blue and yellow lights winked minutely on Indy's collar and the shiny metal door slid open, revealing a cluttered laboratory space beyond. Indy walked in slowly, tail waving as she threaded between lab benches and equipment. She headed for the back of the room, where dim yellow light shone from tall racks stuffed full of devices that Anna couldn't identify.

"Sorry it's such a jumble in here," Indy said as she walked. "We just got everything working again after the move, but it's not very pretty yet." She stopped in front of a set of six metallic pillars that jutted up around the edge of a circular platform maybe five feet across, like a miniature techie Stonehenge on a low, round stage. The big cables that came in through the hallway wall cut parallel tracks under and through the clutter before plugging in around the edges of the platform, terminating in heavy black connectors.

"Well, here it is!" Indy looked at Anna expectantly, ears pricked up. "What do you think?"

"Wait, here *what* is?" Anna looked around. "You mean the henge?" Indy looked blank, so Anna elaborated. "This round, druid altar thing?"

Indy brightened. "Ha! Like Stonehenge! Somehow I never made that connection." She nodded toward the platform. "I forgot that the last time you came, you had to look through that tiny viewport into our old closed field chamber." She paced over to a console and sent commands from her collar that brought it glowing to life. "We've figured out how to stabilize a much larger field since then. Now it's a free-space bubble that's confined by these six wave-guides. The pillars," she clarified, when Anna still looked confused. "It'll appear inside the ring of pillars, floating above the platform. Hang on, it'll make sense when you see it."

Indy mentally tweaked the controls, collar lights blinking, then turned to face the platform. In the center of the henge, the air brightened and grew hazy. "I'll bring up my favorite scene," Indy said as her collar blinked out a final sequence. "It takes a lot of energy, but it's more fun than what your dad wanted me to show you."

Above the platform, the light of a sunny afternoon suddenly shone forth, giving a view onto a mountain hillside. Brownish-white sheep grazed in clumps scattered here and there, cropping grass amid white-petaled flowers, below peaks heavily forested with short pine trees. It was like looking through a window in mid-air that opened down onto another world, and the sun was bright enough to make Anna squint.

"Ancient Greece, as it was 2800 years ago, so a little after 500 BC." Indy smiled widely, panting in amusement as she watched Anna's face. "We're looking at a spot about sixty miles northwest of Athens. On a Thursday, by the Julian calendar. Local time, three in the afternoon."

"Wow." Anna stood for a moment, stunned. "Wow! Last time, it just looked like a dim picture behind a window. Is this really real now?"

"It was real before, too." Indy's face showed what could only be a look of canine smugness. "But back then, we could only form a field bubble in a vacuum chamber behind that reinforced viewport, and you could hardly see anything because we couldn't get the optical gain high enough. Now you can walk all the way around it, with parallax and everything. Watch this."

Indy began a slow circuit of the platform, and Anna followed, staring raptly into the bubble. The view changed as they walked, like they were looking into a cylinder chopped out of another reality and fenced in behind the pillars. On the Greek mountainside nearby, a large falcon-like bird took flight, suddenly huge as it soared off past the edge of the bubble. The scene was eerily quiet, though, as if sound couldn't escape the same way light did.

"You probably shouldn't do that." Indy stopped Anna's hand with a surprisingly rough paw pad where she'd reached out unconsciously toward the bubble. "You can wave a stick right through it with no problem, and we don't *think* it would have any ill effect on you. But this is all new territory, scientifically speaking." Indy's voice turned wry. "I don't want to have to explain to your dad if you pull your hand back and now it's a giant bird claw or something."

Then the big hybrid looked at her more seriously. "Back in the early nineteen-hundreds, X-ray scientists used to show off by waving their hands around in the beam to cast the shadow of their bones on a glowing screen. But after a few years of that, so many of them had lost fingers to radiation damage that they couldn't serve roast chicken at professional dinners anymore. Too many colleagues would fumble their knives and forks! So we're trying to play it safer."

"So wait." Anna was still trying to grasp what she was seeing. "Could you just, like, walk into this thing? Like a wormhole in time or something?"

"No, nothing like that." Indy's collar-voice was dismissive. "You could walk into the field bubble itself, sure, now that it's not in a vacuum chamber anymore. But all our theoretical models say that we can't affect the past, though there's still a lot of experimental testing to do. We're cloning the quantum states of photons from the past, which lets us see what you would have seen back then, but it's a one-way street. Otherwise, it'd be a paradox! Like a movie where you go back in time, ruin your parents' first date and undo your own conception."

Indy grinned impishly at the thought, and her collar lights flashed with more commands. "Let me show you my favorite thing so far." The bubble's viewpoint zoomed down the mountainside from the biggest group of sheep, coming to rest near a spreading tree. Beneath it, a boy lay sleeping, clad in a grubby white tunic belted at the waist. And near *him* lay two shaggy black herding dogs, at ease but with watchful eyes tracking the nearby flock.

"Look at *those* fine specimens!" Indy gestured with her nose. "They could be my distant relatives! Just don't tell my granddam I said so. She always swears we're one hundred percent, never-domesticated wolf on her side, but I've got my doubts." Her canine face grew pensive. "Next semester, we'll have the energy budget to start looking around more, so I signed up for a classical civ course to help understand what we'll be seeing. Your father's been concentrating on the recent past, since we can keep the portal open a lot longer that way. But honestly, that's kind of boring. If I want to see what three hundred years ago looks like, I can watch old videos!"

Anna was still stunned. "When did you get this working so well? Last time, the picture was so dark and fuzzy that I could hardly tell what I was seeing."

"It's been gradually coming together for years," Indy said. "Lately, we've just been putting on the finishing touches. Every overnight success is a decade in the making, et cetera. It finally started working with that version you saw, and this one only came online a week ago." Indy's eyes flicked aside to another console screen, then back to Anna. "We haven't published these results yet, but word's starting to leak out. Professor Reyes is worried someone's going to try to scoop us, so when he got called away to some government hearing yesterday, he almost lost it. I've been up all night writing because he wants to submit this paper way ahead of the conference deadline, so we'll have clear priority." Her eyes flashed. "This is going to be a career-maker, for sure. I could go straight from postdoc to tenure!"

Through the field bubble, the long-ago shepherd boy continued his nap. The smaller of the two black dogs looked away from the flock to gaze longingly at a bag by the shepherd's outflung hand. *Must be lunch in there.*

"Hey, what about the future?" Anna asked. "Can we look forward with this thing?"

Indy barked out a laugh. "Everybody asks that eventually. But no. Think about it—the future doesn't exist yet, so there's nothing there to see."

"But how do we *know* that?"

"Aha, that's one of the most beautiful results of modern temporal theory." Indy's voice quickened with excitement. "There's this interesting duality between the symmetries of—" She stopped at Anna's quirked eyebrow. "Well, and we also tried it, just to be sure, and couldn't see anything," she finished. "So theory and experiment agree."

Anna had never wanted to be part of anything as much as this. At the same time, she struggled to tamp down a queasy feeling of inadequacy. *Indy's got seven years on me. Nobody's going to expect me to walk in here and understand all this stuff right away.* Her upcoming talk with her father loomed larger in her mind, and she clenched her jaw in determination. *This is where I belong!*

"Time to shut it down." Indy glanced over at the nearby console. "Your dad made me promise not to leave it on too long, at least not until after our paper's submitted. I just need to run a couple of quick power-down checks." Indy's collar lights flashed. "I can show you the rest of the lab too, but honestly you've seen the best part." She leaned in to look more closely at the console, collar lights modulating from green to amber and then red.

"That's unusual." Indy's mobile brows pulled together slightly, and her ears swiveled forward in concentration. "The field's showing some oscillatory boundary conditions. It almost looks like that cable cladding problem again, but our techs swore up and down—"

"What does that mean?" Anna tried to interpret the diagnostic messages flashing on the screens nearby, but they might as well be written in a foreign language.

"Probably nothing." Indy turned to look at a different display. "Hold on, I'll just do a cold shutdown. Grad-student engineering, it's not exactly production quality."

Anna's phone and Indy's collar rang at the same time, jarringly loud in the hushed lab.

Anna pulled her phone from her pocket. The call was from her father, so she tapped his icon to answer it. She could see it was answered on Indy's collar at the same time. His face appeared on Anna's phone and on the console near Indy, his features unnaturally composed.

"Indiana. Please turn the field diameter to maximum and crouch down with Anna at the center of the field projector. Quickly."

Anna felt ice crystals stab into her guts. Her father's dead-calm voice meant something was very, *very* wrong.

4

"One moment, Mateo, I was…" Indy spoke distractedly, eyes still scanning the diagnostic messages in front of her. "Wait, did you say *into* the projector? I was just shutting it down." Indy frowned as she said this, belatedly picking up on Anna's father's facial expression and tone of voice. He was standing in a big room full of flashing screens and urgently gesturing people, and he was trying to talk quietly.

"Do it. And hurry. No questions now, I'll explain as you go." His eyes shifted. "Anna, pick up that small bench fab on the table behind you and carry it in with you. It's the black one with the yellow stripe on the door. Indy, you protect her, no matter what."

Anna squelched the weird, jealous feeling of hearing Indy call her father by his first name. She had never seen a look like this on his face, and it scared her.

"What do you mean, protect her?" Indy began making changes to the projector's control console as she talked, but she sounded doubtful. "And why risk walking into the projector at this stage? We still have a lot more safety testing to do."

Anna found the fab her father had mentioned after a few tense moments of searching. It was a compact, one-foot black cube with a door on one side, similar to the one in her family kitchen that had made her breakfast this morning, though this one was free-standing and more industrial in design. She placed her phone face-up on top of it so she could keep her father in view, then lifted the fab from the table and stepped up onto the edge of the platform, coming face to face with the image of the Greek mountainside in the bubble. She stopped, reluctant to touch it.

Her father's voice came eerily through both phone and collar, slightly out of sync. "Indy, please get onto the platform. I need your help."

Indy froze for the briefest moment. Then her collar lights blinked red, and the field bubble expanded hugely, spilling out around Anna, past the six pillars and onto the floor of the lab as Indy turned the field projector to maximum strength. The floor seemed to vibrate slightly, and the scent of ozone rose from the cables.

Indy bounded up through the image and onto the platform, pushing Anna toward the center. The big hybrid sat down and leaned against Anna, who squatted down, resting the fab on the floor.

"What the hell is this about, Mateo?" Indy added a bark to her collar's voice.

Anna's father relaxed slightly as he saw them together on the platform. "Just hold on for a few moments." He looked aside quickly at something else in his field of vision, then refocused on Anna and Indy. "Stay where you are. Hopefully I'm wrong, and nothing will happen. We'll know in two more minutes. I've been doing an emergency data transmission, just in case." Lights were blinking steadily on Indy's collar, Anna's phone, and even the bench fab, showing a huge amount of incoming information of some kind. Anna's phone grew hot in her hand as it struggled to accept a torrent of data.

Anna leaned her head from side to side, looking into her phone's screen at an angle to see more of the scene behind her father. Worried-looking people in suits and hybrids in wide gleaming collars were clustered around console screens in some sort of government facility, pointing and talking intensely. "What's going on, Dad? Where are you?"

"Indy, I got a call from a three-letter agency last night to help them figure out a very strange signal being observed at Mauna Kea," her father said, with an apologetic look at Anna for not answering her question. "It turned out to be some kind of temporal resonance. It was stable for a while, but now it's getting stronger at a worrying rate. We don't know its source yet. It seems to propagate most strongly through dense regions of local spacetime, so the worst of it is taking an odd path to reach us. That gives us some time to react." His laugh was more nerves than humor. "The alarmist politicians might have been right, for once. This could be bad."

He settled himself visibly. "If this resonance is what I think it might be, the field bubble may shield you. The bubble should be pushed retro-temporally ahead of the wavefront that may form when the resonance gets strong enough." He frowned. "As long as the boundary layer isn't too unstable, that is. The potential energy in the field itself should be enough to keep it going for a while after pinch-off from the projector."

"Dad, what are you talking about?" Anna tried to keep the frustration from her voice. Beside her, Indy started a high whine, ears back against her skull.

Anna's father addressed Indy again, speaking more quickly. "The field bubble normally can't move along the temporal axis, but that's because the present anchors it in place. But if that were no longer the case, then—"

The lab around them disappeared with a shattering noise, leaving Anna and Indy surrounded by a rushing inky blackness. Then there was a lurch, and Anna pitched forward onto unseen grass and dirt, squashing her nose painfully and bruising her ribs against the fab in her arms. Beside her, Indy yelped in surprise and pain, then barked fiercely.

The blackness slowly dissolved away as Anna rolled to her side and stood. The platform was gone from underneath them, and there was no sign of the henge or the rest of her father's lab. She stood on grass, in the open air, looking out across a landscape very much like the ancient Greek mountainside that they had seen through the field bubble just minutes before. But now night was falling, and the clouds rolling in promised rain.

5

"Dad?" Anna called out to the empty air, but there was no response. *"Dad!"*

"Professor?" Indy's collar gleamed in the last rays of the setting sun as she looked back and forth, then up at the sky. She cast a worried glance at Anna, then lowered her nose to the ground, snuffling experimentally. She shook her head in confusion at whatever she smelled, then nosed through the grass nearby.

"Your phone." Indy nodded to where Anna's phone had been flung to the ground in their rough landing. Anna bent to retrieve it, while Indy quested in a circle around them. It didn't take long.

"Nothing. No scents except us and wild animals." Indy walked back over to the bench fab and sniffed at the door, which had popped open when Anna fell on it. One corner had been driven down through the tufted grass and into the rocky earth below.

"Nothing here either." Anna turned her phone toward Indy to show the "no connection" icon on its screen.

"My collar says the same thing. No wireless signal of any kind, not even satellites." Indy paced back and forth, eyeing the rain clouds that were sweeping across the mountainside toward them. "It's raining upwind." She raised her muzzle, inhaling lightly. "Smells like it's heavy, too. Wherever this is, we're really here. The bubble can't transmit scents."

"Hold on a second." Anna waved her phone slowly around, letting it see the landscape contours, then pointed it up at a few stars already visible in the darkening sky in front of the clouds. "Maybe my sky map can get a visual match on where we are." She looked at the screen, and after a moment Indy walked over to peer at it too.

"What does 'conflicting observations' mean?" Anna asked. "It's never said *that* before."

Indy's tail stilled. "I hope this doesn't work." Her voice sounded tightly controlled. "But try manually setting your calendar back to around 500 BC."

Anna's fingers tapped at the screen, adjusting the date, and the display changed. "It's got something!" Her face slackened, and the phone dipped in her hand.

"What?" Indy leaned in to see.

"It says it's 74 percent sure that this is central Greece." Anna looked more closely. "Okay, now it says 70 percent. Could it be wrong?"

"I don't think so." Indy's head hung low. "I thought this landscape looked too familiar." Fat raindrops began to patter down around them as the wind picked up, stirring the wet scent of unfamiliar grasses. "We should find some shelter."

"Shouldn't we check around more first?" Anna pocketed her phone and looked around uncertainly in the failing light, blinking as a drop of water glanced from her forehead. "We could have missed something!"

As she spoke, the first real sheet of rain swept over them. Indy snorted and shook water from her fur, and Anna hunched her shoulders as her T-shirt and shorts were rapidly soaked with chill water.

"We won't smell or see anything in this." Indy raised her voice over the rising wind.

Anna's face twisted with indecision. "We'll just have to come back, then." She pointed to a nearby cluster of trees. "Looks like some cover over there, maybe?" She started walking, wet shoes slipping over the newly damp earth.

"Don't forget the bench fab." Indy nodded back to where it lay, now slick with rain.

Anna ran over and picked the slippery thing up, careful not to drop it. The bottom door latch was caked with mud and wouldn't go into its slot, so she held it awkwardly closed as they fled, the storm rising all around them.

Ten minutes later, Anna huddled miserably under some low, shrubby trees in the hollow of a rocky hillside. Indy's soaked fur pressed against her back, her silvery wet collar gleaming in the scarce moonlight.

There wasn't much cover to be had. The mountainside was forested, but the trees were widely spaced, and their piney tops were much shorter than the pine trees she'd seen in movies. The low trees they sheltered under now were in the lee of the hillside, but rain still trickled down her neck every time a gust of wind swept their refuge, and some sort of heavy bulbs rattled noisily up in the dark amid the leaves.

Anna turned to face Indy. "So what do we do now?"

"I don't know yet." Indy sounded defensive. "This wasn't supposed to be possible."

"I thought you were an expert on this stuff!"

"I am." Indy bit off her words, nettled. "If we had a full lab and a field projector, then maybe we could make another bubble and try pushing it forward in time. But it's not supposed to be possible even to push one backward, much less forward." Indy jerked her dripping muzzle upward toward the black clouds. "Your father might be able to create another bubble and push it back to us. Depending on what happened after we left." She paused in thought. "Though if that were possible, you'd think he would've come back to a point right after we arrived, and he didn't." Indy started to shake the water from her ruff, but stopped when she saw she was throwing it onto Anna. "But this whole situation is outside the bounds of our standard temporal model. Perhaps there's some reason you can't come back too close together." She settled down again, paws squishing on the wet ground.

"What did my dad mean? That last thing he said, about the present anchoring something?" Anna hated how scared her voice sounded, and clamped her mouth shut again. It didn't help that she was shivering. Luckily it wasn't *too* cold, but her T-shirt and shorts weren't exactly appropriate for a rainy night outdoors.

Indy's light brown eyes glittered, and water dripped slowly from the tip of her white chin. "It sounded like he was saying, what if *the present itself* disappeared?" She blinked some of the water out of her eyes reflexively, her pale nictitating membranes sweeping across and back as she did so. "Like you could push the field bubble back into the past somehow if there was nothing to keep it moored. But that's ridiculous!" She visibly suppressed the urge to shake the water off herself again. "We're here, so we know *something* must have happened. But the present's not a thing that can just vanish. I'm sure your dad's on his way back to the lab right now, to figure out whatever that temporal resonance was and how it glitched the bubble." She shifted on her haunches and faced out into the rain again. "If we can get *here*, there must be a way to get back. We just need to find it."

Anna shifted, miserably wet and uncomfortable, wrung out by the stress of events. Now that it was dark and the action had passed, it was hard to stay alert, even though her body's internal clock still thought it was early afternoon, Texas time.

The rain eventually slackened, giving way to a chill wind and a dark clear sky. Anna had nodded off, but she jerked awake as she felt Indy's head turn quickly toward her.

"Wait!" Indy looked closely at the fab in Anna's arms. "Which fab are you holding?"

Anna looked down at the fab, but the night was too dark to make out any details. "Um, the black one?"

"They're *all* black. Let me look." A gentle white light shone from the bottom of Indy's collar, and her eyes glowed orange in its reflection. She peered at the fab that Anna had carried with them, and exhaled sharply. "Ha! *Yes!*"

Anna rolled her eyes. "Could you give me a hint here? What

good does a fab do us? Hooray, I can make some dinner now!" She paused. "Though dinner *does* sound like a pretty good idea."

"It's the yellow stripe," Indy said. "This bench fab is restricted technology. Even the famous Professor Reyes had to have a special license for it. We weren't allowed to take it out of the secure lab." Indy dropped her jaw in a smile, wet ears forward. "We used to joke that if this fab ever went past the lab doors, it would send a signal to some secret government agency, and a commando squad would saw holes through the ceilings, slide down on poles, and put black bags over all our heads." She cocked her head as she queried the fab with her collar. "Huh. Your father must have unlocked it while he was talking to us. That's a little bit terrifying."

Indy spoke to Anna's uncomprehending look. "A normal fab has limits, for safety and security. A food production fab like you have in your kitchen only takes water as input, and can only fabricate organic matter. The big fabs they use to make cars can only fabricate the easy parts, like the chassis and doors. They install the complex parts like the repellers after fabbing those separately, with more restricted equipment." Indy grew more serious. "In our research, we use a lot of exotic nanocomposite materials, especially in the waveguides and conduits. Those things are all over the periodic table. Elements that would never appear together in nature."

Anna finally got it. "So I could ask this thing to make an anti-matter bomb, or something?"

"Well, not *that*," Indy said. "It can use almost any substance as input, but it can only make normal matter. Though it can make almost anything out of normal matter." She considered a moment. "Well, given enough time and energy." Indy scraped with a blunt, sparkly-pink toenail at the mud on the fab's door latch where it was holding the door ajar.

"I've got my phone, too," Anna pointed out. "And you have your collar. So we've got something to work with."

"Actually… hmm." Indy looked aside in thought. "This fab could almost *make* more phones and collars. But it can't make the mass-energy conversion power supplies that all our portable devices use. We'd need to bootstrap our way up. Use this fab to make a bigger fab, then store up energy for weeks to run the bigger fab for a few seconds, then use that to make an even bigger fab, and so on." She looked back at Anna. "Eventually, we might be able to build anything you can think of. But it would take an awful lot of doing."

"My dad must have had some idea what might happen to us." Anna looked at the fab's door, still beaded with rainwater. "He told me to pick up this particular fab. He must have guessed we'd need it." Suddenly Anna felt more heartbroken than hungry.

"We're still in big trouble." Indy turned off her collar light, plunging them back into darkness. "Remember, fabs need plans for whatever you're trying to create, and we don't have any network connection here. You could store a huge number of plans in the fab itself if you needed to, but usually they're just pulled in from the network on demand. So this fab will have cached the plans for everything we ever built with it back in the lab, but who knows what's on that list. It may not be as useful as we think."

Anna pursed her lips, trying to bring a memory to the surface of her tired brain. "Didn't my dad say something about sending us some data, right before we came back?" She touched the interface ring of her phone, lighting the screen and navigating through status displays. She held it up where Indy could see. "It shows that my storage is almost full. I didn't even know that was possible."

"Hmm." Indy's collar lights flashed. "I'm seeing the same." Lights blinked on the fab as Indy queried it. "And on the fab too. But it looks like a jumble of unlabeled files, all super-compressed and thrown together without an index." Her face grew pensive. "I'll network us together so my collar and your phone can start trying to sort through it. But our devices can store a *lot* of data, more than we'd normally ever need in two lifetimes. And there's so much packed in there now that it'll be hard to uncompress it or even move it around without writing over something else. We'll have to be careful."

Anna flipped through the list of new files that crowded her phone. "There must be thousands of these things." On a hunch, she tapped the oldest of them, the one that her father had sent first. "What's this?"

"Processing," Alixa's cool voice answered aloud. A progress bar began to crawl across the screen. "Performance degraded due to lack of temporary storage. Can I delete some older files to make room?"

"No!" Anna spoke quickly as Indy shook her head. "We don't know what might turn out to be useful. Just run slow for now."

Anna and Indy waited for several interminable minutes before Alixa finally announced, "This file contains fab plans for emergency survival equipment."

"I knew it!" Anna smiled at Indy. "My dad didn't know when he'd be cut off. So he sent the most important one first."

"We'll analyze the rest of these in the background, but it's going to take months at this rate." Indy's collar winked blue and green in the wet darkness. "Maybe we can fab some memory cubes to make more room. But in the meantime, it looks like we've got just enough space to uncompress that one file... let me try something." She tried to push the fab door closed with one forepaw, but it was still blocked somehow, even after she'd scraped most of the mud from the latch. "What did you do to it?"

"Nothing!" Anna took over, rubbing the remaining sandy grime from the latch with her fingers, wiping them on her shirt to get them cleaner. "I was resting it on the platform, but then we fell somehow." Indy turned her collar light back on and leaned in as Anna tried the door again, but it still wouldn't close.

Anna's heart lurched. "It's hitting something solid." She crouched closer. "The bottom latch isn't lined up with the slot anymore. It must've got bent when it hit the ground." She tried the door again, fruitlessly, and her face felt hot despite how soaked she was. "I shouldn't have set it down. But I didn't know we were going to drop like that!"

"I'm not sure why that happened." Indy's voice mixed tension and defensiveness. "But if we can't get this fab working..." She looked Anna in the eyes, collar light illuminating her face from below. "Well, then we're just stranded."

"Hold on." Anna hunted around with trembling hands, stopping when she found a fist-sized rock. "I can fix this." She snatched up the rock and bent over the fab door again, setting the rock carefully against the metal latch. Then she slowly pressed against it, harder and harder, trying to bend it back into place.

"Careful!" The light bounced as Indy moved closer. Anna's hand slipped, and the rock gouged a scratch into the back of the fab door. "Sorry. But if you snap off that latch, the safety interlock won't let the fab turn on, even if we close the door."

Anna gave Indy a sour look. "No pressure." She shook out her hands, picked up the rock, and carefully pressed against the latch again, stopping every few seconds to check its alignment against the slot. After a few tense minutes, it finally lined up, and Anna opened and shut the fab door a few times experimentally. "It's still scraping a little, but it seems okay. Try it out."

The fab's display lit, echoing the blue of Indy's collar lights. An instant later, the fab went *ding!* and the capacity display on its front panel dropped from seventy-six to seventy-five percent. They looked at each other, Anna smiling with relief.

"Good thing you're handy with a rock." The worried crease faded from between Indy's brows and she popped the door open, revealing a tightly folded insulating tarp, streaming cold fog into the humid night air. "Spread this over us and let's warm up." She yawned hugely and lay down, cringing as her belly hit the soggy ground. "There's no point being cold as well as wet. We'll see if things look any better in the morning."

nna surged awake, gripped with fear from some formless nightmare. She struggled out from under the tarp she had shared with Indy, the reality of their situation sinking in again as she looked around the trees they'd huddled under. The day had dawned clear and beautiful, but she was wet and smeared with mud. And hungry. She hadn't had anything to eat since her breakfast bagel the day before, 2800 years in the future.

Beside her, Indy shed their rain tarp, then walked out to a safe distance and shook the remaining water out of her fur. Tiny droplets flew everywhere, leaving her still damp, but at least not soaked. Then she balanced on her rump, folded up the tarp with her flexible front paw pads, and shoved it back into the fab. She closed the door, and lights flashed on her collar. The fab dinged, and its window now showed an empty cavity. The capacity display bumped back up to seventy-six percent.

"That's my favorite fab trick." Indy looked very self-satisfied, like she'd invented the thing herself. "Industrial fabs can do matter reclamation, though the elements you get back are always a bit lighter than what you put in. This one can store about ten pounds of internal reserves for when it's not hooked to a supply line. But after that runs out, you either have to reclaim something, or add more feedstock through the port on the back." Indy fumbled for a moment trying to get a grip on the fab, then looked up at Anna.

"Carry this thing for a while longer, will you?" She wiggled her front paws, which were much more mobile than those of a natural dog, but lacked opposable thumbs. "We hybrids are fast-moving and good-looking, but not so great at walking while carrying things."

Anna picked up the bulky fab and looked around. "Let's go back and check where we landed again. Maybe my dad found a way to leave us a note or something." She stretched uncomfortably, hating the feel of damp clothes against her skin. "And maybe some breakfast? I can already feel myself working up an appetite carry-ing this thing."

"Just a moment, I've got an idea." Indy stood up on her long hind legs and used her two front paws together to pluck two of the big bulbs out of the tree they'd sheltered under. In the morning light, Anna could see that they were about the size of oranges, but with a smooth, dark-red shell.

"Pomegranates," Indy said. "It can't hurt to try some local food, since our fab options might be limited."

"Good thinking." Anna opened the fab door so Indy could stow the hard fruits inside for safekeeping, and frowned as the latch scraped when she closed it again.

They walked back the way they'd come the night before, and a few minutes saw them back at their landing spot. The ground between the tufted grass was muddy now, the grass still damp from yesterday's rain.

"It seemed like a longer walk last night." Indy sniffed around slowly. "Are you sure this is the same place? The rain washed away all the scent."

Anna set the fab down and pulled out her phone to check. "Yep, we're right at the map marker I set yesterday. Even with no network, the map can at least show us where we've been." She looked around hopefully. "Maybe Dad doesn't know how to send another person back yet, but is there any other way he could talk to us?"

Indy looked up from her check around the area. "Not that I know of. But remember, yesterday I thought we couldn't affect the past at all, much less get thrown back into it."

The pair continued their search, spiraling in and out methodically from their landing point, but another half hour's search didn't turn up anything. Anna's stomach growled, and Indy licked her lips unconsciously. "Your stomach's making me hungry too, now."

Anna rubbed at her face, then sighed. "Okay, let's get some food. I'll just leave a message in case someone shows up while we're gone. Then we can go find some water to wash up, and fab some breakfast."

The rocky soil held an abundance of pebbles and small stones, so it was only the work of a few minutes for Anna to spell out "A&I will be back" on a bare patch nearby. Then she stood and dusted her hands, looking down the gentle slopes around them. "Water flows downhill, right? So I guess if we walk down and across, we'll eventually find some." She made a resigned face as she bent and picked up the fab again. "Hopefully it won't take too long."

Indy trotted out ahead, scenting the air, white-tasseled tail held high. Anna trudged along behind, struggling to hold the fab up at waist level so it wouldn't bang into her thighs as she walked and shorten her stride. The thing only weighed about twenty pounds, and wasn't any wider than her hips, but it was awkward to walk any distance with, and she could feel the pomegranates rolling around inside it.

All around them as they walked, the Greek landscape overflowed with life. There was no sign of the sheep or the shepherd they'd seen through the portal yesterday, and she couldn't see as many flowers, but the forested slopes looked much greener than Anna remembered from pictures of Greece that she'd seen. Wasn't Greece mostly dry and rocky, with lots of goats? This was a verdant landscape, at least by west Texas standards, and the fresh smell of yesterday's rain still lingered in the air.

After a while they came to a narrow rill of water, threading down a crease in the mountainside from a rocky slope high above.

Indy brought her muzzle low and lapped at the cold water for a full half-minute. Anna set the fab down, rinsed her hands, and cupped them to drink likewise.

Thirst quenched, she dried her hands on her grimy shorts and pulled out her phone. She touched it to the fab to pair them together, which surprisingly worked on the first try. Her father must have authorized her back in the lab when he unlocked it. She took the pomegranates out of the fab, then scrolled her phone to her favorites list. "Hmm, most of the foods are grayed out for some reason."

"Remember, right now we've only got whatever fab plans were in that emergency survival file," Indy said. "Plus whatever this fab's made before."

Anna kept scrolling, then stopped at a likely item. "Good thing the survival menu was made in Texas." She poked the phone's screen. "Breakfast time!"

"Wait!" Indy said, just as Anna touched her phone. The fab dinged, and Indy grimaced at the sound. "I should've thought of this before."

"What's wrong?" Anna asked. "I thought we could make whatever. And now that you mention it, I guess we could've fabbed some water earlier, instead of walking all the way down here to find a stream." Anna pulled a face. "It might have been cleaner, too. There could be frogs living in this."

Indy looked worried. "I didn't think this through. This fab is loaded with our custom lab feedstock right now. Heavy elements, exotic materials, chosen to convert efficiently into the complex assemblies we had to make in our lab."

"So what?" Anna asked. "It can convert anything to anything, right?"

"Not exactly." Indy sniffed at the fab door. "The more different your feedstock is from what you're fabbing, the less efficient it is." Indy thought for a moment. "In a perfect world, you could make uranium using grass as feedstock. But the matter conversion process gets exponentially less efficient as the difference between materials increases. And you can only dissipate so much waste heat from a unit this small."

"Meaning…" Anna prompted.

"Meaning, we don't want to fab breakfast from irreplaceable feedstock. We might need it later to make something techy to keep us alive."

"Ah." Anna looked up soberly. "I get it now." She paused, thinking. "But you fabbed us a tarp last night!"

"That was a bad idea." Indy looked chagrined. "Maybe *very* bad." She paced for a moment. "I'm not sure exactly how much and what type of feedstock we would need to bootstrap our way up the technology ladder like I mentioned last night. I'd have to work with our nets and do some experiments to figure it out exactly. But if we're even a little bit short…" Her voice trailed off. "We could never make another fab. And then if this one broke, we'd be stuck with Iron Age technology until we get rescued." She looked up, fear evident in her tucked-under tail. "And what if rescue turns out to be impossible for some reason, and we have to get back on our own? Then we'd have to either work our way through the whole Industrial Revolution again, or die of old age back here."

Anna's stomach clenched with worry. "Yeah, that wouldn't be good. Let's not do that last thing."

Indy shook out her ruff quickly and squared her stance. "Let's at least make sure we don't go any deeper in the hole." She looked over at the narrow stream. "Could you pour some of that water into the feed port on the back of the fab?"

After a bit of fumbling, Anna opened the little hatch covering the feed port. Then she cupped her hands in the chill water flowing nearby and tipped it into the open port. It gurgled quietly, and half the water ran down the back of the machine, but within a few seconds the capacity display had risen to eighty percent.

"It's working!" Anna quickly scooped several more handfuls of water into the machine, wetting the ground beneath it, until no more would go into the port. The fab played a jaunty tune as its capacity display bumped up to one hundred percent. "Success!"

Indy leaned in, collar lights flashing. "I set a safety cutoff so it won't use up the good stuff unless we override it," she said. "Now, try some more food."

"Let me empty it out first," Anna said. "Don't want to waste the most expensive breakfast ever." She opened the fab door, frowning. "That bent latch still sticks a little." She took out a plate holding two chorizo and egg breakfast tacos, complete with a little cup of salsa on the side. She considered, then poked at her phone again. The fab dinged, and she reached in and pulled out another cup of salsa. "No such thing as too much salsa." The box's display showed ninety-nine percent for a moment, then went back to one hundred as she splashed more water into the port. "Works for me."

Anna poured salsa along the top of her first taco and took a bite. Then she grimaced. "Ugh, it's cold!" she said around a mouthful of taco.

"The one disadvantage of an industrial fab," Indy said. "A kitchen fab is specially designed to produce hot objects, but this kind of fab makes everything cold to get more precise outputs."

Anna finished her first bite, then smacked her lips disapprovingly. "Bleh. I'm starving, so even cold tacos taste somewhat okay. But still."

Indy entered her own order via her collar, and pulled out a big plate of cold mini-cheeseburgers a few seconds later. Anna raised an eyebrow. "I didn't see *that* on the survival menu."

"I might have eaten in the lab a few times when I've had a paper due." Indy looked defiant. "Don't judge me." She nipped the top burger from the pile, and mustard squelched noisily as her jaws made short work of it. They were both hungry, so breakfast didn't take long.

"Now, check this out." Indy quickly fabbed a paring knife, its handle oddly curved to fit her thumbless paws. "I learned this from a fellow grad student back at UT. And we might as well have a little fun while we're here." She grabbed one of their pomegranates, nipped off the top with her front teeth, spat it out, then slit down the sides with the knife and levered the pomegranate open into six slices, each one filled with dark, juicy seeds. Her paws might not have the same span as human hands, but they were still dexterous.

Indy offered the open pomegranate to Anna, who just stared at it. "Ew, you got your slobber on the top." She screwed up her face with mock disgust.

Indy rolled her eyes, set the first pomegranate aside for herself, and prepared the second one, this time using the knife to cut off the top. Anna took this one happily and turned it this way and that to look at it.

"Make sure not to get any juice on your clothes," Indy said. "You can't just lick yourself clean like I can."

"Hey, these are good!" Anna bit the seeds right out of the slices, trying not to let the juice drip down her chin. "Definitely messy, though." Indy nodded in agreement as she noisily smacked on her own.

Their plates, the knife, and the pomegranate skins went back into the fab for reclamation. Anna rubbed her hands together in the icy water to clean them, then wiped them on her shorts again with a frown. A thought struck her, and she entered another order into the fab via her phone. After another *ding!* she removed a packet of toilet paper from the fab and tucked it into her back pocket.

"Better to have it before you need it," she said at Indy's amused look. Anna assumed that hybrids must squat like normal dogs, but she didn't feel like now was the right time to ask. Thankfully, like everyone else where they'd come from, both of them could pause their monthly cycles using their neural implants. So there was no need to worry about *that*, at least.

Anna fed more water into the fab to top it up, then closed the port and stood. *Right. Time to start doing more than just asking dumb questions after bad things happen.*

"Um. I've got an idea for what to do next?" Anna fought back her self-consciousness as Indy's ears swiveled forward in attention. They *had* just spent a whole night shivering together under a tarp, and Indy was more approachable than a lot of older scientists, but Anna was still afraid she was going to say something to make herself look terminally dumb in front of her potential future colleague.

"Let's assume my dad will eventually find a way to come back and rescue us." Anna didn't want to think about the alternative. "But we don't know how long that'll take, for whatever reason." She paced, thinking. "We can't just camp out at our landing spot and wait. Anybody could stumble across us, and if this fab gets taken away or someone breaks it, we're stuck here with nothing but our clothes." She hesitated. "Well, *my* clothes. Since you're not wearing any."

"Good point." Indy looked thoughtful, as if what Anna had said was a coherent sequence of ideas. "We need to find some kind of shelter that's not suspicious. We can't set up a tent or build a hut. Somebody might own this land, for all we know. They could show up at any time, and then what happens?"

"Exactly." Anna looked around the empty hillside. "We need to learn more about this place, and we can't do that by hanging around here."

"Sounds like a plan." Indy's collar lights glowed to life. "And step one of every great plan? Go shopping."

7

Ten minutes later, Anna settled the straps of a cold new backpack over her shoulders. The bulky pack had space for their fab and ten pounds of newly fabbed equipment, including a small rolled sleeping bag, a bag of trail mix, and a bottle of water. Kibble, water bottles, and a plastic drinking bowl filled a new pair of saddlebags that clipped to a harness thrown over Indy's back and belted under her deep chest.

"You sure you don't want me to decorate that for you?" Indy looked at Anna's plain backpack pointedly, then back at her own harness and bags, which were chased with silvery patterns. "Even survival gear has *some* customizations you can add."

"I'm okay." Anna shrugged. "I like stuff plain. One less thing to think about."

"Very utilitarian of you." Indy chuffed out a canine laugh. "I thought about making my whole setup pink, to match my nails. But that might be a little much, even for me. And not exactly inconspicuous." Her face grew serious. "It's a good thing you guessed where to look for the fab plans for these. A few little tweaks to an existing plan are one thing, but if we had to design something from scratch…"

"Come on, don't we already have enough to worry about?" Anna gave Indy a look. "Plus, my dad's probably going to show up any minute and yank us back to the future. Then we'll be sorry we didn't enjoy this while we had the chance."

"Maybe you're right." Indy's expression relaxed somewhat. "I might even get our paper in on time, if it turns out that we can go back to right after we left."

After topping up the fab with water one last time, they set off downslope. Indy slowed her pace to match the walking speed of a short human, though she occasionally pulled ahead when she got distracted, then had to stop and wait for Anna to catch up.

They followed the stream toward what her phone said should be the small town of Analipsi. Their original hillside landing spot was in the mountains of somewhere called Boeotia, in central Greece, thirty miles or so northwest of Thebes, which was toward the middle of one of the three main Greek land masses. The regional capital, Livadeia, was supposed to be only a few miles away down the mountain in the direction they were going, but Anna couldn't see any sign of it yet.

Her phone's map was certainly going to be wrong about the minor details of the landscape, but city locations usually stayed the same for centuries or millennia. *Didn't they? Unless a harbor silts up, or a river shifts its course. But how often can* that *happen?* Anna made a mental note to double-check that Alixa was updating her maps as they travelled.

Anna glanced at Indy as they walked along. They'd met once at a Christmas party, and Anna had heard about Indy through her father a few times. But other than that and the events of the day before, they were essentially strangers. It was an unsettling thought, that her only link back to her home was someone she barely knew.

"So, um. Indy." Anna cleared her throat.

Indy slowed and turned her head back toward Anna as she walked. "Yes?"

"I was thinking," Anna said. "We hadn't really talked that much, before. Until this happened."

"Mateo talks about you sometimes. I can tell he's very proud." Indy spoke as she walked, weaving gracefully between tufts of the still-damp grass. "You're starting UT physics in the fall, right? And you're up for some sort of fellowship?"

"Well…" Anna paused, stomach clenched. "Not anymore." She spoke in a rush. "I didn't get a chance to tell Dad, before all this happened. But I just got my entrance exam scores back, and I didn't quite make the fellowship cutoff."

"Oof." Indy winced, then backpedaled when she saw Anna's stricken look. "Hey, but you can recover from that! Hit the books, then reapply next semester. People do it all the time."

"Did you?"

"No." Indy's sympathetic tone softened her blunt words. "But I was pretty well prepared. Mateo—I mean, your dad. He'd been helping me out for years by then."

Anna shoved down another surge of jealousy at how familiarly Indy referred to her father, and the relationship it implied. *How could he help his student more than his own daughter?* She saw her father several times a year, and he'd helped guide her in her studies. But her parents had been divorced almost five years now. She'd never really thought about how much more time his students must spend with him.

Indy must have seen something of that in her face, because she stopped walking and turned fully toward Anna.

"I met your father at an open house at UT when I was in high school in Austin. He offered me a summer internship, where I came in and helped out in the lab. Hard to believe it's been nine years already!" Indy looked thoughtful. "I graduated high school, got into UT physics, and stayed in contact with him the whole time, just doing little projects for him and learning from his other students. We border collies can be pretty obsessive, so once we latch onto something, we can get a lot done. When I was ready to start grad school, your father agreed to take me on as my supervisor."

"I'm lucky to see my dad for an hour a month." Anna tried to keep the bitterness out of her voice, but wasn't quite sure she succeeded.

Indy gave her a regretful look. "Your father's a great man. But none of us at the lab know why he does what he does. I've got no clue why he picked me out of all the others. No professor really needs a high school student as a lab assistant, or an undergrad hanging around screwing things up and asking dumb questions. Especially someone as famous and talented as your dad. A lot of *really* smart people fight for those openings."

Anna stiffened her jaw. "I'm getting in there, one way or the other. I don't care how long I have to study or how many make-up classes I have to take."

Indy gave her a considering look. "If you want something enough, there's always some way to make it happen."

Anna scowled. "Now you sound like my mom."

Indy snorted with laughter. "You take that back! I'm only eight years out of high school, myself."

"Sorry. I'm just..." Anna fought to relax her expression. "Yesterday I was *so close* to everything working out. I can't believe I came up just three points short." She started walking again, picking her way over a rocky hump in their path. Indy joined her, walking alongside now instead of in front.

"So did you ever worry at all?" Anna asked. "That you might not make it?"

"No." Indy answered with bedrock certainty. Then she softened. "But border collies don't really have the genes for self-doubt. So I can't take credit for that."

The pair made their way down the mountainside in silence for a while. From the relatively short grass here, it seemed that these slopes were grazed regularly, at least during the growing season. Indy raised her muzzle periodically, declaring that she could definitely smell the lanolin scent of sheep, but Anna couldn't see any sign of them or their shepherds nearby.

As they approached a copse of trees in a narrow valley, following their original stream downward, Indy's ears swiveled forward, and a few moments later Anna heard a sheep's bleat up ahead. There was no sign of the source, but clearly the animal was in distress.

Anna turned to look at Indy. "Sounds like a lamb got lost somewhere down there. Maybe it's looking for its mama." She felt a pang as she thought of her own mother, now some unknown distance in the future. *Not lost, though. My dad will find us.*

They pressed forward along the stream, which wound down into the trees. Then all at once the trees opened out, at a curve in the stream where it broadened and formed a pool before continuing down the mountain. A lamb had its hind leg stuck in a forked branch, where it must have gotten wedged while pushing forward too eagerly through the brush to drink. A few other lambs and ewes stood nearby, drinking or wandering in search of grass.

A skinny, gray-bearded old man crouched beside the trapped lamb, sweating under the hot sun, trying to work the lamb's leg free without injuring its delicate skin. The same sort of white tunic and sandals they had seen on the young shepherd through the portal flapped loosely over his wiry upper arms.

Wow, bald is not *working for him,* thought Anna. *He should fill it in more on top.* Then she felt a stab of shame. *You're in the past, dummy. If someone goes bald back here, they're just stuck that way.*

Sweat ran off the man's bronzed pate and into his eyes. The lamb must have weighed almost half as much as he did, and it was clear he was having a hard time of it.

Anna called out without thinking. "Need some help, sir?"

The man looked up in surprise, and his eyes took in her unfamiliar shorts and T-shirt. Anna was suddenly aware of how strange she must look to him. *I didn't think to make new Greek clothes. Or even clean clothes. And backpacks probably don't exist yet! Can I get arrested or something for obviously not belonging here?*

The old man called out something unintelligible to her.

Ugh, and I'm such an idiot. He speaks Greek or whatever. But his intent was clear. He jerked his head toward the lamb, calling Anna over to help.

Anna hesitated, then walked over and took hold of the lamb's fleecy body under the forelegs, trying to turn it a little so its hind leg wasn't caught so tightly. The lamb bleated again, much louder now that Anna's ear was right beside its grassy-smelling mouth. The old man kept working with the animal's hind leg. Finally, after a grunt of effort, he slipped it free.

The lamb sprang out of Anna's hands and away from the thicket, shaking out its hindquarters and favoring one hind leg a bit, then joined one of the nearby ewes. They moved off to drink at the stream, regarding Anna suspiciously before ambling away.

The old man straightened up slowly, rubbing his lower back with both hands. Then he looked at Anna more closely. He frowned, and the frown deepened as his eyes found Indy, sitting mutely on her haunches back where the trees ended, like some kind of oversized sheepdog. Anna could swear the big hybrid was smirking at her as she sat there.

The man spoke another long string of syllables, none of which made any sense to Anna. "Sorry, sir. I can't speak your language. I'm not from around here." She looked down at her grubby clothes and muddy sneakers. "I guess *that's* obvious."

The old man thought for a moment, then made an odd overhand flapping gesture with his hand, palm downward, like he was trying to get Anna to back away. She moved back a step. He made the gesture again, more emphatically.

Maybe flappy-hand means follow me? She took a step toward the old man and he looked pleased. He turned away and began walking downstream, checking over his shoulder to make sure she was coming.

He doesn't look *like a murderer, at least.* Anna paused. *But what if he's taking us to the police or something? If they take our stuff, we'll be in big trouble.* She looked back at Indy. *But we can't exactly talk this over in front of an audience.* The old man had stopped, and smiled encouragingly. *And we* do *need shelter.*

She sighed. *What's the worst that could happen?* She followed the old man, and Indy trotted along behind.

8

They never did see the town of Analipsi. Maybe it didn't exist yet in 500-ish BC, or they'd just missed it somehow in the rolling terrain. But after a downward trek of maybe a mile across flowering meadows at the old man's slow pace, the trio came to the upper edge of a lower-lying forest.

A humble white stone cottage stood there where the trees began to cluster together. It was flanked by a smaller stone building, a wood-fenced garden, and a sheep pen, currently empty. The cottage looked like it had been built with care, but a long time ago, and Anna could see that it needed maintenance. A few chickens clucked nervously nearby, scattering at Indy's approach.

The old man called out to the cottage as they arrived, and a girl a few years younger than Anna appeared from behind it, carrying a wooden bucket brimming with water. She set it on the ground and waved, walking over to greet her… grandfather? Anna had no idea, since the language they spoke was still gibberish to her. The girl had braided, medium-brown hair, and she wore the now-familiar white tunic and sandals, though hers was much longer than the old man's, coming down almost to her toes. She wasn't as thin as the old man either, but she looked like hunger was no stranger to her.

Anna felt acutely self-conscious. She didn't exercise especially diligently, but her muscles still showed the effects of good nutrition.

The girl's eyes narrowed as she took in Anna's odd clothing and pack, then widened again as she saw just how big Indy was. Anna was suddenly glad for Indy's black and white coloring. *At least no one'll think she's a wolf! That's probably no joke around here.* Indy had wisely hung back thirty yards or so, hiding her true size, but the Greeks could see her plainly enough now.

The girl was leaning in and talking to the old man, obviously getting the story of his meeting with Anna and Indy. She seemed skeptical, but the old man replied in a clearly admonishing tone. She picked up her bucket again, emptied the water into a nearby stone trough for the animals, and went in the cottage's front door, leaving it open behind her.

The old man gestured for Anna to doff her pack and follow him through the open wooden door. She laid it aside reluctantly, trying not to show how afraid she was to let it out of her sight.

Inside the cottage, the girl crouched by a smoke-stained white stone hearth, stirring a small pot that bubbled beside a low-banked fire. Anna's stomach growled. *Lunchtime, maybe?*

Setting her wooden spoon aside, the girl hurried to the back of the cottage, where a curtained doorway hid what looked like a small enclosed room. Anna could hear the girl speaking quietly inside, and a softer voice answering.

Meanwhile, the old man gestured Anna over to a wooden table, plain but carefully made, with a long bench on either side. She took a seat across from her host and looked nervously back for Indy, who was sitting on her haunches, almost filling the doorway of the cottage, but making no move to enter. *Probably best. She can watch our stuff. And hopefully nobody's wondering too hard why my dog is wearing customized saddlebags and pink toenail polish.*

The girl emerged from the back room's curtained doorway, supporting a thin old woman who held the girl's arm lightly for support.

Huh, she's old too. Then Anna mentally smacked herself. *Of course she is. When you get old in the past, you* look *old.* She'd seen what people in the past looked like before, in videos and books, but it was different somehow being here and seeing it in person.

The old man called out something to the woman, who started slightly when she looked up and saw Indy in the doorway. But she came the rest of the way to the table steadily, if slowly, and sat down next to the old man with the ease of long familiarity.

The girl went to a cupboard and filled a shallow bowl with water from a nearby jug. Then she brought it over to the table and handed it to the old man, who gravely held it out to Anna, speaking a few words as he did so.

Anna took it with a nod of thanks. *I guess they drink out of bowls here. Well, when in Rome!* She raised it to her lips, but stopped at her hosts' shocked expressions, and lowered the bowl to the table again uncertainly. The old man made an ambiguous gesture toward the bowl and said something. Anna looked around at a loss, then her eyes lit on Indy at the door. *Oh, I get it. It's* dog *water! That's why it's in a bowl, and why they freaked out when I was about to drink it.* She got up and walked over to Indy with the bowl. *It's so considerate of them to make sure Indy has something to drink!* She placed the bowl in front of Indy, who looked at it, nonplussed.

The old man called out from behind her, then rushed over hastily, retrieving the bowl before Indy could drink. He placed it on the table again, then mimed dipping his hands into the bowl and rubbing them together. Beside him, the old woman was stifling laughter.

Anna's cheeks burned with shame. *Oops. Okay, so I just tried to drink the hand-washing water.* She dipped her hands and rinsed them, careful not to spill any water on the table. The old man offered her a clean cloth to dry her hands, then he and the old woman washed up likewise, their motions oddly formal. He said a few more words, looking relieved, and Anna gave him an embarrassed smile. *Sorry!*

The girl had watched the whole situation open-mouthed, but she recovered well, washing her own hands after the three of them were done and setting the bowl aside. She went back to the fire to check on lunch one last time, using her stirring spoon to daub a tiny bit of whatever it was in front of a little statue of a man with shaggy goat-legs that occupied a tiny shrine built into the hearth. Then she began gathering simple pottery bowls and cups from the cupboard and setting them out on the table.

Anna felt a vibration in the front pocket of her shorts. She slipped a thumb into her pocket and felt around for her phone, ignoring the old couple's curious looks. Once she touched the interface ring, she heard Indy's mental voice. *Come outside for a moment.*

Anna pulled her thumb from her pocket and rose from the table, making a brief "stay put" gesture to the old folks. The old woman said something questioning, but they stayed seated, turning to speak to each other as Anna retreated out through the cottage's front door. A muffled *ding!* sounded from inside her backpack as she walked past it, but a quick glance back through the door showed that none of the Greeks seemed to have noticed.

She and Indy edged a couple of feet to one side, out of sight of the cottage's occupants, and Indy mutely pointed to Anna's pack with her muzzle. Anna pulled it over to her, opened it, and saw on the fab's display that there was something ready inside. She opened the fab door and pulled out a tastefully small gold stud earring, sized to fit a human ear. Indy gave her a look with raised eyebrows and a jerk of the chin, clearly indicating that Anna should put the earring on.

Good thing it's a stick-on, and not one of the stabby ones. Anna had always hated the idea of poking anything through her flesh, so her ears weren't pierced. She warmed the fab-chilled metal between her fingers, then stuck the smooth backing to her left earlobe and squeezed it gently into place, looking back at Indy.

Anna realized afresh just how ill-prepared she and Indy were for this. *We're bumbling around like clueless tourists trying to find a hotel without their phones. Note to self: come up with a better plan before the next time you're thrown back into the past.*

Indy raised a paw and folded down one flexible digit, then another one. Anna felt a brief tingle from where the earring met her ear, then flinched as she heard phantom sounds flit from one side of her head to the other. Indy counted down the last two digits on her paw and looked at Anna expectantly.

Can you hear me now? Indy's voice appeared in Anna's head.

Of course! Another good idea Anna should have had sooner. *Yes, I can hear you*, she thought back. The earring was just a smaller version of the interface ring on her phone that let it communicate with her neural implant. This way they could talk without Anna having to constantly fiddle with her phone. It would certainly be much less suspicious.

The earring used a bit of our special feedstock, but it can't be helped, Indy said softly in Anna's head. *We need to find shelter, and soon. Which means you need to be able to convince people we're harmless.* Indy gave her an exaggeratedly innocent, big-eyed look, then spoiled it by snorting. *Though I think your bit with the washing bowl might have done that already.* Her eyes twinkled in amusement. *I've had my collar's net working on their speech, and it's close enough to the ancient Greek we knew that we can translate it, more or less. Thankfully there was still a fair chunk of the* Iliad *cached on my phone from when I was researching that classical civilization class I'm taking next semester. That was enough for my collar net to put together a rough dictionary, though there are probably a lot of gaps in it.*

Indy glanced toward the door. *They're probably getting suspicious by now. Go on back in, and I'll stay here in the doorway. When you want to say something, just think the words to yourself, and you'll hear them translated in your head. Then repeat them out loud.* Indy dropped her jaw in a smile. *No guarantees on the accuracy, though.* She pointed toward the cottage door with her chin. *Try not to say anything too crazy!*

Anna took a deep breath, then squared her shoulders and walked back into the cottage. She was met by three sets of curious eyes, between the old couple at the table and the girl filling a bowl at the hearth. She was suddenly thankful for her Mexican heritage. If she'd been a six-foot, blue-eyed blonde, her origins might have needed even more explaining. As it was, she could probably pass for Greek if she had been wearing the right outfit and hairstyle.

"This one's for you." The girl held a bowl filled with some kind of mush out toward Anna. "Sorry about my cooking."

"She doesn't understand us, Iole," the old man said.

It was very weird hearing Greek words outside of her head, and then English words inside of it a fraction later, but it was understandable enough. She thought of her response in English, then listened to the Greek translation in her head and repeated it haltingly aloud. "Thank you."

Iole stepped back a bit at this, but then smiled hesitantly and offered the bowl again. Anna took it and sat across from the old couple at the table. She scooped out a bite with the wooden spoon and found it to be a bland but hearty porridge, made of some kind of boiled grain with a hint of gamy meat flavor. Iole served the old couple next, then carefully scraped out the last of the food into her own bowl and sat on the end of the hearth instead of at the table, perhaps too shy to sit on the same bench as a stranger.

"So you *can* speak Greek." The old man looked at her, curious. "Why didn't you say so?"

"My Greek is bad." Anna kept her sentences short, since she had to repeat each one aloud before she forgot the first words, and the lilting tones were hard to emulate. "I have to talk careful."

"'Speak carefully,'" corrected the old man.

Great, I probably sound like an idiot. She hoped the nets in her phone and Indy's collar were noting the corrections.

"My name's Leitus, and this is my wife Helene." He gave his wife's arm a gentle squeeze, and Anna watched the crepey old-people skin wrinkle and compress with fascination. He waved his other hand toward the girl sitting on the hearth. "And this is our grand-niece, Iole."

He inclined his head toward Anna formally. "Thank you for your help earlier. It seems like these lambs get heavier every year." He rubbed at his forearms with knobby, work-roughened hands. "It's a job, keeping them out of trouble, especially once they're a few months old and running amok. We should get a dog to help us again, but that idiot Gryllus from around the mountain still won't trade us for a good one."

"Hush, Leitus, she doesn't need to hear all our troubles in the first sentence." Helene's voice was soft, but steady, and her eyes were still bright in her weathered face. "What's your name, girl?" she asked, not unkindly.

"My name's Anna, ma'am." Anna had no idea how Alixa's translator rendered "ma'am" into Greek, but using the word to her elders was like a reflex to the Texas girl. She'd just have to hope they responded well.

"Indy—my dog—and I. We're travelers. And we're a long way from home." Anna's throat closed up with emotion as she realized the old woman's name was almost the same as her mother Helena's. Anna looked down and took another bite of the porridge, chewing slowly while her heart ached behind her ribs.

Helene glanced at her husband, asking a question without words the way long-married couples could. The way Anna's parents had done, back before they had split up. Then Helene looked back at Anna. "You've washed at our table and shared our food, so you're already our guest. We don't have much, but you're welcome to stay here until you find your feet. We could use some help, to be honest. I can't work much anymore, so poor Iole has to cook now. And Leitus here isn't as strong as he used to be."

"I'll show you strong, old crone," Leitus shot back with a smile. It sounded like an old shared joke between them.

Anna noticed Iole staring apprehensively at the doorway behind her, and turned to look. Indy was standing and watching intently as they ate, a long strand of saliva hanging from one side of her muzzle.

"I think your dog is…hungry?" Iole sounded scared. "There's no more food, though."

"Wait." Anna looked around at the family. "Are you guys afraid of Indy?"

No one said anything, but the guarded looks on their faces were eloquent enough.

"Don't worry." Anna tried to look reassuring. "She's very well behaved. Here, let me show you." *And don't you dare say a word,*

Anna warned her via the earring. Indy smirked mutely, and drooled even harder.

She went outside briefly to retrieve a bowl of kibble from Indy's saddlebags, then added a dollop of her porridge and held it in front of Indy. "Can we do a trick for our dinner?"

I know you didn't just ask me to beg for food. Indy's silent voice was outraged. *I am not a house pet!*

I'm so sorry! Anna's face heated with shame. *I didn't mean it like that! I just wanted you to show them something so they'd know you were...*

Well-trained? Indy gave her a stony look.

No! Anna was even more mortified. *Just some kind of sign that you're not going to eat them! You're huge and scary, and we're in their house! We need a place to stay, remember?*

Indy's posture softened as she thought this over. *You're right. They don't know who I really am.* Her eyes flashed again. *I'm not begging, though.*

Indy looked slowly around the room at the Greeks, then nodded deliberately to Anna. She raised one forepaw to gently touch the bowl, then the other. Then she sat down, waiting.

Anna put the bowl down in front of Indy, who came to all fours to eat, chewing open-mouthed but daintily. *Not bad,* she said silently to Anna. *Boiled barley, maybe? We'll have to see about some seasoning, though.*

"See?" Anna sat back down with Leitus, Helene, and Iole, who looked reassured. "Nothing to worry about." She picked up her own bowl again and dug out another spoonful of the cooling porridge. Then she realized that she was the only one still eating. The others had scraped their bowls clean, and were watching her finish.

"You guys are done already?" She looked at her bowl, which was still half full.

They gave you the lion's share, Indy said. *You're their guest.* She crunched a bit of kibble. *Then you gave some away to your dog!* Her mental voice sounded amused. *Which was actually the right thing to do, since I'm also their guest. But they don't know that.*

Their cooking pot was barely big enough for the three of them. Anna's guts knotted with anxiety. *And the two of us are probably twice the weight of everyone else here. I'm such an idiot!*

"Um, hey. Guys?" Anna thought fast. "This was really delicious, but I'm getting kind of full." She hoped her stomach didn't growl and give away her lie. "Would you like some more?" She held up her bowl.

Leitus looked slightly abashed, but he took the bowl with a small nod, and split up the remainder between himself, Helene, and Iole.

Anna took her bowl back when Leitus offered it, and carefully scraped every last bit of porridge out to match her hosts. *I can't believe I let them give me so much, even after I saw how thin everyone is here.*

We're not used to thinking in terms of scarcity. Indy's bowl rattled on the dirt floor as she licked it clean. *But there's plenty of daylight left today.* Her mental voice gained a taunting edge. *I'm sure we can figure out some way for you to earn our keep.*

nna woke up the next day in a cold sweat, frantic from a dream where she'd been wandering the streets of a surreal, unfamiliar version of the UT campus, fending off her father's increasingly irritated texts as she tried to find his office and make her guilty confession about her test score.

The ceiling of Leitus and Helene's rustic cottage confused her for a few moments before she remembered where and when she really was. *Really, a dream about being lost? Real subtle, subconscious.*

She groaned, hurting in a dozen places. She'd spent the last half of the previous day doing chores inside and outside the cottage, with Iole shyly supervising. Indy had sat there and watched, occasionally pretending to scratch at a flea, just to rub it in. *I'm just a big dumb dog,* she'd mocked over their mental link. *I don't know how to do human things.*

After hours of hard labor, another too-small meal, and a night of sleeping on a hard-packed dirt floor in front of the hearth with Indy and Iole, Anna's future-soft muscles ached. Plus, the cool night air had leaked in around the door and window shutters, with the banked fire doing little to offset it.

It'll probably be even worse tomorrow. She grimaced as she carefully stretched out where she lay. *Isn't the second day after a workout supposed to be the worst one? Or is it different with subsistence labor? Maybe people in ancient times hurt every day!*

Indy stirred beside her on the dirt floor, extending all four legs in a luxurious stretch and splaying her paw pads wide. *Good morning, Anna!* She let her tongue hang insolently. *Ready for more chores? Iole's already out there feeding the chickens, so I'm sure there's something you could help with.*

Anna fixed her with a glare. *Don't get too comfortable here in front of the fireplace. I'm sure we'll figure something out for you.*

At least we get eggs for breakfast, Indy said. *I think Iole's coming back with some.*

Ugh. Anna's stomach turned over, despite its empty state. *I just realized that eggs here come out of a chicken's butt instead of a fab.*

Can I have yours? Indy sounded amused. *Can't let those chickens' hard work go to waste.*

Leitus swept aside the door curtain and walked stiffly out of the back room, nodding a greeting to Anna as he walked to the hearth to poke up the fire. Helene followed slowly and settled into a blanket-wrapped chair nearby where she could soak up some warmth.

Leitus poured her a cup of some herbal infusion that Iole had left heating near the coals earlier, then looked at Anna. "Could you come along with me this morning? It's about time to move the sheep over to the western slope, and having two people will make it a lot easier."

Anna groaned inwardly. But then inspiration struck.

"Um, sir? I have an idea." Anna turned and looked at Indy with a wicked grin.

The old herdsman measured Indy with his eyes, approval growing on his face.

What? Indy said over their link. Her ears perked up. *Did I miss something?*

10

Not so saucy now, are we? Anna taunted silently.

Indy looked up from where she was gulping down cold water from a stream. Her black-and-white sides heaved as she panted, her red tongue lolling when she paused between draughts.

I thought those stupid sheep would never go where we wanted, Indy complained. *I'm sure my great-great-granddogs never had to deal with animals this annoying.*

Leitus walked up and rubbed Indy on the neck and shoulder as she drank, backing away respectfully when she stiffened at his touch. "You did good out there today, girl." He turned and spoke to Anna. "She just needs to hang back a bit more when we get a group of sheep together. She's so big that if she gets close, they'll scatter every which way. Stay further back, and the sheep'll clump up on their own. Then she can push 'em along." The old herdsman smiled fondly.

"I'm glad we could help, sir," Anna said out loud. Silently, she said, *Indy? You taking notes?* Indy took a moment from her drinking to shoot Anna a murderous look. Anna smiled sweetly for Leitus' benefit.

Leitus looked over Indy's legs with a practiced eye. "Give her a quick check for burrs, and we'll head back home for the day. I could use some dinner, but a good shepherd always takes care of his partner first. Make sure to feel up between her legs and under her tail especially. A burr up there'll rub them raw before you know it."

Anna looked at Indy uncomfortably, and Indy gave her an unmistakable look back. *No offense, Anna, but there's no way that's going to happen. You need to at least buy a girl a drink first.*

Anna looked back to Leitus. "Um. I think she still needs to cool down a little more?" She spoke quickly as Leitus' expression grew more skeptical. "Don't worry, I promise I'll make sure she's okay."

"Well, could be you know her best," Leitus admitted slowly, obviously unconvinced. "Let's get back then, and we'll get you both some food." He set off, Anna joining him a few moments later after waiting for Indy to shake the dust out of her coat.

More porridge tonight, you think? Anna's mental voice was rueful. It had been a long day, and cold porridge from the night before had made a meager lunch.

Not sure what else they'd have, Indy replied. *They've got eggs from the chickens, and probably get a little produce from their garden. Staple goods like grain must come from a town somewhere nearby. They might trade eggs, or the occasional sheep.* She licked her lips unconsciously as she picked her way along. Then her voice turned mournful. *Look what I've done to my beautiful nails!*

Anna glanced over. The sparkly pink paint was flaked away or covered with mud, and Anna shared a sympathetic look.

Though who knows what the Greeks thought if they noticed them earlier, Indy added. She froze, then sat down and scratched furiously at her flank with a hind leg. *I think I just felt a flea bite me!* She glared back at her side, then stood and shook out her coat, sending dust flying. *Maybe we could convince them to have mutton for dinner tonight?*

But they'd have to kill one of their sheep! Anna said, her mental voice horrified.

You're right. With a flock this size, they probably only slaughter one every few months, if that. Indy sounded disappointed. *Mutton's probably a luxury around here.*

Anna walked along, pensive. Life in ancient Greece seemed pretty marginal. With food so scarce, she hated to think what this landscape would feel like in winter. She did a quick check with Alixa via the earring link that she was still getting used to, asking questions and listening to the answers. It didn't freeze that often in Greece, or at least it hadn't in the modern era. Still, forty-degree winter nights on this mountainside didn't sound fun at all.

As the three slowly made their way back to the cottage, Anna had a thought. *Indy? I've got another idea for you.*

I'm still recovering from your last one. Indy stopped and shook out her coat again.

Hey, I slaved half of yesterday, so today was your turn. Plus, I gave you my gross eggs. Anna suppressed a shudder. *But why don't we use the fab to make some food for all of us tonight? I'm starving!* Her stomach growled, emphasizing the point. *We can say we have to go off alone to wash up, or something, and take our packs with us. Then we fab some food, and just tell Leitus and Helene that we had it with us before. All five of us are going to starve if we try to keep eating like they do. And you're too big to eat so little.*

Maybe we could make some mini-burgers? Indy sounded hopeful.

How do I explain us rolling up in ancient Greece with a bag of two dozen little cheeseburgers? Anna laughed, then suppressed it when she saw Leitus give her an odd look. *I don't think our translator's that good yet.*

They don't have to be in a bag. Indy grumbled audibly. *But anything's better than more porridge. And let's fab some flea repellent while we're at it.*

nna was half-afraid that some sort of ancient rules of hospitality would forbid guests from contributing anything, dooming them all to another night of grumbling stomachs. But Helene agreed right away when Anna suggested that the travelers might share some of their own food with the family.

Anna and Indy snuck off with backpack and saddlebags to the stream where the Greeks fetched water for the cottage. Under cover of the trees and the gathering dark, Anna used the fab to create a washcloth and a chiton, a long, high-belted tunic like those worn by Helene and Iole. They were simple, one-piece garments, so even though their survival gear fab plans didn't include them, Anna was able to cobble one together by using her phone to reshape the picture of a linen shirt that they did have the plans for, then asking Alixa to crudely hack the fab plans to match. A pair of similarly made leather sandals completed her new outfit. After stepping behind a tree to clean herself up and dress, she reclaimed her old clothes, shoes, and the washcloth in the fab. *Is that bottom door latch sticking a little worse than before?* She shoved the thought down. They had enough to worry about already.

"Anna?" Indy kept her voice soft in the darkness, since the cottage was not that far away.

"Yeah?"

"I can't believe I'm asking you this, after how I shut you down earlier. But could you help me out with something?" Indy sounded embarrassed, which Anna hadn't heard from her before.

Anna walked over to Indy, who was biting at a point high up on her back. "I've got a burr up here, and it's just out of reach. It's driving me crazy!" Indy looked away. "Could you get it for me?"

"Hey sure, not a problem." Anna stuck her hand into the fur nearby, and immediately yanked it back out again. "Ew! You're all slobbery!"

"I was trying to bite the burr out." Indy looked away again, sounding miserable.

"Sorry." Now Anna felt like a jerk. "It's not your fault, I was just surprised. Hold on a sec though, I've got an idea." She tapped her phone, the fab went *ding!*, and a moment later Anna held a king-sized slicker brush. She dug around for a few moments in Indy's wet fur with her fingers, finding the offending burr and teasing it out. Then she used the brush to groom the tangles out of the hair nearby. "There we go," Anna said. She patted the area, still a little hesitant. "Good as new!"

"Could you do the other side too?" Indy asked. "I hate to admit it, but Leitus was right. And I can't reach back there very well without any grooming-drones to help out." She looked down.

"I got you." Anna transferred the brush to the other hand and started working. "Girls have to look out for each other."

Indy gave her a look of gratitude and shook out her ruff when Anna was done. "Luckily for both of us, there are no burrs under my tail," she said with a hint of her usual sass.

Anna laughed and packed away the brush, some of the tension that had grown between them over the past few days dissipating. The two of them huddled companionably over her phone for a few minutes, trying to work out what foods two travelers in ancient Greece might plausibly have been carrying with them and which of those were fabbable. They hit a lot of dead ends without a network connection, but by this time Alixa and Indy's collar had deciphered a few more sets of fab plans, two of which contained food items they could draw from. They fabbed a few of them, making crude changes here and there to try to make the packaging seem more Greek, and reclaimed some of Indy's earlier supplies to make room in her saddlebags. Then they packed up their new food and returned to the cottage.

Helene and Iole noticed Anna's new clothes right away, but thankfully didn't ask any difficult questions about why she hadn't dressed like a Greek before. Leitus did give Anna an approving nod when he saw that Indy's fur had been brushed out, and all three of the Greeks looked on expectantly as Anna unloaded Indy's saddlebags. The fab had produced two thick, oval loaves of bread, a small clay jug of brined olives, another jug of olive oil, a crumbly white cheese wrapped in cloth, some chili powder and salt in a tiny jar, two hard smoked sausages, and two small jugs of wine whose stoppers were sealed with wax. The chili powder had been Indy's idea. *We've traveled from far away, right? Who's to say where this came from?* Anna had been pretty sure chilies were originally from Mexico, but she let it slide. More unseasoned food didn't sound good to her either. Iole helped set everything out on the table alongside the usual porridge, looking like she hadn't seen that much at once for quite a while.

Helene's eyes lit when she saw the wine jugs. She rose and went with halting steps to the cupboard, where she took out a large jug and four small, shallow pottery cups. Judging from the layer of dust on them, they hadn't seen much use lately. Leitus rose to help her. Apparently, the jug was heavy even when empty.

After rinsing the dust off the vessels with water from the big storage jar in the corner, Leitus set the jug on the table and arrayed the four cups around it. He looked at Anna and gestured at one of the wine jugs. "Would you mind if I served it out?"

"Sure, go ahead." Anna realized at that moment that she had no idea how ancient Greeks served wine. *I really need to learn to ask Alixa about these things beforehand,* she thought to Indy.

Leitus carefully cracked the wax seal from the jug and pulled out the stopper. He sniffed with interest. "Never smelled one like that before."

Hope they like California cabernet, since that's the only wine we can fab right now, Indy thought. *And wait, who's Alixa?*

That's what I call my phone's net when I talk to it. Anna was a little embarrassed. *My grandfather always called his net Alexa, which was some kind of old in-joke. I copied a lot of custom software from his net, so I call mine Alixa. Like our nets are sisters or something.* She picked up one of the cups and held it out for Leitus to fill.

He looked at her oddly, and Anna got the feeling she'd committed another faux pas. "Um, sorry? We're not from around here," she said, putting the cup back down. Indy snickered over their link.

Leitus smiled tolerantly, then lifted a small flat dish that Anna hadn't noticed before and poured a tiny bit of wine into it. He set the wine jug aside and lifted the dish solemnly, bowing his head. Helene and Iole did likewise, as did Anna and Indy after a moment's hesitation. After a few seconds, Leitus emptied the flat dish onto the dirt floor of the cottage and waited for it to soak in.

Pouring out a libation to the dead, Indy thought to Anna.

Anna's mouth twisted down in sorrow. Was everyone she cared about dead? Had they ever even existed at all, now? Her eyes burned with hot, unshed tears. Just two days ago, she'd been a high school graduate in El Paso, Texas, and her worst problem had been the lack of three points on a test. And now she was here, exhausted and hungry, almost completely alone, and scared about what might happen next. Anna tried to force her features back into an expression that wouldn't invite unwanted questions, but it was hard.

Leitus poured the rest of the little jug of wine into the bigger jug, then tilted it around and smelled the aroma rising from it. He held it over to his wife, who also inhaled deeply. "Maybe a little more water in the krater than usual," she suggested.

Huh, so I guess the big wine jug is a krater, Anna thought to Indy.

Leitus got up and brought over a cup of water, then poured some into the krater carefully. After swirling it around to mix it, he added more water, then swirled it again. At last, he poured some of the diluted wine from the krater into Helene's cup. She sipped, then nodded her satisfaction, so he went on to pour into Anna's cup first, then his own, and then Iole's.

Anna saw Indy's hangdog expression from the corner of her eye, and turned to Leitus. "Sir, can Indy have some too? That's how we do things, where we come from."

Leitus was briefly taken aback, but then he smiled. "She's the one who carried it, so it's only fair." He got out one of the bowls from the night before, poured a generous measure of watered wine into it from the krater, and placed it on the cool side of the hearth where Indy could reach it.

"Before we enjoy this feast." Leitus raised his shallow cup. "To those who've left us, and those we still cherish." He clasped Helene's hand tenderly, and both sipped from their cups. Iole followed, then Anna, and she could hear Indy lap once at her bowl.

Then he gestured at the food. "Now, let's eat! A temperate man should never drink on an empty stomach."

At that, four humans and one very large dog set to with an appetite.

"I still can't get over how much death there is, back here in the past," Anna said to Indy.

It was two hard, chore-filled months after their dinner party with the Greeks. Yet another check of their landing site had come up empty, and now the two of them were ranging out through the sparse mountainside forest on the way back to the cottage, gathering fallen wood for the hearth. The task didn't take much attention, so they talked as they rambled along to distract themselves from bellies that never seemed full enough.

"Don't you think that's a *bit* dramatic?" Indy nosed at a bush that held some kind of interesting smell, the bundles of firewood strapped to her harness rattling as she did so. "Leitus has only killed three chickens the whole time we've been here, and those went into the stewpot and got stretched out for days." She licked her lips. "It's not like we've been feasting on fried chicken every night. Unfortunately."

"It's so unfair. I'm not even a vegetarian!" Anna tested a fallen branch, then dropped it when it proved too rotten to burn well. "I've eaten meat all my life. But until we got here, everything I ate came out of a fab. No animals had to die for it."

"You'd probably have a hard time finding genuine dead-chicken fried chicken in the future even if you wanted to." Indy left the bush she'd been sniffing and walked up beside Anna again. "Most of the animal species that humans domesticated over thousands of years have either reverted back to their original types or died out, except in a few special preserves. A *lot* of land has re-wilded since your ancestors invented matter transmutation and started our modern way of life."

"I guess the chickens here don't have it *too* bad," Anna admitted. "They can mostly cluck around and do whatever they want. But still, it's just… weird and gross to think there's something dead in my dinner." She spotted a small dead tree and picked her way toward it. "It's a pain coming up with excuses to carry my backpack out into the woods, but I eat from the fab as much as I can."

"My kind are less sensitive about the issue." Indy's tone was matter-of-fact. "Look at your teeth. Even you monkeys—" she used the term jokingly now, after months of daily banter "—have sharp teeth in the front, and little pointed teeth on the sides. You evolved to eat meat when you could." She flashed her own three-inch canines in a frightening grin. "I still have the instinct to snatch up my prey and shake it violently from side to side, to break its neck or its back so I can eat it. We can't erase how evolution made us."

Anna sighed. "Yeah, I know." She picked up a short length of dry, jagged wood and added it to the growing bundles strapped to Indy's harness. "I never thought about how much my idea of right and wrong depended on our tech." She loosened the strap on one of the bundles to make more room, then went back to gathering.

"In the future, I'd never even kill an insect." Anna thought back on all the beetles she'd rescued in her front yard. "For real, I'm probably responsible for saving whole bug dynasties." She picked up a long stick and struggled to snap it down to size, finally cracking it under one sandaled foot. "It's easy to take the high road when you have fabs and everything else. But what are Helene and the rest of them supposed to do when they get hungry?"

"I can tell that Leitus is beginning to notice that we're both heavier than our food intake in their house would support." Indy walked closer to Anna, concern on her face. "He may start asking difficult questions soon."

"My dad really needs to hurry up with that rescue." Anna stuffed the snapped stick in with the rest of the bundle on Indy's back. "And what do we do if Leitus kills a sheep for our dinner before then? They're poor, so it can't happen that often. For them, it'll be like a party! You've seen how hungry they are. I can't just say, 'Sorry, sheep is against my religion' or something. They'd look at me like I sprouted a second head."

"Maybe it's against *your* religion," Indy said. "For me, I can't help wondering what a bit of real mutton would taste like." Indy smacked her lips with relish, then turned to look at Anna more seriously. "If it helps, think of it this way. As the shepherd of the flock, you protect the sheep and their lambs, and give them a life free from struggle and danger. You dedicate part of your life so they can live and play according to their nature, here on the mountainside. In return, when they reach the right age, they dedicate their lives back to you." Indy sat down, careful of her load of firewood. "You respect their sacrifice, and you make sure their ends are without cruelty. That's the bargain."

Anna looked at Indy curiously, hesitating. "Do… hybrids have a religion?"

Indy looked aside, ears back and tail set low. "We usually don't speak much about it with outsiders."

"I'm so sorry, I didn't mean—"

"No, it's all right. I think in our current situation, it's good for you to know." Indy lay down on the pine needles, letting the firewood bundles rest on the ground, and Anna sat down beside her.

"Your kind raised us up," Indy said. "Made us into what we are today. The first few of us were created under suspicious circumstances, and there are still questions about how such an unusual technology was developed so quickly, and by whom. The very first one of us started life as a dog named Luke, about one hundred and fifty years ago. He's very old now, but he came to speak to some of us in Austin when I was younger. He smelled like he knew more than he was telling, but it seemed like even he didn't know the whole story."

She huffed. "But after a bad start, humans always, always gave us a choice. As soon as we could understand the question, before we even had a full language, they asked us, 'Do you want to go on? Or do you want to go back?'"

"Some of us, when they heard that question, chose to go back. They bred back to earlier lines, and lived out their lives, their little spark of sentience just barely enough to understand and choose for themselves. Their pups became closer to what we were before, and their grandpups even closer, and then there they were, back in a state of nature. They're some of our greatest heroes." Indy looked up solemnly. "We preserve their memory today, and their descendants live among us with honor. Now we are *their* shepherds, as your kind were ours." She swallowed and an unreadable look came over her face. "When we finally do get back to the future, you probably shouldn't talk about this to anyone." She took a steadying breath, then let it out.

"Others of us chose to go onward, which led to my own family, and me being here today. But that's a story for another time, maybe." She heaved herself back upright and stood, leaning carefully from side to side to settle her load of firewood. "So what I suppose I'm trying to say is, we hybrids have got a different perspective on the relationship between those of us at the different levels of existence." Indy raised a huge front paw and patted Anna's back like you'd pat a dog's fur. "Animal welfare here is actually not so bad, compared to most of human history before the invention of the fab." Her expression darkened. "I hate to say it, but we've got bigger problems. Like why there's still no sign of any message from your dad or anyone else from the future."

"There's no way we could have missed it." Anna stood up, brushing pine needles from her chiton. "We've checked our landing site every couple of days for the whole time we've been here.

Why is it taking so long?" She turned a pained look on Indy. "I don't even care anymore if my dad freaks out about my test score, or if I have to take remedial classes. I just want to go home and start my real life again."

"You think I don't?" Indy's brow furrowed, eyes flashing. "Back home, I was one paper away from making a real name for myself. A whole new phase of my life was about to open up. And now look at me!" She twisted her body, shaking the firewood violently. "I'm a pack animal! I can't even speak out loud when there's anyone around to hear."

Anna sighed. "That sucks. It really does." She gave Indy a sympathetic look as she re-checked the firewood straps. "And we've been so busy with chores and surviving, it's been hard to figure out what else we could be doing." She started back toward the cottage, Indy beside her. "But something's bound to happen soon." She looked around the empty forest. "I can feel it."

13

Winter came, and it was a hard season. But with Anna and Indy there to help, their little household was thriving, even though any sign of rescue was still worryingly absent.

They mowed hay for the sheep, dried it, and stacked it in the little stone outbuilding, then harvested and stored root vegetables in bins under its floor. And even in the winter there was still some forage for the sheep and chickens, since ancient Greece didn't exactly get a lot of snowfall.

They had a few visitors up on the mountain, mostly old friends of Leitus and Helene. And once, a brash young man came to visit Iole, which left her smiling secretly for days, though it seemed to worry her guardians.

Indy's winter coat came in full and shaggy, and she pranced in the chill air. But Anna, who had grown up with central heating, was shivering before December had even begun. Months of labor and short rations had left them both lean as well as toughened, so the cold bit harder than Anna expected. She had grown more skilled at using Alixa's custom software to hack and remix what fab plans they had. So she carefully noted their visitors' clothing, and after some trial and error produced a rectangular woolen cloak and a few other garments that wouldn't look out of place in their surroundings. She even secretly reinforced the wool with modern insulating fibers, though there was a limit to what she could make without standing out too much. It was a good thing Indy hadn't set the portal to ancient Norway or Iceland!

She also went down to the nearby town of Livadeia—which was called Lebadeia here in ancient times—occasionally with Leitus. Each time, they would bring a few chickens or a sheep to barter for olives, olive oil, barley, honey, figs, and other staples and items they couldn't make for themselves. With Anna's and Indy's labor added to the household, they could raise more chickens and feed the animals better, creating more of a surplus for trade. Anna still felt a pang when she traded each chicken or sheep on to an uncertain fate, but she couldn't deny that with the extra goods they could afford now, they were all better fed than before.

Indy would drive the sheep, handling them adroitly now that she had learned to let her instincts do most of the work. Sometimes she would even show off, detouring around the sheep to scent the road before them, then predicting for Anna how many others they would see once they got to town. She got a few looks for her unusual size, but sheepdogs were not uncommon in ancient Greece. Many of them were large and fearsome-looking, having been bred to guard their flocks from wolves, so Indy didn't attract as much notice as Anna had feared.

One cold but sunny day in January, Anna, Leitus, Iole, and Indy drove two sheep down the mountain trails and into town to trade. Iole's real reason for coming with them was to see her young paramour, whose name had turned out to be Neleos. Iole's parents had died some years before, after which she had come to live with Leitus and Helene, who was her great-aunt. Their family tree was narrow, so Iole had only distant relatives to visit in town, but Neleos' family were prominent there. His mother promised to chaperone Iole and Neleos properly at their home for the hour or so it would take Leitus to do his business in town.

After Leitus, with a hint of reservation on his face, dropped off an eager Iole at Neleos' family home, they wound the rest of the way down out of the mountains toward Lebadeia. Once they reached the valley floor, they passed a long, heavily forested hill on their right, and this time Anna glimpsed brightly painted stone buildings up near the top.

"The temple of Demeter the broad-browed," Leitus said, noting her look. "That whole hill is her sacred grove, off-limits to us average folks."

"Broad-browed?" Anna usually avoided asking too many questions about Greek religion for fear of giving offense, but this one popped out before she could think better of it. Her ancient Greek had improved, growing in fluency as Alixa's translator gained accuracy in the local Boeotian dialect, and she tried to dig into new words and concepts whenever she had the opportunity.

Leitus laughed. "I can see how it might sound strange. Every temple worships a different… idea of Demeter? I don't know what you call it, exactly. Our Demeter has a big beautiful face, like a full moon. And she was the nurse of Trophonios, who was a hero from Orchomenos out across the plain, back in the old days. Her priestess here has a lot of pull with the government, and people really like her. Probably only the priestess of Demeter at Eleusis would be more famous, since she's the keeper of the Mysteries." He laughed again at Anna's confused expression. "Sorry, sometimes I forget how little you know about Greece." He nodded back up toward the mountain. "When we get back, we'll ask Helene to tell you the story of how Demeter's daughter Persephone was stolen away to the underworld to be the unwilling bride of Hades. She's a much better tale-teller than I am. I always seem to get things out of order and spoil the ending!"

After passing the sacred grove, they crossed a bridge over the narrow, rushing Herkyna River, which took them into the town of Lebadeia. The city center was mostly civic buildings of brightly painted limestone surrounding a central market square, with more modest shops and houses spreading out onto the lowlands beyond. The river came down out of a gorge in the high, rocky cliffs on their right, and the tall plane trees along its banks were bare of leaves for the winter. But even though the morning market had already wound down, there were still a good number of people coming and going in the fair weather.

It's still weird to me, seeing such a range of older folks, Anna said over their link. *That, and how skinny some people are.* She tried not to stare too obviously, but it was hard not to gawk at the unfamiliar.

Agreed, Indy said. *Nothing they can do about old age, of course. And they're not even too malnourished, mostly. But it doesn't look right to me, either. They even* smell *hungry.*

As they passed in front of an open-fronted warehouse, a well-dressed young man who'd been idly lounging with a pair of friends looked up at their approach. He said something to his friends that brought an ugly laugh from one of them. Then he stood up and called out to Anna.

"Girl! I haven't seen you around here before." He tried out a gap-toothed smile as he looked her over. "And I would've remembered." His gaze lingered where her chiton clung to her body, and behind him, his friend laughed again, eyes bright.

"Not interested." Anna pushed past, tugging her cloak tighter, and Leitus moved to put himself between them.

"Oh, so grandpa's renting himself a foreign bedwarmer then?" The young man cackled. "You old pervert! Probably just letting her grow cobwebs, at your age." He reached down, as if to pull up the hem of his tunic. "Let me show her what she's missing."

Anna rounded on him, but before she could say anything, she felt as much as heard a deep growl beside her. Indy had left her brace of sheep behind and come up to face the man, teeth bared and ruff bristling.

He flinched briefly, but then anger bloomed on his face. "You think your farm mongrel is going to scare—"

Indy charged the man, snapping ferociously, teeth an inch short of his flesh. He jumped back with a wordless cry, trying to hide behind one of his friends, who scrambled to get out from between them. She snorted in contempt as they fled, then backtracked a few paces to retrieve her sheep before rejoining Anna and Leitus further down the street.

"I'm sorry about that." Leitus was shaking his head as they quickened their step. "Those young men should've been taught better manners." He glanced back at Indy, who was once again herding their sheep alertly. "Maybe Indy's lesson will help them develop some."

I'll develop them a bite in the ass if they try that again, Indy said over their link. She swiveled her ears and stole a glance back behind them, but the men were wisely nowhere to be seen.

"It's okay," Anna said. "I wasn't scared. I was just surprised." She made a disgusted face. "Does that approach *ever* work? For anyone?"

"Even in a small town like Lebadeia, there are sons of privilege with nothing better to do." Leitus sighed. "The ringleader back there is the son of a former archon, which gives him and his wastrel friends some foolish ideas." He looked back at Indy again, then over at Anna. "Don't worry. Once word gets around, his kind should know to keep their distance."

After a few more minutes they came to a prosperous-looking shop, with what looked like a broken-handled plow mounted over the open front doors in place of a sign. Inside, the place was neatly stocked with many varieties of staple foods and household wares. The shopkeeper, a muscular, tough-looking man in his early middle age, stepped forward and clasped hands with Leitus, who greeted him familiarly before turning to introduce him to Anna.

"Echetlus, this is Anna, who's been guesting with us these last months," Leitus said. "Anna, this is Echetlus. His family have dealt fairly with ours for many years." He laughed. "More years than I care to admit!"

"Though not so often, lately." Echetlus spoke with businesslike good cheer. "I'm glad to see you around town again, and looking well-fed, too." He nodded to Anna, and lifted an eyebrow in mild surprise at the sight of Indy out in the street, expertly keeping their two sheep in place with the occasional glance. "I see you finally got that sheepdog you'd been wanting. She's remarkable!"

Leitus laughed. "I can't take much credit there. She's Anna's companion. I helped with her training, but she took to herding so quick, I hardly had to do a thing." He turned to Anna. "Echetlus here's a bit of a hometown celebrity. You'll have to ask him to tell you some of his stories sometime."

Echetlus waved it off good-naturedly. "Only if you don't mind being bored, young lady." Seeing that Indy had backed a few paces away from the sheep, he moved to the window and made a peremptory gesture to a short-haired older woman in worn clothes, who silently guided the sheep away.

The rest of their shopping was concluded quickly, the terms of this sort of trade seeming fairly standard. They arranged for the delivery of three large sacks of barley, and packed up some of the delicious local pork sausages and a variety of compact household items to take with them. Then they headed back up the long valley trail toward Neleos' family home, which lay close to the foothills of their mountain.

Ah, I finally get it, Indy said over their link.

Get what?

The plow over the shop entrance back there. My collar net says that the word for 'plowshare' in Greek is echetlon, *which sounds a lot like the name Echetlus.* Indy sniffed at a branch hanging low above the trail as she walked past. *It's a clever way to let illiterate people know whose store it is.*

Lots of possibilities there. Anna smiled. *What if your name sounds like the Greek word for 'buttocks'?*

Indy gave Anna an amused chuff. *We're lucky my collar had a few bits of ancient Greek literature cached when we showed up here, or we would've had to learn the whole language from scratch. Our nets are scraping together everything they can about ancient Greece from all our jumbled data, but we weren't lucky enough to get a history textbook. There's more historical drama and ancient legend in there than facts.* She trotted forward to sniff at a clump of bushes as Anna shifted her pack, nodding to Leitus as they kept to their slower pace.

With no sheep to tend, Indy ranged far ahead, off the well-travelled path and out of sight, sniffing after dormant field mice or whatever other interesting scents she could find. They both knew the way home, so Anna wasn't worried about keeping up with her, and they could always communicate via their mental link if need be, though they tried to avoid it if others were around to see them react to each other's words. Anna and Leitus walked the trail side by side, enjoying the pale winter sun and the mountain air.

They rounded a curve and came to a fork in the path, the right side of which would lead them up toward home. A young man reclined there, thin with winter hardship, but still dark-bearded and handsome, cushioning his head on a ragged bundle propped against the trunk of a bare-branched tree. Leitus slowed his pace in surprise, but then sped up and passed the man with a quick nod, continuing without a word along the trail. Anna hurried to follow him.

They walked on for a few moments before hearing footsteps behind them. Anna turned first, and then Leitus, to see the young man who they had passed at the crossroads.

He smiled easily. "Pause a moment, grandfather? Could you spare a bit of food for a poor traveler? It's been a hungry winter this year."

"It has. And I suppose we have a little to spare." Leitus reached for the bag slung across his back, then half-turned as he heard the crunch of sandals on the rocks behind him.

A second man lunged out of the nearby thicket and seized Leitus' bag from behind. This man was older than the first, and wore a floppy-brimmed hat that shifted on his head as he tried to pull the bag away.

The younger man's fake smile vanished as he ran forward, drew back a fist, and drove it into Leitus' belly, doubling the old herdsman over. Then he grabbed Leitus' arms and held him while the older robber tried to unwind the bag's strap from his body. Leitus twisted on his feet, vainly trying to pull free.

"Let him go!" Anna tugged at one of the young man's arms, but he was much stronger than he looked. Anna let go of his arm and clawed at his face instead, one finger catching the corner of his mouth.

The young robber released Leitus, fought for a moment to get a hold on Anna's arms, then threw her to the rocky trail, his greater weight impossible for her to resist. Anna bit off a cry as she hit the ground with bruising force. She scrambled away, her long tunic tangling her feet.

"You better not have marked my face." Her attacker looked her over, his initial rage turning into a leering appreciation. "Man's got to make a living, you know."

"Shut up and get her pack." The older robber now held Leitus' bag by the strap, and straightened his hat before shoving the old man away to stumble to the ground. "And no more than that. This is supposed to be a quick snatch, we don't need some blood debt on us." The young man swallowed some angry reply and reached for Anna.

A shaggy black-and-white blur hurtled from the trees and smashed into the young robber before he could touch her. Huge jaws gripped one of the man's forearms and twisted, snapping it like a wet branch, and Anna gaped in horror at her first sight of real-life violence done at close range. Indy took hold of the young robber's other arm, planted her forelegs, and whipped her head back and forth, using her full weight to fling the man from his feet and dump him screaming to the rocky ground.

The older robber reacted quickly, stepping away from Leitus and turning to run back into the brush. But he wasn't quick enough. Indy surged toward him and slammed both huge forepaws into his back, throwing him from his feet. His head hit the ground with a hollow *thud*.

Indy turned back to the young robber. He put one hand to the ground and tried to lever himself upright, then screamed when his arm bent sickeningly below the elbow. She advanced on him slowly, head held low and menacing.

"Indy, wait!" Anna called out.

Indy paused and stood still with her ruff bristling, growling deep in her chest.

Anna picked herself up and straightened her clothes, trying to gather herself mentally as she did. Then she addressed the younger robber. "You. Your friend's still moving over there." She nodded to where the older thief was beginning to roll over, hands clutching his head. "Get him to pull your arm out straight. Then tie a straight stick to it. If you're lucky, it'll heal up okay." The man glanced at her briefly, then froze again when he looked back at Indy's menacing light-brown eyes.

Anna shook her head, then went to check on Leitus. The old herdsman was gray with pain, but he took her hand and rose to his feet slowly. She handed his bag back to him from where the older robber had dropped it. There was blood on one of Leitus' hands where his fragile old skin had torn on the rocky ground. She turned back to Indy. "Come on, leave these two. They're no threat to us now."

"Letting them go would be a mistake," Indy said out loud. Her eyes bored into those of the younger thief, who looked back in horror. "Dogs will snap and snarl over a bone. But once it's settled, they'll get along together again in the pack." Her ruff bristled higher. "These two might slink away now, but how do we know they won't come back for a second try?" Indy straightened up from her menacing crouch. "It will only take a moment for me to snap this pair of scrawny necks. Go on ahead, and I'll catch up when it's done."

"Wait. Wait!" croaked the older robber. He pushed himself up to all fours, then slid haltingly across the rocks to throw his arms around Indy's forelegs in supplication. Indy looked down at him, nonplussed, lip curled against his smell.

"I beg you, mighty one. Spare our lives. I am called Thrasius, and this young idiot is Nicon. We're—" The man paused to swallow with a bitter grimace. "We're poor, and hungry. And we've lost our place in this world somehow, and now we're thieves. Grant us mercy, and the gods will smile on you." The older robber lowered his face into the dirt in front of Indy's forepaws and held it there. His younger companion looked on, mouth agape and working, face blotchy white and red with the pain from his broken forearm.

Indy panted as she glared down, saliva dripping from her heaving red tongue onto the older robber's thinning hair.

Anna walked over and placed a hand on Indy's shoulder, her face troubled. "We can't just kill them in cold blood."

Indy glanced over at Anna, then back down to Thrasius. "Leave, and take your accomplice with you." She picked her forelegs up out of the man's grip and backed away a few steps, her ruff falling slightly, but still raised in a threat display.

The robber rose stiffly, pausing to recover his hat from the ground and settle it back on his head. Then he moved to his younger companion and gripped his unbroken arm around the biceps to help him up. The two left without a word, making their way unsteadily back along the trail toward the town with many a backward glance at Indy.

Once they were out of sight, Indy let out a huge breath and lay down on the trail, panting and shivering with delayed reaction. Anna threw her arms around her friend's neck, hugging her close. Her mind replayed the sight of the young robber's arm breaking with a horrible grinding crunch, and she squeezed her eyes shut to banish the image, laying her cheek against Indy's fur.

"We should get moving." Leitus made his way over to them. "Iole and Neleos will be expecting us soon. And no matter what that one robber said, I wouldn't trust them not to come back after us." He rubbed his bruised belly with one hand and winced. "I'll bet they've done that little act before, with the young one distracting you while the other one grabs your things from behind. If they miss the mark somehow, then they cry out for mercy and move on to try again somewhere else. You were more merciful than they deserved, Indy."

Anna suddenly realized Indy had been speaking aloud through her collar this whole time, and turned quickly to Leitus, who looked back at her fondly and held up a hand to forestall her explanation. "I've known you two were more than you seemed for a long time now. Like when the two of us would agree on how to move the sheep, and then Indy would run straight off and do it, with no commands." Anna felt a stab of embarrassment at this. *Clearly we're not as discreet as we thought we were.*

"At first I thought you might be two gods in disguise, funny as that sounds." Leitus smiled wryly, then looked pained as he rubbed his belly again. "There's this legend where Zeus and Hermes visit an old couple in disguise. And that first night we shared your food together, when you and Indy went out and came back with more wine after we ran out, it was just like Hermes did in the story!"

Then Leitus regarded Anna more soberly. "But you living with us these past months since the fall, we could see you were only a girl, and one who hardly knew a thing about how the world worked. Good thing you have a giant magic dog to guide and protect you."

Indy snorted at this, then stood and shook the dust from her coat. "It's not magic. I was born with great fur and loads of talent, but the rest is all hard work." Her tail waved high and proud.

Leitus grinned as he regarded Indy. "Finally hearing your voice is going to make Helene laugh herself silly. I'd have never guessed your voice would come out of the collar while your mouth just sits there." Indy panted a laugh of her own at this as they set off slowly along the trail toward Neleos' home.

Would you really have killed them? Anna asked silently as they walked. *When you burst out of the trees and broke that robber's arm, I almost ran away myself!*

Indy bared her teeth. *After the way that younger one looked at you, I wanted to shake him by the neck like a rat and drag his body into the woods.* She settled again, reluctantly. *Back when I started college, things were still pretty ugly for us hybrids in Texas, sometimes. So I took a self-defense class that first semester. They told us 'Break the arms so they can't hurt you; leave the legs, so they can run away.'* She shook out her coat again, then continued walking. *But that was advice for a more civilized place and time. Giving those robbers a second chance puts our own lives in danger.* Her words boiled with anger. *This is not a game!*

You're right, Anna said, looking down. *If those robbers came back and found us, we'd all be in danger, even Helene and Iole.*

It's not your fault we were attacked. The anger began to leave Indy's mental voice. *And it's not something we were prepared for.*

We should have been, though. Anna's fist clenched at her side, twisting her cloak. *But this whole time, I've been walking around thinking that all we had to do was wait, because my dad would show up any minute and fix everything, and then this would all be over. Like we were just on some weird vacation gone wrong.* Her heart felt leaden. *But that's not going to happen, is it?*

Well… I can't say I wasn't hoping for the same thing. And I wasn't any more ready than you were. Indy walked in silence for a long moment. *But we need to start working on getting ourselves back home. We need to start acting like we're on our own.*

Anna nodded. It was the simple truth, and she couldn't avoid it any longer.

"Let's go pick up Iole," Indy said aloud for Leitus' benefit. "Then we'll send her out for water, and tell Helene what happened."

14

ack at the cottage, with Iole sent off to fetch water from the stream, Helene anxiously tended to Leitus' minor hurts. But she was remarkably unruffled about hearing their story told by a giant dog with a magic talking collar.

"I could tell you understood us, right from that very first night," she said, laughing at Indy's surprised expression. "You'd turn from one person to the other as we talked. Then you'd look off into space, and Anna would look up and say something." A youthful grin brightened her weathered features. "It was hard sometimes, pretending not to notice. But a good host doesn't press her guests for their secrets."

Anna and Indy looked at each other, chagrined. *Is there any part of this scenario we didn't mess up?* Anna thought.

"I'm sure you'll tell us more about yourselves when you're ready." A look of caution flitted across Helene's face. "But it might be best to keep Indy's secret just between the four of us, for now. Even after knowing the two of you for months, hearing her voice with my own ears is a bit unsettling. And many people are fearful of what they don't understand. There's a legend of an immortal horse named Areion, the foal of Poseidon and Demeter, who had the power of speech and was a friend to our kind. But we also have darker legends of the Centaurs, who were half-savage and dangerous when provoked." She put her frail hand on Indy's big paw where it rested on their trestle table and patted it reassuringly. "You've been nothing but a blessing to us. Best not to risk anyone else's reaction if you don't have to."

"I wasn't sure what would happen if we ever got found out." Anna had to swallow a lump in her throat. "Thank you both. For being so understanding." She frowned. "But I still feel bad for Indy. She's had to stay quiet around you guys for so long. Can't we at least tell Iole?"

"Iole's a good girl. She'd never hurt anyone." Leitus sighed. "But Helene's right. She's got friends in town, and her young suitor." His gaze grew troubled. "It would only take one word in the wrong ear to cause a lot of trouble."

Anna opened her mouth to object, but Indy spoke first. "Agreed." She regarded Leitus and Helene seriously. "You're both risking enough, just by sheltering us. I'll keep my silence around her."

I feel bad that you're the only one who has to sacrifice. Anna kept her face unnaturally still, self-conscious now that she knew how obvious they'd been before. *It's not fair!*

You're right, it isn't, Indy said. *And thank you. But it's the right thing to do. And even so, I hope Leitus and Helene aren't signing up for something they'll regret.*

15

For the rest of that day and late into the evening, Anna's worried thoughts kept circling between their near-robbery and their seemingly vanished chances of rescue. The cottage was completely insecure, without even a bar on the door. What if those robbers came back and attacked them in their sleep! With their illusion of safety broken, passively waiting to be saved seemed like a terrible risk. So the day after their talk with Helene and Leitus, they picked up their packs and went out to begin what they had put off for far too long.

First, they fabbed two tiny spy-drones they'd decoded the fab plans for. Small as bees and dull-colored for camouflage, the drones flew all around the mountainside and down onto the lowlands, far enough to see workers planting winter crops on the more fertile land there, updating their maps for a few miles in every direction. Then they alighted along two different pathways to the cottage, which would hopefully give them some warning if anyone approached.

Even though the spy-drones used tiny, low-tech wings instead of antigrav repellers, each one had still required a smidgen of their precious lab feedstock to create. Indy still wasn't quite sure they could afford it, but they felt like they had no choice. Even so, the drones had a limited range and had to fly back to them every so often to recharge, since creating even a tiny drone-sized mass-energy converter was still far beyond their abilities. For now, the converters in the fab, Anna's phone and Indy's collar were their only power supply, and any drones would need periodic access to one of them to top themselves up.

As their spy-drones filled in the details on their map, Anna and Indy scoured it for a good hiding place. They needed somewhere they could build and store things that they didn't want others to see. And it should be hard to stumble upon by accident, but not too hard for them to get to on purpose. They finally decided on a shallow fissure that led back into a cliff face a little way up the mountain from where the cottage sat. The fissure was only about eight feet deep, but it opened out into a tiny cave at the back, just high and wide enough for Anna to crouch down and duck-walk into.

The next day, they packed up their precious fab, hiked up to the fissure, and smoothed out a flat area at the back where it dead-ended, Indy's huge forepaws making quick work of the loose gravel and piles of debris.

Indy sneezed and shook her head. "It smells like a cat used to live in here." She resumed digging, flinging everything as far out of the cave entrance as she could. "I'm going to need to rinse my paws after this."

They placed the fab on the ground inside the cave, sheltered from the elements and from prying eyes. Then Anna pulled out her phone and called up the fab plan for the new mining-drone she and Indy had been laboring over for the last two days.

"Still look good to you?" Anna held it up for Indy to see.

"Well, it looks as good as it's going to." Indy raised an eyebrow at the image of a brown Texas June bug rotating on Anna's phone screen. "I still can't believe you just happened to have the body plan for this thing."

"What can I say? I like June bugs." Anna smiled and stopped

the image with her finger. "I rescue these guys all the time back home, since they're always getting stuck on their backs. I must have looked them up so often that my phone stored everything anyone ever knew about them."

"I *really* wish we had the compute power to run some real design software." Indy sounded worried. "You're not supposed to bash together fab plans for different things like this."

"Eh, I've done it plenty of times now," Anna said. "My clothes are all made from bits of different stuff that me and Alixa hacked together."

Indy made a skeptical face. "Clothes aren't the same as mining-drones." She shook her head. "But it's not like we have any other option. At least there's room inside that big round body for a matter former. We fabbed those all the time back in the lab. We just never tried putting one inside a bug." She exhaled. "I guess there's no point delaying. We've prepped as well as we can. Time to see if it works."

Indy's collar lights flashed in the dimness, answered by the lights on the fab. But instead of the usual ding, the fab buzzed ominously. Its display said *Feedstock mix insufficient.*

Anna's stomach dropped. "How bad is that?"

"Well, it's not good," Indy said. "But hold on. There's a trick I can try."

She looked off into space for a few moments, collar lights blinking, then looked back at Anna, ears lowered in frustration. "I was afraid of that. We don't quite have enough feedstock for this. We need to shrink the whole beetle by about five percent." She held up a paw to forestall Anna's suggestion. "This can't just be a chop job, though. We need to run at least one constraint solver pass over the design, or it might fall apart at the seams after we fab it. But to do that, my collar needs a lot more temporary storage space to work in."

"But what about all that fab plan data my dad sent us?" Anna scrolled through the list of files on her phone, frowning. "We were almost out of space when we got here, and indexing it is making it even bigger."

Indy looked pained. "We may have to get rid of some of it."

"But there could be things in there that we'll need to survive!"

"Most of it's still unanalyzed, so we've got no way of knowing." Indy's ears went back, then tentatively spread again. "Let's try some triage. Maybe we can delete enough trivial stuff out of our caches to give us the room we need."

Both of them spent the next few minutes clearing out their caches. Anna felt a pang as she flagged for deletion movies, music, and anything else she thought they could survive without. *Well, at least it won't be gone forever. I can always fetch it from the network again when we get back.*

"All right, let's try again." Indy's collar lights blinked, and she frowned. "We still don't have enough space. Are you sure you've flagged everything you can?"

Anna looked guilty. "I still have some pictures of my family and friends in there. How important is making this June bug?"

"Very." Indy's brow furrowed as she paced around the tiny cave. "This is our first step up the technology ladder. Without a mining-drone, we can't collect the right feedstock. Without feedstock, we can't make a bigger fab. Without a bigger fab, it's impossible to build a field projector, which means we can't even *try* to get back to the future on our own. So unless we want to just keep waiting around for rescue…" She let her voice trail off rather than re-state the obvious reasons why they couldn't.

"This is our best and only option." Indy stilled her pacing with an effort. "Your pictures won't be big enough to make a difference, though. We're going to have to delete some of your father's data."

Anna scrolled through the long list of unanalyzed files on her phone, dismayed. "How do we choose, though? Any one of these could be the thing that helps us get out of here!"

Indy looked conflicted. "I would guess that the biggest files are fab plans, so we should try to keep those. Other than that, it's anyone's guess how things are packed together. I'd say just pick a few medium-sized files and hope for the best." Her collar lights blinked, and a list appeared on Anna's screen. "I had my collar select these at random. Deleting them will free up the tiniest bit more space than we need."

Anna looked over the list of files, their names computer-generated gibberish that gave no hint as to their contents. "These are as good as any, I guess." She shrugged helplessly. "We didn't have enough space to finish analyzing everything anyway. I really hope there's nothing life-saving in there." She gave Indy a worried look, then tapped her screen to confirm the list.

Indy's collar lights went dark. "Deleted. Now I'll have my net try to shrink the beetle again." Indy stared into space, and complex patterns swirled over her collar. "Tether your phone to my collar, will you? We need more compute power, or this could take forever."

Anna did so, and her phone immediately grew warm, then hot in her hand. A progress indicator appeared, but didn't show a completion time. "Why isn't it moving?"

"There's no certain way to do a design change like this." Indy lay down on the floor of the cave, head on her forepaws. "Our nets have to explore the solution space until they find something that works." She gave Anna a worried look. "There may not even *be* a solution. It might run for a week and come up with nothing."

Anna sat down on the dirty floor, her expression resigned. "Well, we'll just have to—"

Operation complete, Alixa's voice said silently. Indy sat up at the same moment, and she and Anna looked at each other.

"Huh," Anna said. "Well, *something* about this had to be easy."

"It looks like it found a size-reducing solution," Indy said, collar lights winking. "And it passes all the sanity checks." She looked at Anna. "The only thing left is to try it out." She looked at the fab and took a deep breath, collar lights flashing once more.

Ding!

The fab's capacity display dropped all the way to zero percent. Anna couldn't see anything in the fab window, but the cooling fins on the back were visibly radiating heat, which had never happened before, so it seemed to have done *something* this time. She jerked open the fab door, revealing one crawling beetle-drone, small but still recognizably a June bug, wreathed in mist where its cold body met the still air of their little cave.

Anna and Indy both exhaled in relief. "Wow, am I glad *that* worked," Anna said.

The beetle-drone crawled out the fab door, seized the nearest small pebble from the floor of the cave, and held it up between dexterous forelegs. The drone's waving antennae glowed a dim yellow, and most of the pebble flaked away into gray dust, leaving behind a whitish marble almost too small to see. The beetle-drone slowly carried the tiny marble over to another pebble. Holding the two together, the yellow glow surrounded its antennae again, and the second pebble fused into the marble, making it fractionally larger and leaving more gray dust behind.

Anna watched, fascinated, as the beetle-drone spent the better part of fifteen minutes gathering up a perfectly spherical marble maybe the size of a pea. Then the drone laboriously rolled the marble around the back of the fab and up a crude ramp that Anna had carefully packed together from loose rock and dirt. With a final effort, the beetle-drone pushed its hard-won marble into the intake port on the back of the fab. Anna heard it rattle down into the fab's guts.

A moment passed. Then the fab's capacity meter flickered, but stayed at zero.

"Why isn't it working?" Anna tried not to let her anxiety make her voice quiver. "Did we break it?"

"Pups these days." Indy shook her head. "Don't worry, the zero just means we have less than one percent of what it would take to build another beetle-drone. We didn't use up ten pounds of mass on this one drone, we just used up all of our stock of a few very rare elements. That was way, *way* too close."

She smiled reassuringly. "But the result is a miniature example of our whole modern industrial economy. Our mining beetle here"—she nudged at it with her nose—"picks up whatever is densest, discarding the dross, rolling up the good stuff, and bringing it back to the fab's intake port. Once there's nothing useful left in the cave itself, they'll start tunnelling back into the rock, trying to follow veins or strata toward more dense material underground." She indicated the funnel on the back. "Once the fab's matter store has enough of the right elements, it can make another mining beetle. Then we get eight marbles per hour going into the hopper instead of four."

"Aha, I know what's next!" Anna said. "Exponential growth, right? Like one of those sci-fi stories where evil nanomachines escape the lab and eat the whole planet!"

"Well, hopefully not *quite* like that." The former physics post-doc and current sheep herder sat back on her haunches and thought for a moment. "We still only have one fab to make new beetles with. But once we build up enough good-quality feedstock from these beetles, then we can make a bigger fab, and that can make more beetles. Assuming there's enough of the right minerals under this mountain somewhere."

"How long can a beetle go before it runs out of power?" Anna asked. "Seems like a beetle-sized battery wouldn't hold much juice."

Indy sighed. "It's not ideal, but for the time being, the beetles will have to recharge themselves from the fab's power supply after they make a drop-off. It's the same situation we have with our spy-drones. Back home, every portable device has its own power supply, but that kind of mass-energy converter is the hardest thing to fabricate, by far. To make another power supply like the one in this fab, we'll need another fab as big as a house, and we'll have to store up power for a month to run it for two seconds." She stood up and shook the dust from her fur. "We'll get there, but we have to pyramid our way up. We could have some useful stuff in a month or so, but getting to our full potential could take years. Assuming nothing goes wrong." She sniffed at one forepaw and wrinkled her nose at the lingering smell of cat. "And we'll need to keep things well hidden, too. I don't want to gamble on how this technology might change the future if it got out. Time travel was supposed to be impossible, so the consequences are still anyone's guess."

"I'm just glad to be doing something, for a change." Anna flashed a smile. "And all this will look great on my college re-application when we get back. The best extracurricular science project ever! So nothing better go wrong with this little guy." She eyed their lone beetle worriedly. "I really don't want to be eating bland porridge and using dry leaves for toilet paper for the rest of my life."

Indy tossed her head in agreement. "You should be glad the wintertime has fewer household chores for us to do. Because we'll be coming back out here every day for quite a while." At Anna's quizzical look she continued. "This fab isn't an industrial model. It was made for manual use in a laboratory setting." She showed her lower teeth in a smile. "Every time its matter store is full enough, it'll create a new beetle-drone and go *ding!* But then one of us has to come back and open the fab door to let it crawl out."

Anna groaned, and Indy's ear-tips shook with laughter.

16

n the pre-dawn blackness the next morning, Alixa's voice shocked Anna awake.

Unexpected interference with drone operation. Drone taking damage!

She rolled over in front of the hearth, tangled in her blanket, then gasped as Indy jumped up and planted a stray forepaw in her belly as she scrambled out the cottage door.

Drone captured!

Anna made a calming gesture to Iole, who had raised her head at the commotion, and who gratefully sank back to the floor again. Then she hurriedly strapped on her sandals, threw her cloak over her shoulders and ran outside.

Indy? Indy! Even though the moon was unusually bright, Anna couldn't see her friend anywhere in front of the cottage. Her breath steamed in the still, cold air.

Alixa's voice sounded in Anna's mind again. *Drone signal lost.*

I'm on my way to the cave. Indy's breathless-sounding voice came over their link. *It's the mining beetle. Something's gone wrong.*

Anna froze in dread, then began to run toward the cave herself, going as fast as moonlight and safety would allow.

Wrong how? Anna asked. *Alixa said it's been captured?* Anna's heart pounded as she ran, mind still fuzzy with sleep. *Who's going to steal a beetle out of a cave at five o'clock in the morning?*

Whoever it was, they're going to wish they hadn't, Indy said. *If we lose that beetle, it could be a slow death sentence for both of us.*

Anna ran faster, charging along the half-remembered path. She brought herself up short just in time to avoid slamming into Indy's upraised haunches outside their cave.

"Stay back!" Indy's voice was urgent. "Don't trample the scent!" She swept her head back and forth, nosing in and out of the cave entrance. "Damn it! That cat's nest that I swept out of here is spoiling the trail." She paced out widening semicircles around the entrance to the cave, nose low, but then shook her head and snorted. "I can't smell any human here except for you."

Anna's stomach sank. "Uh oh."

"What?" Indy's voice was frantic. "Do you see someone?"

"This is all my fault!"

"How could it possibly be your fault?" Indy sounded puzzled.

"Why did I have to pick a beetle?" She pulled up a video of a June bug on her phone, bumbling and buzzing along the ground, and showed it to Indy. "If you were a cat, what would this look like to you?"

"How would I know? Maybe a—" Indy stood still. "A *cat* toy! Yes!" She waved her nose slowly around, gently sampling the air, then lowered her head to the ground again, pausing on a flat stony outcropping. "Here! It went this way!"

Indy walked forward a few paces, then sped along as she grew confident of the trail. Anna set her phone camera to night-vision mode and followed more cautiously behind.

There was a cat's nest in the cave. Anna swept her camera from side to side said as she walked. *We put a shiny, moving toy into its house.*

And cats are active at night, Indy finished from somewhere ahead in the dark. *But I've got his scent now.* Her voice turned uncertain. *Smells… different from the cats I'm used to, though.*

The path wound crazily across the mountainside, which was

mostly smooth rock in this direction, and pitched downward at a dangerous angle. Anna could imagine some playful tabby batting their precious beetle down the slope, its wiggling legs and glowing antennae an irresistible temptation. Her phone pinged, outlining a tiny bit of metal on the ground, too small for Anna to make out even in the bright moonlight.

Anna bent to retrieve it, giving her phone a closer look. *Found a beetle leg!* She straightened up and looked for Indy, who was scrabbling down the treacherously smooth rocks toward a line of trees at the bottom of a gully. Indy charged as she reached the trees, disappearing between the trunks.

Almost got him, just another—aaah! Indy's mental exclamation was echoed by a yelp from somewhere ahead.

What's wrong? Anna had followed Indy into the trees, but even with her phone's camera it was too dark to move quickly in their shadow. *What's happening?*

Look out! Indy's voice held real fear for the first time Anna could remember. *Get out of there!*

Anna retreated, stopping when her back hit a tree. She heard something tearing through the underbrush ahead of her, and pulled her phone up in time to see a pair of glowing eyes coming straight for her.

She shrieked, dropping her phone and reflexively covering her face with her arms. An instant later something heavy hit her in the stomach, knocking the breath out of her, then clawed its way up her body, over her arms, and into the tree above her head.

She ducked away from the tree, clutching at bright lines of pain across her abdomen and forearms. *Indy! Where are you?* Blind in the shadows without her phone, she felt in front of her, desperate to get away but afraid of running headfirst into another tree.

Got him! Indy shot past and ran from one side of the tree to the other, bouncing her forepaws against it and barking angrily. She stepped over something on the ground. *Oh, your phone's over here.* She looked up into the branches and barked again.

Anna retrieved her phone and aimed it up toward the tree's

shadowy foliage. Its camera outlined a furry silhouette with a lashing tail, and she heard an angry hiss and growl from above.

Quarry identified as felis silvestris, *or European wildcat,* came Alixa's voice over their link. *Large male, approximately thirty pounds.*

"He seemed bigger in the dark." Indy sounded sheepish. "I thought you were about to get mauled by a lynx." She looked at Anna, muzzle welling blood from a scratch on one side. "One minute I think I'm chasing a housecat, then this monster rears up and nails me on his way back here. I *thought* he smelled funny somehow." She lowered her front paws to the ground again and began to circle the tree, sniffing the underbrush. "Cats!" she said, exasperated. "Maybe I'm prejudiced, but I've never liked those smug little jerks." Another growl drifted down from above. "You don't even eat beetles!" she called up at the cat. "Which means he was doing this just out of spite."

Anna walked around the tree, pointing her phone camera down and slowly waving it from side to side. "Nothing here yet." Her forearms throbbed where the wildcat had raked her on its way up the tree. "Ow."

Indy widened her circle, then caught the scent trail again, moving off downslope. Anna followed, stumbling over an unseen rock, then stopped as her sandaled foot splashed into shockingly cold water. She stifled a curse and swept her phone around again. The screen's night-vision mode showed a tiny stream trickling over mossy rocks.

"Water's hiding the scent," Indy said. Her collar glowed dimly to life, illuminating the ground beneath her, but not brightly enough to hurt their dark-adapted eyes.

"It's gotta be here somewhere." Anna tried to cover the ground slowly and methodically so she didn't miss anything. "If I were a cat, what would I have done with it?"

"Probably pooped on it and buried it," Indy grumbled. "You and your beetles!"

"Hey, we didn't exactly have a lot of choices." Anna's phone camera caught a glimpse of shiny chitin, almost lost in the glint of moonlight on water. "There!"

She ran over to a patch of mud, and after a moment of fumbling, dug their beetle-drone out of the soggy ground between her sandals. It was missing two legs, and lay in her hand, inert.

Indy trotted over and sniffed at the beetle-drone worriedly. "Most of it's here, at least. Recharge it a little so we can check its status."

Anna flipped her phone screen-downward and placed the dirty, wet beetle on top of it to charge. "It must have used up all its energy trying to escape."

Indy growled, and was echoed by another hiss from the treed wildcat. "If you messed up this drone, we're having cat-meat fajitas for breakfast!" Indy called back over her shoulder. "You hear me, little monster?" The cat growled again, seemingly undaunted.

The beetle-drone's four remaining legs began waving feebly, and Anna released a breath that she hadn't realized she was holding in.

"Just one more thing to check…" Indy's voice was distracted. A pale yellow glow surrounded the beetle-drone's antennae for a few seconds before fading out. "It's still too low on power to do a full diagnostic, but it seems functional."

"I've still got the leg, if that helps." Anna pulled the tiny limb from her belt where she'd stashed it, holding it up between thumb and forefinger. "And we can search for the other one once it's light enough."

Indy looked up from the beetle-drone, ears relaxing into something more like their usual spread. "The matter former still works, and that's the only irreplaceable part." She looked toward the wildcat's tree and bared her front teeth briefly. "That cat managed to crack the drone's carapace, though. This could have been much worse."

"We're lucky he got tired of playing with it." Anna looked around the hillside for a moment, then put her hand over the beetle-drone to hold it in place while she flipped her phone over to check the map. "Let's go back up this way." She pointed along the little stream. "The way we came down was so steep, I'm surprised I didn't break my neck."

Indy spared another growl for the wildcat as they passed by its tree for the last time, but he just sat up in the branches, serenely ignoring both of them.

"I guess he figured out that you can't climb trees," Anna said.

"Damn cats," Indy grumbled. She licked at the cut on her muzzle and continued walking, footsteps sure in the moonlight.

Another fifteen minutes saw them back in their cave, where they quickly fabbed a replacement for the beetle-drone's second missing leg. They also fabbed a shock deterrent device to attach to its back, which would hopefully make any animal avoid touching the drone a second time.

"Ugly, but it'll have to do." Indy leaned in to watch as Anna carefully pressed the adhesive new parts into place with her fingers. "I can't believe we have to glue things back together in a cave now, like literal cavewomen." She looked around at the rough stone walls. "Back home, we'd just re-fab the whole drone and it'd be as good as new. But here, if we reclaimed it, we wouldn't get enough feedstock back to fab it again." She sighed. "So one way or the other, the die is cast. Either we make this drone work, or we're screwed."

Anna set the completed beetle on the rocky floor of the cave and dusted her hands. "All done." She backed out of the narrow entrance, then stood up and tried to brush some of the dust off her chiton. She stifled a cry as she hit the bleeding scratches the wildcat had left across her body. It was close enough to sunrise now that she could see spots of blood here and there on the fabric. "We need to block up this entrance somehow. This feels way too vulnerable after what just happened." She eyed the narrow opening. "I wish we could fill it with rocks, but then we couldn't get in ourselves." She glanced around them quickly. "I'll try shoving it full of dry brush. Maybe I can make it look natural, like it grew out from inside." She looked up at the slowly lightening sky. "Then we should get back. Iole and the others will be wondering where we are." She plucked at her bloody chiton. "And I need to clean up and change."

"Hmm." Indy looked thoughtful. "I'll be right back. I'm going to run back down to that little stream and tank up on water."

"Isn't there cleaner water on the way back to the cottage?" Anna was already pulling dead branches from a nearby tangle.

"Yes, but I've got an idea." Indy smirked. "And you're the only one with hands, anyway."

Anna shrugged and continued her work. When Indy returned several minutes later, she had the lower part of the fissure reasonably well blocked with dead brush arranged to look like it had grown out naturally, and was using a small leafy branch to brush out their tracks from the area.

"Okay, I'm ready," Indy said. "One large dose of organic cat repellent, coming up."

Anna looked puzzled for a moment. Then she wrinkled up her nose. "Ew. You're not talking about what I think you're talking about, are you?"

"No wildcat's going to go poking around in what smells like a wolf den. Especially after I treed him." Indy squatted at one side of the fissure, and Anna quickly turned around. Trickling sounds came from behind her.

"Ew, come on!" Anna stepped further away. "We could have fabbed some kind of chemical for this, you know."

"Probably." The trickling sound stopped, then started again on the other side of the fissure. "But this is much more satisfying." The noises stopped again, and Indy appeared beside Anna a moment later. "Ah! Much better." She shook out her coat. "Let's go get some breakfast."

17

Being on drone door duty for the following month wasn't hard, but it was stressful. Every twenty hours or so, the fab would *ding!* silently via phone and collar, and one of them would find an excuse to trek out to the fissure in the cold, pull out all the dead brush blocking the entrance, open the fab door, let the new beetle-drone out, close the fab door again, replace and re-arrange all the brush, and walk all the way back. All the while trying to disguise what they were doing from Leitus and Helene, who had already proved themselves uncomfortably sharp. But on the good side, their steadily increasing army of beetle-drones meant that they were now starting to create parts for their next, larger fab, in addition to making more drones. They tried not to let their hopes run too high, but it was hard not to be excited by their progress.

Returning from the fissure one day, Anna walked into the cottage in the middle of a tense conversation between Iole and her guardians. Indy was already there on her bed in front of the warm hearth, tongue lolling as she tried not to eavesdrop too obviously.

"—so his family thinks I'm not good enough for him," Iole said.

Anna raised her eyebrows at this as she went to the water jug for a drink before sitting down on the hearth. She reached out unconsciously to scratch Indy between the ears, but stopped short. It was easy to forget she wasn't just a big dog sometimes, especially when she was being quiet around Iole.

"Give them some time to get used to the idea." Helene put a comforting tone into her words. "You two have only been serious for the last few months. It takes a while to change people's minds."

Iole snorted dismissively at this, but Leitus spoke up to support his wife. "Iole, I know that to you and Neleos, it seems like you've known what you wanted since forever. But there's no harm in taking things slowly. You're a wonderful young girl, and any family would be lucky to welcome you into their house." Leitus raised his hands in a placating gesture. "Please, just trust us. Things will work out for the best, you'll see."

Iole didn't sound happy. "I hope you're right." She rose to her feet and headed for the door. "I'm sorry, I've got to go feed the chickens." The young girl fought to control a sob as she swept past Anna and Indy and out the door of the cottage, letting in a draft of cold air as she went.

At the table, Helene looked worriedly at her husband, then over at Anna and Indy. "I hope she listens to us." Seeing Anna's quizzical expression, she went on. "As far as Neleos' family is concerned, Iole is an orphan. Her parents were poor, and they died young, without passing anything much on to her. Leitus and I have done our best to take care of her, but we haven't been able to do much more than keep her fed and clothed."

"What more would they want from you?" Indy asked. "Iole seems healthy and happy enough."

"Things aren't quite that simple." Leitus frowned. "When a family has a daughter, it's their duty to save up a dowry to set her up in her future husband's household." He sighed and sat back. "A dowry's supposed to be a gift, to help get a young couple started in the world. But the family has to give permission for a son to marry. So if they have a choice of two daughters-in-law, one with a dowry and one without, which one are they going to pick? Their son's going to take care of them when they get old, so a better dowry helps them in the end."

"It's a shame, but it's the truth," Helene said. "I hope that Neleos' parents put their son's happiness first. But I wouldn't be too surprised if they went the other way." She paused for a moment. "We'll leave her everything we have, of course. We don't have any children of our own. But you can see that doesn't amount to much." She gave a rueful look to her husband. "And I'm not sure if Iole's thought of this yet, but if she left to join a husband, we'd have a hard time of it here by ourselves."

Leitus looked sad. "We might even be part of the reason Neleos' family are cool to her. We'd be a drag on their household if they had to take care of us."

Helene put a comforting arm around her husband. "We never thought we'd have a responsibility like this. But life has a way of handing you more than you expect." Her eyes sought Anna's. "It's something you might have to think about too, if you haven't already. We're glad to keep you and Indy as long as you'd like. But if you ever did want to establish yourself here, you'd need to find a husband."

"A husband?" Anna looked at Helene and Leitus, nonplussed. "What for?"

"Don't worry," Leitus said. "A young girl of your obvious quality would have her pick."

"What for—" Helene paused, looking wan, and put a hand to her side before continuing. "What for, is that under the law, only the men of a family can control its property. Even if a wife comes into a marriage with a dowry, the husband controls it after that, though it goes out with her again if she leaves him."

Anna's consternation must have showed on her face, because Helene went on hurriedly. "It's not unheard-of to have a household without a man in it, but it's mainly in unusual circumstances, like a widow with no other family to take her in."

"We'll do whatever we can," Leitus said. "Introduce you into society, help you make connections. Put an end to some rumors."

His expression darkened. "There's been some idle gossip in town about the two unmarried young women we have living with us here, with no father around to speak for them." He held up a hand, embarrassed. "That young wastrel who catcalled you is the one who started it, most likely. Once more people come to know you, they'll realize there's nothing to it."

Great. Anna tried not to let the fear show on her face as she spoke to Indy. *I can either get found out by the authorities, or live a double life hiding all my time-traveler secrets from some weirdo would-be husband.* Aloud to Leitus and Helene, she tried to stay noncommittal. "You've given me a lot to think about."

With any luck, we'll be back home safe in the future before it becomes an issue, Indy said.

Helene had grown paler and paler as they spoke. Now she slumped forward in her seat with a cry. Leitus caught her as she crumpled to the table, face twisted in pain.

Anna and Indy looked on helplessly as Leitus rocked Helene in his arms, humming to her softly until her face gradually eased from its rictus. After a while, with Helene dozing fitfully against the table, Leitus rose and placed his arms gently around her back and under her knees.

Anna feared the old man's strength wouldn't be up to the task, and made as if to help him, but Leitus gestured her instead to push aside their bedroom curtain at the rear of the cottage. With Anna in place there, Leitus straightened up carefully, his wife held tightly in his arms, and carried her back to their bed.

Anna had never seen the inside of their bedroom, and was surprised at its comfort and beauty. Every surface was brightened in some way, whether with strings of carved stone beads, small pottery disks with bucolic scenes pained on them, or tiny pots with the mosses and other plants of the mountainside bursting forth despite the season.

Leitus laid his wife gently on the bed, which was a simple wooden frame, though with an abundance of soft woolen blankets piled on it. Anna hadn't noticed it before, but one of the hearth walls of the cottage's main room made up one side of the bedroom. This turned what might have otherwise been a cold, windowless box of a room into a snug enclave, well-shielded from the weather outside, with one wall radiating heat, but without choking them with smoke from the fire.

Helene nestled down weakly into the bed, and Leitus covered her carefully with one of the blankets, making sure not to tuck her in so tightly that she couldn't move. Then he nodded to Anna, and they retreated out into the main room of the cottage to rejoin Indy.

"Helene has had attacks like this twice before. But there hadn't been one since you came to join us." Tears formed in the old man's eyes. "We'd started to hope that we'd seen the last of them." He blinked the tears away. "We can't change whatever thread of life Lachesis has measured out for us." He nodded to them both. "I'm going to lie down with her for a while. I'll see you all at dinnertime."

After Leitus retired to the bedroom to join his stricken wife, Anna joined Indy in front of the hearth, putting another log on the waning fire.

Could we get sick here, too? Anna spoke through their link, wary of Iole's return. *What would happen if we got exposed to some kind of old-fashioned plague or something?*

Hard to say, Indy said. *Our genetic enhancements were designed to protect against diseases from our own time, not the ancient past. Though hopefully they'd give us* some *protection.* She turned her head toward Anna. *Our enhancements do make us somewhat stronger and faster for our size than a natural person. But we have to burn through more food to stay that way, so that's probably a drawback here, with food so scarce. Without the fab, we'd struggle to keep ourselves fed.*

Anna looked back at her friend soberly. *My father told me once that some professors get their hair grayed when they get tenure, because they feel like people won't take them seriously if they look the same age as their students. But people here just look like they look, or get sick when they get sick.* She swallowed hard. *Or die when they die. And there's nothing they can do about it.*

We can't do a whole lot about it ourselves, at the moment. At least not if there was an emergency. Indy shifted on the folded blanket which served as her makeshift day bed. *We might live two hundred years here in good health, even without our medical technology. But our bodies can't regrow severed limbs on their own. Or heal punctured organs, if we're stabbed by robbers in our sleep.*

Well, thanks for those *images.*

We'll add medical care and personal safety to phase two of our plan, Indy said. *We'll just have to hope that tonight isn't a stabbing night.*

The past sucks. Anna sat back against the hearth. *Phase two can't come soon enough for me.*

18

fter another month of secretive but steady work, Anna could hardly recognize their little cave anymore. The outside was still the same narrow, rocky gap she could barely squeeze through even after the disguising brush had been removed for good. But inside, the fissure now dead-ended in a false wall that could pivot aside like a door, which they had fabbed out of thin panels disguised to look like natural stone.

She unlocked the door with her phone and pushed on the right side, opening it just far enough to slip through into the cave beyond. Inside, it was bigger than it had been when they started, since they had programmed their army of crawling beetle-drones to enlarge it as they burrowed their tiny tunnels in search of rare minerals. But it was crammed full of stuff, especially since Anna had finished assembling their new fab the week before.

The new fab was a five-foot cube with a spindly, unfinished look. They'd had to hack the design to save on materials and to allow it to be fabbed piecemeal by their old, smaller fab. They had also removed the door, to allow new mining drones to crawl out unimpeded. The new fab had to be permanently wired to the old one, since they still couldn't make their own power supplies, but it worked well enough as long as they didn't try to run them both at once.

"Hey, Indy," Anna called out as she walked in. "Ooo, this is new."

Indy looked up from a large display screen that sat propped against the cave wall. Its background image showed a large extended family of hybrid canines posing for a picture, apparently on vacation in front of the Alamo. Anna recognized a younger Indy in the photo, jaw agape in a smile, and she felt a pang as she thought of her own family.

"I've wanted a screen for a while, but couldn't make one until we finished the bigger fab." Indy had been lying sphinx-style on a wide mat while using the screen, but sat up as Anna walked over. "I can control our machines with my collar, but it doesn't give the same visual feedback as your phone. The collar is more instinctive, like a phantom limb that you can move without knowing exactly how you're doing it. A screen makes precision work much easier."

"I'm just looking forward to finally making enough spy-drones," Anna said. "The bats are leaving the newest ones alone now, after I did that last design tweak. But now crows have started stealing them! And every time we lose one, that's a hole in our lookout around the cottage."

"Once we're done here, we'll know everything that's happening on this whole mountain." Indy looked self-satisfied. "Even with the new fab, our drones will still have to be small, and they'll still have to fly back here frequently to recharge. But we'll have enough of them so we can even put one on permanent station back at our landing spot. I know we've been checking as often as we could, but I don't want to miss it if your dad figures out how to pop a camera out and take a look around somehow."

"Good thinking," Anna said. "We're so wrapped up in our tech plan now, sometimes I forget there might be an easier way to get home. It would be nice if my dad just showed up and rescued us." She grinned. "But it'll be much more impressive when we rescue ourselves."

Indy snorted. "Let's not get too far ahead of ourselves. Now that we've got surveillance almost sorted out, we need to start working on personal security. Take a quick look in our index under 'Military equipment, individual, defensive' and choose a couple of things you like. Most of them will need hacking to make them rechargeable instead of self-powering, and fabbing that kind of equipment will take a while, so we should get started now." Lights glowed on her collar. "I've got plenty more to work on here, so just let me know when you're done."

Anna pulled out her phone and lay down on the mat beside Indy, scanning through the growing list of fab plans that they'd managed to decrypt from the mass of data her father had sent them. Now that they were more flush with feedstock and had a new fab online, that opened up whole categories of items that had been grayed out before, most of which Anna hadn't had a chance to look through yet.

She flipped through a few pieces of defensive equipment, trying to figure out which of the unfamiliar items might be useful. But she got sidetracked looking up all the unfamiliar terminology, and her curiosity took over. She backed out to "Military equipment, individual, offensive" and scrolled down that list instead, just to see what was there.

The first few items she was familiar with: "knife, utility," "knife, Bowie," "truncheon, weighted." But it quickly escalated into unfamiliar territory. "Assault rifle, basic." "Assault rifle, heavy." "Proton cannon, personal." "Proton cannon, man-portable." "Proton cannon, crew-served."

She stepped back out to the parent list, "Military equipment." The categories there were "individual," "squad," "battalion," "division," "army," "planetary," and "solar." She looked under "division," which Alixa said was a group of ten thousand or so soldiers in an old-style army. This list held items like "theater defensive photon projector" and "anti-metropolitan kinetic missile." This was getting very weird.

She stepped back out and chose the "planetary" category this time. There were only a few items on the list. "Thetavirus precursor, aerosol." "AQT-1198-23-Z-2 (human-specific)." "Oceanic azootic catalyst (undeployed)." "Crustbuster (undeployed)." Her finger trembled as she stepped back out to the top level of the list again, and this time chose the last category, "solar." It showed only two items, "nova initiator (undeployed)" and "doomsday machine (undeployed)."

'*Doomsday machine*'? *Who ever thought* that *was a good idea?* She exhaled and closed the entry. Then she abruptly selected it and clicked "delete." Her phone displayed a box that asked her, "Are you sure?" She hesitated.

"I thought about doing that too." Anna glanced up from her phone to see Indy looking over, her own screen now dark. "That's what I meant back when we first showed up here, about how scary it was that we had an unrestricted fab." Indy regarded Anna calmly, their heads at nearly the same height as they lay side by side.

"Your father probably only had a few moments to write the query that selected the data to send us. And he must have an *insanely* high security clearance. Running a query like that, on-site at a top-secret government facility? It must have swept up a lot more than he intended." Indy looked pained. "Probably forty percent of what we've decrypted so far is like this."

"We could've deleted these to make space, earlier!" Anna felt sick. "What if we got rid of a complete history of ancient Greece, but left all this stuff?"

"There's no way we could have known." Indy shook her head. "Our indexing wasn't done. It still isn't, and won't be for quite a while. We made the best decision we could. And anyway, it would take us years to build up the manufacturing base to fab most of the things toward the end of the list. I've never even *heard* of half that stuff." Indy licked her black lips nervously. "I have to believe a lot of those things are just designs or prototypes, left over from before demilitarization. They were probably never used in anger." Indy exhaled noisily. "But still. Even knowing this information exists makes me afraid. I don't want to think about what it means about the world we came from."

Anna cancelled the deletion on her phone, and then looked Indy in the eye. Brown human irises surrounded by white sclera met golden canine eyes showing only a thin white rim.

"How about this, then?" Anna thought a few commands to Alixa, then turned the screen to show Indy. "For anything above the level of 'personal, offensive,' both of us need to sign off two weeks before it can be fabbed."

"Hmm. I don't know." Indy hesitated. "What if your dad knew something we don't?" She laid a rough paw on Anna's shoulder. "Or what if one of us gets killed, and the other one really needs that equipment to survive?"

"You're a good person, and I trust you." Anna looked into Indy's eyes steadily. "But having stuff like this just lying around, one click away? What if we run into some terrifying danger, and a huge weapon seems like the only way out, but we mess up and commit some kind of war crime? Or what if one of us gets taken hostage and tortured, to get access to this stuff? What would it take to force one of us to push the button?" Anna put her finger to her phone's screen where it asked for a signature to make the contract binding on both of them. "Neither one of us should have to be responsible for something this big alone."

After a moment, Indy raised her paw and put one pad beside Anna's finger on the phone. The phone chimed and recorded the contract, and Indy's collar glowed in response.

"You're right." Indy placed her paw back on the ground, then shook out her fur in relief. "It would be irresponsible of us not to put some guardrails on. And with any luck, we'll be long gone from here before we can find out if we need them." She glanced over at their new fab. "In another month or so, assuming our beetle-drones keep finding the right mix of materials, we should have what we need to start assembling a small field projector, like a miniature version of the one we had back at the lab in Austin." She looked over at Anna. "And then, if all goes well, we put it together, turn it on, and start figuring out how to make contact with our own time again and get the hell out of here."

"Fingers crossed," Anna said fervently. "And I'll go back through that weapons list and pick some stuff, now that I'm not freaking out about it." She smiled. "Crustbusters may be off the menu, but we need some options besides 'border collie beat-down' in case we hit another bad situation."

At this, Indy struck a ridiculous kung-fu pose, turning from side to side and chopping at imaginary enemies with her paws. Anna laughed, her voice ringing off the walls of their cave. For the first time in a long while, it seemed like things really were going to turn out all right.

19

Through the cold winter days, Anna and Indy continued to build out their secret lair. Their beetle-drones tunneled out more space under the mountain, and they bootstrapped again to an even larger third fab. This one could fabricate items taller than Anna, though they were still limited by the power their original fab could supply.

In the six months they'd been stranded, they hadn't seen a thing at their arrival site to indicate that anyone was looking for them. They'd had a spy-drone stationed there continuously for many weeks now, but no one else had appeared on the mountainside, and their drone hadn't detected even the faintest sign of a probe or camera sent through a portal from their home.

But they'd been building what they hoped would be a portal of their own. It was only a fraction the size of the one they'd come back through, since they were still far away from being able to recreate the entire lab setup and power supply they'd had back at the University of Texas. Their mini-henge was only about eighteen inches high, but that should be plenty to create a small portal, assuming they could figure out how to duplicate the time-travel effect that had sent them back to ancient Greece. Then they could try to send a message back to the future, to tell Anna's father where they were, and hopefully enable their long-delayed rescue.

The day finally came when everything was ready. They had fabbed a sparrow-sized spy-drone and set it up beside the henge, ready to fly in once it opened. And they had carefully charged up a large bank of power cells for a ten-minute test, since their original fab's power supply wasn't strong enough to run even this mini-henge without saving up for it first.

Indy looked at Anna one last time. "I *really* hope this works."

"Me too." Excitement and sick fear warred in Anna's belly. "Ready when you are."

Indy's collar lights blinked, the power lines to the mini-henge buzzed quietly, and Anna could see a field bubble forming at the center of the ring of posts, just as it had back in the future. A light shone from the bubble, but it was gray, rather than the expected color of room lighting, and the fuzzy portal didn't clear to show them an image of their future lab.

Anna fought down disappointment. "Are we sure it's set to the right time?"

"As nearly as I can tell." Indy's collar lights twinkled out a query. "We might be off by a few decades plus or minus, since we don't know exactly what year it is here, but that shouldn't matter. Wheeler Hall is more than two hundred years old. There should be *something* there." She fiddled with the controls, checking and cross-checking. "I'm not sure what's wrong. We *should* be able to look forward in time from here, since we got back here ourselves somehow. Though temporal theory's going to need some major revisions once we figure out how this all works." She nodded at Anna. "Go ahead with the drone test. We might as well see what happens."

Anna picked up her phone and gave their spy-drone the command to hover beside the mini-henge. Then, once it was stable, she told it to fly into the bubble.

The moment it entered the field, the drone's lights went out, and it moved forward sluggishly, as if pushing through water instead of air. It drifted, slower and slower, into the center of the bubble, and came to a stop, hovering there somehow despite its inactive repellers.

"What's it doing?" Anna put down her phone and reached forward to prod the little drone, but then pulled her hand back quickly before Indy had to stop her. "I know, I know!" she mocked. "No monkey paws in the dangerous machinery."

Indy made a quick gesture with her muzzle, oblivious. "Just a moment, let me figure out what's going on here. It's not behaving like it should." Indy stared into space, sending the spy-drone commands through her collar. She looked at the drone expectantly, but nothing happened. "Hmph. You try giving it some commands."

Anna picked up her phone again and told the drone to return to its starting place. But the drone's control app was red-tinged, showing that it had lost the connection.

Indy glanced at Anna's screen. "That's what my collar says too. But that doesn't make sense. We walked into the bubble back home, and nothing strange happened. Plus, it's only three feet away!" She got up and padded around the mini-henge, observing it from all sides.

"Wait a second. I've got an idea." Anna got up and walked over to the workbench where they'd assembled the mini-henge, returning with a thin metal bracing rod that they'd used to hold some parts in place during construction. She held the rod out cautiously, making sure to keep her hand well outside the grayish field, and poked it against the hanging drone.

The spy-drone moved sluggishly. Anna could feel it trying to move back toward the center of the field, but not very forcefully. She pushed harder, until the drone slowly slid out of the field on the other side of the mini-henge, where it fell to the floor of their makeshift lab with a clatter. After a few seconds, its lights came on again, blinking as it restarted itself.

A few seconds later, the spy-drone was responding to Anna's commands again as if nothing had happened. She flew it around the lab a few times experimentally, but it seemed unaffected by its time in the field.

"Huh. That's really weird," Anna said. "What do you think happened to it?"

"I have no idea." Indy looked thoughtful. "Let's try sending it in again, and see if it's repeatable."

"Good thinking. Once more for science, little buddy!" Anna flew the spy-drone back into the field, slightly faster this time.

Exactly the same thing happened. The drone's lights died, it slowed down, and it came to rest in the center of the field. And this whole time the mini-henge behaved normally, its field perfectly steady on her phone's control screen.

Anna tried out a hopeful look. "I'm sure we'll figure this out." She sagged as she exhaled. "I'd feel a lot better if it had just worked, though."

"We should design a more systematic set of experiments." Indy's expression was neutral, but disappointment was clear in her voice. "Varying some of the conditions may give us a clue what's going wrong. And honestly, things like this rarely work on the first trial." She sounded like she was trying to convince herself. "This is pretty normal, for science."

Anna poked the drone back out of the field again. "Let me try one more thing before we run out of power." She waited for the drone to reboot, then shot it back toward the mini-henge at greater speed.

The drone's lights went out again, but this time it was moving too fast for the field to stop it. It slowed down as it went through, but it slid out the other side and skittered across the floor for a foot or so before coming to rest. It cycled through a reboot just as it had before, and it was functioning again in a few more seconds.

"Huh. Okay, I guess that doesn't tell us much." Anna looked back at Indy sheepishly. "Maybe systematic experiments *would* be a good idea." The mini-henge's field winked out as the power cells ran down, and Indy set them to recharge for the next shot.

They spent the next few days shuttling between chores and sleep with Leitus, Helene and Iole at the cottage, and grimly working through experiments in their hidden lab up on the mountain.

By the end of that time, they had a pretty good idea of *what* their little henge was doing, but they still didn't know *why*.

Anything they put into the field bubble experienced a huge temporal slowdown, running about five hundred thousand times slower than normal speed. At that rate, a minute inside the field would seem like a year to those outside. If they flew or pushed a drone into the field during operation, the drone would glitch and shut down. But if they parked a drone in the henge *before* turning the field on, it would continue to work afterward, though its lights would become invisibly dim from outside the field. Then when they turned the field off again, the drone's internal clock would be behind their lab clock, but otherwise it would be perfectly normal, seemingly unaware of anything having happened.

Living plants placed in the field seemed unaffected. Insects could crawl into the field, but then they'd come to a stop until the field was shut off, and continue their crawl unharmed. It was baffling.

After a week, they finally figured it out. Instead of trying to set the mini-henge to open onto the future, they set it back into the past. Their *current* past, weird as that sounded.

At first, nothing seemed to change. But as they turned the year further and further back, the field bubble started to brighten and clear, losing its grayish color. Once they had set it back two hundred years, they could see through the portal fully, just as they'd been able to see through the full-sized henge back in her father's lab, and drones could fly through the bubble with no effect. The portal in their little henge showed their own mountainside, as it had presumably appeared two hundred years ago. It looked not much different than it did today, though perhaps less grazed by sheep.

"The field seems to be working perfectly. I just don't know why we can't set it to view our original time." Indy growled in frustration. "Even if you can't set it closer than two hundred years to your current time, that shouldn't prevent us from setting it twenty-eight hundred years forward." She got up to pace around. "We still hadn't done a comprehensive set of future-time experiments like this back at the lab, so we never saw this stasis effect. The math seemed to rule out future viewing, and quick checks confirmed it didn't work, so it wasn't a priority. And for the past, we thought it was a viewing portal only. There wasn't supposed to be any way to affect anything through it. It should be completely undetectable on the non-projector side." Indy sat down from her pacing and looked at Anna. "I'm not sure what to try next. We can go through more possible settings to try to learn what's going on, but it could be a long process."

"Have you tried searching our nets?" Anna asked.

"There's no point!" Indy got up to pace again, her voice short with frustration. "This was our own cutting-edge research, remember? I know more about it than anyone in the world besides your father."

"That's totally true," Anna said, palms raised defensively. "But remember, the whole time we've been back here, we've had your collar and my phone trying to sort out all that data my dad sent us. We're still not quite done, but what if our nets decoded something useful that we haven't asked about yet?"

"Hmm." Indy looked thoughtful. "I'm co-author on all our papers, so I don't know what there could be that I don't already know about. But it can't hurt to check." Indy gazed off as she accessed her collar. "So far, everything's been straight copies of existing data. Mateo didn't have much time to set up the transfer, and we already know it dragged in large amounts of unintended data. And the transmission most likely got cut off in the middle of something when we were thrown back here, though we haven't seen that part of the data stream yet." Indy's collar lights winked in a complex pattern. "Hold on, still looking." Her tail raised and began to wave slowly. "You're right, I found something! Search for both of our names together, and you'll see it."

Anna hurriedly searched for the names "Anna" and "Indy," changing to "Indiana" when the first didn't work. And there was a hit! She opened it with a trembling finger.

"It's a message from Dad!" Anna said. It looked only partially written, and it had apparently never been sent, but it was addressed to the two of them. She had just started reading it when she heard Indy say, "Oh, no."

20

"What? What!" The bottom dropped out of Anna's stomach as she tried to read faster.

The beginning of the message said, "Anna, I love you. Indiana, please take care of my daughter. Notes below, calling you now." The rest of the message looked like handwritten rough notes, hastily pasted in. He must have written them the night before their cancelled lunch appointment, or while he was at that government lab he had called from right before they got sent back.

Anna tried reading the notes, but it was all impenetrable abbreviations and math. Occasionally a word or phrase was underlined for emphasis, like "Temporal rollback?!" But she had no idea what to make of it.

"Indy, what does all this stuff mean?" She looked at the big hybrid, who was standing with her head hanging low, mouth clamped tightly shut. "Indy?"

"It's bad news." Indy's voice was quiet and flat. "Our original temporal theory was right after all. Just incomplete. It really *is* impossible to travel in time, either forward or backward." She raised her head and looked at Anna, ears laid back against her skull.

"But... if we can't travel in time, how'd we get back here?"

Anna asked. "We're *in* the *past!*"

Indy inhaled deeply, then exhaled, her tail curled under her body as she spoke. "Imagine time is like a coral reef. The living layer at the surface is like the present, building up moment by moment. The dead, rocky part inside is the past. You can't change it, but if you cut into the reef, you could see what the surface used to look like. And the future hasn't grown yet."

She looked off to the side. "Now, imagine you trimmed off the outer surface of the coral, carefully following every little crevice and bump, removing precisely the last 2800 years' worth of growth. Afterward, fresh coral polyps from the ocean start landing on the exposed surface again, so now it's growing just like it was before." Her mouth tensed. "It would be like time restarted itself from some point in the past. Like the trimmed-off part never even happened."

"But that still doesn't explain how we got here," Anna said. "*We're* from the future, and you can't travel through time, you said."

"Technically, Mateo's notes are saying that a tiny bit of the present, containing the two of us and everything inside the field bubble, got grafted back onto the past during whatever happened when we got thrown back here." Indy lay down on the floor of the lab. "But the timeline that led up to our existence is gone. And the future from this point onward is the only future there is. We can't travel forward into it, because it hasn't happened yet."

Anna felt suddenly nauseated, and sank to the floor as the realization struck her. They were not only stuck in the past, the future they had come from didn't even *exist* anymore. Everything and everyone either of them had known was gone.

"How could this happen?" Anna asked in a small voice. "What could do this?" All the hopes she'd built up over the last few optimistic months were draining out of her, leaving only emptiness behind.

"Mateo's—your father's notes were a work in progress. I don't think he knew. That new instrument at Mauna Kea saw something happen out in space, and he put the pieces together somehow in time to warn us. To save us." Indy sat up and leaned against Anna. "He didn't know whether it was some natural phenomenon, or something else. He didn't have time to figure it out before it hit them."

Tears ran unnoticed down Anna's face as she thought of the last time she'd seen her mother Helena, at a hurried breakfast in their kitchen in El Paso, so far in the future. The thought that she'd never see her mother and father again sat hollowly in her chest. It was such a terrible revelation, she almost didn't know what to feel. *At least now we don't have to worry about messing up the future,* came the thought from some dark corner of her mind. *And as an only child, I was really only close to my parents, so—* She drew a sharp breath and turned to Indy. "Oh, Indy, I'm so sorry! Your sire and dam, and…"

"Littermates," Indy added. "Cousins. Boyfriend. Everybody." She lay back down, resting her muzzle on her paws. "Would you mind if we just… stayed here for a while?"

Anna slowly lay down beside her friend, on the hard floor of the lab beside the now-dark mini-henge, and silently cried for her whole world.

For the next several days, Anna hardly felt like she was connected to the world at all. There was always plenty of work to be done, so she and Indy still headed out with Leitus to move sheep, helped Iole around the cottage, and did all the other normal daily tasks that had become part of their lives here. The two of them had taken on a role in Leitus' and Helene's lives that would be sorely missed if they just stepped away and disappeared. So they moved forward, a few hours at a time, and tried to cope as best they could.

But the grief of what they had discovered lay unspoken between her and Indy every moment. Indy grew snappish and critical, and spent much of her time alone, out watching the sheep even when there was no herding to be done, her fur growing shaggy from constant exposure to the elements. Anna often found herself simply numb, unable to process what had happened to them. During the day, they would throw themselves into their chores, trying to keep their minds occupied. But at night, in front of the cottage's warm hearth, they huddled together in their spot on the floor, silently reliving the realization that they were trapped here forever, and that there was no home for them to go back to.

Leitus and Helene must have noticed a change in them, though they seemed too respectful of their guests' privacy to ask uninvited questions. Iole also seemed to sense that something was wrong, and she went out of her way to try to make their lives easier where she could, even preoccupied as she was with her own troubles with Neleos' family.

Sometimes, Anna would trek back out to their secret lab alone. Their mining-drones still buzzed with activity, but now they were building up feedstock for an unknown future, just going through the motions like Anna and Indy themselves. Their experimental mini-henge lay abandoned on the floor where they had left it. Anna felt like she should be doing something. Anything. But it wasn't clear what. So after a while she'd turn out the lights and go back to the cottage, still sunk in depression.

Finally, though, she had an idea. Maybe it would end up being a dumb waste of time, but she badly needed a task to keep her mind from constantly dwelling on everything she'd lost.

She'd come to realize that winter was a bad season for personal hygiene in ancient Greece. For the first few months after arrival, she had bathed the same way their hosts did. The stream they got their water from went over a short, narrow waterfall a little way below the cottage, and then widened out to form a natural pool that one could bathe in. But once the season turned to winter, nobody particularly fancied the idea of splashing cold water on themselves out of doors.

Of course, you *could* carry water from the pool back up to the cottage one jug at a time, heat it at the hearth, and use it to take a kind of sponge bath. But that was so much trouble that people usually just bathed less often in the winter. Which was really starting to gross her out.

Indy was unsympathetic. "Just don't wear so much cloth wrapped around you, and you won't smell so rank." Her own sanitary habits mostly consisted of daily swims across frigid, muddy streams in pursuit of unruly sheep, and the occasional roll in dry grass. She wasn't exactly clean, but she at least wasn't that smelly.

Which was more than Anna could say for herself. It felt like she had dirt seamed into her skin that would never come out.

So Anna decided to do something about it. She talked through a few alternatives with Alixa, entered a fab order, and picked up the resulting small bundle the next time she visited their dark and lonely cave. Then she went down to the waterfall one cool, late-winter afternoon and set to work building a hot tub.

Anna had fabbed two things: a heater pipe and a rock molder. The heater pipe was just a metal pipe, about a foot long and two inches across, which would heat water passing through it up to a nice hundred degrees or so whenever its hidden sensor detected your presence.

The rock molder was a common landscaper's tool that looked something like an ice-cream scoop. It would let Anna carve easily through the crumbly limestone of the Greek mountainside with the scoop end, and then pack the tailings into place with the handle, which subtly re-formed them to look like natural rock again. Indy had fabbed the rock molder earlier to disguise the door to their cave, so Anna had only had to re-fab a human-style handle onto it.

Alixa had drawn up the hot tub plans to fit a location slightly to the side of where their natural waterfall tumbled down to feed their bathing pool, and Anna had made sure they were straightforward enough that she could follow them by hand. Programming their beetle-drones to do the work would've been easier, but Anna couldn't risk having a huge swarm of them running around in the open. Plus, the whole point of the exercise was to give her something else to think about besides their desperate situation, so the harder it was for her to build, the better.

With the rock molder, Anna quickly carved a deep slot into the stony ground, leading from the stream over to a dry limestone shelf six feet above the ground beside the pool. She placed the heater pipe carefully into the lower end of the slot, so that water diverted from the stream would flow through it and out onto the shelf, where it cascaded down in a narrow shower. Then she packed rubble back over the slot using the molder's handle, careful to make it look natural, and went to work carving out a tub below.

In moments, she was soaked to the skin by the cold shower she had just made.

Nice job, genius. She shivered as icy water ran down her back. *Next time, carve out the tub first, and* then *route the water into it.* She quickly turned the heater pipe on and dialed the temperature up until it was barely warm enough to be tolerable, not wanting to use up all of its stored power too quickly. Then she wiped the water out of her eyes and went back to work, holding her phone in front of her periodically so she could see the plans overlaid onto the scenery and know where to carve next.

A few stolen afternoons of work later, she had created something she had dreamed about for months. A little of the stream's natural flow now bypassed the waterfall and fed into the heater pipe's intake. The warm outflow rushed out of a natural-looking hole, ran off the rock shelf and splashed down onto a wide ledge which Anna had carved beside a rough, oval tub. The overflow from the tub gurgled over one wall and down into the original stream's pool, which continued its course through the forest as it had before. Anna scattered the leftover chunks of rock around in plausible locations after reshaping and disguising it with the molder's handle, which took the user's motions as guidance, but filled in the surface details using its internal library of natural shapes and textures.

She felt proud but a little foolish, standing in front of her creation. Had this really been the best use of her time? Arguably she should be spending every spare moment running new mini-henge experiments, or coaxing Indy out of her funk to find a loophole in her father's analysis that had shown them to be hopelessly stranded in the past. But those tasks were so big that it felt like she couldn't even find a starting place. Whereas with a tub, you just start scooping out rock, and eventually it's done.

Finally, Anna pinged Indy her location via their link. *Come take a look what I made!*

I'm sure it's great. Indy's mental voice came over in a depressed monotone. *I'll check it out later, whatever it is.*

Dammit Indy! Anna fought back a hot rush of tears. *We can't just lie around forever. Come on!*

Fine. Indy signed off abruptly, but at least it sounded like she was coming.

She quickly stripped down to her fake, fabbed-from-modern-materials-but-made-in-Greek-style undergarments, cranked up the water temperature, and got into the tub before her friend arrived. She was still a little shy in front of Indy, which didn't make a lot of sense, considering. *Indy's a whole different species from me. Plus she's naked all the time, herself! But still.*

Indy found Anna there a few minutes later. The human girl lay utterly relaxed in the newly created hot tub, her soiled outer clothing hanging from a tree nearby, with freshly-fabbed dry clothes folded up out of the way to don after she emerged.

"Come on in!" Anna called out. "I made it big enough for three or four people, and it's plenty rough so nobody will slip."

"You made this?" Indy goggled, caught totally off guard. "You made... a hot tub?"

"I needed something to keep my mind off of—" Anna's voice caught. "Well, you know."

Indy's expression softened. She made her way over to the tub and unclipped her harness with a dexterous paw. Then she dipped a pad in to test the water before wading in slowly.

Anna laughed as the water level rose, sloshing out into the stream and slowly refilling with hot water from the shower above. "Isn't this the best thing ever?" She lifted a brown forearm out of the hot water and held it up for Indy to see. "I haven't been this clean since before we got here!"

Indy sank down fully into the water, submerging herself to the neck. "Ahhh!" She closed her eyes in contentment. "I won't pretend this doesn't feel pretty fabulous. I can *tolerate* bathing in cold streams, but that doesn't mean I *prefer* it." The big canine sank even lower, wetting her neck up to the bottoms of her ears. "You should've built this a long time ago."

"I know, right?" Anna put her arm back into the water. "Don't take this the wrong way, but sometimes it feels like I'm really just your assistant when we're working on the really hard problems. It's nice to make a difference on my own, too." She peered down into the water and made a face of mock disgust. "Ew, look how dirty you are!"

Indy opened her eyes and looked down. They could both see the mud sluicing from her paws and streaming up over the edge of the pool in the current, clouding the formerly clear water as it washed away.

"Some of us have to work for a living," Indy said with great dignity. Then she spoiled it with a big, sheep-eating grin. "I admit it, this is indeed the best thing ever." She paused a moment. "But how are we going to explain this? If there were a hot spring here, people would have known about it already."

"Who's to say a new one can't pop up?" Anna looked guilty and defiant together. "Yeah, maybe it's a little suspicious." She looked down. "But it's not like we have to worry about messing up the future anymore."

"Well, I suppose we still need to carefully consider what we do here. Even if it can't affect our original future anymore." Indy looked down somberly. She rubbed her paws together under the water, releasing more mud in a murky cloud. "Decisions that seem small to us could end up having big consequences for the people around us. But if we take that kind of thinking too far, we'd just have to lock ourselves in our cave and never come out." She relaxed again, watching the water clear as the current pushed it up and out of the tub. Then her ears pricked forward. "Wait, how are you heating this water? Our only stationary power supply's in the original fab up in the cave." She looked around. "Is your phone plugged into it somewhere?"

"The heater recharges itself from the energy of the water flowing through it." Anna spoke with more than a trace of pride. "It'll probably take a week to charge back up if you run it all the way down, but there'll be enough for at least a shower every day or so. For now, the only way to adjust the temperature is my phone or your collar. But we don't have to tell Leitus and Helene about that part. I don't know if hot water would help whatever disease Helene's got, but it would probably at least make her feel better." She felt a pang of guilt. "I know we've got bigger problems. But it's nice to work on something for the here and now." She sighed, but couldn't feel too unhappy when enjoying her first hot bath in many months. "Our problems might seem a little smaller after we're clean."

"And we need to get Iole down here, too." She looked at Indy awkwardly. "Her blanket's on the other side of the hearth from ours, but sometimes I'll still get a waft of something a bit… sheepy. Not that that's a bad thing," she added quickly.

"No offense taken." Indy leaned over to rub her flanks against the rough walls of the tub. "It's normal for a herding dog to smell a little bit like sheep. But when a human does, that's just not right."

22

few days later, on a fine sunny afternoon when the first stirrings of spring had finally begun to brighten the air, Anna invited all three Greeks down to the pool to show off her new creation. She told them only that it was a surprise, and that they should bring their usual bathing supplies, regardless of the fact that the water would normally still be far too cold for comfort at this time of year.

Leitus escorted Helene down the path to the pool, with Iole, Anna, and Indy close behind in case the old man needed assistance. But on this day Helene's steps were less hesitant than usual, and she made it down to the pool mostly under her own power.

"It's very well made, Anna." Leitus looked approvingly around the new setup, running a hand over the edge of the tub. "How did you find the time to do all this? And the tools?"

"It'll be wonderful, once the season's warm enough." Helene's eyes were bright as she spoke.

"Well, you haven't seen the surprise yet." Anna smiled. "Put your hand in the water, up there where it falls."

Anna had programmed the sensor to turn it on when any of the three Greeks approached, and Leitus, Helene and finally Iole marveled at its new warmth. Leitus opened his mouth to ask the obvious question, but Anna quickly cut him off.

"It turns out that there's a hot spring here now." She tried to keep her statements true, though incomplete. "I channeled it over here, and carved out a tub for it."

Helene looked at Anna slyly, then nodded to the other Greeks. "We're not going to ask any questions." Her face creased in a smile. "Especially not about something this useful."

"What questions?" Iole looked confused. "Hot springs just pop up, sometimes."

"They totally do," Anna said. She added a mental smirk to Indy. *See?*

"Shall we try it out?" Leitus asked.

"You guys go ahead," Anna said. "Let us know if you need anything."

Ancient Greeks didn't seem to be especially modest about bathing in their underclothing, but nevertheless Anna and Indy withdrew out of earshot to the edge of the clearing, leaving Iole to assist Leitus and Helene. Anna had left one side of the tub with a natural slope, so one could walk down into it without having to negotiate any steps. And the look on Helene's face as she sank into the steaming water made all of Anna's earlier efforts worthwhile. Leitus helped her lather up gently with a light soap they had bought in town months ago, but after that Helene simply lay back against the rocky ledge, smiling blissfully.

It's weird. If I hadn't asked my dad for a lab tour that day, I'd be gone along with all the rest of the future. Anna looked over at the Greeks, trying to steer her thoughts away from the dark spiral that always tugged at them. *But at least something that I built here is doing good for somebody.*

It's my fault that we're stuck so far back in time, Indy said, her mental voice bitter. *If I had just showed you what your father asked me to, we'd at least be stranded in a more modern civilization.*

You can't take that all on yourself, Anna said. *I wanted to see ancient Greece too.*

I'm still not sure how our lab settings could've affected something as big as the temporal resonance your father saw coming. Indy frowned in thought. *Why did the timeline get cut off right around where our one little experiment was looking?* She sighed. *We'll probably never fully understand what happened.*

Why 'never'? Anna didn't look at her friend directly, since Iole might see. *You can keep developing the theory that you and my dad were working on.* A bit of hope flickered in her heart. *One day I could help, too. You can train me, and we'll figure it out together.*

Science doesn't work like that, Indy said. *Even a genius can't work in a vacuum. It takes a community of dozens or hundreds of scholars working for decades to make those kinds of advances.* She tried for a more upbeat tone. *We can probably add on a bit here and there. But it's not something two people can do alone.*

But what if— Anna cut off her reply as Iole walked over to join them.

The young woman looked both of them in the eyes, laying one hand on Indy's shoulder and the other on Anna's arm. "There's no way I can pay you back for what you've done for my great-aunt and uncle." She pulled a small, stoppered tube out of a fold in her waistband and held it out to Anna, looking at Indy as she did. "But I noticed when you first got here, Indy had the nicest pink paint on her toenails! I don't know where you got it. I've never seen a color like that before. So when Neleos gave this to me, I thought of you two."

Anna accepted the tube gravely, not knowing what it contained, but touched by the gesture.

"Whatever I can do for the two of you, I'll do." Iole looked down, embarrassed. "Hopefully someday when I amount to something, that'll mean more than it does now. I know I must sound pretty foolish."

Anna gave Iole a measuring look. The younger woman had placed her hands equally on her and Indy. Perhaps Leitus and Helene's grand-niece was more perceptive than they'd given her credit for.

"Leitus and Helene took us in when we didn't have a friend in the whole world." Anna's heart wrenched because of how literally true that was now. "We're glad to do whatever we can to help make their lives easier." Too late, Anna realized she'd said "we" instead of "I," but she let it stand, not wanting to draw attention by correcting herself.

Iole gestured toward the hot tub, where Leitus was helping Helene emerge from the steaming water, covering her thin shoulders with a heavy woolen robe. "I need to go see if they need any help. But remember what I said."

"We will," Anna said. And Indy nodded, almost imperceptibly.

23

Helene made it most of the way back to the cottage on her own, only leaning on her husband here and there when the footing was uncertain. But Anna could see that the old woman's strength had been taxed by the short trip. Iole went outside to tend to the chickens while Leitus settled his wife into bed in the back room. He emerged a few minutes later, looking both happy and resigned.

"I haven't seen her feeling so good in a long, long time." The old man settled himself at the table. "Thank you two, again." He sighed, lightly. "I can't help thinking there won't be that many more golden days like this for us." His lined features grew serious. "All the years we've been through together, I never thought about what it would be like, if one of us went before the other." His brown eyes were sad. "I can't say I like the idea."

"So. About that." Anna shared a look with Indy. "Back home—" She stopped, fighting to keep her composure as she thought of everything she'd lost. She cleared her throat. "Back home, we have special… treatments, I guess you'd call them, that can help keep people healthy. We thought about it after we saw Helene's… attack, or whatever it was. These treatments aren't usually used like this, but…" Anna struggled for the right words, looking to Indy for support.

"Think about it this way, Leitus." Indy spoke matter-of-factly. "Say that each person has a set lifespan that they'll eventually reach, assuming nothing goes wrong. So as long as you don't fall off a cliff or catch a fatal disease, there's some best-case age that's different for each person. But for any two people, those ages are going to be different," Indy went on. "Usually, you'd treat each person separately. But if you gave a stronger treatment to one person than the other, you could make their lifespans closer to equal."

"We'll take it," Leitus said.

Indy looked nonplussed. "But I haven't explained the drawbacks yet."

"I don't care about those." Leitus rubbed at his eyes as they grew red with emotion. "If you can do something to make sure that neither of us has to live without the other, well… that sounds pretty good to me."

"Leitus, we need to tell you both sides," Anna said. "Otherwise, you wouldn't understand what you're agreeing to. It wouldn't be right."

Leitus thought for a few moments. "All right," he said slowly. "Tell me."

"If we do this, you'll both live longer than you would have otherwise, but Helene more so than you," Anna replied. "If we gave you both the same treatment, you'd benefit from it more. So you'd be making a sacrifice to stay together."

"I'm sorry we don't have a better option for you," Indy added. "We're not yet in a position where we can work to our full potential."

Leitus shook his head. "Even your bad option sounds pretty good to me."

Anna felt an irrational stab of jealousy. *I wish someone could just come through like this for us,* she thought to Indy. *It feels great to help people. But still…*

Indy put a sympathetic paw on Anna's arm. *We feel our own hurts more keenly when we see someone else made whole.* Anna nodded in reluctant agreement.

Leitus grinned, unaware of their exchange. "Do you remember that story I mentioned to you, back before we knew Indy could talk?"

"Yeah, the one where Zeus and what's-his-name disguise themselves and visit an old couple, right?" Anna vaguely remembered that conversation.

"Zeus and Hermes, yes, that's the one. At the end of that story, because the old couple treats them so kindly, Zeus gives them a gift. The gift of one never having to live without the other." Leitus chuckled. "Of course, in that same story Zeus also destroys the nearby town where he and Hermes couldn't find any hospitality. But the rest of it matches up pretty well!" He grew serious again. "We should explain all this to Helene. She needs to agree too. But say that she does. How does this boon of yours work?"

"That part's easy." Anna went to her backpack and dug out a tiny, carved wooden box they'd fabbed earlier. She came back and opened it to reveal two smooth green pills. "To start it, each of you swallows a green pill." At Leitus' quizzical look, she said, "Yep, that's all there is to it."

You make it sound so easy. Indy's mental voice was dry. *If we hadn't found fab plans for these pills, there's no way we could have invented them ourselves. I guess with me being a 'magical talking dog,' they just assume we can do anything.*

"How long until—" Leitus stopped abruptly as Indy's ears flicked toward the door.

"Iole's back," Indy said. "We'll talk more later."

The three of them rose to greet Iole, and they easily slipped into their usual routine of dinner preparation, though the evening's meal was quieter than usual. Leitus brought food to Helene where she rested in the bedroom, and the two talked in low voices behind the curtain. Anna shared the dining table with Iole, which meant awkwardly ignoring Indy over at her usual spot near the hearth, since Iole still wasn't privy to their secret.

Finally, to have something to talk about, Anna pulled out the small gift Iole had given her back at the pool, and admitted her ignorance. "Sorry Iole, but how does this work? It seems like this little tube should open, but I can't figure it out, and I don't want to break it."

Iole laughed and held out her hand for the tube. "Here, let me show you." She twisted the cap end a quarter-turn and pulled it off, holding it so Anna could see a bright red powder inside. "It's red ochre. It doesn't take much, so there should be enough to do all of Indy's nails. Assuming she likes the color?"

Oh, Indy likes, came the thought over their link. Anna looked over her shoulder and saw Indy suddenly sitting right behind her, with a gleam in her eye and one forepaw already raised. Anna laughed, heart lighter than it had been for many weeks as her friend gently placed her paw on the table.

Anna looked at Iole. "I'd say that's a yes."

"Easy there, it takes a few minutes to get it ready!" Iole smiled as she brought over a tiny brush, some short twigs, and two small bowls from the far side of the table. "I saved a couple of egg yolks from dinner, I just need to mix everything together." She tapped some of the red powder into one bowl already stained from previous use, and deftly mixed in egg yolk and water, stirring it with a twig. Once the mixture was smooth, she took the brush, sat down beside Indy and pulled the white fur aside from one blunt nail. "You brush it on like this." Iole dipped the brush and coated the nail in one smooth stroke.

Indy sat stock-still as Iole painted each nail on one front paw, then the other, wedging a length of broken-off twig between each toe to keep the nails separated. The she stood back to admire her work.

"Not bad!" Iole looked from Indy to Anna. "Do you think she likes it?"

Tell her it's wonderful, Indy said. *Just looking at it makes me feel more like myself again!*

"She thinks it's wonderful," Anna said out loud. "And so do I." She hugged the younger woman, who looked surprised but pleased. "It was a very thoughtful gift."

Anna released Iole as a thought occurred to her. "How long does this stuff take to dry?"

"Not too long," Iole said. "Maybe don't walk on it for fifteen minutes?"

Indy froze. *Fifteen minutes?*

"We'll get her to put her paws on the hearth, the heat'll speed it up," Iole continued. "Then we can start on the back feet."

Anna and Iole laughed together as Indy's ears drooped.

Still totally worth it, Indy said.

24

The next day, Anna and Indy were returning to the cottage with water for the evening when they saw a half-recognized man in a floppy-brimmed hat walking up the slope from town. He had been heading in the general direction of the cottage, but he stopped when he saw them emerge from the woods, and held up his hands to show they were empty. Then he waited for them to come to him.

As they neared the man, Anna's heart clenched with dread. It was the older of their two robbers from a few months ago. *What was his name again?*

"Thrasius," Indy growled. "There's a face I hoped I'd never see again." She lay down briefly, and Anna unloaded the heavy waterskins from Indy's saddlebags and laid them on the ground, along with her own pack, so they'd be able to move quickly if they needed to.

"He must've walked right between our spy-drones somehow." Anna looked around. "Indy, could you use your collar to call them all in closer? Someone else might still be hiding out there."

"Done," Indy replied. "And it was the squirrels this time," she added. "My last design tweak finally got the crows to ignore our spy-drones, but now the squirrels are burying them, and it left a hole in our network."

"At least they have trackers in them now." Anna took stock of her equipment, regretting too late that she hadn't accelerated their preparations for this day even more. She had carried a small knife for a while now, for daily use as well as protection, but that didn't stop her from feeling vulnerable. Still, the man seemed unarmed, and Alixa whispered in Anna's earring that their drones couldn't see anyone else coming up the trail. Fortunately, Iole was visiting Neleos and his family again today, so they didn't have to worry about watching out for her too.

Anna and Indy closed the distance to the older man warily, expecting the worst, but he waited for them without moving, keeping his empty hands raised.

"Thrasius." Indy's guttural growl contrasted eerily with her collar's voice. "I can't think of a single good reason for you to be here." She stared at the man as she advanced stiff-legged, tail high, and he wavered back in fear.

"I can tell you, I never wanted to come back here." Thrasius stopped backing away, though he carefully avoided looking Indy in the eye. "But you need to hear what I have to say. I came to warn you."

"Warn us about what?" Anna asked.

"Could I address your household?" Thrasius motioned upslope toward the cottage. "This is something you all should hear." Anna shivered at the old robber's tone when he said that, and looked over at Indy questioningly.

Indy paused a long moment, then nodded. *He's no threat on his own. And he obviously already knows where we live. We should hear him out.*

"Wait here," Anna said to Thrasius. She looked around again to make sure there was no one else approaching, then walked back with Indy to retrieve their waterskins and her pack. Then they guided Thrasius to the trail, which he must have missed on his way up, and flanked the older man as they walked the rest of the way to the cottage.

As they approached the front door, which was open to the cool afternoon breeze, Anna called out. "Leitus! Helene! We have a visitor!" After a few moments, the old shepherd appeared in the doorway. His smile turned neutral as he saw who their visitor was.

"What brings you here, Thrasius?"

"I apologize for coming unwelcome to your home." Thrasius squared his shoulders, defensive. "But I'm bringing you a warning. A warning about a danger that I'm partly responsible for. I understand if you want me to stay out here, but I'd feel better if I could talk to you all at once." At Leitus' quizzical expression, Thrasius added, "They mentioned you had a wife when I asked directions in Lebadeia. This concerns her too, sadly."

Indy and Anna looked at each other questioningly, then over at Leitus. After a moment, the old shepherd made up his mind. "Come in. And be welcome in my house." Leitus led the way back into the cottage, and Thrasius doffed his hat and followed. After shucking off her pack and unloading Indy's, Anna entered a few moments later. Indy trailed warily behind, frequently glancing back out at the trail and at the forest's edge.

As they sat, Helene emerged from the bedroom and nodded a greeting to their guest, though her displeasure at seeing her husband's attacker was plain on her face. She was looking better, with more color in her face and a steadier step. *Looks like someone took her green pill yesterday,* Anna thought to Indy. *I didn't think we'd see a difference already.*

Helene must have heard the scene at the door, because the old woman went to the big water jug and dipped out a cupful, then tore a piece from that morning's flatbread. She brought both over to Thrasius, who rinsed his hands with a bit of the water. Then he ate the bread solemnly, and drank the rest of the water down in a few swallows. He handed the cup back to Helene, who welcomed him with the same words her husband had used, though with markedly less sincerity.

At Leitus' gesture they all sat, Leitus and Helene closest to their visitor, Anna near the hearth, and Indy at the doorway. The old herdsman gestured to Thrasius. "Speak." He gave Indy a significant glance. "And have no fear. I'm the master of this house, and none living here will break peace with a guest."

Indy, who had been looking daggers at their former robber this whole time, took the hint and adopted a less menacing expression, though one still anything but peaceful.

"Well, the best thing is just to say it." Thrasius rubbed the back of his neck, ill at ease. "I've come to warn you that you're all in danger. The man who was with me a few months ago—"

"Nicon," Indy said grimly. All heads turned to look at her. "I marked both their names well."

"Yes, Nicon," Thrasius went on. "I told him I was done with robbery, and that he should quit too if he had any sense. He skulked off to Thebes for a while, where his people are, to lick his wounds. I set his arm for him before we parted ways, but he was always careless. It didn't heal well." Thrasius looked away from Indy. "He's not a cripple, but... well, that arm'll never be the same again."

"Forgive me saying so, Thrasius," Leitus said, "but it was no more than he deserved, and less than he might have gotten."

"Hard, but true," Thrasius agreed slowly. "But he didn't see it that way. Got angrier the more he dwelled on it. I didn't see him for a while, but next time I ran into him, he was full of talk about how he was going to come back out here and cut all of your throats for you." He sighed. "So that's why I'm here. To warn you."

"I'm so sorry that we brought this on you guys," Anna said to Leitus and Helene. She'd been worrying about something like this for months. Now that it was happening, she felt sick with fear and guilt.

"I told you we should have killed them," Indy said. Anna looked sad at this, but said nothing.

"Well, I'm glad you didn't," Thrasius said. "And short of that, you couldn't have done much different than you did. *I* knew we weren't going to kill you, but there's no way you could have known that." The former thief looked down. "You do a few robberies, you start to forget all the things that might go wrong. It's easy to convince yourself it's not such a big thing. Marks get a little bruised up, then they get over it and go on with their lives. But I was wrong." He swallowed. "More than wrong. Nicon and I were in with some dangerous people, back in Thebes. I cut ties, trying to make myself a new start, but they don't let you just walk away clean. If they found out I was here…" He looked uncomfortable. "Well, it doesn't matter. I couldn't live with myself if I didn't warn you. I've known Nicon long enough, I'm afraid of what he might work himself up to."

"Then the question now is what *we* should do." Indy looked like she had some ideas, none of which would be pleasant for Nicon.

"Leitus, Helene, could you please excuse us for a few minutes?" Anna gestured Indy toward the door. "Indy and I need to go discuss a few things. We won't go out of sight of the trail."

Leitus nodded, and Indy got up to accompany Anna as she picked up her pack again outside. Behind them, Anna heard Helene tell Thrasius that he was welcome to join them for dinner, and to stay the night if he needed shelter.

Weird, how making someone a guest flips the whole situation like that, Anna said over their link. *I wouldn't invite my ex-robber to dinner!*

The host-guest relationship seems to be very important in this culture, Indy replied as they walked. *Which I suppose I can't argue with, since it worked in our favor when we first got here.*

Anna and Indy kept walking until they were out of earshot, around the edge of the little storage building where they couldn't be seen from the cottage door, but they could still monitor the path approaching it. The sun was setting, throwing lengthening shadows from the edge of the forest across the cleared pasture toward the household.

Anna opened her mouth to speak, but Indy beat her to it. "I'm sorry, Anna. But mercy for those two was a bad idea." She glared back toward the cottage. "And now everyone here is in danger, not just us."

"I know." Anna drooped miserably. "I know. I just couldn't say yes to killing two people right on the spot like that." She hung her head. "But maybe you were right."

"I was," Indy said. "But that moment is past." She relented, and her gaze softened as she looked at Anna. "You've got a gentle soul. That decision was too much for you." She flicked her glance around, looking for danger. "Things may get ugly this time."

Anna straightened up and raised her chin. "They might. But I have a plan." She gathered her thoughts. "And we do have a few things prepared." She set her pack down on the ground. "This morning, Alixa and I finally finished those two personal shields I talked to you about. I was afraid my weird style requests were making them un-fabbable, but it eventually worked out." The corner of her mouth bent upward. "I also added a little surprise. I just hadn't had the chance to deck us out yet."

She dug deep into her pack and withdrew a silvery crescent, curved to match Indy's collar. "Yours clips on, like a decoration. I tried to make it pretty, that's why it took so long." Anna held it up tentatively.

Indy's eyes brightened. "It's beautiful!" She hopped from one foreleg to the other. "Put it on, put it on!"

Anna smiled with relief, reaching under Indy's collar to secure it in place. "I'm glad you like it. It seemed like it fit your style." Her face took on a hint of their recent sorrow. "And we haven't had a lot to feel good about for a while, now."

Indy shook out her ruff and tried to look down far enough to see the new addition, then gave up. "Too bad ancient Greek shepherds don't have mirrors. I'll have to wait until we get back to the lab."

"Don't worry, silver looks great against white fur." Anna smiled tightly as she fastened her own shield around her wrist, where it looked like a dull silver bracelet. "I'm not much into jewelry, so I made mine boring. Just remember, these shields can only block one small area at a time, when they sense something fast about to hit you. So try not to get hit from two directions at once, and hope no one tries to stab you slowly." She twisted the shield bracelet on her wrist. "And one more thing. These'll only work for a minute or so before we have to recharge them, and that'll take most of an hour. I tried to keep the shield effect small and close to the body, but even tiny shields suck down a *lot* of energy."

"And here's the surprise." Anna dug further down into her pack and withdrew two more items, narrow wooden rods about six inches long. Each was wrapped with leather on one end, and capped with a silvery metal on the other. "Stunners," she said, clicking the rods together lightly. "These'll run for a good long time on a charge, at least."

Indy bared her teeth in a frightening rictus. "I'm already armed, remember."

"You can always go there if you need to." Anna looked sad. "I was just trying to give us a softer option." She pulled out a small black leather holster. "This clips to the front of your harness, on your right side, so you can reach back and grab it with your mouth."

Indy raised an eyebrow. "An interesting choice."

"I figured you'd prefer that instead of trying to be Quick Draw McPaw." Anna tucked her own stunner under the wide belt of her tunic. "People don't seem to carry weapons openly around here, but no one will know what yours is, so it should be okay."

Anna drew a nervous breath, then let it out. "Now. Here's the *rest* of the plan."

Two days later, Anna and Indy walked down the path to meet Nicon.

Their re-deployed spy-drones had seen him coming. But Anna didn't like the idea of the man even getting a look at their home, so she quickened her step to make sure their meeting place was well away from Helene and the rest of the family.

"Are you sure you want to do this?" Indy scented the air as they moved. "I still don't like the risk. One mistake, and one of us could end up maimed. Or dead." She looked at Anna. "There's still time to do things my way."

Anna's mouth was set in a grim line. "If this doesn't work, your way may be our only choice."

The breeze shifted and Indy's steps slowed on the path, her nose questing.

What is it? Anna said over their link.

Indy's lips peeled back from her teeth in a silent snarl, and a moment later Nicon came around a corner in the trail ahead. The man flinched back abruptly as he saw Indy. His left arm was visibly scarred and twisted, and even though they hadn't meant for it to happen, Anna's stomach roiled with guilt at what they'd done to him.

Nicon recovered quickly and reached down to a quiver at his left hip. In an instant, he fitted an arrow, tip-down, to a short bow held stiffly with his bad arm. Then he drew and loosed at them before Anna could even cry out.

Indy leaped to one side, disappearing into the brush. But Anna froze in place, mouth open in surprise, feet rooted to the rocky trail. Fortunately, the arrow flew wide, disappearing into the trees somewhere behind her. Anna helplessly watched Nicon pull another arrow from his quiver, his features twisted with rage. He drew and loosed again.

This time Nicon's aim was true. Blood rushed in Anna's ears as she felt the arrow strike home low in her belly.

With an odd, metallic *ting* of impact, the arrow sprang away and rattled on the hard ground, spent. Anna's hands flew to her abdomen, feeling for a wound, as she finally flung herself to the side, too late.

Then she remembered her shield bracelet. Its pinpoint barrier had sprung up and knocked the arrow away, exactly as it was designed to. Relief flooded her, though her heart still pounded with fear. She turned back toward Nicon, just in time to get an arrow to the cheek.

Ow! That one hurt! She rubbed her cheek as she backed away down the trail. Her hand came away only spotted with blood, so her shield must have turned the second arrow too, mostly. But the sound had been noticeably lower-pitched this time.

Anna held her hands uselessly in front of her as she continued to retreat. Nicon was only a few yards away now. Was he close enough that his arrows could punch all the way through her shield? And how many arrows could it deflect on one charge? Nicon looked frightened now as well as angry, but he walked closer and pulled out another arrow, ready to skewer her at point-blank range.

Behind him, Indy stalked silently out of the forest, stun-baton gripped in her jaws. Anna's eyes must have given it away, because Nicon started to turn. But before he could complete the motion, Indy lunged forward along the trail and jammed the baton into his back. He stiffened, then crumpled forward with a groan, gouging his forehead on the rocky ground when he hit. He struggled to rise, and Indy stood close, ready to stun him again. But then he slumped down, motionless.

Indy twisted her head back and holstered the stunner, then trotted over to Anna. "You okay?"

"Yeah, I'm fine." Anna blew out a shaky breath. "I just wasn't ready. I didn't mean to let him get so close. But I couldn't move!"

"It was *your* plan," Indy reminded her. "And I must admit, it worked beautifully."

"Yeah, but I really underestimated how scary it is to get shot in the *face* by an arrow!" Anna wiped off another spot of blood that had welled out of the tiny puncture in her cheek, then rubbed it away between her thumb and forefinger. "Especially when the shield's so close to your skin that you can feel it." Anna was shaking with reaction now, and struggled to slow her breathing. "It's one thing to know you're safe, but you never really *know* know. It's not like I've ever been shot at before." She felt sick, so she leaned over and put her hands on her knees. "Maybe we should've practiced this a few times or something."

"You did perfectly well." Indy sniffed at Anna's cheek, making sure the damage was minor, then walked over to Nicon. "And hopefully now he believes there's no point even trying to attack us, since our 'magic' makes us invulnerable." She wrapped a heavy paw around Nicon's shoulder and rolled him over on his back. His head rolled loosely, but he was still breathing. Blood pooled on his forehead where he'd hit the ground.

Indy took Nicon's bow in her mouth and flung it out of reach, then did the same with the arrow he'd dropped when he went down. Anna straightened up and joined her friend, unfastening the strap for the small quiver at Nicon's hip and pulling it off him. There were three more arrows in it, which she cast aside as well. He was also wearing a knife at his belt and a short cudgel studded with bronze. Anna took those and put them in her pack. Then Anna tied Nicon's hands and feet with a thin rope they'd brought.

She looked at his crippled left arm as she did so. It was fully healed, but twisted and seamed with thick scar tissue, and some of the muscles were oddly wasted, like he couldn't use it fully. But apparently it was enough to hold a bow, with the good arm to draw it.

She took a steadying breath and let it out. His behavior still made no sense to her. What could drive someone to robbery and attempted murder? Crime was rare where she had come from, and not something she had ever thought much about. Maybe the future's material abundance reduced the motivation for wrongdoing? She shook her head. Whether she understood it or not, she still had to deal with it here and now. She backed away, sat down, and waited for him to wake up from the stunning.

It didn't take long. In five minutes or so, he began to stir. Then he jerked up suddenly, eyes wide, but fell on his side when he couldn't steady himself with his hands bound together. He lay there on the ground, chest heaving, glaring at them hatefully. Indy growled low in her chest, and he froze, then lay still.

"So, what now? Going to finish the job, I suppose?" He tried to lift his scarred arm toward them. "This wasn't enough for you?"

"In case you've forgotten, *you* tried to beat and rob *us*," Indy said in a flat voice.

"You would've been fine." As Nicon spoke, blood from the gouge on his forehead slowly ran down and dripped onto the dirt. "Couple of hits to the gut, we grab your stuff, and we're out. You come up with a few bruises, maybe a knock on the head if you're trouble."

"And what happens to the ones who give you trouble?" Anna asked. "What if someone pulls a knife?"

"If they don't have the sense to go along, that's their own fault, isn't it? They act right, there won't be any problem." He tried a smile, but it came out closer to a grimace.

When Anna saw Nicon's expression, she remembered the leer that had been on his face when he'd knocked her sprawling and looked her up and down. Her heart hardened. She'd be willing to bet that Nicon wouldn't stop at robbery, at least not if his blood was up. She rose, face set, and reached into her pack. Indy rose to all fours beside her.

"Just make it quick." Nicon's face went dead, eyes resigned. "Don't throw me to your demon dog." He spat on the bloodied ground. "And watch yourselves. You're not exactly hard to find. My crew knows where I went."

"You sicken me, Nicon." Indy grunted in disgust. "You slithered all the way back here to try to kill us, because you crippled yourself trying to rob us. If I hadn't been there, there's no telling what you'd have done to Anna. If you had taken care of your arm properly, it would've healed fine. And if anyone cared enough to come looking for you, they would have come with you instead." She looked down at Nicon and bared her teeth. "You're lucky Anna's a better person than I am."

Anna finished her rummaging and pulled a bronze bracelet from her pack, along with a translucent green pill. She held them both up in front of Nicon. "We're going to make you a deal."

"Which you don't deserve," Indy growled.

"Of course he doesn't deserve it," Anna said. "But what kind of place would the world be, if we only ever got just what we deserve?" She turned back to Nicon.

"Here's the deal." Anna held up the green pill. "You eat this, and it'll fix your arm. It may take a long time, but eventually it'll be like it never happened."

Nicon slowly heaved himself into a sitting position, using his bound hands for leverage. "Say I was stupid enough to believe that." The blood trail across his forehead began running downward toward his eye. "What's the catch?"

"The catch is that you also put on this bracelet." Anna looked Nicon in the eye. "It won't come off. In a few minutes, it'll start to hurt. But it'll hurt less, the farther you get from here. Once you're twenty miles away, you won't feel a thing."

"But if you ever come within twenty miles of this place, the pain will start again." Indy bared her front teeth in a malevolent grin. "It'll get worse and worse, the closer you come. I'm fairly sure you'll pass out from the pain at around five miles away. I wouldn't advise letting that happen, though. The bracelet isn't supposed to cause you permanent harm, but I didn't test it as carefully as I might have." Anna frowned at her companion but stayed silent. "The safest thing for you," Indy continued, "is to stay far away."

Nicon blinked the blood away from one eye and looked up at them. "What if I say no?"

"Then you can try out *my* deal." Indy glared at Nicon, fur beginning to bristle. "But I think you'll like it less than Anna's."

"We can see you coming," Anna broke in. "If you came here again, we'd just catch you. And we can't let you hurt anyone. Don't make us choose between you and our friends."

"What gives you the right to do this to me? No, don't bother," Nicon said as Anna opened her mouth to answer. He screwed his mouth up and spat to one side. "I can't believe I'm arguing with a girl and a giant talking dog." He briefly tried to stand up, but couldn't do it with his legs bound, and he thumped back to the ground.

"Well, cut me loose," he growled. "I can't take your damn pill if I'm tied up."

Indy circled around behind him while Anna untied his hands. When she reached for the ropes securing his feet, Indy said, "That's enough, until he's done his side of the bargain." Anna held out the green pill in one hand, and the bracelet in the other.

Nicon took the pill between thumb and forefinger and held it up to look at it.

"Just eat it," Indy said. "If we wanted to kill you, there are much easier ways." The scarred thief looked at her sourly, but put the pill in his mouth and swallowed it dry.

"Now the bracelet," Indy said.

Nicon slipped it over one wrist and twisted it around uneasily. Anna reached forward and touched it with one finger, and its open ends drew together and joined, leaving no seam.

"What's it doing?" Nicon asked, eyes wide.

"Don't worry, it'll leave some space," Anna said. "It adjusts itself."

"But make sure you don't get too fat," Indy said with relish. "It can only stretch so far."

Anna shot her a look, then began loosing the rope from Nicon's ankles. He rubbed them briefly and then levered himself to his feet, favoring his twisted arm.

"How long until this gets better?" Nicon held the arm toward them.

"It should feel better within an hour." Indy sounded displeased with the prospect. "The scarring may take months to go away. And the badly set bones will take longer. But as long as you don't get it cut off entirely, it should eventually be back to normal."

"You should leave now," Anna said. "That bracelet will start hurting soon, and the further away you are, the less painful it'll be."

Indy advanced on Nicon, who cowered back. "You could always stick around a while to help us test it out first. But if I were you, I'd follow her advice."

Nicon hesitated, glancing over at his pile of possessions.

Anna shook her head. "No. Don't press your luck. Remember, you shot me in the face with an arrow, not half an hour ago." She rubbed at her cheek, which felt like it was swelling into a bruise.

Indy whuffed in amusement. "At least you have *some* sense."

"You bitches are going to regret this," Nicon said. "I know people. Dangerous people."

"Yes, you mentioned that before," Indy said. "And you're lucky that I think you're all bark." She glared at him. "Are you *trying* to give us a reason where we have to kill you?"

Nicon opened his mouth as if to say something more, but then looked at Indy and reconsidered. Without another word, he turned and walked quickly away down the trail.

Anna and Indy watched him go until he vanished around a bend in the trail. Then Anna pulled out her phone, and they watched him on their spy-drones' cameras as he continued walking back toward Lebadeia. After several minutes, he clutched the wrist with the bracelet on it, then quickened his step.

Indy laughed. "He'll have a painful few hours, but he'll be past the worst of it before dark. If he turns around, he'll regret it, though." The big canine yawned and stretched out her forelegs. "Let's go home. Our spy-drones will tell us if he gets up to anything. And I'm hungry. Getting shot at works up an appetite."

"He didn't even graze you!" Anna rubbed her sore cheek, which had stopped bleeding. "*I'm* the one that should be hungry." The two friends turned to walk back up the mountain trail toward the cottage.

Indy smirked. "It's not my fault if you're too slow to dodge an arrow."

"Gah!" Anna stopped suddenly. "I'm such an idiot."

"Why?" Indy looked back. "Don't feel bad. I was only joking about dodging arrows."

"No, I just realized." Anna started walking again, shaking her head. "We could've made a tiny mosquito-drone or something, and had it bite Nicon and knock him out with some kind of drug." She looked sheepish. "I got shot for nothing!"

Indy laughed. "Well, not *totally* for nothing. Nicon thinks we're invulnerable to arrows now, which can't hurt." Her white-tasseled tail swayed as she walked. "And besides, I didn't think of it either."

26

ater that night, Anna and Indy lay in their places in front of the hearth, with the remnant coals of the evening's fire glowing behind them. Iole was snoring gently in her spot near the wall, but that wasn't why Anna couldn't sleep.

She called out to her friend over their link. *Indy?*

Shouldn't you be asleep? Indy's voice held a teasing note. *You've had a long day of getting shot with arrows.*

That's what I wanted to talk to you about. Anna shifted under her blanket. *Well, our whole situation, not just getting shot at. We really need to get out of here.* She rolled over and looked at Indy in the coal-glow. *Sure, we solved the Nicon problem, which we caused in the first place. But there's still the whole issue of people here expecting me to get married. Even if I wanted to get hitched with some local guy, it'd only be a matter of time before they saw or heard something they shouldn't. And any trouble would come back on Helene and Leitus.*

There's also my secret to consider. Indy uncurled and sat up, sphinx-style. *Just because the first few people have taken it well, doesn't mean that everyone will. And I'm bound to be found out eventually.*

Yeah, exactly. Anna looked down. *If the wrong people found out about you, who knows what could happen? They could burn us all for evil sorcery, or something. It's not fair that you have to hide, just because people are stupid.* She sighed. *But where could we go that would be any different?*

I do have a sort of… *radical idea.* Indy cocked her head as she looked at Anna. *It might be possible to leave here, soon, and travel back to our own time.*

But… the portal won't open on the future! Anna said. *And we still haven't figured out how to go through it again.* Excitement bloomed on her face. *Or have we?*

Don't get your hopes up before you hear how it would work. Indy took a deep breath and huffed it out through her whiskers. *You remember how our field projector experiments came out, right? The ones where we tried to set the projector for the future?*

Sure. Anna tucked her blanket around her feet where they lay far from the hearth. *It didn't work, it just glitched out our drones and stopped bugs from crawling.*

That's the whole point, though. Indy's eyes grew animated as she spoke silently. *To us, it looked like the bugs were sitting still once they got to the center of the field. But to the* bugs, *it would've looked like time outside was passing much, much faster. A minute for them would've been like a year out here.* The big canine sat up on her haunches. *So what I'm saying is, we* could *travel through time after all. Sort of. But it would be a one-way ticket. We could only go forward.*

Oh. Oh! Anna said, getting it. *We could get into the field and wait, and then pop out of our cave in our own year!* Her hopeful expression turned to worry. *But hold on. What about the event that sent us back here?* She sat up and put her back against the hearth, pulling her blanket around her shoulders for warmth. *We know that something bad happens, way in the future. At the end of our time.* Her eyes stung as the familiar sadness rose in her, but she fought it down and continued. *If we jumped right back there, wouldn't the exact same thing be cued up to happen all over again?*

Maybe. Indy frowned. *We're still not sure what caused the temporal anomaly in the first place. If it was a random phenomenon of some kind, it might not happen again, now that we've perturbed the timeline a little. Though that might also make the whole future totally different from what we remember.*

Could be. Anna tried for a lighter note. *Or maybe the anomaly was some aliens rolling through and messing up our timeline by accident, putting in a hyperspace bypass or something, and we just missed the email. If we looked harder next time, maybe we'd figure it out.*

We also wouldn't have to go all the way back to our time in one big jump, Indy said. *We could try to trickle some of our knowledge out over the years, so that the world's tech is more advanced when we get back. That might give us a better chance to stop the temporal anomaly or whatever it is from happening.* Her eyes got a faraway look. *I remember reading something like that in an old sci-fi book when I was a pup. At the time, it seemed like fast-forwarding across millennia while shaping the future would be quite the adventure.* She looked down. *But think about what it would mean to really do that. Leaving aside whether we could even keep a field projector running and hidden for thousands of years.* She lay back down again and looked over at Anna. *What would it be like to live that way? Could we really leave everyone and everything behind, over and over again? And what if we made a mistake? We still couldn't go backward. We might even make things worse than they were before. And…*

And what? Anna said.

It still wouldn't take us back home. Indy's ears drooped. *We might get back to the same year, the same place. But it wouldn't be home. Everything, the timeline and the people, would be different. We can never get back what we've lost.*

Anna laid a comforting hand on Indy's forepaw, and they sat silently for a few moments.

Do me a favor? Indy raised her head.

Sure, just name it.

Let me look at some of my pictures on your phone. Indy looked around the dark cottage. *No one's awake, and it makes me feel better. When I see them, I can almost…* She left the thought unfinished.

Anna fought to swallow, her throat gone tight. She set her phone to show whatever Indy's collar sent, and propped it where

Indy could see the screen. Images flashed by, most of them showing what must be Indy's family and friends, but some of them pictures of the university, her classmates. And then one of Anna's father, posed proudly beside a younger Indy, holding her diploma high and smiling. She turned away, unwilling to reawaken her sorrow just when it seemed she was finally starting to heal.

You're right about not skipping ahead in time, Anna said. *I'm not ready to butcher the whole timeline like that. We might still figure out a better idea someday.* She shifted in her blanket cocoon, eyes still avoiding the images Indy displayed on her phone. *But that still leaves us with the same problem of making sure Leitus and Helene don't get in worse trouble because of us.* She sighed. *What we really need is to find some way to live our lives here. I don't want anyone to get hurt because of us. But I want my life to mean something, too.*

I don't want to hide in a cave forever, either. Anna's phone went dark as Indy stopped the stream of pictures.

We'll figure something out. Anna sounded more doubtful than she liked.

Indy stood, looking like she wanted to say more. But then she scratched at the blanket and turned in a tight circle a couple of times before curling up and closing her eyes. *Let's sleep on it.*

27

A few days later, Anna and Indy were working on the cottage's storage building, clearing away weeds, checking the roof for cracks, and making repairs where many seasons of running water had damaged the mortar between the blocks up near the roof. The family stored staple foods like dried beans and barley there to survive the winter, so it was important to make sure the building was absolutely dry and mouse-proof.

Indy was cleaning up the small limestone blocks, since only Helene was there to see. They'd fabbed a faux-authentic chisel and mallet for the task, which looked clumsy in Indy's huge paws, but she found solace in the painstaking work, chipping off bits of old mortar to smooth the blocks so they could be re-laid and made watertight once more. Anna handled any detail work that needed fingers, but was more than happy to leave the worst of the old-school masonry to her friend. Using a rock molder was one thing, but doing it with a chisel was beyond ridiculous!

Iole was out foraging in the woods, trailed invisibly by one of their spy-drones. And instead of leaving after they'd seen off Nicon, Thrasius had stayed on for a while as a laborer and assistant, having struck a deal to pay his hosts back somewhat for his earlier actions. Leitus had taken him to town a few hours ago to collect supplies and bring them back up the mountain for storage. Helene was on walkabout in the garden, checking the health of the plants and plucking insects off the leaves here and there. Anna smiled, glad to see that the old woman was continuing to improve after taking their green pill. She could walk steadily on her own now, and her whole personality had brightened now that she no longer suffered from the crippling bouts of pain they'd seen earlier.

Helene inspected one final leaf, then walked toward where Anna was dry-fitting one of the small blocks that Indy had prepared. They had taken the top of one corner of the building apart, removing the old mortar and smoothing the blocks, following directions from phone and collar for this unfamiliar and archaic procedure. The next step would be mortaring and re-laying, but they'd wait on that until the blocks were all ready to go. The instructions said that this "mortar" stuff dried quickly, and Anna didn't want to mix more than one batch, since they were doing everything the old-fashioned way.

Alixa told Anna through her earring that Leitus and Thrasius were approaching, spotted by one of their tiny drones along the path. Indy stopped her work at almost the same moment, notified by her collar, and put the chisel and mallet down beside the mostly-cleaned stones.

The knowledge Anna and Indy had brought with them had proved invaluable here, allowing them to help out around the household without having to explain away any advanced technology. But doing things this way was hard work!

Anna put down her block as Helene approached and went to the water jug, which they'd moved outside before starting the day's work. Indy walked over to join them.

"I'm feeling better every day." Helene spoke as Anna dipped out a bowl of water for Indy, placing it on the ground a few feet away. The big black-and-white lapped noisily as Anna filled a cup of her own and drank it down. "I can't thank the two of you enough for what you've done for us."

"You took us into your home when you didn't have a thing to spare." Anna wiped the sweat from one eyebrow with the back of her knuckle. "I'd call us even. Though if there's much more masonry to do, we'll have to start charging by the block," she joked. Anna pointed to the trail where Leitus and Thrasius were just emerging, and Helene's face broke into a smile when she saw her husband.

Leitus waved to the three of them, then took custody of the supplies from Thrasius, who had carried the lion's share, and went into the cottage to store them away. Thrasius acknowledged them with a nod before walking off to check on the sheep. Iole emerged from the trees a few minutes later with her foraging basket, calling out a greeting as she approached. She handed the basket to Helene and went straight to the garden to glance along the rows, looking for weeds and ravenous insects, not realizing that Helene had been there only minutes before.

Helene watched Iole fondly. It was hard work, pulling out tiny weeds before they could put down thick roots, and picking caterpillars and other pests off their vegetables. But Iole had the most dexterous hands of all of them, and she made it look easy.

"I hope things work out between her and Neleos." Helene's voice was wistful as she shifted the foraging basket in her hands, sorting through the contents quickly, then setting it down beside her for Indy to sniff at with interest. "She doesn't need to be trapped out here with two old folks the rest of her life. She's almost fifteen years old! It's time for her to start a family of her own."

Anna still cringed inwardly at this sort of talk. She could never see herself giving up her independence the way women were expected to here. And the idea of becoming a mother at fifteen still sounded very strange to her. *I guess it makes sense, though. If hardly anyone lives past seventy or so, you have to get started early!* Leitus and Helene still seemed old to her, but they couldn't be past their early sixties, which would still be considered young where Anna had come from. Life in ancient times wore you down quickly.

"What's to work out?" Anna asked. "She and Neleos seem pretty into each other. Can't they just get married?"

"It isn't only a matter of love." Helene's face showed an odd sort of disappointment. "There's the dowry to consider as well. We spoke about that before, and her inheritance will be worth more now that you and Indy have helped us in so many ways. But there's no shortage of girls from town whose families aren't poor shepherds who live in tiny cottages, high up the mountainside." Helene looked sadly over toward Iole, who was almost finished with the garden already. "That's the world we live in, unfortunately. Who wants to start a new life and a new family with someone who's only got the clothes on her back, and hardly any family to support her?"

Anna thought for a long moment, then spoke hesitantly. "Um, Helene? I'm still not sure how your customs work, and I don't want to break any rules or mess anything up for Iole."

"And that's very worthy of you, Anna," Helene said.

"But let me put an idea out there," Anna continued. "If it won't work, or would make you guys look bad or something, just tell me and we'll pretend I never said it." Indy looked up from the foraging basket, clearly curious about what Anna was going to say next.

"Well, now you have me interested." Helene smiled fondly. "Out with it, then."

"So..." Anna twisted her hands together awkwardly, then blurted it out. "What if me and Indy gave you a box full of money. Like, coins. And you used *that* for Iole's dowry. Would that be okay?"

Helene considered for half a second, at most. "That would be perfectly fine, dear. I'm not one to look a gift horse in the mouth." She gave Anna a sly look. "Though if you had so many extra coins lying around, you might have mentioned it before now."

"Really?" Indy asked, *sotto voce* so Iole wouldn't overhear. "A box full of money?" The big canine snorted and shook her head in amusement.

"I can't believe I'm even talking about selling Iole to Neleos' family." Anna looked embarrassed. "Or paying them to take her, I guess."

"Don't worry, dear." Helene spoke with a wry smile. "Think of it more as a bribe, if that helps."

"What about Leitus?" Anna nodded toward the cottage, where the old herdsman was still putting away the supplies from his and Thrasius' shopping trip. "I feel like a real idiot for asking this, but isn't there some sort of honor code or something? Where you couldn't accept help for this sort of thing?"

"Leitus might have some ideas along those lines," Helene said, "but don't worry. I'm sure I can talk him around." She smiled. "And a box full of money will certainly help."

28

t actually ended up being two smaller boxes of money, since a single box would've been an uneven load in Indy's saddlebags. Fortunately, there were trace amounts of silver in the rock their beetle-drones had been tunneling into all this time, though Indy had to spend a few hours fiddling with Greek coin designs before they could fab anything from the accumulated metallic dust. They had pictures of a few coins from this time period in their library, but they couldn't very well deliver dozens of absolutely identical coins that looked like they'd been dug up two thousand years ago. At least coin designs were relatively easy to tweak with their limited computing power, unlike mining drones or personal shields.

Working with her collar's net and the big screen in their lab, Indy had come up with an assortment of coin denominations and weatherings that an exceptionally thrifty Greek herdsman might, just barely plausibly, have accumulated over a lifetime. The total value of their hoard was maybe ten years' income for a middle-class man, which was a lot of coin for this neck of the woods, considering that people around here didn't get paid in cash, and transacted much of their business as barter.

They'd fabbed the coin boxes to look like the small wooden

boxes that Helene kept her modest jewelry in, and they packed the coins tightly so they didn't jingle and attract unwanted attention. But even small boxes full of dense metal were *heavy*.

The whole family walked down to the small compound where Neleos lived with his parents and younger siblings. Leitus and Helene led the way, followed by Iole, with Anna and Indy in the rear. Thrasius had stayed behind at the cottage, quickly volunteering to keep an eye on things before Leitus could feel awkward about asking him to stay behind.

I really hope this works, Anna said to Indy. *What if Neleos' parents think it's weird, us just showing up with a suspicious amount of money?* She looked worriedly at Iole, who was wearing her best clothes and trying not to look nervous. *If Leitus and Helene had this much saved up, someone probably would have noticed before now. Maybe we should have minded our own business.*

At this point, we're committed. Indy walked on unhurriedly, not showing the least strain from carrying the many pounds of metal in her saddlebags. *And don't forget, everyone else agreed to this plan too,* she added. *We'll have to trust their judgement.*

Their party was expected, so Neleos was there to greet them in the courtyard of his family home. He quickly ushered them inside, where his father Timais, a tall slender man just beginning to gray at the temples, and his mother Nephele, shorter and dark of eye and hair, stood to meet them.

They shook hands in greeting, Leitus with Timais and Helene with Nephele. This gesture still struck Anna as oddly anachronistic, though the Greeks had told her previously that hand-shaking dated back at least to the legendary times of Homer's *Odyssey*, if not before. While they exchanged pleasantries, a servant of some kind—a thin woman with short-cropped hair—circulated among the guests to offer each of them water to refresh their hands and a thick cloth to dry them on. Then, formalities concluded, they got down to business.

"So, Leitus, we've heard through Neleos, and he from your grand-niece, that you wished to speak to us about some important matter." Timais' light tenor voice held a hint of wariness.

"And I confess to being curious about what could bring you all here together." Nephele eyed Anna and Indy discreetly. "I had heard from Iole that your guest of these last months is nothing like the rumors one might hear in the marketplace." She raised an eyebrow, and Anna cringed inwardly. "But I haven't yet had the pleasure of meeting her."

"I'm Anna, ma'am." Anna stepped forward and shook Nephele's proffered hand. "And this is Indy." She gave a pre-arranged and unnecessary hand signal, upon which Indy trotted forward, sat, and offered up her right paw to shake.

Nephele laughed and shook the paw firmly, while Timais looked on with amusement. Anna and Indy had hit upon this strategy of pretending Indy was merely a specially trained herding dog, which gave her an excuse to be present and go through the social niceties, while not appearing *too* out of the ordinary.

"Anna and Indy," Nephele mused. "Interesting names. Where did you come to us from?"

Anna hesitated. They hadn't thought to come up with a whole back story. And she didn't want to lie, because Leitus and Helene were standing close by, listening with interest. She went with true but vague. "We were born a long way west, and a little to the south, of here."

"Ah, you do have the look of Iberia about you." Timais looked over Anna's light brown skin, dark hair done up in now-familiar Greek braids, and darker eyes. "Fellow merchants have told me that we have some little trade with that far land, and have described its people to me." He considered a moment. "The story of how you came to be here must be an interesting one."

Iberia? Anna queried Alixa through her earring. Then she almost laughed aloud. Iberia was what the Greeks called Spain, which was indeed far to the west and a little south of here. Anna had been thinking of Texas when she said that, but Spain would do just as well. For all she knew, some of her Reyes great-ancestors were living there now!

"I'd be happy to tell you all about it," Anna lied, "but I don't want to take away from the real purpose of this visit."

"Indeed," Leitus broke in, more smoothly than Anna would've expected from a rustic herdsman. "Timais, I've known you for some time now, and you and Nephele have grown acquainted with our grand-niece. Helene and I never had a daughter of our own, but Iole has filled that role in our lives for many years now since her parents passed from us." The old man hesitated, no doubt saddened by painful memories. "Since Iole is like a daughter to us, we've come to tell you that we intend to fulfill the traditional role of the parents of daughters." Leitus looked to Anna, who gestured for Indy to rise and walk up to the old man.

Leitus reached out and opened Indy's saddlebags, which were on a level with his chest. He pulled out the two small but heavy wooden boxes, one at a time, and set each of them on the table with a solid *thud*.

"We are not a wealthy family," Leitus said, "but I have some small inheritance from my parents, and Helene from hers. And over many years of toil, I've always tried to put aside what I could for the future."

He's actually a very good actor, Indy said. *I'm glad he's the one delivering this speech and not you.* Anna could hear the smirk in her friend's voice, though her face remained impassive. This whole story was completely untrue, of course. Leitus and Helene hadn't had a tiny silver coin to their names when Anna and Indy arrived. But it had just enough of a ring of plausibility that hopefully it would pass.

"And as our adopted daughter, Iole's inheritance will be all that we own." Leitus reached out and opened the lids of the two boxes. Inside were packed many dozens of small silver coins, of a variety of sizes, some smooth with apparent use, others newer and shinier.

Anna had inspected their hoard earlier. She still couldn't read Greek fluently, but she could mentally sound out the letters for Alixa to translate. The coins represented a sampling of smaller denominations minted by local city-states. Most were tiny, only fractions of an ounce, but taken together they came to a considerable weight. Timais' and Nephele's eyes widened at the sight.

Ha! They weren't expecting that! Anna thought to Indy.

Then Timais' eyes narrowed again. "How deep are those boxes?"

Trust a merchant to think of false bottoms, Indy said.

But Leitus was ready for this. He lifted one box and poured it carefully onto the table, making sure that none of the coins went rolling off onto the floor. Then he held up the box, showing its full depth.

"Would you mind one final check?" Timais asked.

"Of course not," Leitus said. "The entire reason we came here was to set your mind at ease about Iole's inheritance."

"Thank you for your understanding, Leitus," Timais replied smoothly. "Rest assured, I have no doubt as to your honesty. I only aim to ensure that you have not been the target of deception yourself."

It sounds like he's had a lot of practice saying that, Indy said.

Timais held out his hand, and their short-haired servant rushed forward from where she'd been standing at a discreet distance. She handed a small bag to Timais, eyes downcast, then withdrew. From the bag, Timais drew out a flat, palm-sized piece of dark rock. Its surface gleamed dully, as if it had been lightly oiled, and it showed a few whitish streaks on one side. The merchant turned to his wife and said, "If you would, my dear?"

"Of course, my darling." Nephele closed her eyes and reached out to Leitus' coin pile, withdrawing two coins at random after a few moments of sifting. She handed the coins to her husband, who rubbed them gravely against his touchstone, making a pair of small streaks beside a set that already marked the stone's dark surface. Then he held the stone up to the light of the nearby window, tilting it back and forth carefully. He paused for an uncomfortably long moment.

What did we miss? Anna struggled not to glance over at Indy. *Maybe he's onto us!*

But then Timais smiled. "Friend Leitus, your coins are of excellent purity," he said happily. "In fact, they're better than I would have expected, especially this Theban coin." He held the offending disk up before replacing it on the pile. "Their master of the mint must have been short of lead the day this one was struck."

Oops, Indy said. *I forgot that people in the past were less than scrupulous about this sort of thing. At least I didn't make them all completely pure!*

Shush, you're making faces when you talk, Anna said. *Let Leitus do his thing.*

Timais gestured to the coins, and Leitus began gathering them up again. They clinked dully against each other as he replaced them in the box. "I'm very glad you've come to see us, Leitus," he continued. "A man such as yourself, prudent in his finances, must find that in our small settlement, opportunities to put one's money to work are few and hard to come by."

What does he mean by that? Anna asked.

It means we've hooked our fish, Indy replied.

"Indeed, that is how I find it, friend Timais," Leitus responded with apparent confidence. "I often find myself in need of good advice. How might Helene and I best provide for our old age?"

"How indeed!" Nephele said. "Our family has much experience in such matters. Perhaps our interests may coincide to some extent."

"This visit was merely to inform you as to our situation," Helene said. "But we welcome the opportunity to discuss this subject in the future." The four elders clasped hands again, the gesture warmer this time then it had been at the outset.

Wait, what just happened? Anna asked Indy.

I'll explain on the way back to the cottage, Indy said with a mental smirk. *But I think our job is done here.*

hat followed was apparently somewhat unusual for an ancient Greek marriage arrangement. Instead of Iole moving in with Neleos' family after their wedding, it was agreed that Neleos would instead come up to the cottage and expand it to support his new, extended family. Then he and Iole would gradually take over from Leitus and Helene, as circumstances dictated.

I think your new 'natural hot spring' helped to seal this deal, Indy thought to Anna. *I've never seen people so excited over a bathtub.* The two of them were watching while a group of workmen from Lebadeia deposited loads of stone and lumber beside the cottage, the raw materials to add another room for the new couple.

Don't sell the tub short. We grew up with them, but for these guys, it's a real luxury. Anna's brows drew together with concern. *Hopefully nobody will go digging into the rock and figure out that it's not a real spring. I probably should've buried the heater pipe a little deeper.*

Who would even bother to look? Greece has plenty of hot springs. Ironically, Indy's worries about the tub had faded as Anna's grew. *Neleos' father said there are more of them out on islands in the Aegean Sea, but they're not uncommon on the mainland.* She stood and shook out her fur. *And in any case, you and the other humans need bathing badly enough that I'm willing to risk it.*

We *need bathing? What about you?* Anna feigned outrage. *You come back from herding with sheep poop up to your ankles!*

Hocks, corrected Indy. *They're called hocks. And I can just walk across a stream a few times, and I'm clean.* She looked up and down Anna's long linen chiton. The fabric was still mostly its original undyed light brown, but discolored here and there, as befitted the guest of poor herdsfolk. *If you didn't have so much cloth wrapped around you, you'd air out better.* She sniffed theatrically. *Anything that smells bad is bound to dry up and flake off, eventually.*

Ugh. Anna cringed. *I really didn't need* that *image.*

I suppose not all species can be blessed with the glorious fur coats of us Canidae. Indy preened and flicked her ears, licking the side of one paw and using it to rub her face.

We'll see how well you like your fur coat when summer gets here, Anna said. *We monkeys lost our hair for a reason.*

Speaking of hairless simians, how about that wedding? Indy darted a glance toward Neleos, who was supervising the unloading of the building materials over by the cottage. *Presumably our little girl Iole finally got to see her beau in his full, naked-monkey glory!* Indy's mental voice roared with laughter.

Anna blushed as well as her dusky complexion would allow. *I'll admit, naked might not be our best look.* She'd had an almost-serious boyfriend in high school, but she'd always given her schoolwork and science projects the best part of her time and attention. She probably wasn't much more experienced than Iole had been, and the Greek girl had never been alone with Neleos without a chaperone present. At least not until her wedding night.

Their choice of foods was interesting. Anna kept her mental voice nonchalant as she tried to change the subject.

Apparently dates, figs, nuts, and the rest of what they served symbolize fertility, somehow. Indy waggled an eyebrow, a very un-dog-like expression. *We'll see how well it works.*

I hope they'll be happy. It seems like they're getting off to a good start, at least. And Anna was surprised to feel a twinge of jealousy at the thought. Iole was younger than her, but she was already moving on to the next stage of her life, complete with a home and a husband.

What about you? Indy asked. *Have you got your eye on anyone? I've seen a couple of likely young simians checking you out in town, when they thought you weren't looking.*

You mean besides my harasser and his creepy friends? Anna made a face. *I've noticed a few. A couple were kind of cute, maybe. But a relationship… I don't know.* Her throat tightened with emotion. *That almost feels like admitting that we're never going to get back home again. I mean, I know we're not, but… still. And marriage here? I want to control my own life, not keep house for some guy.* She frowned to herself. *Plus, the education gap would be a killer, even just for dating.*

It might not be as bad as you think. Indy gave Anna a knowing look. *None of my boyfriends had PhDs, but they still managed to add something to the equation. If you know what I mean.*

How could I not *know what you mean?* Anna blushed again. *That's like a single entendre.*

As the workmen deposited the last of their burdens and turned to go, Anna saw Iole place a hand on Neleos' arm and say something, smiling. He answered her with a smile of his own, but Anna couldn't hear what they were saying from this distance. *Probably something about how she can't wait for him to move in, and how their new room is going to be much nicer than sleeping in front of the hearth.*

We're going to have more room in front of the hearth soon. Indy spoke as if reading Anna's mind. *It's kind of sad! I've gotten used to sleeping with our little pack. Even Thrasius,* she added grudgingly. *He's been good about getting up and putting more wood on the fire, at least.* Her ears pricked up, then lay back as she saw Thrasius emerge from the cottage and head their way. *Speak of the devil.*

Be nice, Anna reproved mentally. *He's square with Leitus now, after helping out for all this time. And he never laid a hand on me.*

He's lucky he didn't, Indy grumbled as Thrasius walked over, but her words were without heat. The older man raised a hand as he approached.

"Hello there, Anna, Indy." He spoke to both of them, but only looked at Anna, since they'd cautioned him that Indy's true nature was still a secret from everyone but Leitus and Helene. And Nicon, though hopefully he was far away and trying to forget he'd ever met them.

"Big changes coming here, it looks like," Thrasius continued.

"Good changes, at least," Anna said. "Iole gets a husband. Leitus and Helene get some more help."

"Indeed." Thrasius paused a moment. "I've already told Leitus this, but I thought I'd speak to you as well. Now that I've done what I came here to do, I had a mind to head back to Athens."

Anna had given Thrasius an edited outline of their encounter with Nicon, emphasizing that he was none the worse for wear, but wouldn't be coming back. *All of which is hopefully true,* she thought guiltily. She didn't have the best track record of foreseeing all the consequences of her and Indy's decisions.

"My family's from Athens." Thrasius shifted his weight from one foot to the other before speaking again. "Thought I might make a start at getting right with them."

"That sounds like a good idea." Anna sobered as she thought of her own lost family. "You should cherish them while you can."

"I'm sorry." Thrasius' face turned sympathetic. "I didn't mean to remind you of anything painful." He rubbed at his chin. "What I came out here for was to see if you might want to come along. You know, see a little more of Greece? I'm sure my family would put you up." He looked embarrassed. "And to be honest, traveling alone can be a dangerous thing. I sure wouldn't mind having a, uh… formidable presence, like Indy here, along just in case."

Indy's ears pricked up. *I saw that!* Anna said subvocally. *At least try to act like you don't understand human speech. Iole and Neleos can see you!*

Indy made a rude noise over their link, but kept her face carefully blank. *How's this?* She let her jowls droop vacuously.

"That could be a very interesting idea." Anna ignored Indy and focused on Thrasius. "We—I mean I—hadn't thought much along those lines yet." She cursed inwardly as Thrasius smiled at her lapse.

"I'd feel safer in Athens, too." Thrasius lowered his voice, though nobody was remotely close enough to overhear. "Those dangerous characters that Nicon and I fell in with? They're all Thebans, born and bred. And Thebes lords it over this whole region, with Lebadeia only a junior city. There's not much to keep the Theban mob from just walking in and doing whatever they want, if they cared to. Whereas a powerful rival city like Athens controls a whole separate region of its own, where outsiders have a lot less freedom to operate." He rubbed the back of his neck. "You'd think the mob wouldn't bother looking too hard for a small-timer like me, but I'd just as soon not make it easy for them."

And there it is, Indy said. *The real motivation behind this suggestion of his.* She sighed. *But he has a point. If all three of us left here, it seems that much less likely that some kind of Nicon-related trouble would come looking for Helene and the rest.*

And it'd also save them from stressing about their reputations in town, Anna said. *With Iole married, I'm the only loose end. A foreigner, living unmarried in their house while my weirdo stalker son-of-the-ex-archon spreads who knows what kind of rumors about me.* The injustice of it made her grit her teeth. But Leitus and Helene hadn't asked for any of this, and it was kind of her fault.

"When were you thinking of leaving?" Anna asked Thrasius out loud.

"Perhaps in a week?" Thrasius said. "I could use another few days of square meals and country air."

"Sounds good," Anna said after Indy's silent assent. "We'll be ready."

30

It turned out they were more ready to leave than they thought. To avoid attracting unwanted attention, they would need to travel as lightly as the Greeks did, which meant carrying not much more than the clothes on their backs. Indy and Anna had fabbed a variety of gear over the last several months, but they'd have to leave it all behind except for the absolute essentials. However, Anna did fab a new cloak for herself that had a discreet waterproof layer under the woolen outer layer, which could also serve as a bedroll in the mild Greek climate.

Their technology still couldn't create a drone big enough to carry any substantial amount of weight without having to recharge frequently at their fab or phones. So for this trip at least, they couldn't count on any sort of resupply from home. But they would be able to direct the ongoing process of enlarging their secret lair remotely, as long as they deployed a tiny solar-powered communications relay drone every twenty miles or so. These relay drones would have limited range, since large solar cells would be impossible to hide, but they should be sufficient to keep them in contact with their base of operations.

On the day before their departure for Athens, Anna waited

outside the hidden door of their cave while Indy gathered up a few final things and sealed the entrance. Then they checked it over, making sure it was still undetectable from the outside. They'd set some of their mining-drones the task of creating hidden drone-only exits higher up on the mountain, where people would never happen across them. These would take a few more weeks to be ready for use, but that was no reason to delay their departure.

Much harder than leaving their lair was taking leave of Leitus, Helene, and Iole. The herdsfolk had insisted on throwing a feast in their honor on the night before their departure, and despite their relative poverty, Anna hadn't had the heart to refuse. Leitus had slaughtered and dressed out a juicy lamb, with Thrasius' help, and Helene used her new-found energy to prepare a few specialty dishes and add finishing touches to Iole's simpler fare. Thrasius had even contributed a bottle of wine that he'd picked up in town.

At the end of a long night of eating and drinking, Leitus raised his bowl in one final toast. "To Anna and Indy! May their journey be swift and safe."

"And may they feel free to come back and let us know how it went!" added Helene. The old woman's eyes grew moist as she went on. "You two be careful. Once you get to the big city, things aren't nearly as nice and neighborly as they are out here on our mountain."

"That's good advice, Anna." *And Indy too*, Leitus' look seemed to say. "Be on guard, and don't be afraid to take to your heels if you need to."

"I will." Anna's voice caught. "It's so strange. When we first came here, everything was so different from what we were used to. But now after all this time, it feels weird to leave."

"Never fear, my gracious hosts," Thrasius said. "I know the road well from my earlier days, and I have family in Athens, as you know. When we've arrived safely, I'll send word to you. I can pay a merchant to pass a message along to Neleos' father Timais, and from him to you." His face grew sober. "You and yours have treated me far better than I had any right to expect, and I owe you a debt of honor that can never be repaid. No harm will come to Anna, that I swear to you."

Iole spoke up last. "Anna, and Indy too—" Indy's ears pricked up at this "—I'll never forget everything you've done for me and my family." She hugged her new husband Neleos close, and smiled at Leitus and Helene. "As long as I live here, you'll always be welcome in this house." She raised her bowl and sipped, and Neleos, Leitus, and Helene did likewise, followed by Anna and Thrasius.

Indy lapped from her own bowl of watered wine on the floor without so much as a glance from the Greeks. She saw Anna looking, and gave an amused shrug. *Apparently, wine-drinking dogs are old news now.* She took another lap from her bowl. *But we should still give them a little longer before we introduce margarita night.*

31

The next morning, the three travelers shouldered their packs and saddlebags and set out early. They had said their long goodbyes last night, so they parted briefly, with heartfelt embraces, and were on their way before the sun had fully cleared the treetops.

As they walked away, Anna noticed Indy looking back at the sheep up on the hill, where Leitus was chivying them along with a slender branch. "I have to admit, there's something to be said for the pastoral life." Indy looked reluctantly away from the scene behind them and picked her way forward along the path. "Chasing sheep all day, eating well at night, sleeping by a warm fire. What more could you want?"

Anna felt a pang herself. "We got pretty lucky, didn't we?" She left it at that, though, not wanting to say much more in front of Thrasius about how they had come to be there.

They were already well provisioned, so instead of going down into the valley and through Lebadeia, they cut straight across the mountainside, which would take them south of a mountain called Granitsa on their maps and shave a mile or so off their trip. Athens was only about sixty miles south and east of them as the crow flew, which would have only taken a few minutes in the flying cars they were used to. But on foot, moving at what felt like a snail's pace, it seemed like anything they could do to shorten the journey was worth a try.

"Are you two sure about this?" Thrasius looked skeptical at their choice of direction. "I've never seen anyone go this way before."

"Don't worry," Anna said. "We've been all over these mountains." This was mostly true, since they'd hunted all around looking for evidence that anyone from their own time was searching for them. But they had never come this specific way before. They were simply relying on their maps to show them a reasonable path.

As they got further from their usual haunts, the trees closed in, and game trails offered the easiest way to proceed. But these twisted about unpredictably, making it difficult to make progress in the direction the map said they should go.

After a few minutes of this, Indy surreptitiously sent one of their tiny relay-drones to scout ahead and find which of these trails went in the right direction without changing their elevation too much. *If not for these drones, we'd be in a world of trouble.*

Yeah, I can see Thrasius' point now, Anna said. *It looked so easy on the map. But once you're under the trees, it's confusing! A local would have to navigate by the sun or something, just to make sure they didn't end up going backward.*

And we're still inside the area where our drones updated our modern maps, Indy said. *We didn't think to send them under the tree cover to find every little footpath, but they're still helpful. But in another hour or so, we'll be outside the updated area, and our maps could start being drastically wrong about everything but basic topography.* She indicated the surrounding trees and brush with her chin. *I found a reference in our files by a guy named Plato, written a hundred years or so from now, talking about how deforested he thought Greece was already getting. By the nineteen hundreds a lot of it was bare rock. It had started to bounce back by our time, but it was still nothing close to this! So keep alert.* She eyed the thick vegetation suspiciously. *We can't exactly get lost, but we could run into some unpleasant surprises.*

After a tense few miles of hiking, the land finally began to open up in front of them as the mountains gave out onto a wide plain, and Anna relaxed inwardly. "There it is, Thrasius! Once we get down to the edge of the plain, we'll be on the road you're familiar with."

"I never doubted it." Thrasius spoke with the smile of someone glad to be proven wrong. He pulled his floppy hat out of his pack and settled it over his thinning hair now that the sun had risen higher in the sky, and they picked their way down out of the mountains and onto the plain in companionable silence, enjoying the clear early-spring weather.

Bulbous yellow crocuses bloomed here and there atop short green stems now that the trees were more widely spaced. Indy sniffed these and the other spring flowers with interest as they walked along, though to Anna's nose most of them didn't smell like much. A squirrel shot out of the brush as Indy approached, and she tore off after it by reflex, plowing through a cluster of bluebonnet-like purple hyacinth and skidding to a halt underneath a tree before remembering herself and sheepishly trotting back to rejoin the group.

"What? You're just jealous that humans aren't fast enough to play 'sniff the squirrel.'" Indy shifted in her harness to get it to lie straight again. "I could've caught him too, without these heavy saddlebags."

Anna laughed and brushed a stray flower petal from her friend's fur as they continued walking, the squirrel chittering abuse from the tree behind them.

Once they came to the road, Thrasius quickly oriented himself, then looked back the way they had come. "I'm not sure I'd try that way again without a guide." He smiled. "But you're right, we did save ourselves a few miles, going south of Mount Laphystios instead of north."

Another name difference, Anna noted silently to Indy. *Like Livadeia being called Lebadeia back here. Alixa, could you update the map please?*

Change noted, came Alixa's cool reply. *Laphystios to Granitsa, sometime after 500 BC.*

This is going to be really annoying if every name on our map is wrong. Anna felt like that shouldn't matter so much, since they at least knew the general features of the land. But somehow not knowing what to call the places they were traveling through made her feel weirdly unmoored.

Thrasius set off at a modest pace along the road to the right. "You two aren't used to walking long distances, so we'll take it easy at first."

Indy snorted. "I think we can handle this."

"Take it from an old traveler." Thrasius held up his hands in a placating gesture. "Walking all day might not sound that hard to you youngsters. But if you go too hard without working up to it, you'll regret it. We'll have to spend two nights on the road regardless, so there's no point pushing it and ending up with blistered feet."

"And one more thing, before we meet any other travelers." Thrasius paused, glancing both ways along the road. "It's probably best not to talk about your origins too openly where we're going. In Lebadeia, Leitus was sort of your unofficial sponsor, and in smaller towns people aren't too strict in any case. But in Athens, foreigners need to have a citizen sponsor within a month, and they're required to pay a special yearly tax. It's not a very big tax," Thrasius added at Anna's look of concern, "but you don't want to get on the wrong side of the law."

Indy looked at Thrasius. "What would the wrong side look like?"

"It shouldn't be an issue," Thrasius said. "If you end up staying longer than a month, I could ask my brother for help, or I could even sponsor you myself, if need be. Though I might not be the best choice, if anyone in Athens has heard about my checkered past." He looked uncomfortable. "In theory, you could get sold into slavery if your status wasn't in order and someone forced the issue. But we won't let that happen."

"Is slavery that common in Athens?" Anna lowered her voice, though there was no one to hear but the three of them. "I don't remember seeing any slaves in Lebadeia."

Thrasius sighed, taking off his hat briefly and rubbing his head before resettling it. "This is too nice a day to spoil with such a topic. But I promise," he said quickly as Anna opened her mouth, "I'll tell you everything you need to know before we get there."

They continued walking, the mood more sober now. The road was not quite what Anna had expected, more of a wide trail than a surfaced road. It was cut here and there by narrow streams running right to left, but these were mostly small enough to step across. Thankfully the spring rains hadn't been too heavy so far, or they'd probably have been ankle-deep in mud in some places. Still, the going was mostly good.

There wasn't a lot of traffic on the road, which suited Anna fine after Thrasius' warning. Off to their left, they had initially passed farms and fields at some distance. But now the plain on that side was narrowing, with a haze of greenery coming closer as they walked.

Indy stopped and scented the air. "Thrasius, is there water around here somewhere?"

"You could say that," Thrasius said with a smile. "Just a little further and you'll be able to see it more clearly."

Why would water be a surprise? Anna said. *I can't check the map on my phone with Thrasius here.*

My collar says there should be nothing but a much wider plain off to the left, Indy said. *But I definitely smell moisture.*

Anna shaded her eyes, beginning to see sunlight glinting off water up ahead.

"Lake Kopais." Thrasius made a sardonically grand gesture. "It's still a bit hard to see until we get closer, but that's where they catch some of the best-tasting eels in all of Greece, or so I'm told. Not partial to them myself, but you'll find them for sale all over these parts."

The lake grew on their left as they continued, though the road skirted widely around it to avoid what looked like marshy ground that was quite overgrown in places. Where streams ran down to the shore, wading birds hunted in the reeds, and the bushes were full of their cousins calling out to each other.

Ah, found it! Indy said. *Finally, all our useless modern history data is coming in handy.* She grunted with disgust. *It sounds like some idiots drained this whole lake in the late 1800s to grow cotton. I've noted it on our map, though we'll have to send out drones to trace the shoreline.*

They should have left it, Anna said. *What kind of person would want to destroy this?* "It's beautiful," she said out loud to Thrasius.

He smiled back. "This is one of my favorite parts of the trip. Bit of a pain to live too near it, though. It floods in the winter some years, and there'll be mosquitoes soon." He looked around, gauging their position. "Another half hour, it'll be time for a break."

Anna was relieved to hear it. After a few hours of walking, Anna could see the wisdom of Thrasius' earlier advice to take it slow. Her feet had toughened to Greek sandals over the last months, and she'd walked all up and down their mountain, but she wasn't used to walking long distances at a steady pace.

I'll be glad for a break, Indy said, echoing Anna's thoughts. The big hybrid didn't look tired exactly, but her tongue hung out in a steady pant. *Working sheep was good for my endurance as well as my soul, but adding heavy saddlebags changes the equation.*

By and by, the road swung away from the lake, and they began to see signs of habitation as they neared a town their maps called Aliartos, which Thrasius referred to as Haliartos.

"Ah!" Thrasius perked up as a delicious smell wafted across the road. "I was hoping he'd be open by now." He made off to the left, where Anna could see a small cluster of buildings, with a thin stream of white smoke rising from one.

Anna cocked an eyebrow at Indy, but the two followed behind their guide. After a few moments, it was obvious that the savory smell was coming from straight ahead. Anna's stomach growled loudly, and drool began to hang from one of Indy's jowls.

Thrasius walked straight up to the compound, which consisted of a low cottage, a few sheds, and a small barn, all fronting stock pens and gardens that were further away from the road. The smoke was coming from a low stone structure outside one of the buildings. A man stood nearby, working at a table with some sort of utensils, and a few travelers stood about, eating something held in two hands.

"Doros!" Thrasius called out. "Is that the first pig of the season I smell?"

"The second!" Doros called back, looking up from his table with a smile. He was a small man, browned from long labor out of doors, but with an open face and an easy manner. He set aside a carving knife and fork, and strode over to clasp hands with Thrasius.

"Good to see you again! It's been a couple of years, it seems like." Doros looked at Anna. "And who is your fellow traveler?" Indy grumbled mentally at being left out of the greeting, but held her peace.

"This is Anna, a traveler and guest of some old friends from near Lebadeia," Thrasius said, rolling out the story they had agreed on previously. "And this is Indy, her doughty companion." He indicated the big hybrid with a wave.

"She's a big one, sure enough!" Doros spoke with obvious admiration. "Size like that, I would've thought she was a wolf, if not for the coloring and the sturdier legs."

I'll show him sturdy legs, Indy groused. She smacked her chops to clear the saliva from her lips.

"Too big for herding, but she could probably rival Kerberos at guarding a flock!" Doros continued, undaunted. "And look at those muscles! She must be strong as a horse!"

I like this one, Indy said, instantly reversing her opinion of the man.

Doros walked around Indy to admire her lines, then withdrew, shaking his head in wonder, though dog-wise enough not to try touching her. "Young lady, if you ever think you'd like to get a litter from her, just come back here next time she's about to go into season. I'll put my big boy Argos to her. He's as fine a herder as you ever saw, and even-tempered to boot. Quite the ladies' man, too, though this big bitch might be a challenge even for him!" Doros laughed aloud at the thought.

I don't think that's so amusing, Indy said sourly. *As if I'd mate with a common dog, out in a field somewhere!*

Shush, Indy, you can tell he means well, Anna said. *And who knows,* she added impishly, *maybe this Argos is a* very *handsome dog.*

"Thank you, friend Doros." Anna grinned as Indy spluttered in outrage over their link. "I'll be sure to keep your kind offer in mind." Then her stomach growled again at the delicious smell, embarrassingly loud. "I'm sorry, we haven't eaten since this morning, and it's been a long walk. What is everyone eating?"

Doros smiled again, obviously on familiar territory. "We've got a special way of cooking meat, down here on the plains." He indicated the small stone building that they'd seen earlier. "You build a low fire in there, and throw in some seasoned wood chips every so often, for the smoke. You hang the meat up over the fire, not close enough to burn, so you can leave it in there for half a day or more. Then you take it out, carve it, and wrap it in one of these pitas." He picked up a flat round of brown bread from his table to demonstrate, carving thin slices of pork from a platter on the table, laying them on the pita, then slathering on some sort of thick paste from a bowl. "Garlic paste, with a little vinegar," he said at Anna's look. He handed the whole thing to Thrasius, who already had an eager hand out.

Thrasius bit into his pita with relish, meat juices running down his chin. "Ah, just as good as I remember! My life took a bad turn last year." He looked briefly shamefaced, though Anna thought he covered it well. "But I'm recovering. I should've come back long before now."

"Agreed," Doros said with a smile. "And for the young lady?" He looked back at Anna. "We've got eel too, fresh out of the lake yesterday and nicely smoked. We even have roasted vegetables for a humbler snack."

"I've only ever had the pork, myself," Thrasius commented between bites. "I always tell myself I'm going to try the others next time, but then when I get back here that smell always changes my mind for me."

"I'll have two of the roasted vegetable," Anna said. Then she wavered. "Well, make that one vegetable and one eel." *Somehow eel doesn't seem as bad as pork, even though I know they're both animals,* she said to Indy.

"Oh, and another eel and a pork, please," Anna said, catching Indy's thought midsentence. "But easy on the garlic for the last two. They're for this one here." She pointed to Indy.

"Good thinking, young lady." Doros filleted more eel with practiced gestures. "Some people call me extravagant for feeding Argos on meat, but the bigger breeds need a good amount to keep up their muscle." He smiled. "Plus, my boy loves it, and I can't deny him anything. I like to feed lamb myself, but pork's just as good." He put together their pitas in moments and handed them over smoothly. "That'll be one hemi for all five, please."

Anna fumbled one-handed for a moment in her pouch, then handed Doros a small silver coin. *Good thing I did my homework on this weird money before we left.* A hemiobol was one half an obol, which itself was one sixth of a drachma. A half-drachma per day was enough for a poor person to live on comfortably, so a twelfth of a drachma for five pitas seemed perfectly reasonable. *Besides, I'm really hungry!*

"Thank you, Anna." Thrasius spoke around a mouthful of his pita. "I'll pay for us next time. I was too busy stuffing my face!"

"Thank you for leading us here," Anna said. "These things remind me of the way they cook at home." She reached into one of Indy's saddlebags and pulled out a wide flat bowl, then placed it on the ground and put Indy's two pitas in it, since she couldn't very well use her flexible paws to eat in front of strangers. Indy leaned down and daintily nipped a bite out of one of the pitas, chewing it thoughtfully. Then she quickly snapped up the rest of the pita and smacked on the whole thing open-mouthed.

Doros laughed. "Now that's an endorsement!" Then his eyes flicked to something over Anna's shoulder. "Excuse me, but business calls. Nice to meet you, Anna. Remember my offer! And good to see you again, Thrasius!" Doros moved back to his table, then hailed the next two approaching customers with a loud greeting.

"Doros probably knows the name and favorite order of every-one who travels this road," Thrasius said to Anna. She was just biting into her pita as Indy noisily started in on her second. "He opens up shop here when the weather's good, and does a pig every few days. It's a good way to make money, since you're getting the price of a finished product instead of selling the whole animals at market. And with the road to Thebes going right past here, it's a good location." He frowned ruefully. "I hadn't come by here since I went broke, and… well, you know. Forgot how good they were."

"These *are* really good." Anna finished her vegetable pita, then took a tentative bite of the eel, chewing it carefully so she didn't choke on one of the tiny, thin bones. The garlic had been roasted before being whipped into a paste, so it wasn't too strong, and a dash of vinegar cut the fatty flavor of the eel nicely. She finished it with guilty relish, then wiped her fingers on a rag. She picked up Indy's bowl, which had been polished clean, and tucked it back into her saddlebag. The three of them waved goodbye to Doros and walked on, a low fence beside them on their left. Beyond the fence lay pastureland, dotted with sheep cropping the spring grass, and out past that the brush that must mark the edge of the marshland around the lake.

"An excellent lunch, Thrasius." Indy spoke once they were out of earshot of the other travelers. "Feel free to schedule as many stops like that as you like."

Anna laughed, and Thrasius did too, after a brief moment of surprise at Indy addressing him directly. "Don't worry, I know all the best places from here to Athens," he said with a smile.

He's gotten used to you pretty quickly, Anna said. *But you can tell that sometimes he's still not expecting you to talk.*

For a lunch like that, I can forgive a lot, Indy said as they walked. *And besides, you can hardly blame him. If cats could suddenly talk, I don't think I'd ever get used to it.*

Out in the distance, Anna saw a big herding dog look up from his sheep and spot them. He watched them go for a moment, then trotted toward them lazily, long legs covering the ground with ease, before slowing to a walk as he matched their course on the other side of the fence.

He was a brown-and-black shepherd, with a shaggy mane of hair and a noble bearing. A huge dog, he must've weighed in at one hundred and forty pounds if he was an ounce, though Indy still had thirty pounds and a few inches on him at the shoulder. His calm eyes looked them all over, but then fastened on Indy and stayed there. He matched her pace smoothly, gazing at her through lowered eyelids.

"This must be Argos." Thrasius smiled knowingly. "Doros was right about him being a ladies' man."

Anna snickered and looked at Indy, who was walking along with an elaborate lack of concern. Argos chuffed as he walked, then chuffed again when Indy didn't respond. Then he trotted forward a few steps, sniffed at the next fencepost, and backed away slightly.

"Oh, all right," Indy said with mild annoyance.

Argos' ears oriented on her when she spoke, but he stood his ground expectantly as Indy bent her path over to the fence and sniffed at the same fencepost. After a moment, Argos stepped forward again and joined her, keeping the side of his head toward hers, not going face to face. They sniffed the post lightly together, then Argos backed away a step. He shook to fluff out his mane, then backed up a step more, still gazing at Indy. Then he flicked his head, turned, and trotted away, back to his flock.

Indy rejoined Thrasius and Anna, and they walked together in silence for a moment. "He seemed very nice," Thrasius ventured.

"I'm sure he's a very good herder." Indy's tone didn't invite further comment, but her eyes hadn't left Argos' retreating form. She pulled her eyes away with a guilty sideways glance, then shook out her fur and trotted on ahead, leaving Anna and Thrasius to share a smile as they hastened to catch up.

32

aliartos turned out to be a walled city near the shore of Lake Kopais, backed up against low hills and commanding a number of passes that led out of the lake's broad valley. They had already eaten lunch, so they bypassed the city proper and turned right toward someplace their maps called Thespies, which Alixa duly corrected to Thespiai after Thrasius mentioned its current name. The road out of Haliartos climbed gradually up into low hills, but it was still relatively easy walking.

The mid-afternoon sun was beginning to descend when they came to a monument of some kind by the roadside. Anna could see a stone pillar, man-high and rectangular with what looked like a ball on top. As they walked closer, she could see that the ball was actually the carved head of a man with a full beard.

"It's a herma," Thrasius said, seeing Anna's look. "A statue of Hermes," he elaborated.

"Is it some kind of milestone?"

"Usually they mark a crossroads." Thrasius gestured to illustrate. "This time it's just a path crossing this main road, but this is our turn-off."

"I hate to be the one to ask," Indy said dryly, "but why is this statue a completely featureless rectangle except for a head and what look like male human genitals?"

Thrasius barked out a laugh. "What kind of genitals do *you* think a statue should have?"

"This *would* be a little unusual, back home," Anna said. "Most statues I've seen have arms and legs. And are maybe less, um… heroic?" She gestured vaguely to the statue's endowment, and Indy snorted in amusement.

Thrasius reached into his pack and pulled out a small bottle of oil. He poured a tiny bit on one finger, then walked up and dabbed it on the statue. "For good luck," he explained. "Hermes is the god of luck and travelers. And fertility," he added, nodding at the statue's midsection. "And the number four is his lucky number, hence the four sides of the pillar."

Indy examined the statue. It sat amid a pile of small stones, but otherwise there was nothing unusual about it. "So, what do you need to do? For the good luck?"

"Most people either add a stone to the pile, or anoint the statue with oil." He suddenly burst into laughter. "Just don't pee on it!"

"I *have* been known to pee on things. Anna can vouch for its cat repellent properties." Indy laughed at Anna's disgusted expression, then sniffed at the statue's base. "And it smells like I wouldn't be the first. But why do you bring it up?"

"Sorry, sorry." Thrasius fought to contain his mirth. "That might have seemed in bad taste. I forgot you two aren't from around here." At Indy's questioning look, he continued. "Aesop wrote a fable about a dog who was going to salute a statue of Hermes with a lift of his leg. The real Hermes noticed and had to speak up for himself quickly, to avoid the wrong kind of anointing."

Indy laughed again. "Well, Hermes has nothing to worry about from me. Women don't lift their legs!" She raised a forepaw toward Thrasius. "I could use some of that oil, though."

Thrasius obligingly dabbed a bit of his oil onto Indy's outstretched paw, and she used it to solemnly anoint the statue in the normal way, lingering as she did so.

Thrasius stoppered the oil bottle and gestured along the trail that crossed the main road. "This way! Not much further now." He led them along the path for a short while, then off it and back into the trees. After a few minutes of walking down a brush-choked side track, they came to a small clearing. Anna could see the faint remains of a fire pit in the center, which Indy sniffed around with interest.

"This is a good place to stop for the day." Thrasius doffed his wide-brimmed hat. "There's no water, but we can get more along the way tomorrow when we cross the Asopos River." He tilted his head around to indicate the surrounding trees. "And this isn't a place where travelers often stop, though someone might see a fire from the road if we lit a big one." He unslung his bag from his shoulder, laid it aside and dropped his hat on it, then sat down on the soft ground underneath an oak tree with a grunt. "I think I may take a little nap, if you don't mind. No point moving around in the heat if we don't have to." He pulled his folded cloak from his bag, tucked it under his head and lay back.

"That sounds like a great idea." Anna dropped her pack a few yards away, then squashed it into shape where she could recline against it comfortably. Indy settled down beside her, nose curled to tail.

Oh, and one thing for you to be aware of. Indy's voice sounded in her mind as Anna's eyelids began to droop. *Thrasius hasn't given me any reason to doubt his good will toward us. Regardless, now that we're alone with him, I set my collar to keep watch anytime we're asleep. If it thinks we're in any danger, it'll wake us both, and turn on our shields if need be.*

I hadn't thought of that. Anna looked at Thrasius' reclining form uneasily. *Do you really think we need to?*

You're a good person, Anna. Indy curled up more comfortably, re-settling without opening her eyes. *But there's no reason to take any chances. Remember, he and Nicon tried to rob both of us just a couple of months ago. If that had come out badly, we wouldn't be here to talk about it today. And I didn't smell any sign of anyone when I sniffed around here earlier, but that doesn't mean we shouldn't be cautious.*

Anna wrestled with those disturbing thoughts as she settled back again, but eventually she nodded off and dozed away the rest of the afternoon, waking as the sun sank low in the sky.

After arising, they set about gathering fallen branches to make a small fire, more for the light and cheer than because they needed the warmth. Anna thought that Indy went about her tasks more quietly than usual, but her friend seemed fine otherwise, so she let it be for now. They unpacked some fabbed cold-smoked mutton, which wouldn't last much longer without refrigeration anyway, and made a meal of that with bread and cheese, all washed down with heavily watered wine.

After dinner and a quick clean-up, Thrasius settled down with a contented sigh. "Ah, this is the life! A nice leisurely walk in the spring weather, two fine meals. A man could get used to this." He looked up at the sky through the trees. The stars weren't visible overhead yet, but the sky was already a deep purple, shading quickly to black.

"Thank you for guiding us, Thrasius," Anna said. "I'd feel much more nervous about traveling with just myself and Indy in a strange land, not knowing all the ways we could get into trouble."

"That goes for me as well." Indy smacked her chops. "And those pitas were an especially good idea."

"You're most welcome." Thrasius thought for a moment. "Tomorrow, we'll cut across country south of Thebes, then rejoin the high road to Athens a few miles later on." He rubbed at his beard with one hand. "Usually we would've gone straight along the main road from Haliartos to Thebes instead of coming down this way. But now that I'm out clean, I want to stay as far away from Nicon and that unsavory bunch as I can." He looked at Indy. "I'd rather none of them got word that a young woman and a huge black-and-white dog walked right through the market on the way to Athens." He sighed. "Once enough time has passed, maybe I can settle things somehow. But for now, I'll take us far around the city. It'll add a few miles to our trip, though."

We'd probably know before Nicon got within five miles of us, Anna said to Indy over their link. *That bracelet we put on him should have plenty of range.*

True, Indy said. *But I'd rather not try to explain that to Thrasius. I think my speaking abilities are about all he's ready for at this point. And since the bracelet's only powered by body heat and motion, it may not be able to ping us as often as we'd like. If it's running low, and we get unlucky, we could bump right into him in a crowded city. I'd rather not bet on it if we don't have to.*

"Sounds good," Anna said aloud so Thrasius could hear. "We've got plenty of supplies to reach Athens, so we might as well play it safe."

"I'm glad you agree," Thrasius said. "Athens should be safe enough, since Nicon has no family or friends there. And Athens and Thebes are rivals, so a Theban who's fallen to banditry"—he looked pained for a moment—"should avoid being seen there, in case anyone should recognize him."

It's too bad, Indy said. *We never did get much detail from your dad's data, but from what I can tell, Thebes was one of the most famous cities in ancient Greece. I suppose we can always visit it later.*

"If you ladies don't mind, I think I'll turn in early tonight." Thrasius settled back. "I'm not as young as I used to be." He closed his eyes contentedly.

"Good night," Anna said, echoed by Indy a moment later.

Anna unpacked her cloak and folded it over to make a sleeping pad. Even with the heat of the day past, it was warm enough that she didn't need any covers, so she simply lay back, comfortably close to their small fire. Indy settled down beside her, the leaves of the forest floor sufficient to cushion her. Anna wasn't quite sleepy yet, so she was content to look up at the deep purple sky and let her mind wander.

After a few minutes, Indy spoke in her mind. *Anna? Can I ask you a personal question?*

Of course, Anna said. *It sounds like Thrasius is asleep already, but I was just relaxing.*

Indy's mental voice paused for several long moments. *Have you ever thought about… having a family?*

Um, I guess not specifically? Not yet, anyway. I always figured I'd have one someday, assuming I met the right guy. Anna grew pensive. *Though being here in the past does complicate things.* Anna rolled toward Indy. Her friend was a fuzzy, sphinx-like silhouette in front of the dimming fire. *I probably wouldn't have much to talk about with some guy from Backwoodsville, Ancient Greece,* Anna continued. *But once we meet some people in the larger towns, it might be different. Awkward at first maybe, but doable. Human nature's more or less a constant, right?*

I can't comment on that, Indy said dryly. *But think about this: where did hybrids come from?*

Well, I guess humans created them a few hundred years ago, Anna said. *Back before the rules were so strict against that sort of thing.*

Indeed, Indy said. *So, how many hybrids are there in this whole world, right now?*

Oh. Anna's mouth opened in silent horror. *I didn't even think…* Anna's mental voice trailed off.

Exactly, Indy said gently. *When we found out that we could never get back home… I can't begin to describe that feeling. Everyone like me who ever lived was out there in the future.* Her eyes gleamed in the firelight. *What if I never meet anyone who can really understand me, ever again?* She exhaled slowly. *Can I live a whole, long lifetime like that?*

They lay there in the warm night for a few moments, considering, before Indy continued. *So when I saw Argos today, it made me think. Up to now, we've been busy coming to grips with what's happened to us, just trying to get by. But what about our future?* She laid her great head down on her front paws. *I don't want to be alone forever.*

Anna's heart broke. *Indy, as long as I'm here, you'll never be alone.* She sat up and put her hand on Indy's furry shoulder. *And we'll find some way to make things work out. For both of us.* Anna stroked her friend's coarse fur comfortingly, forgetting cross-species etiquette in the face of a friend's pain.

Thank you, Anna. Indy exhaled deeply and leaned into Anna's hand. *And some problems are so big, there's no point worrying about them. But I wanted you to know.*

I'm sorry I was so selfish. I can't believe I didn't think of this earlier. Anna's mind raced, trying to think through possible solutions, but she calmed herself with an effort. *We're not going to solve this tonight. But there's got to be a solution out there somewhere.*

Could you set your phone up for me again? Indy asked. *Looking at my pictures always makes me feel better.*

Of course. Anna quickly propped her phone where Indy could see, but where Thrasius wouldn't notice it if he awakened. *And we'll see what tomorrow brings, and take it from there.*

Agreed, Indy said.

33

When she woke the next day, Anna was glad they'd taken it easy the day before. She'd thought her muscles were pretty tough after eight months of their new life, and they'd probably walked less than twenty miles. But walking in one long stretch, up and down hills, seemed to work different muscles than walking around rolling mountainside pastures. She got up slowly and stretched, taking stock of her aches and pains. Thankfully, her feet felt only slightly tender. She'd been worried about walking so far in sandals, but apparently her feet were tougher than the rest of her.

"Feeling a little road-sore?" Indy taunted. She rose smoothly, then bowed in a deep stretch fore and aft, looking none the worse for wear as she padded over. "Don't worry, it's not your fault." She looked irritatingly smug. "Wolves travel long distances, chasing large prey. Whereas monkeys spend a lot of time roaming and foraging, but don't really cover much ground."

"We'll see how you do if we have to climb a tree." Anna smiled, glad that her friend seemed to be feeling better after their conversation last night. "You'd better hope there's nothing dangerous on the ground. There could even be bears in these woods."

Indy looked around, scenting the air carefully. Then she snorted in disgust when she realized Anna was just tweaking her.

Noticing that Thrasius had apparently gone off in search of privacy, Anna quickly pulled one of their little solar-powered relay drones from her pack, then asked Alixa to send it up to the top of the tallest tree nearby. Once it found the right spot to cling to, it would hopefully be invisible from the ground, even with its tiny solar cells exposed to keep it active. Then it would serve as the first link in their chain of communication back to their secret cave and its machinery.

After a few more minutes, Thrasius appeared at the other side of the clearing, throwing his cloak over his shoulder. "Ready to get moving?"

"Just a minute." Anna's face heated in embarrassment. "I need to go find a bush." She moved off out of sight, Indy trotting after her. In the future, it was not unknown for hybrids to relieve themselves in the open, as a matter of ancient custom and privilege, but Anna needed more privacy. And even Indy had become paradoxically more modest in the past. "After they heard me speak, Leitus and Helene started giving me the weirdest looks when I peed in front of them," she had explained.

The party re-formed and set out after a last bit of packing. Thrasius snacked on the last of the mutton as he walked along, and Anna did likewise, handing a bigger piece to Indy every few minutes. The day had dawned clear, and the walking was good. Once they broke out of the trees near their campsite, the terrain was wide and rolling, with low purple mountains far off in the distance ahead. Sheep and goats grazed here and there, and small farmsteads dotted the plain. The slopes of the low hills were terraced with grape vines, their fruit still too small to see at this distance. Lower down were groves of olive trees, the straight rows standing out against the jumble of uncultivated forest.

As they walked, they saw men laboring in the fields and orchards. Some looked like normal Greeks to Anna, but others wore humbler clothes, or foreign features. Many appeared wiry and thin from their toil, even thinner than the native Greeks, and were clad only in loincloths.

Anna turned to Thrasius as they walked. "Who are those workers? They look a bit different to me."

"Just laborers," Thrasius said. "The spring harvest is starting, so there's always plenty to do in the fields."

"But why are some of them so poorly dressed?" Anna carefully didn't gesture toward them, to avoid drawing attention. "And thin! They don't look strong enough to be farmers."

"Ah. This goes back to yesterday's conversation, and the explanation I promised you." Thrasius rubbed at the bridge of his nose wearily, though it was still early in the day, and the corners of his mouth turned down. "Those men are mostly slaves, with some freedmen among them. A few might be non-citizen foreigners, which we call metics, though we don't see so many of those outside Athens." He paused a moment. "Are things so different in Iberia? I admit I've never been there, so I don't know much about the place."

"Iberia is not as well-developed as Greece," Indy broke in smoothly. "So there's not the same need for agricultural labor as you must have here." *And slavery must be a sensitive topic,* she said mentally to Anna. *Since he keeps avoiding it.*

Right, Anna said. *Slavery never even occurred to me before he mentioned yesterday that we might get sold into it. I guess the folks back in Lebadeia were too poor to own any?*

Or we saw slaves there, but didn't recognize them as such, Indy said darkly.

Anna froze. *Of course! Echetlus' assistant at his shop, Timais and Nephele's servants at their house… they were all slaves!*

Many of them, probably. Indy sounded resigned. *I wasn't ready to see it either.*

Slavery just seems so unthinkable. Anna was stunned. *Like human sacrifice or something.* She thought for a moment. *But if it's normal here, we need to know more about it.* She turned toward Thrasius, forestalling Indy's half-voiced objection. *Don't worry, I'll be careful.*

"Could I ask you a few more questions?" Anna put on her most guileless expression as she addressed Thrasius. "We still don't know much about how things work here, and I was a little scared yesterday when you mentioned how we might get into trouble if we're not careful. I don't want to be clueless when we get to Athens!"

"Of course, of course!" Thrasius spoke with forced heartiness. "Ask away! I don't own any slaves, so I have no skin in the game, you might say." His smile lost some of its width. "Though my brother will certainly still own some, in Athens."

"Um, so…" Anna searched for the right words. "Where do they even come from?"

"It depends. Many of the men would have been captured in wars among their own people somewhere, and sold on to Greeks by the victors. Those with money can get ransomed back to their families, so these would be the poorer ones here." Thrasius considered briefly. "Some, especially girls, might have been sold as children by their families, if they couldn't afford to feed them." He frowned. "There are also some unsavory Greek traders. They'll take anyone they happen upon, poor immigrants or even children or the old who've been left to die from exposure in the hills."

"Couldn't they just run off, though?" Anna asked. "I can't see any chains on them."

Thrasius snorted. "They couldn't work very well in chains, could they? And some do manage to flee, especially if they're somewhere near where they were captured." He frowned more deeply. "But most slaves are sold far away from their homes. These were probably captured somewhere near the mouth of the Istros River, or elsewhere around the Black Sea. Returning to their homelands would mean a journey of hundreds of miles on foot, with many dangers and little help along the way."

"I imagine they'd also be hunted down by their former owners," Indy said. "To make an example of the runaways, so the rest wouldn't get the same idea." She raised her lip in disgust.

"In Athens, our freedoms are the envy of Greece!" Thrasius looked a touch defensive now. "Slaves can work for pay, and can ply a trade if they have one. Freed slaves can even get rich, though they can't own land. Whereas if a Spartan helot so much as talks back, he'll get a beating or worse." His face grew sad. "Still, I'm glad I was born a free man. And it's hard not to sympathize, after spending some time close to the bottom myself."

Thrasius paused in their conversation, nodding to two well-dressed travelers they could see coming the other direction on the path. The men gave their party a short greeting and only a cursory glance as they passed, to Anna's silent relief.

Once the men were out of hearing behind them, Thrasius turned back to Anna and Indy. "How do these things work in Iberia? I'm eager to know more about your mysterious homeland."

Indy spoke up first. "We're not from Iberia proper, though Anna's ancestors came from there. Our land is some distance further to the west, but the climate and terrain are similar."

"It's almost as dry as this, some years." Anna looked around at the relatively sparse vegetation of the Greek plain around them.

"But to your question," Indy continued, "our land did enslave people, long ago. They worked the soil just like they do here, though the crops were different. And like here, most of them were sold abroad after being captured in wars among their own people, far away. They were sold to traders who brought them to our land to sell." Indy kept her tone carefully neutral as she spoke. "They had even fewer liberties than these Greek slaves, I'm ashamed to say." She worked her mouth as if she'd tasted something sour, whiskers bristling.

"So what happened?" Thrasius looked at Indy with interest. "Did they revolt?"

"A few did, here and there. Never with wide success. Their descendants were kept in bondage for hundreds of years, even after the international slave trade was banned." Indy huffed sadly. "To make a long story very short, only one part of our country allowed slavery. Eventually there was a civil war between that part and the rest. The slave-holding part lost, and slavery was outlawed everywhere after that." Indy looked straight ahead as she walked. "But by then, the formerly enslaved population had been gone from their homelands for so long, generations in many cases, that most couldn't very well return even if they had the means. It took hundreds of years for them to integrate fully into our society after that, and even now their descendants still suffer at a disadvantage."

I should really go read up on that stuff, Anna said to Indy. *It's hard to believe America was like that only five hundred years ago.*

Most of my kind know this story by heart, Indy said. *Though you can probably find more details in the data your father sent us, since it's relatively recent history. It's ironic though. In some ways, the worst parts of our history may be the most helpful to us here.*

"Hundreds of years…" Thrasius mused. "Strange to think that something so common here could be so far in the past in other lands." He looked at the farms spread out nearby. "And if a war like yours ever happened here, it would be a disaster! Athens is probably one-third slaves. Where would they all go? Would they all be set free at once? Who would do their work? What happens if they take revenge on their former masters?"

"Our ancestors struggled with the same questions," Indy said. "Rebuilding afterward was slow and painful, with plenty of false starts and mistakes. I can tell you more about it if you like, but it's a long, sad story."

Indy's head turned sharply toward the field they'd been walking beside. A moment later, Anna heard a cry of pain. When she turned to look, she could see one of the field slaves, a painfully thin young man wearing only a grubby cloth around his hips, crouched on the ground, holding the side of his head with both hands. Another, stronger slave stood between him and what looked like an overseer, a better-fed man wearing a tunic instead of a slave's loincloth, holding a short wooden cudgel in one fist.

As Anna watched, the overseer drew back his cudgel to strike the young man again, and the stronger slave grabbed his arm, struggling for control of the weapon. When the overseer called out for help, the slave released his arm and ran, coming directly toward their group. The overseer gave chase, and two more of his kind ran in from the other corners of the field to aid him. Indy growled and stalked forward in a low, menacing crouch.

Thrasius reached out toward her in alarm. "Don't!" he hissed, as quietly as he could. Indy dismissed him with a shake of her head and took another step. "Remember what I said yesterday!" he added. Indy stopped. "We could be enslaved ourselves for aiding a runaway!"

Indy looked over at Anna, who watched in horror as the first overseer tackled the runaway in a cloud of dust just twenty yards from where they stood. The other two overseers caught up seconds later, and rained kicks on the hapless slave as he rolled on the ground, covering his head with his arms.

In moments, the runaway slave was subdued and dragged off, held tightly by a man at each elbow. The original overseer who'd tackled the runaway walked a few steps toward their party, dusting his tunic with his hands, but stopped short when he saw Indy's murderous glare directed at him.

"Sorry about that, sir, miss." The man's eyes narrowed. "Don't worry, we'll teach him a lesson." Indy rumbled a growl low in her chest at this, and the man gripped his cudgel but didn't look away. "You have a nice day now," he said shortly. Then he turned and followed the other two overseers, looking back over his shoulder as he did.

Indy's growl turned into panting, and her posture lost some of its stiffness. "They're lucky there were three of them," she said, quietly enough so the retreating overseer wouldn't hear.

"There are more than that," murmured Thrasius. He glanced significantly out toward the edges of the neighboring fields. "If the call went up, there could be ten men here in minutes. Neighbors would run to help. I've seen you in action, but one against ten is poor odds. And there's Anna to consider."

"You're right." Indy grunted in disgust and shook out her lowering ruff. "But that doesn't mean I have to like it."

Anna watched as the first young slave who'd been struck by the overseer was pulled to his feet by his fellows, who'd paused in their labor to watch the brief scuffle. All of them set back to work quickly as the overseer swept his gaze over them. The overseer looked back toward Indy again, this time more consideringly, and glanced around to check the positions of his comrades nearby.

"Time to go." Thrasius forced a smile for the distant overseer's benefit. "We can talk more about this later," he said, his smile slipping. "But please, we need to move on before that one gets any ideas."

I hate it too. Anna looked at Indy. *I'm with you. But we're outnumbered and in the open here. There's nothing we can do.*

Indy growled wordlessly and stalked off down the road, Anna and a grateful Thrasius following behind her. Anna looked back every so often, and every time she did, the distant overseer was looking toward them. She shivered to herself, and hurried on.

They walked in silence for a while, eventually coming upon the Asopos River. It hardly lived up to the title of a river though, being only a few tens of feet wide where they forded it at a shallow, rocky spot. They filled their waterskins on the far side, with Anna filling Indy's and replacing it in her saddlebag, since they were out in the open, and you could never tell who might be watching. Then they forged on, paralleling the river for a while, then gradually climbing up into another series of the low mountains that seemed to be so common in this part of Greece. Conversation between the travelers was sparse and somber after earlier events, but as they finally left the Theban plain behind, Thrasius pointed out an unimposing stone marker beside the road.

"We're now leaving Boeotia, the region controlled by Thebes and the smaller cities of the Boeotian League like Lebadeia and Haliartos." He pointed ahead along a narrow plateau, its sides hemmed in by mountains. "Ahead is Attica, the region controlled by Athens." He smiled slightly, emotions warring on his face. "My home. It's been a long time."

They traversed the grassy plateau from one end to the other, a distance of ten miles or so, the few travelers they met outnumbered by grazing sheep and goats. As they climbed up into the surrounding mountains at the far end, they stopped for the day, this time at a secluded hollow Thrasius knew of on a side track away from the main path. Anna dropped her pack gratefully, then popped the clasp on Indy's saddlebags so she could crawl out from under them.

Anna sat down wearily and watched while Indy writhed around

on her back in the dry leaf litter. Eventually the big hybrid stood up and shook out her coat forcefully, sending dust and leaves flying. "Ah, much better! That harness makes my fur feel like it's matting up." She cocked an ear, then dove toward her left thigh, biting at the fur there. "You little—" She stopped, then attacked a different part of her leg, hind paw wiggling frantically. "I *know* that's not a flea crawling on me. There'd better not be fleas in this forest!"

Anna rose again. "Hold on a sec. I got you." Anna's dexterous fingers made quick work of the flea, winkling it out of the fur and crushing it between thumb and fingernail. Then she pulled the brush from her pack and quickly ran it over the fur of Indy's chest where the harness strap ran.

Indy shook out again afterward with a satisfied sigh. "Thanks, little sis."

Thrasius had unslung his own bag and squatted down to rummage through its contents. "It's not much further now to Athens. Just one more easy morning's travel over the crest of these hills and down onto the plain." He pulled out a few wrapped packages of food and laid them on the ground. "We could get there tonight if you didn't mind walking another dozen miles or so. But there's no sense pushing on too hard and getting there in the dark."

"I'm good with resting." Anna rubbed at one of her heels where her sandal strap was chafing. "It's been a stressful day. And it's going to take me more than two days to harden up into a real traveler like you two."

"I'm sorry about what we saw today." Thrasius closed his pack and began unwrapping the food, looking down rather than at Anna and Indy. "It doesn't represent the best of what Greece is about."

"It wasn't you who beat those poor men," Indy said. "And you were right. It was hard to just stand there and watch, but there was nothing we could have done."

At least not yet, Anna said over their link.

Dinner was a simple affair of sausage, cheese, and bread, and none of them felt like gathering wood for a fire. Thrasius seemed preoccupied as they ate. "Sorry, I'm a little anxious about tomorrow," he finally said. "Which must seem ridiculous at my age, I know. But I haven't seen my brother in years. There's no telling how it'll go once we're face to face again." He stretched, then winced slightly as he hit some bit of soreness. "I know there's going to be an 'I told you so.'"

"An 'I told you so'?" Anna finished eating and dusted her hands, looking around, but there was no cleanup to do since they hadn't cooked anything.

"From my older brother." Thrasius made a rueful face. "He always warned me that Nicon was no good. But I didn't want to hear it. Nicon and I were both the youngest sons of well-off families, though I was from an older generation than he was. And we both felt that urge to strike out on our own, to prove that we were as good as anyone. I could see a lot of myself in him." He looked down. "But Nicon had a bad streak that I just kept excusing. Being born rich wasn't enough for him, his success had to be at someone else's expense. Finally, my family cut me off for getting tangled up in one too many of Nicon's schemes, something that would've reflected badly on them if it'd come to light. After that, I didn't have any way to support myself. Then Nicon was cut off too, after we fell in with the wrong sort." He frowned in disgust. "Our first few robberies were just for the thrill of it, back when we didn't even need the money. But you met me a while after that."

Anna tried to find something good to say. "I think your brother will be able to tell that you've changed."

Thrasius smiled tightly. "I'm sure you're right."

The conversation trailed off after that. As the sun set behind the hills, they laid out their cloaks for the night. And though Anna felt a twinge of guilt about it, she was also glad that Indy's collar was set to watch over the both of them as they slept.

34

The next morning, Anna awoke excited. *Okay, I'm officially freaking out right now,* she said to Indy after they'd had a bite of breakfast and set out again. *I still feel bad about yesterday. But we're about to see* ancient Athens!

Well, we have *seen plenty of pictures,* Indy said. *But a lot of those were fictional, from movies and such that got lumped in with our data. The few real pictures we have of buildings from around this time just show ruins.* Her words notwithstanding, she seemed enthused by the prospect of seeing for herself, and trotted along with a spring in her step, ears bobbing and tail riding high.

They crested the low mountain pass in less than an hour of relatively easy walking, with Anna discreetly setting up another relay drone near the highest point. Then they started their descent toward Athens. Eventually, after they had wound down out of the hills and almost onto the plain, Thrasius pointed out ahead. "See up there? That tall, rocky hill way off in the distance? That's the Acropolis. You can almost see it now, though we're still too far away to see the temples on top. Athens is spread out all around that."

He waved his hand to the right. "Out past the city is Piraeus, the seaport. That's where all the foreign trade comes in and pays its taxes, at least since they switched from the old port at Phaleron. We won't be able to see it from here, though."

Soon their trail joined with others to become a full-sized road, still not paved with stones, but dry and flat from the pounding of many feet and hooves. The volume of traffic increased, with individual travelers, groups of two or three together, and farmers leading donkeys piled high with baskets of produce to sell in the city. Anna looked away from one wagon stacked with chickens in wicker cages, not wanting to think about the fate they were probably headed for. Indy trotted from one side of the road to the other, sniffing deeply at stone road markers and piles of animal dung.

After a while they crossed a low, wide bridge over what Alixa told her was the Kephissos River. Groves of olive trees lined the river here, knobby trunks holding up branches that reminded her of the live oak trees back in Texas.

"Peisistratos planted those, must be more than sixty years ago now," Thrasius said when he saw Anna looking. "My father always said he was a great leader, regardless of what Solon thought about him. He died when I was just a boy, though."

Incredible, Indy said. *I checked my net. Some of these trees were still alive in our time!*

Hard to believe. Anna reached out to touch the rough bark on the nearest one as they passed. "Reminds me of home," she said to Thrasius. She felt a pang of longing at the thought, but pushed it down, not wanting to darken her mood this morning.

One thing that didn't *make it to our time,* Indy continued, *is Plato's Academy, which will be off to our right somewhere… in another hundred years or so.* Anna could hear the smile in her friend's voice.

They could see the Acropolis straight ahead in the distance, with a glimpse of buildings of some sort on its crest, tall stone columns and shallow roofs glowing blue and red in the morning sun. All around them the farms and fields had given way to homes, ever more densely populated the closer they came to Athens. Indy had given up sniffing around at some point and now walked beside them. *There's more poop here than I could smell in a dozen lifetimes,* she thought to Anna. *It's olfactory overload!*

There was no sudden transition, but at some point Anna became aware that they were in Athens, and not just walking through smaller and smaller farms. They walked beside a small stream, through what seemed to be a pottery and sculpture district. There were cemeteries here as well, where grand monuments with metal-crowned and armored statues shared space with the humbler grave-markers of ordinary folk.

Anna looked around. "I kind of thought there'd be a wall around the city, like we saw at Haliartos."

"There's been no need," Thrasius said. "Even the mighty Persians only made it as far as Marathon, many miles to the northeast. And that was some years ago now." After a moment's consideration, he continued. "Besides, can you imagine how much effort it would take to raise a wall all the way around this city? Look at the size of it!"

Anna was impressed despite herself. The great cities of the future were far larger, of course. Even her relatively small city of El Paso was many times the size of ancient Athens. But you couldn't compare by size alone. Athens in this time felt like New York or Tokyo did in her time, a city at the edge of what was supportable, bursting with possibilities.

In our history, they do build a wall at some point, after a Persian invasion, Indy said. *At least as far as we can glean from our fragmentary data. Our nets found an off-hand mention of it in the dialogue of a much later play.*

Anna swung her head from side to side, taking in the sights. No one else around them on the road seemed impressed, but it was hard for Anna not to goggle like a country turnip on her first trip to the big city.

The road had consolidated itself by this point into a paved surface, which wound deeper into Athens. Presently they slowed, as traffic backed up in front of them at some unseen barrier. Anna could see that there were some sort of uniformed guards up ahead, asking questions of travelers, handing out some sort of tokens, and taking money in exchange.

"The farmers that come here to buy and sell have to pay a fee to do it in the agora," Thrasius said, seeing where Anna was looking. "They can trade out in the countryside if they want, but it's more profitable to pay the fee and do it in the main marketplace."

As their party reached the guards, the left one spoke out. "Sorry, miss, but guard dogs aren't allowed in the agora."

Anna was taken aback. She hadn't thought there might be sections of the city off-limits to dogs. She opened her mouth to object.

"My dear sirs," Thrasius said smoothly. "Our faithful hound Indy is no mere guard dog, but a highly trained member of the family! Allow me to demonstrate." He walked forward as Anna closed her mouth.

"Indy, sit!" Thrasius called out. Indy sat promptly, jaws agape in a doggy smile. Thrasius grinned with success, looking around at the guards and the travelers behind them.

He turned back to Indy and called out, "Indy, shake!" Indy raised her right paw gravely, placing it in Thrasius' hand for a slow shake. The guards smiled and relaxed, and a man behind them applauded briefly.

Thrasius puffed out his chest and faced the guards again. "Indy, salute!" he cried. He must have meant for Indy to raise her paw in a military salute to the guards. Instead, Indy jabbed her paw out and spread her toes in an immediately recognizable Greek rude gesture toward Thrasius.

The guards stared in surprise, then burst into raucous laughter. The left one doubled over, whooping for breath, as Thrasius reddened in embarrassment.

"Go on ahead, sir, miss," the guard said between breaths. He handed Thrasius a red clay token with a dog's head drawn on it in black. "I can see that your dog is… *very well trained!*" He bent over laughing again, one hand on his knee.

Thrasius gathered his dignity, gestured to Anna and Indy, and swept on past the guards, laughter receding in their wake.

"Sorry about that, Thrasius," Indy whispered once they were out of earshot. "I knew what you were going for, but my subconscious saw the shot and took it. I didn't realize the guards would think it was *that* funny."

Thrasius smiled, his embarrassment fading. "It got you a pass, didn't it?" He handed the dog-token to Anna. "I couldn't have planned it better." He looked around. "Too bad about all this traffic, though. I overheard someone say the City Dionysia started today, so the city's packed. I had forgotten the calendar here's offset from the one in Boeotia. But on the good side, they should announce the newest play premieres tomorrow! I saw a great one by Aeschylus here, many years back. When we arrive, I'll ask my brother which ones have the best word of mouth this year."

They continued along the road, which by this point had become a wide avenue, packed with people going in both directions. In a few moments they crossed the narrow stream they'd been paralleling, which Thrasius offhandedly referred to as "the Eridanus." The stream was bridged at many points now and covered over with stone in other areas, but Indy's nostrils still narrowed as they crossed, and Anna held her breath, her gorge rising at the unmistakable smell of raw sewage. Then the road opened out onto a grand marketplace.

The agora of Athens was a wide plaza surrounded by brightly painted stone buildings, some of which were still under construction. The plaza's main area was occupied by all manner of stalls, tables, piles, carts, baskets, and any other way you could display goods for sale, divided by tiny winding paths and wider makeshift thoroughfares. Indy held her head as high as she could, taking in the unfamiliar and fascinating scents, while Anna gawked at the wide spectrum of noisy humanity thronging the place, old, young, sick, lame, and healthy jostling and jumbled together like nothing she'd ever seen. Her translator earring seemed stunned into silence, unable to render such a cacophony into anything intelligible, and struggling with the change from the Aeolic dialect of Boeotia to the Attic of Athens.

Thrasius waved a hand around at the buildings, white stone accented with bright colors. "City offices, tax collectors, merchant associations, that sort of thing. A lot of this wasn't here until recently, but the agora's been getting larger and larger, and the city's tax collectors have to keep pace." He pointed out a pair of bronze statues nearby, each one a cloaked man holding a sword in a dramatic pose. "Those are the Tyrannicides, who killed Hipparchus the tyrant and set the stage for our democracy." He looked like he wanted to say more, but got distracted weaving through the crowd. "It's a great story, remind me to tell you about it later."

Barkers and touts called out to them from all sides as they walked the gauntlet. "The freshest olive oil, free samples!" "You look thirsty, Uncle. Our finest vintage, right here!" "Delicious roasted haunches, fresh from the Isle of Frogs!"

At this last, Indy sat and flicked her eyes back at Anna, giving her a look that needed no interpretation. Anna smirked, then stepped forward.

"How much for the frog legs, sir?" She quickly haggled out a price, trying to imitate how she'd seen it done back in Lebadeia, and returned with four steaming legs, rubbed with aromatic spices and impaled on thin wooden skewers. She handed one leg to Thrasius, who nodded in thanks, then tore bits of meat from the remaining three with her fingers, giving most of it to Indy but sneaking a couple of bits for herself as they walked along, bumping shoulder to bony, skinny shoulder with the marketplace crowd.

As they walked, on their left Anna could see a hill, in front of and lower than the Acropolis, but still impressive, topped with limestone buildings painted in brilliant, contrasting shades. "The Areopagus," Thrasius said. "Where the city council meets, and where legal cases are argued." As they passed around it, he swept his arm to the left. "And here, the jewel in Athens' crown," he said with mock pomposity. "The Acropolis!"

From this distance, the Acropolis loomed over them, the limestone hill itself more than one hundred feet high. The top was covered with grand temples, most of their walls faced with brightly colored columns of carved stone. Trees clustered around its base, and some sides of the hill had been built up into walls, while other sides were sheer natural rock.

"The building under construction in the front is our new temple of Athena Polias. Our city's patron goddess," Thrasius added at Anna's questioning look. "Looks like the columns are two or three drums high already, so it's coming right along."

It doesn't look much like the pictures we have, Anna thought to Indy.

Fewer temples, at this point, Indy thought back. *The ones we know about came later. I think I read that these are due to be destroyed by the Persians in a decade or so.*

"And look! You can see the last of the sacrificial parade too, going into the Theater of Dionysius." The throng of people Thrasius pointed at were laden with all sorts of odd items, with girls and young women bearing grain sheaves and baskets of food, boys and young men leading animals, and adults carrying aloft curiously decorated poles or statuettes. "We're going to miss the sacrifice, but that's all right. My family traditionally holds a private feast on this day instead."

I'm just as happy not to see a sacrifice anyway, Anna thought to Indy. She guiltily recalled the frog legs she'd sampled earlier.

They crossed the mouth of a narrow alley, where a thin, pock-marked beggar held out his hands toward them, mumbling words that Anna's translator couldn't make sense of. Thrasius walked past without seeming to notice the man.

"We can go up and take a look at the Acropolis later if you like, but it's a fair walk. I'll need to spend today catching up with my brother, but then I can show you the rest of the sights after we've settled in for a day or so." He tipped his floppy hat back and grinned like a much younger man. "It's strange, like being a tourist in my own city."

It's all so big! thought Anna to Indy. *I thought the past would be much smaller, somehow. And less smelly,* she added, wrinkling her nose at the press of sweaty humanity. *Look at all these people, all these temples, all this* stuff! Anna suddenly felt very small. *Where would we even start to make some kind of life here?*

Don't worry about that for now, Indy said stoutly. *One step at a time.* She yawned widely. *Let's start with a good afternoon nap. And tomorrow, maybe some more of those frog legs.*

35

nce past the Acropolis they walked another few hundred yards along progressively less-crowded streets, bearing back toward the east edge of the city. At last, they stopped in front of a substantial but not princely house, two stories high and built of mud brick with a red tiled roof. It wasn't precisely run-down, to Anna's eye, but it looked overdue for a fresh coat of paint. The two-story house was built in a U shape, with both stories surrounding a courtyard on three sides. On the fourth side was a one-story wall, whose metal-banded doors stood open to the street. To the right of the courtyard doors was a small shopfront built into the house, through which Anna could see shelves stocked with jars of various shapes and sizes.

"I'll keep quiet for the time being, like we discussed," Indy reminded them quietly as they arrived. Anna nodded in affirmation as Thrasius stepped toward the house, hesitating just outside the courtyard entrance.

"I never thought I'd be nervous outside my parents' old home," he said. "My brother was the one who finally cut me off, but he did say that the door was open if I mended my ways." His brows pinched together. "Though it has been a long time. Hopefully he still remembers."

Anna shared a worried look with Indy as Thrasius drew a deep breath, blew it out, and then clapped his hands together. "Hello, the house!" he called out. He waited, but there was no response.

"If we did get turned away..." He threw a worried look at Anna and Indy. "There were some lodging houses back nearer the market. We could stay the night, then decide what to do in the morning." He glanced back over his shoulder toward the market. "Though with this festival crowd, they may already be booked up." He turned back to the house and repeated his hail. "Hello!"

After a few more moments, a slender, middle-aged man appeared from the shopfront, wearing an apron over the ubiquitous chiton, which was dyed with a subtle decorative pattern at the edges.

"Ah, Thrasius! Sorry to have kept you waiting. We weren't expecting visitors today." He spoke with perfect politeness laid over an almost undetectable air of disapproval. "I'll let your brother know you've come. Please come in and rest a moment in the court-yard with your companion." He nodded to Anna, then turned and walked away smoothly toward the back of the courtyard, disap-pearing through a wooden door into the rear part of the house.

Thrasius followed the man into the courtyard, with Anna and Indy close behind. Stairs on one side led up to a wooden balcony running around the inside of the U-shaped second floor, and the red tile roof overhung the balcony by a foot or so all the way around, giv-ing the enclosed courtyard plenty of shade from the midday sun. The inner door to the front shop was open, and through it, Anna could see more shelving, stacked with a variety of small boxes and bundles in disarray. Gauzy hangings stirred in the windows that opened onto the courtyard, but there was no one else in sight.

"Still the same old place." Thrasius looked around. "Built by my father many years ago, business and home in one." He squinted at the peeling paint covering the wooden posts supporting the bal-cony. "My brother has fallen a bit behind on maintenance, perhaps, but it's still sound."

The rear door opened again, and the slender aproned man emerged, this time bearing a small tray. He was followed by an older man who showed a clear resemblance to Thrasius in the eyes and set of the jaw, though he was somewhat taller and more prosperously fed, and his hair showed more gray as he approached.

"Thrasius. Brother! By Zeus, it's good to see you again!" The older man reached out and embraced Thrasius, slapping his back heartily. But as he stepped away again, his face grew grave. "Hopefully you've come to make things right between us, and not for... some other purpose?"

"I have forsworn my old ways, and I come to make amends," Thrasius said formally. "May Hermes, or any god you choose, call down punishment upon me if I speak false." Thrasius held out one hand to his brother, who clasped it, his earlier smile returning.

"This is Anna, my friend and travelling companion, and her trusty hound Indy." Thrasius indicated the pair with a sweep of his arm. "Anna, this is my elder brother Oresus, the head of our family."

"Pleased to meet you, sir." Anna stepped forward and shook hands with Oresus in the accepted fashion, trying not to look too obviously relieved at their positive reception. Indy came up beside Anna and offered her own paw mutely.

Oresus shook it with a delighted laugh. "A dog of great refinement, I see!" Anna flashed him the dog-token they'd gotten at the agora, and Oresus laughed again. Indy opened her mouth in a doggy smile, but remained silent.

"Anna, this is my steward Kepthos." Oresus indicated the aproned man, who nodded to her as he stepped forward with the tray, which contained a cup of water, a few squares of bread, and a bowl. Anna was familiar with the guest ritual by now, so she carefully rinsed her hands over the bowl, then sampled the bread.

"Be welcome in my house, Anna," Oresus said gravely. Anna nodded in response.

"By your leave sir, I should get back to the inventory." Kepthos stepped back. "Phaia will be here by sundown to take our order." At a wave from Oresus he turned and walked back to the shop, taking the guest tray with him.

"Phaia is one of our suppliers," Oresus explained, gesturing toward the shop. "And weekly orders are a curse, but it's always better in this business to have fresh stock." He waved for them to follow as he turned to walk up the stairs to the balcony. "I need to help with the inventory, but I'll show you upstairs first."

"Will there be enough space?" Thrasius asked. "There was only the one extra room."

"What's that? Oh yes, I forgot that we changed things since you were here last." Oresus walked carefully up the wooden steps, holding the rail as he did. "After the last of the children moved out, we split the room on the left into two smaller ones, so we can put you in one, and Anna and her dog in the other." A well-worn sorrow ghosted across his face. "And after Sophia passed, I found I didn't need as much room as I did before, so I divided the downstairs bedroom as well. It gives me more flexibility when I have guests."

He walked over to two doors set side by side, and opened them both with a flourish. "And here we are!" The rooms were modestly furnished and almost identical, with a low, narrow wooden bed placed against the wall in each one. Small windows set high in the outer walls let a breeze blow through the rooms and out into the courtyard through wider, inner windows hung with sheer coverings.

"The privy's still downstairs where you remember," Oresus said to Thrasius. "I'll leave you to unpack and rest from your journey while I finish up downstairs. Dinner will be at sundown in the dining room, but I expect you'll smell it cooking before we call you. And you've arrived on an auspicious day, so it will be a feast!" He clasped Thrasius by the arm. "I'm glad you've come home, brother. Even unexpected, it's good to have family back in the house again." Then he walked back down the stairs and disappeared into the back room with a wave.

"A quick word." Thrasius stopped just inside his door and gestured Anna to move closer after his brother passed out of sight. "Things seem to be going well. Better than I had hoped, really." He looked embarrassed. "One small thing to be aware of. My brother likes to talk, once he's had a cup of wine or so. And based on our conversations on the way here, you may feel that some of his views… well. Just remember that he's a good man, who provides a good living for his household." He looked aside. "In any case, I'll see you two at dinner." He excused himself and closed his door.

"Good to have a… heads-up, I guess?" Anna looked at Indy, who snorted and walked through the other door. "A little family drama is still probably better than having to go find a hotel."

It didn't take them long to settle in to their own room. They had Anna's pack and Indy's saddlebags, but those could be laid aside in a few moments. Anna did unfold a clean chiton from her pack to replace the one she was wearing, which was crusted with three days of travel dirt, and she refreshed herself with water from an ewer in the room and a clean linen washcloth.

With the door closed and no one there to see, Indy unclipped her own harness and wiped it clean of dust, her big paws much more dexterous and flexible than those of a dog. Then she sat patiently while Anna checked her for burrs and gave her fur a quick brushing, a comfortable ritual between them by now.

So, this is a real guest bedroom in a real house in ancient Athens! The door was closed, but Anna still spoke over their link, since there was no telling who might overhear them through the open windows and thin curtains. *If you squint a little, this could be the inside of a cabin out in the country, anywhere in Texas. Like going to visit grandma and grandpa for the summer.* She sighed and reclined on the bed, letting her feet dangle over the end. *It's weird how something so foreign can seem so familiar.*

Indy looked up, indicating the undersides of the red tiles of the roof, held in place by wooden cross-braces. *You probably wouldn't see that in Texas. But point taken. It's much more modern-looking than the cottage back in Lebadeia. A wooden floor instead of packed dirt, curtains in the windows. It's bound to cause some cognitive dissonance when we remember where we really are.*

Indy whuffed out a slow breath, then turned around three times and lay down on the floor, groaning as she did so. *I don't know about you, but I could use a nap before dinner. Not that I'm tired or anything,* she said at Anna's smirk. *But we canines like to stay well rested. We sleep more hours per day than humans, you know.*

Anna slipped off her sandals, then lay back on the bed again and closed her eyes. *I think I'll join you.*

36

As Oresus had promised, the savory smell of cooking began to drift through the house as the sun sank lower outside their window. After pulling her sandals back on and re-blousing her chiton over her belt, Anna was ready to explore.

Thrasius' door stood ajar and his room was empty, so apparently he was already out and about. Across the open courtyard, the other side of the second floor looked to be more living quarters, and Anna didn't want to barge into those uninvited, so she and Indy headed for the kitchen. The smell led them downstairs and toward the back of the house, away from the shop out front.

As they came down the stairs, they saw Kepthos the steward in the courtyard passing a small wooden tablet coated with what looked like wax to a short-haired young woman. She took it with a nod, then noticed Anna and Indy coming down the stairs as she turned to leave.

Anna stepped forward and offered her hand. "Hi, you must be Phaia." Phaia hesitated, but at a nod from Kepthos, offered her own hand in return. "I'm Anna, a friend of Thrasius. This is my friend Indy," she said with a nod to her companion. This time, Indy merely nodded gravely instead of offering a paw.

"I'm very pleased to meet you, mistress." Phaia's voice sounded strong, but not accustomed to social use. "Please excuse me, but I have to run. I need to collect three more orders before the sun sets."

"Of course!" Anna said. "It was a pleasure meeting you."

Phaia looked at her strangely, but not unkindly. "Likewise." With a final nod to Kepthos, she turned and strode away, mind already on the next task.

You greeted a slave as an equal, Indy said. *I think that's why the odd looks.*

A slave! Anna felt her face go pale. *How could you tell?*

Let's talk about it later, Indy said. *But be careful. Dinner sounds like it could be a minefield.*

"Mistress Anna." Kepthos turned to Anna and nodded, looking more relaxed now that the inventory and ordering were finished. "You're just in time for dinner!"

Indy smacked her jaws together eagerly, and Kepthos laughed at the sight of the drool beginning to dangle from the corners of her mouth. "Come with me. And don't worry, there'll be enough for everyone." He glanced pointedly at Indy.

Kepthos led the way across the courtyard and through the door on the left, which opened into a small dining room. Oresus and Thrasius were already reclining on low couches and laughing together, two shallow cups of watered wine set aside for the moment.

"Ah! Our guests have arrived!" Oresus nodded to Kepthos, who disappeared through another door into what looked like the kitchen. "Please, please! Make yourselves at home." Oresus indicated two more couches. Anna perched on the edge of one, and after a moment Indy sat in front of the other with an expectant expression. Oresus laughed again.

Anna could hear the sounds of preparation from the kitchen. Soon, two young women emerged bearing trays, each one heaped with roasted lamb, grilled fish, vegetables, flat cakes filled with sesame and cheese, and wheat bread instead of the coarser barley bread Anna had grown used to. They laid the trays on two tables, then served out portions onto plates which they first handed to

Anna, then to Thrasius, and finally to Oresus. And then, after a whispered consultation with Thrasius, another plate was laid on the floor in front of Indy, to her much-satisfied expression.

Oresus rose and dipped out another cup of wine from a krater nearby, handing it to Anna. Then he poured a smaller bowl for Indy and set it before her. Thrasius must have already briefed him on the unusual customs of Anna's homeland.

Hopefully they'll never host any actual Iberians here, Anna said over their link. *Or both sides will be very confused!* Indy laughed mentally, but kept her features composed and her eyes on the food, which was steaming mere inches in front of her muzzle.

"Friends!" Oresus raised his cup high. "Tonight, we have much to celebrate. As always, we mark the beginning of the City Dionysia with our own feast. But also, we celebrate the return of my brother, and the meeting of our new guest. Guests!" he amended, with a nod to Indy. "To your health!" He took a lusty swig from his wine.

"To your health!" echoed Thrasius and Anna, sipping their own wine in answer. Indy lapped a bit of hers from the bowl, and Oresus laughed again. "Delightful! Why can't the hounds of Athens be so well trained?" He settled back into his couch with a satisfied air, propping himself on one elbow. "Let the feast begin!"

After having set out the food, the two young servers retreated to the other side of the dining room, where they were joined by Kepthos, an older woman who Anna assumed must be the cook, and two other men who looked like members of the household staff. They loaded their own plates and began to eat, seating themselves on simple stools.

Seeing the three women together, Anna finally made the connection that she'd been missing. *Short hair!* she said. *Slave women all have short hair!*

I think you're right, came Indy's reply. *For the men, it must be something less obvious, though.* She nibbled a tiny bite of her fish, smacking in approval.

Thrasius addressed Anna just as she took a bite of one of the flat cakes. "Before you arrived, I was telling my brother about our journey here, and a little of our circumstances before that."

Anna must have looked uncomfortable at this, because Oresus immediately broke in. "Don't worry, young lady. My brother has told me only the most complimentary things about you and your stalwart companion here." He raised his cup to Indy, who lazily took another bit of food from her plate in response.

Oresus laughed again. "And I understand I have you to thank for my young brother's reformation."

"I think he was already a good man." Anna shifted awkwardly on her couch. "Maybe we helped him remember it again, that's all." She took a sip of her wine. "And he might not have told you that he saved me and my friends from a very dangerous man afterward."

"He told me indeed." Oresus' face flushed red. "And I was very glad to hear he'd finally parted ways with those Thebans! The way they act, it seems like they're hoping for the Persians to sweep in and conquer us all!" He shuddered theatrically. "If we hadn't dug up enough silver out at Laureion to pay for more warships, we'd be trying to fend off the emperor with nothing more than fishing boats."

Anna shivered, remembering their frightening encounter with Nicon. A quick check with Alixa didn't come up with much of an answer for what Thebans had to do with Persians, but the way Oresus said it didn't sound good. "We went around Thebes on the way here, and didn't run into any trouble."

"Well done, young lady!" Oresus said. "There's nothing there worth seeing anyway."

Thrasius snorted at this, and Oresus amended his statement. "Well, perhaps seven-gated Thebes does have a few things to recommend it," he admitted. "But it can hardly compare to Athens. Tell me, what did you think when you entered the city?"

"It wasn't like anything I'd ever seen before," Anna said truthfully.

"Exactly!" Oresus said. "You won't find a city in Greece with our refinements. We're on the very cutting edge of human freedoms here!" He took another sip of wine. "I know you avoided Thebes, but if you should ever pass through it, or Athena forbid, if you should ever see Sparta, compare how the slaves are treated here and there."

He gestured to the other side of the dining room, where Kepthos and the rest paused in their chewing and looked up from their stools anxiously. "Here in Athens, slave and master break bread together, united by their common humanity! In Sparta, they're lucky not to get cut down in the street if they look at an aristocrat the wrong way."

Oresus sipped his wine. "In Athens, the enlightened master always acts in his slaves' best interests, even when they don't have the perspective to see it for themselves." He leaned forward on his couch. "My brother may have told you already, but one reason we've always had our own private Dionysian feast in our family is so the slaves can celebrate with us, since they don't receive a share of the city sacrifices."

This kind of talk must be what Oresus was hinting at earlier, Indy said.

Um, Indy— Anna's mental voice sounded nervous.

Don't worry, I'll keep my mouth shut. She growled silently. *For now. He is our host, after all.* Her voice turned hopeful. *Plus, I think another course is about to come out.*

Oresus continued speaking as Kepthos and the other slaves studiously applied themselves to their food. "Why, our best drug compounder Phaia is a slave herself. She rents her own room in the city, and is likely to buy her freedom any year now." He motioned to Anna. "You must have seen her in the courtyard earlier. She's a prime example of how here in Athens, the only thing limiting your success is your desire to work hard and better yourself." He drained the last of his cup. "If it wasn't for slavery, she'd still be living in a grass hut with her people on the banks of the Istros somewhere, instead of here partaking of Greek science and culture. We're doing her a favor!"

"Really?" Anna spoke without thinking, one eyebrow raised as she pulled a skeptical face.

"Of course!" Oresus seemed taken aback. "I'll send for her, and she can tell you herself. Or any of my household will tell you the same."

I thought we were keeping our mouths shut. Indy's mental voice sounded amused. *Though it needed to be said.*

"Stolos!" Oresus pointed at one of his slaves, who froze uncertainly, food halfway to his mouth. "Tell our guest what you think of your situation."

Thrasius raised his hands quickly in a placating gesture. "Brother, please. Let's not overwhelm our guest on her first night. She hasn't seen much of Greece yet, so many of our customs are foreign to her."

Oresus seemed keen to continue, but his empty cup caught his attention as he raised it to make his next point, and he conceded. "Fair enough, fair enough!" He motioned with one hand, and one of the young women rose from her stool and brought the wine tray around again, this time grating a little of what looked like cheese into Oresus' cup. He sipped from his new cup of wine approvingly. "I don't mean to rant. If you can stay with us a while, you'll see for yourselves in any case. Athens can speak for itself."

"I'm looking forward to seeing more of your city," Anna said, grateful for a change of subject. "Maybe tomorrow we'll wander around and see the sights."

"I highly recommend it!" Oresus said.

"I'll show you around." Thrasius swallowed the last of one of the sesame cakes. "I promised my brother I'd run a few errands for him, so I can just take you along."

And we can get some more frog legs! Indy said. She licked her lips, still looking hungry despite having devoured a sizeable portion of bread and roast lamb.

You can tell him yourself, once the rest of the household can't hear you, Anna said.

Just then the cook re-emerged from the kitchen, bearing a tray filled with narrow white slices of something. "Ah!" Oresus beamed. "Our cook's specialty, served in honor of our new guests."

"Ooo, what is it?" Anna leaned over to look, and Indy sat up with keen interest.

"Cheesecake, young mistress." The cook spoke with obvious pride. "My mother's own recipe. Won't find better in Athens!"

Cheesecake? Anna tried not to look surprised. *Is this dessert from the future?*

Surprisingly, we have a reference for this. Indy's ears still flicked as she consulted her collar, though she kept the lights off around the Greeks for secrecy's sake. *It says that ancient Greek cheesecake was served at the Olympics, and at weddings. I never realized I was eating a three-thousand-year-old dessert!*

Oresus served out the pieces himself, with even the slaves getting an equal share and a cup of wine to go with it, and conversation ceased for a few minutes while everyone enjoyed it. It was sweetened with honey instead of sugar, but it was the first dessert Anna had had since the future, and it was delicious.

Afterward, the conversation turned to matters of local politics and old shared acquaintances of the two brothers, which Anna and Indy lacked the context to follow along with. And after a big plate of food, a cup of wine, and dessert, Anna felt her eyelids drooping, and from Indy's glazed expression she looked mentally checked out as well. The staff had long since collected the dishes, cleaned up, and retreated to their own quarters, leaving the room to the two brothers, Anna, and Indy.

Just as Anna was finally about to stand up and excuse herself, Oresus noticed her expression and cut himself off in the middle of a long tirade to Thrasius, something about how some guy named Solon had gone too far when he reformed Athens' debt slavery laws.

"Dear guest! Please excuse my rudeness as a host." He looked at his empty cup, bemused, then set it aside and reached for water instead. "I can see that you are weary, so feel free to retire at your leisure. I'm afraid that my eagerness to catch up with my brother has overcome my manners."

"Sorry, I guess our journey was more tiring than I thought." Anna rose. "I'll go get some sleep and see you both in the morning." She walked to the door, closely trailed by Indy, who'd roused from her stupor when Oresus had spoken. Anna could hear the conversation resume as they left the dining room, growing more heated, but in a genial way.

My brother and I could argue politics right through a holiday dinner too, Indy said. *He could be pretty annoying sometimes, but that's the sort of conversation with family that you don't miss until it's gone.*

Too true, Anna said with a sigh. *Well, I was an only child, but I know what you mean.* She left it there, not wanting to rekindle her feelings of loss now, in a strange house in a strange city. *Let's get some sleep. Ten more minutes and I would've fallen off the couch.*

37

ronically, after using the facilities in the small, surprisingly non-smelly room downstairs and cleaning herself up, Anna lay in bed sleepless. She tossed for a while, then gave it up.

"Hey Indy. You still awake?" The staff seemed to be asleep, and Thrasius and his brother were probably still down in the dining room catching up, but she still spoke softly to ensure that her voice wouldn't carry outside the bedroom.

"Yes." Anna heard her friend's jowls smack in the dark, close air of the room. The night breeze had died down, leaving their room slightly warm, but not uncomfortably so. "I'm finding it hard to sleep." Faint snatches of drunken song drifted in through the window from the city's continuing Dionysian revelry somewhere outside. "And that's not helping."

"Your hearing's better than mine," Anna said. "But I'm having a hard time sleeping too. We saw so much stuff today. It's a lot to take in." She rolled fully onto her back and looked up at the shadowed rafters, faintly illuminated by moonlight that fell through their high outer window. "Back home when I couldn't sleep, I'd watch a video on my phone. Something calm, like a nature documentary. But now, watching videos from home reminds me of stuff

I'd rather not think about when I'm trying to sleep." She shifted in the bed, trying to straighten her twisted blanket. "It still doesn't seem real that we're lying here in someone's guest bedroom in their house in *ancient Athens*."

"When you say it that way, it does seem pretty remarkable." Indy stretched where she lay, then exhaled as she curled up again. "What did you think of our host?"

"Well…" Anna cast around for words. "To the folks here, Oresus probably seems like a nice enough old guy. He could be anyone's embarrassing uncle who likes his wine a little too much."

"I kept thinking that too. But then I'd remember I was being waited on by his household slaves." Indy's voice took on a mock-chiding tone. "Which I had thought we were trying to hide our opinions about?"

"Yeah, sorry. I kind of put my foot in it." Anna looked pained. "But it was so ridiculous when he said that slavery was actually doing people a favor! My mouth just popped open without me even thinking about it."

"At least Thrasius diverted him before he made that poor man lie to us about how much he loved being enslaved." Indy snorted quietly. "And did you notice how tight-lipped all of them were while Oresus was ranting on about how debt slavery shouldn't have been abolished, because it meant that now people could weasel out of the consequences of their own irresponsibility?"

"I must have dozed off during that part." Anna looked chagrined. "So it was pretty hypocritical of him to talk about how liberated Athens is, then."

"Oh, I don't doubt that Athens is quite liberated, compared to the rest of Greece," Indy said. "But we're twenty-eight hundred years in the past, here. There's still twenty-three hundred years or so of slavery left to go."

"Ugh. What a depressing thought," Anna said. "And the whole world is like this?"

"I'm a physicist, not a historian," Indy said. "And we don't have a lot of high-quality information about this time period, even after piecing together every scrap we could find in the data your father sent us. But from what I've read since we got here, Athens seems like one of the brighter spots."

The two of them fell silent for a few moments, each lost in thought. Then Anna took a breath and spoke again. "We've done some good here, right? Back in Lebadeia?" She stared up at the dim ceiling. "We healed whatever was wrong with Helene, and made it so Iole could marry Neleos and have him move in to help them. We built them a nice bathtub, even."

"Yes." Indy's voice was guarded. "Though I'd hesitate before trying more of the same here in Athens. Remember, we also almost got them all killed when Nicon came back for his revenge."

"Yeah, that one was on us." Anna took a deep breath and let it out. "But we learned our lesson. And after everything we've seen on this trip, I can't help but wonder if we could make more of a difference, somehow."

"What kind of a difference?" Indy asked. "With just the two of us and what we can fab right now, we don't have a lot of excess capacity yet. But say we decide to try making healing pills, like the ones we gave Leitus and Helene. We do the calculations, and figure out that we can make ten of them per month. Sounds good, right? We can help ten people who otherwise would've had nothing." She leaned closer to the bed, intent. "But think about it. A limited supply of something life-and-death valuable like that? It would cause riots once word got out." She lowered her voice, which had risen as she spoke. "And even if we could keep something like that a secret somehow, how would we decide who gets them and who doesn't? Do we interview people to find who's the most worthy? Hand them out at random?"

"I hear you. And you're right." Frustration crackled in Anna's voice. "But I mean, look at this whole slavery situation. Can we really live our whole lives here and just look right past *that* every day?" Anna rolled onto her side to face her friend. "I heard how you growled at those overseers beating that poor guy in the field yesterday. If Thrasius hadn't been there, you would've taken on all three of them."

"Maybe. Probably." Indy shifted uncomfortably on her blanket. "Many of my kind have very… personal feelings about slavery. We were never slaves ourselves, exactly. But many bad things happened to us that we had no choice in. Slavery strikes a nerve with us." She looked at Anna pointedly. "Thrasius was right when he told me to back off. I could've gotten us all imprisoned, or worse."

"I hate it, but yeah. Fighting head-on like that, we'd lose for sure." Anna sat up. "Whatever we do, it'd need to be a lot more subtle. But this place is so much *bigger* than I thought!" She paused, embarrassed. "I mean, of course it's *big*. It's a whole planet, right? But travelling here to Athens, it really hit me hard." A breeze shifted the curtains, letting dappled moonlight spill across her face. "We're not in some ancient-Greece amusement park. These people aren't actors wearing costumes, and we can't just walk back to our hotel restaurant for a nice lunch." She exhaled in frustration. "This is a real city, in a real, full-sized country. And it's not even the biggest country on the continent. How would we even make a dent?" Anna paused for a long moment. "Sometimes I really wish my parents were here." She swallowed against a tightness in her throat. "My mom, especially. She was really good at finding ways to work within the system to make things better. She mostly helped animals instead of people, but still."

"Your mother sounds like someone I would've liked to meet." Indy sat up and put a paw on Anna's shoulder. "And I know just how you feel," she said quietly. "Though my dam was more about finding a back door when the front door was locked." Her eyes gleamed in the moonlight. "She always told me that if the system didn't work for me, that I should either work around it or build a new one." She went still, thinking. "Hmm."

"Sounds like good advice," Anna said. "How would we apply it, though?"

"Actually, I had a thought about that." Indy looked for a moment like she was reluctant to say more. "It's a huge risk, mind you, and I'm not saying we should do this. But making a difference isn't just about things that we physically create." She stood up, pacing their small bedroom. "We brought a great deal of knowledge with us from the future. Knowledge that could be very valuable, if we put some of it in the right hands." She looked back at Anna. "You heard Oresus this evening. Slaves can buy their freedom. Maybe we could give them the currency to do it."

38

The next morning dawned clear and bright, but Indy and Anna slept in, exhausted from their long journey and late conversation. By the time they left their room, breakfast was already done, but thankfully there were still some leftover loaves in the kitchen when they made their way downstairs.

Anna sat in the courtyard, alternately munching on the coarse brown bread and ripping off pieces to hand to Indy. It was still before ten in the morning, but the air was already heating up. She could tell it was going to be another hot day, even if it wasn't Texas hot.

The rear door onto the courtyard rattled open, and Oresus and Thrasius strode out, deep in conversation. "Ah, there you are!" Oresus said. "None the worse for your trip, I see! Hopefully you're feeling rested?"

"We're feeling much better, thank you." Anna blushed, feeling bad that she and Indy had slept so late while the rest of the household was obviously up and working. "And we're looking forward to seeing more of Athens!"

"Ha! About that!" Oresus aimed a considering look at Thrasius. "If you wouldn't mind, there's a little errand I could use some help with. Kepthos had to run off to deal with a minor emergency for me this morning, but we still need to pick up our delivery from our compounder before noon today if we're going to get it stocked and ready for the afternoon market." He tapped the side of his head with a satisfied expression. "I expect to do a brisk business in headache and digestive remedies today, after last night's festivities."

"Of course," Anna said. "It's the least we can do. But we just got here yesterday! Does Thrasius know the way there?"

"I've got another task that could use my brother's help this morning. Nevertheless! For a young lady of your obvious intelligence, I think this should be sufficient." Oresus pulled out a small wax tablet and quickly scratched a few lines on it with a stylus, then held it out to her.

Anna could see it was a crude map of Athens. The Acropolis was clearly marked as a blob in the center, and Oresus' house was an X along a long street. There was another X marked, which didn't look like it was too far distant.

"You go from here back through the market to the other X, which is the workshop of our compounder Phaia." Oresus indicated the route with one finger. "I believe you met her yesterday? She'll recognize you, so just pick up our order and load it into the saddlebags of our friend here." He slapped a startled Indy on the withers. "See some sights on the way, walk back here. Everyone's happy! What do you say?"

"Give us another minute to finish breakfast, and we'll get going," Anna said.

"Excellent! I knew I could count on you." Oresus turned to Thrasius, who looked bewildered by the speed of the transaction. "By the time they get back, the two of us will have reorganized the front shelves, and we'll be ready to take delivery."

"Take delivery, right." Thrasius smiled with bemusement. "You know, part of the reason I left Athens was that the business life was a little too busy for me."

"Nonsense!" Oresus said. "And don't worry, this revisiting of your salad days will be purely temporary. Normally we're well on top of things here, but with Kepthos gone we're a little short today."

He turned back to Anna. "You're still here?"

"On our way." Anna bolted the last of her bread and threw a final piece to Indy. "Just let me get Indy into her harness."

I notice no one asked Indy what she thinks of this, her friend said over their link. *What if Indy wants an after-breakfast nap?*

Shush up, you, Anna said. *It'll only take us an hour or so, and then I'll feel better about eating Thrasius' brother's free food. Even if his politics are horrible.*

It does seem like the honorable thing to do, Indy groused as they headed back up the stairs to their room.

Five minutes later, with Indy's saddlebag harness secured and Anna's small day bag slung over her shoulder, they headed out the open courtyard doors and onto the busy morning streets of Athens.

As they exited, Anna saw a nondescript man further down the street flick his glance away from them, then walk unhurriedly away. *Hey, Indy?*

Yes? Indy stopped walking and looked back over her shoulder.

Huh. Anna looked at the man's retreating back, but there wasn't anything particularly strange or threatening about him. *Never mind. Probably just someone checking out how big you are.*

Well, I am very impressive. Indy's mental voice sounded pleased. *I'm sure they've never seen anything like me.* She tossed her ruff and set off again, Anna following a moment later.

Superficially, the morning scene in Athens looked the same as any ancient city center that had survived to Anna and Indy's own time. The cobbled streets and narrow alleyways could have belonged to any number of places, and Anna could easily imagine the gaily colored linen chitons of the Athenians replaced by more modern clothing. Still, the reeking garbage in the corners and the skinny stray dogs that slunk away at Indy's approach marked it as being truly of the ancient world.

The map guided them back toward the market they'd passed through yesterday. If anything, the streets were even more crowded today, with steady streams of people, animals, and carts going in both directions in the wider stretches. Anna was more or less used to seeing older people by this point, but Athens added a whole new dimension of the sick and lame as well. She was also beginning to distinguish the large underclass of slaves by their dress and hairstyle as they went about their business.

And it was *loud!* Wooden wheels clattered on stone, and voices shouted and cursed back and forth between the buskers, shopkeepers, and customers that lined the street. Anna's translator couldn't make sense of the cacophony, repeating *"a brabble of voices"* every so often in her head until she silenced it.

Anna groaned when she finally saw the entrance to the market up ahead. *This is ridiculous,* she said. *Look at that crowd!* She tried to squeeze out of the main stream of traffic and huddle against a wall, but even there she was still jostled by the stream of people going past. She held up the map tablet again. *This path shows us going straight through the market, but I think Oresus forgot about the traffic from that city festival thing. Let's try to cut around.*

No argument here. Indy sneezed and looked at the crowd pushing past them. *I don't think I've ever smelled so many bad things simultaneously in my life.*

The two of them walked back away from the market to the first side street that seemed to go in the direction they wanted. Once they were off the main way, the crowds thinned considerably, though there were still some plain shop fronts here and there. But shortly the street ended in a small square with several alleyways branching off it. Anna stopped, considering.

My collar's mapping the streets as we walk them, Indy said. *So we can always go back the way we came. And it's got a rough idea where we're going. But we don't know what the streets look like between here and there. There's nothing to do but try one and see where it leads.*

I so wish we could just call a car. I never appreciated how nice antigrav was until now. Anna looked around the little square. Traffic was light, but there were still people coming and going. *I can't pull my phone out here. Which of these alleys does your collar say points the most toward where we want to go?*

This one. Follow me. Indy walked forward and left, entering a narrow way between two buildings of rough limestone. There were doors here and there, the open ones giving views into packed rooms or grimy courtyards where people watched them pass with a little too much interest. Anna glanced nervously behind her after they passed one, and saw a slender man lean around a corner to take a look at them. He ducked out of sight, then reappeared a moment later with another man who looked somehow familiar. Both of them began to slowly walk in their direction.

Maybe they're just going this way? Anna quickly checked ahead of her. Indy was still leading, but she couldn't see the end of the alleyway. It made little jogs left and right to make its way around buildings, so there was no sightline longer than a dozen yards in any direction but up. When Anna looked behind her again, the two men were still following, and had gotten closer. The first man put two fingers in his mouth and gave a loud whistle.

We've got company back here, Anna said. *Probably not the good kind.*

I think we're almost through, Indy said. *I can smell fresher air up ahead.* She glanced back briefly at the two men, then increased her pace. *Maybe twenty more yards.*

A third man stepped out of a crossway ahead of them. He was dark-haired and slightly built like the first two, but looked tough and wiry. His expression, initially a confident sneer, faded as he saw Indy's size. He nodded quickly to the men behind them, then reached into a fold in his tunic.

Indy rocketed forward with a scratch of claws on stone, accelerating far faster than Anna could have, and slammed both forepaws into the center of the man's chest. He flew backward, clipping his head on the alley wall and dropping a wickedly curved small knife.

Go! Indy shouted over their link. She was past the man instantly, with Anna right behind her. They scrambled around a corner, only to confront a solid wooden door at the end of the alleyway. A large iron-barred window exhaled a fresh breeze, and through it, Anna could see the clutter of some sort of workshop, with a glimpse of the sunlit traffic of a busy street on the far side. She grabbed the door handle and pushed, but it didn't move even a fraction of an inch. The door felt distressingly solid and well-made.

"Hello? Hello!" Anna called through the window, but there was no answer. At Indy's low growl, she turned in time to see three men come around the corner of the alleyway behind them. One of them was the man Indy had just bowled over. He'd recovered his knife, and advanced with a menacing glare. The second man was the whistler, who drew a heavy weighted stick as she watched. And the third man…

Anna gasped. *That guy was watching us come out of the house this morning! He must've followed us here!*

Well, he's going to wish he hadn't, Indy said, hackles raised.

But her threat rang hollow. Three armed men had them trapped at a dead end, and someone was going to get hurt, or worse.

39

The whistler spoke first. "It's them, all right." He threw a derisive look at the knifeman, who was rubbing the side of his head where Indy had bounced him off the rough stone wall of the alley. "Idiot. Didn't I tell you to watch out for the dog?" Then he spoke to Anna. "You're coming with us. Someone has some questions for you." He glanced aside at Indy, her teeth bared in a snarl. "And you'd better muzzle that thing, or I'll bash its head in. Boss wants it brought in too, but he's not paying me enough to get a hand bit off."

Anna felt like she couldn't catch her breath as she fought down a rising panic. It struck her that the men's voices were familiar, somehow, though she couldn't place why. Her mind blanked, mouth gaping as her back pressed against the door behind her.

Then she felt as well as heard the door's bolts clunk open. She stumbled as the door swung inward, and she felt the outgoing breeze strengthen as it opened fully.

"Young lady." The voice was deep, but mild. "Come through the shop. I will deal with these."

Not wanting to take her eyes off the three men in front of her, she darted a glance backward. A huge man of early middle years nearly filled the door, wearing a scorched leather apron over a brown tunic. A square-headed hammer rested easily on one shoulder, long haft gripped in a massive fist. Anna hesitated, taken aback by the sight of him.

The smith stepped through the door, squeezing between her and Indy to confront the three men. "A hammer this size is a very dangerous weapon in the right hands." He swung it down from his shoulder and dropped the head onto the ground with a thump that Anna felt in the soles of her feet. One of the men began backing away unconsciously. "It would be wise of you all to—"

Anna didn't wait to hear the rest. With a confirming glance at Indy, the two of them broke and ran through the door, dodging another, younger smith who was carrying a heavy iron bar on his way to aid his comrade. His mouth opened in surprise as they split and ran around him.

They ran a short distance past tool racks and a glowing forge, out the front of the shop, and onto a major street, plowing into a knot of beggars holding out their hands and calling to the festival passers-by. Indy slowed slightly, then forced her head between two surprised beggars and shoved them roughly aside as they emerged.

"Sorry!" Anna said to one of the beggars, who'd lost his crutch and was hunting about for it. The man glared as he found it and took up his spot again. Anna bobbed aside to try to see what was happening at the back of the shop they'd just fled, but she couldn't get a clear view without going back in herself.

Let's keep moving, Indy said. *I think two burly smiths are more than a match for whoever those three were, but there's no sense waiting here to find out.*

Down that way! Anna looked left along the street, heart pounding. *Isn't that the other side of the market?*

My collar map thinks so. Indy made her way urgently, pushing through traffic but glancing behind frequently to make sure Anna was still there and that they were free of pursuit.

They reached the market entrance in a few moments, the throngs of people around them reassuring now instead of annoying, since any further attack would have dozens of witnesses. Anna lifted the map tablet to check their location, but had to lower it again and breathe slowly for a few minutes before she could calm herself enough to make sense of it. Finally, she traced their route with a trembling finger.

Okay, we go straight away from the market, then take the third right. She exhaled deeply and looked around. *And I promise, no more shortcuts.* She put a hand on Indy's shoulder. *You saved us again back there. We almost got caught between the three of them!*

That's what friends do. Indy laid her head against Anna's arm for a moment, then started walking. *If that smith hadn't let us through, things might have gotten dicey.* She glanced around, ears flicking alertly. *But our shields would have turned those sorts of small knives and cudgels.*

Maybe once or twice. Anna shivered. *But I wouldn't want to try to fight my way out of a narrow alley, surrounded. Even with us being armed, it's too risky.*

Armed? Indy looked back at the inconspicuous holster on her harness that held the little stun-baton, then shook her head. *Oops. I forgot we had those. I was just going off pure instinct.* She panted a laugh. *At least I remembered not to talk out loud this time!*

What do you think that one guy meant? Anna slowed. *When he said his boss had questions for us?*

I don't know. A furrow grew between Indy's brows. *And you said it was the other one who watched us come out of Oresus' place this morning. So they were tracking us down as a team, probably from our description, and waiting until they could get ahead of us and cut us off.*

Anna shook her head, bemused. *Why would anyone bother tracking down a poor-looking young woman and a big herding dog?*

There's only one possibility that makes sense. Indy's voice was grim. *It's starting to look like Nicon actually might have had the powerful friends he claimed, after all.*

But... Anna thought back to what Thrasius had said before they set out on their journey. *I thought the Theban mob or whoever couldn't just run around free in Athens.*

It did seem like they were keeping to the back alleys. Indy walked steadily, keeping her gaze moving over the crowds. *But maybe Thrasius was underestimating them.*

Crap. Anna looked around warily. *We need to tell him about this when we get back.*

And keep a sharp eye out, Indy said. *Even if they're really trying to avoid making a public scene, that doesn't mean they might not try for a quick snatch if they know where we're likely to be.*

This dire possibility hung over them as they kept moving, trying to put more turns and more distance between themselves and the scene of their ambush. Anna consulted their map carefully at each intersection, but she needn't have bothered. It turned out that if you kept to the main streets and didn't try to take any shortcuts, it was hard to get lost. It only took the two of them another half an hour to find their way to the front door of a narrow building tucked down a side street. There was a small row of narrow hand-painted Greek signs beside the open door, one of which said "Phaia's drugs" when Anna sounded out the letters.

Indy's stomach grumbled audibly, and she looked back over her shoulder at the street they'd turned off of. *We're going through the market on the way back, right? Now that we're sticking to the map?* Her lips curved in a doggy smile, taking the reproach out of her words. *Because I could really use a couple more of those frog legs.*

Definitely. Anna smiled back, finally starting to shed the jitters from their earlier close call. *Though it still seems unsportsmanlike to me, eating such a small animal.*

Indy snorted as though such an idea was completely ridiculous. *Smaller just means more tender.*

The open door of the building gave onto a narrow hallway with a couple of rooms on either side. The first one on the left looked like a sewing workshop, but the seamstress went straight back to work after an incurious glance up at Anna. The right-hand door seemed more promising, smelling strongly of strange herbs.

Anna stuck her head in the door and called out. "Hello, Phaia? We're here for Oresus' delivery?"

She couldn't see anything inside at first glance except for stacks and stacks of boxes, bundles, jugs, and who knew what else, with a narrow path leading through the clutter. She stepped forward along the path, toward the back of the room. "Hello?"

"Back here, heard you the first time," came Phaia's strong contralto voice from the back of the room.

Anna moved forward tentatively, with Indy close behind. The path opened out into a small work area, which held a small table with a few stools around it, surrounded by huge but orderly stacks of jars and bags. A curtained-off nook in the back corner of the room looked like it held a small cot and a few personal belongings. Phaia was hunched over a mortar, carefully grinding some sort of dried herbs. She glanced up at them and nodded in recognition. "Just one more moment."

With a few final motions she finished the grinding, then carefully tipped the resulting powder out of the mortar into a small jar. Then she set the mortar aside and rinsed her hands in water from a nearby ewer, drying them on her long chiton before using them to tuck her short hair back behind her ears.

"Sorry about that, but this henbane is dangerous." She picked up a wax seal and placed it over the mouth of the jar, tying it tight with a string. "And stopping in the middle of a grind is a good way to forget what you're doing and get some in your eye when you forget to wash up." She set the covered jar aside.

"So, Oresus has you running errands already? Not surprising." Phaia turned to a pile of bags and pulled a large one from the top. Opening it, she showed that it was full of small jars, individually sealed and packed in straw. "You got a way to carry these?"

"Um, will these saddlebags work?" Anna asked. Phaia gave her a quizzical look, then seemingly noticed Indy for the first time, her saddlebags empty on either side of her harness.

"Oh! I forgot you had a dog." Phaia frowned in thought. "Was she this big yesterday?"

"Yeah, pretty much," Anna said wryly. Indy stood panting, keeping her fake vacuous expression firmly in place. "Can we put half of those jars in each side?"

"Of… course. Yes, that should work." Phaia pulled a smaller empty bag from a pile, then quickly transferred half the jars from the original bag to the new one, adding a bit more straw.

Anna took one bag and placed it in Indy's left saddlebag. Phaia started to do the same on the right, then stopped. "This workmanship is extraordinary!" She held the spring buckle to the saddlebag between her fingers. "Where did you get this?"

"Oh, it's just a normal bag. I brought it with me," Anna said. "From Iberia."

Phaia looked at Anna skeptically. "This buckle is so thin, but it bends right back into shape when you release it." She flexed it a few times. "And I can't see a single mark of a file or hammer on it." She moved her head to view the surface at a better angle. "Do you know how it was made?"

Uh oh, Indy said. *We didn't think to make every little detail of our gear look believably ancient!*

"Sorry, I don't know much about that kind of stuff." Anna tried to look unconcerned.

Phaia frowned at the buckle. "Hey, Themis!" she called out toward the door. "Come take a look at this!"

Anna's heart lurched. She waited tensely for a moment, but no one replied.

"Guess she's not there." Phaia shrugged, then carefully put the bag of jars into the saddlebag and secured it. Her fingers stroked the fine leather surface of the bag, lingering on the unnaturally even stitching and touching the other metal fixtures on Indy's harness. "Hm. I thought I was better-informed about metalworking." Her face relaxed into a less intent expression. "I guess that just means I have more to learn. I'll ask my friend later, she's the real expert."

Anna cast around quickly for a change of subject. Her eyes roamed over the bins of plant stems and leaves, then alighted on a box of green pods. "Hey, so what are these?"

"Poppy pods." Phaia picked one up and handed it to Anna for a look. The sides were scored with precise slashes. "I use these for the seeds. And you can grind up the pulp to infuse an anesthetic sponge. This is the real stuff, right here." She picked up a smaller box and held it out. It was full of small blobs of a dark brown resin. "Opium. It oozes out of those slashes on the pods. The right amount of this, and a patient will be telling you jokes while he's getting his bladder stone cut out."

That sounds absolutely terrifying, Indy said. *I keep forgetting that they have to vivisect you for surgery here. And I'm almost afraid to ask my collar what 'opium' is.*

"How did you learn about all this stuff?" Anna asked Phaia. "There must be dozens of different plants and things in here."

"It wasn't easy. Physicians are a close-mouthed bunch." Phaia smiled tightly. "But they're also lazy. They can't be bothered to collect, dry, grind, powder, mix, and whatever else. So I worked my way into the business, and gradually figured out what was what."

Phaia turned her head at the sound of another customer at the door. "I need to get back to work. Just sign your receipt, and you're ready to go." She held up a small fragment of pottery that already had the name "ΦΑΙΑ" written on it in some brownish ink, then handed it to Anna along with a reed pen dipped in ink.

At Anna's confused expression, Phaia said, "Write your name beside mine. Or you can draw some sort of picture if you can't write." Indy snorted a laugh over their link at that.

Anna carefully wrote her name, thankful that the Greeks of this time hadn't invented lowercase letters yet, so "ANNA" looked the same in Greek as it did in English. Or at least it looked similar enough so that Phaia didn't remark on it one way or the other. She deftly cracked the shard across both their names, and handed one half back to Anna.

"Just give this to Oresus when you get back. The invoice is in the bag." Anna heard a man clear his throat somewhere behind her, and Phaia spoke without looking up. "Come on in!" She gave them a significant look. They took the hint and headed for the door.

40

On the way out, Anna carefully squeezed past a thin young man who looked like he had five more errands to run that morning. Indy brushed past him with the magnificent unconcern of a beast that outweighed him by forty pounds. Then the two of them stood for a moment outside the shop, plotting their next move.

"Don't even say it." Anna sighted on the Acropolis, then pointed. "The market's off that way, and I'm sure they have plenty of frog legs left."

Indy lunged forward, her new burden not slowing her at all. Anna followed, laughing at her friend's eagerness. Together they wound their way through the streets, more at ease now that their errand was done and they knew the way back.

This quarter was definitely rougher than where Oresus' house was. The wine shops were already half-full before noon, some patrons rolling dice and cursing or cheering loudly, others reclining on couches with their cups, watching scantily clad women playing odd double flutes as they danced suggestively. The skirling of their flutes and the rattle of accompanists' hand drums added to the din.

This festival thing, what did Thrasius call it again? Anna asked.

The City Dionysia, I think, Indy said.

Seems like it's a big deal. Anna looked around. *This place is hopping!*

Well, Dionysus was the god of wine, Indy said.

One especially raucous wine-shop game seemed to involve throwing the dregs from one's cup at a small statue, trying to knock a tiny disk out of its hands to make it ring against a larger bronze disk below. Anna quickly learned to walk on the other side of the street after a near-miss from one drunken player.

They found their way back to the market, and after a few minutes' search, discovered another frog leg vendor. This one sold *two different flavors*, salted and garlic, and Indy insisted over their link that she wanted one of each. Anna also picked up a skewer of roasted artichoke for herself.

They made their way slowly back toward Oresus' house, keeping to the main thoroughfares this time. They were still wary of another meeting with their earlier pursuers, but gaining confidence that they didn't seem to want to try a direct confrontation on a crowded street. Anna was still nibbling at her first chunk of artichoke as Indy crunched up a whole pair of frog legs with relish, bones and all, then licked her scalloped black lips. Ahead of her, a pedestrian crossed the street at the sight.

So, are you thinking what I'm thinking? Indy asked.

Anna laughed. *I'm pretty sure I'm not thinking about how to find Frog Island or whatever and devour its whole population.*

Very droll, Indy said. *No, I was thinking about our talk last night. About how we could improve things for the enslaved people here.*

I liked your idea about using our knowledge somehow. Anna sobered, her good spirits dampened by the magnitude of the task. *I just don't know how we'd get started.*

Don't you? Indy smiled, her whiskers pouching with self-satisfaction. *The perfect idea was right in front of us a half-hour ago.*

I know you won't give me any peace until you tell me how I missed it. Anna gave her friend a tolerant look as she chewed another piece of artichoke. *So go ahead, let's hear it.*

Bear in mind, I'm still not sure this would be wise, Indy said. *But how about medicine? Think about it. Of all the bodies of knowledge we have access to, medicine is probably the least likely to be abused.*

True. Anna spoke slowly as she thought it through. *I guess you could poison people with medicine, but there'd be no point, since they already have actual poison here.* She stepped around a questionable-looking pile of trash in the gutter, its smell contrasting unpleasantly with her food. *But there's no way we could teach people to make pills like we made for Leitus and Helene, right? I thought modern medicine had nano and stuff in it.*

It'll need to be something far less advanced than that. Indy glanced over at Anna as they walked. *But medicine's easily monetized, like we saw at Phaia's earlier. So we teach a few enslaved people to make some kind of valuable drug, on the condition that after they buy themselves out, they pass the knowledge on to others to help them do the same. They could even form a guild or union to help, once there were enough of them.*

But what kind of drug, though? Anna brushed against Indy's saddlebags as she moved to avoid an oncoming cart. *If we give people something less than a panacea, wouldn't we be sort of responsible for all the things out there that we could have healed, but didn't?*

Maybe? I'm a physicist, not a philosopher. Indy paused for a long moment. *But even if we had the fab capacity to just hand out panacea pills like candy, it would help a lot of people, but it wouldn't have the effect we want. If we do something that benefits everyone equally, we leave the current system in place. We're talking about changing their society because we believe that slavery is morally wrong. If we have the power to do something about it, and we don't, wouldn't we be responsible for that too?*

Huh. You'd think that helping people would be much more clear-cut than this. Anna blew out a breath. *Let's say you're right, then.* She double-checked the map, then kept walking. *What could slaves make on their own that's valuable enough to make this work?*

Well, it turns out your dad actually sent us a good bit of data on the history of medicine, Indy said. *I don't think he meant to, but it probably got swept up along with medical technology in general. So I did a quick search while I was acting dumb at Phaia's, looking for some lower-tech possibilities.*

Ooo! Like penicillin or something?

That was my first thought too. Indy sounded disappointed. *But it turns out the penicillium fungus was a pain to grow and purify even with the twentieth-century tech they had when they discovered it. The whole process seemed way beyond what anyone could do here.* She glanced at an alley as they passed its mouth, still wary after the morning's misadventure. *Though I guess we could start by teaching them how to make some simple lab equipment and try to work our way up.*

Hold on, though, Anna said. *Just because something was hard back in the old days, doesn't mean we have to do it the same way. Couldn't we fab some better kind of fungus that's easier to work with?* Anna chewed on that thought. *Or is that even possible? I still don't have a good feeling for what we can design for ourselves here and what we can't. Our kitchen fab back home, if we wanted a new kind of steak or something, we'd just search for a fab plan with a lot of good reviews and download it. But I never really thought about where those plans came from.*

Creating a new fab plan completely from scratch can be extremely compute-intensive, Indy said. *Even in our lab at UT, we'd try to start from existing plans whenever we could. But we've probably got enough compute power here to tinker with something small like the penicillium fungus in simulation to try to get a better version. Though this could potentially be very dangerous.* Indy fell back behind Anna for a moment to avoid oncoming traffic, then walked up beside her again. *Imagine what would happen if we made a mistake. We'd be engineering a fungus to make it easier to grow. What if we accidentally create a strain that grows out of control in the wild and eats up all their crops? We could cause a famine, or worse.*

So we change it so it needs some really special food or something, Anna said. *That way if it got loose, it would die on its own.*

That's a good idea. But there are always going to be failure modes we don't anticipate. Indy whuffed and settled her saddlebags more comfortably. *Not to mention all the non-technological ways we could screw up a scheme like this.* She walked along for a moment without speaking. *And if we make a mistake, we'll be the ones responsible for the consequences.*

You're right. Anna laid her hand on her friend's broad furry back as they walked. *You're right! But what's the alternative? We can't just live out our whole super-long lives here, eating fabbed Mexican food in our cave in Lebadeia and trying to ignore all this.* Anna gestured around at the ancient city. *Greece's got to be twenty percent slaves. It sounds like they're always at war. We saw starving people sleeping in the alleys this morning who looked like they probably had worms! It'd be hard to make things any worse.* She smiled. *Plus, it's a chance to finally do some science!*

Well, applied research maybe. Indy sounded like she was being drawn in, despite her better judgement. *I guess it can't hurt to look into it, at least. We just need to be careful.*

Anna smiled and handed Indy the second pair of frog legs.

47

ver the next few days, the three travelers began to settle into a routine. Anna and Indy ran errands during the day for Oresus, getting to know the city and its people and helping to earn their keep. Thrasius found himself drawn into helping his brother expand his business, handling some dealings with more elite clients who preferred to deal with a full citizen instead of with Oresus' steward Kepthos. Thrasius also arranged for a message, written in Anna's laborious Greek letters on a leather scroll, to be delivered to Leitus and Helene back in Lebadeia to let them know that things were going well in Athens. Indy was content to dictate her part of the message, rather than stain her fur with ink trying to use a pen not suited to her giant paws.

One night there was a knock on Anna and Indy's bedroom door just as they were about to go downstairs for dinner. Anna raised an eyebrow toward Indy, who gave the canine equivalent of a shrug. Anna walked over and opened the door, revealing Thrasius standing outside on the courtyard balcony.

"May I come in? This will only take a moment."

"Um. Sure?" Anna stepped back beside Indy.

Thrasius came in and closed the door behind him. Then he got down on his knees and bowed his head low, the gesture formal and far more assured than when he'd abased himself for mercy in front of Indy at their first encounter, months ago.

"My deepest thanks to you both," he said. "For making me realize just how low I'd sunk with Nicon. You gave me the kick I needed to cut myself loose from that whole crew in Thebes and start pulling myself back up. If it wasn't for the two of you, I wouldn't be standing here today, reunited with my brother, my blood." He stood up, brushing at the hem of his chiton. "That's all. I thought it needed to be said, and I haven't had a chance to talk to the both of you alone in a while."

"You're welcome." Indy put her paw out, and Thrasius took it gravely. Anna laid her own hand on top, echoing her agreement.

"I'm just sorry that my mistakes have followed you all the way here," Thrasius said. "I never meant for my benefit to be at your expense." Anna and Indy had told him about their near-kidnapping by the Theban mob the same day it had happened, though there wasn't much any of them could do about it except avoid going out alone or at night. "Now that they've seen I have the full support of my family, they shouldn't try anything more. At least not here in Athens, where they could expect summary justice if they were caught."

"Athenian houses seem to be built with defensibility in mind." Indy nodded up at one of the high, slit-like exterior windows into their room, which was too narrow to allow ingress from the street, even if an attacker could climb that high. "And people around here bolt their gates at night." She shrugged. "The Thebans might have given up now that we're on our guard, regardless of whatever Nicon might have told them. Though we should still watch ourselves."

"Definitely." Anna nodded, fingers unconsciously feeling for her stunner where it lay hidden behind her belt before she pulled them away.

"And while I'm apologizing…" Thrasius pulled an embarrassed face. "I'm sorry for putting you in the uncomfortable position of having to listen to my brother spout off every night. He wasn't like this before. Well... at least not as often. I think since his wife passed, there's just been nobody here who'll tell him when he's being tiresome. I'm working on him, but older people can be slow to change." He sighed, his expression rueful but accepting. "Anyway, that's all I came for. I'll see you two downstairs." He bowed briefly, then left and closed the door behind him.

Anna and Indy looked at each other. "So," Anna said. "I guess sometimes doing the right thing pays off?"

"I admit, your way worked out pretty well," Indy said, thoughtful. Then her stomach growled. "Sounds like dinnertime." She made a wry face. "Maybe tonight we can get it without a side of politics."

42

nna and Indy tried their best to stay on Oresus' good side, since they would eventually need a citizen sponsor to gain legal status. But their life in his house became less tolerable by the day. Social convention required that Anna and Indy share in the household's evening meals, where tension lay just under the surface of every conversation. Anna had to grit her teeth and remain non-committal about slavery, women's rights, and a list of other hot-button issues to avoid offending their host. And keeping Indy's true nature hidden was a constant worry. They'd already had a few close calls with Oresus' household staff, and Anna knew it was only a matter of time until someone saw something she couldn't explain away.

The secrecy was taking a toll on Indy, too. *I hate having to watch myself every moment to make sure no one sees me pick up a bag or unclip my own harness,* she told Anna one day after almost being caught repacking her saddlebag in their bedroom. *And not being able to tell Oresus what I think about his nightly rants is giving me an ulcer. Apparently, whatever Thrasius is trying with him isn't working.*

Yeah. Anna tilted her head back and closed her eyes, frustrated. *This is killing me too.* She looked at Indy. *We still have some of that money left that we made back in Lebadeia. And Athens is a big town, there's got to be someplace better we can stay.* Anna's resolve firmed. *Let's get out of here!*

Indy dropped her jaw in a doggy smile, and her tail came suspiciously close to wagging.

Three days later, Anna and Indy moved their meager belongings into the very first house that they didn't have to share with anyone else. It took a lot more work than they'd expected, since it turned out that non-citizens weren't allowed to rent property on their own in Athens. But Thrasius volunteered to sponsor them, his citizen status having been rehabilitated by Oresus' accepting him back into the family. And Oresus connected them with a successful acquaintance who had recently moved his family out of their small house in the city to larger quarters in the countryside. Getting set up on their own felt like a victory, like they were finally making things happen for themselves that *they* wanted, instead of just taking whatever opportunities drifted by.

The house wasn't as spacious or as nicely appointed as Oresus' house. It had plain mud-brick walls instead of whitewashed, and a thatched roof instead of tile. The courtyard was barely large enough for Indy to turn around in, and there was only one big U-shaped room upstairs and two rooms downstairs. But it was more than big enough for the two of them, and most importantly it was secure, with solid gates, thick walls, and narrow, barred outer windows. There still hadn't been any sign of the Thebans who had almost abducted them, but they didn't want to become complacent.

Neither of them wanted any live-in staff in the house, for privacy reasons. Through a referral, they found house cleaners who would come by once a week, though they had to pay a premium to hire resident foreigners instead of slaves. They could buy their own food in the market and cook it in the small kitchen downstairs, but the open fire was tricky to handle, and neither of them was a particularly good cook yet. So much of the time they bought already-cooked food instead, or paid one of their cleaners extra to bring over some of her family's cooking.

In their new home, Anna and Indy could finally work in the open with Anna's phone and Indy's small screen that they'd kept packed away until now. They took the opportunity to work remotely on their hidden cave back in Lebadeia, trying to figure out the best way to jump-start ancient Greek medicine.

Since they'd left it, their cave had kept growing on its own, running on instructions they'd set up before leaving. "It's like a secret superhero base!" Anna marveled to Indy. Images relayed through the drones they'd strung behind them on their journey to Athens showed lightless underground galleries where the rock had been mined away and re-compacted in search of rare ores, and the hulking form of their latest industrial-sized fab, its hopper rattling as their mining beetles dropped in concentrated pellets to feed it.

In between their other tasks, they also manually reviewed the drone surveillance footage of their landing site, just in case there was something to see that their nets had somehow overlooked. But after almost nine months stranded in the past, and given the revelations in the unsent message they'd found from Anna's father, neither of them was surprised that there was still no hint of any rescue. They left the monitoring drone in place, because neither of them could bear to completely give up hope. But at this point, it felt like a formality, like honoring their past, whereas their plan to improve medicine for the Greeks at least gave them some optimism about their future.

The easiest part of that plan turned out to be the penicillium spores. Thanks to the foresight of Anna's father, their nets already held a library of every sort of plant and drug imaginable, along with bio-engineering software to tailor it to their needs, and spores were easy to fabricate since they didn't require heavy elements or high energies. Score one for nature!

Much longer in the making had been new shield projectors for both of them. They'd learned their lesson from the confrontation with Nicon months ago, so this new pair of shields was much stronger than the last, though they were still far short of what the future could have achieved. The shields had turned out distressingly boxy and ugly, since no amount of computing power could produce a design that packed the energy storage they needed into elegant jewelry. But they did have the added ability to project their invisible force out a few feet from the wearer, which could be used to manipulate nearby objects as well as form a barrier. These shields had each taken a full month to fabricate due to their specialized high-density batteries, and they would probably only be able to run full-out for a few minutes before needing many hours of recharging from phone or collar. But they had started fabbing these before they left for Athens, so now they were finally ready for service.

The hardest part was getting any of this stuff delivered to their rental house in Athens. Their little solar-powered relay drones couldn't carry much extra weight, and couldn't fly far from their roosts without breaking their communication chain. And a bigger drone couldn't fly more than a few miles from their base without a recharge, which was no good since their only power sources were in their original fab, Anna's phone, and Indy's collar.

But in the process of searching through their vast library of plants, they'd also realized that their earlier drone designs had been hopelessly naïve. Instead of hiding tiny solar cells under the wings of an insect-like drone, it made much more sense to create a drone that looked like an insect while flying, but which unfolded larger solar cells disguised as plant leaves after landing. Since relay drones didn't need to move very often, they could produce much more solar power this way without fear of detection.

After a few days of refining these ideas in simulation, with Anna talking out loud to Alixa and Indy subvocalizing to her collar's net while they watched the results on a screen, they finally had a workable solution. They remotely fabbed and dispatched a string of new relay drones, with their foldable solar cells patterned after the leaves of the native trees they would roost in. The first drone flew out to the limit of its short range, found a hiding spot, spread its leaves, and recharged. The next day, it re-folded its leaves and did the same thing again, moving further toward Athens, while the next drone in the string emerged from the base and flew to occupy the previous drone's spot.

After two weeks and a dozen new drones sent out, they finally had a line of closely spaced, solar-powered charging stations that a bigger carrier-drone could use to make the trip straight through from Lebadeia to Athens. It was a precarious solution, and Indy grumbled about the risk of someone catching sight of the carrier-drone itself and getting suspicious. But it was better than walking the 120-mile trip to Lebadeia and back. And it worked well enough, though slowly, since each carrier-drone trip needed a week of accumulated sunlight along the route to power it.

The carrier-drone itself was only as long as Anna's forearm, and less than that in height. But it was far too large to pass for any kind of insect, and even a bird with a body that size would need a memorably enormous wingspan. So they had just given the drone an irregular outline to avoid drawing the eye, and had it fly over Athens at high altitude in the dead of night, then drop directly toward their house from invisibly far above.

Even with the drone's safety lights extinguished, Anna could still see it gleaming faintly in the dark night sky, and hear the low humming of its repeller field once it got close enough. During every delivery, her heart would be in her mouth until they unloaded its tiny cargo bay and sent it back aloft with a double-pat on the side.

Over the course of several weeks, the carrier-drone dropped off their new shields and the experimental penicillium spores in their tiny courtyard. They barely had any weight allowance left for silver coins to pay their rent, so they had to scrimp to make up the difference, but the extra freedom of having their own house was worth it.

Culturing their new variety of penicillium proved to be simplicity itself. They'd engineered it to use olive oil as a growth medium, since it was widely available in ancient Greece. And as a safeguard, the fungus required a small amount of ground olive pits to survive, to make sure that if it got loose somehow, it wouldn't be able to eat everything in its path. Anna and Indy grew a batch of it in their upstairs room in only a few days, using olive oil and a shallow pan they'd bought at the market, and were so excited by the results they went to see Phaia again the day after.

It was a week or so since they'd seen her last, but they had run errands for Oresus frequently enough now that they were an expected sight at the rented house that Phaia shared with a few other crafters and slaves who worked a trade. Phaia had lost some of her gruffness toward them as well. *Or maybe I've just gotten used to it,* Anna thought with a smile.

Phaia looked up from her worktable as Anna and Indy walked in. "There's no delivery due, is there?" She frowned. "What did I forget? Did somebody die?"

"No, no, nothing like that," Anna said quickly. "We brought you something from our homeland. Something that might be useful in your business." She handed over two small linen pouches, one containing penicillin tablets, and the other containing their specially engineered penicillium fungus spores. "This is a treatment for infection—"

"Why did you say 'we'?" Phaia asked.

"Sorry, what?"

"You said '*we* brought you something.' Not '*I* brought you something.'" Phaia looked at Indy, who stared back innocently, pretending to scratch at a flea.

You really need to watch your words, Indy thought to Anna, digging in behind one ear with a back paw. *Remember, this one's very clever about noticing details.*

"Oh. Oh yeah, sorry!" Anna said. "Where I come from, we treat our dogs just like people. You can ask Oresus! Indy comes to dinner with me every night. She even drinks from her own wine bowl."

What else would I drink from? Indy said. *The toilet?*

Phaia still looked suspicious. "You said this is a treatment for infection?" She held up the two pouches, looking inside each one, but careful not to disturb the contents.

"Yes. The first pouch is finished pills, samples we made to get you started," Anna said. "A patient should take one every six hours, for eight days in a row. For bad cases, double the dosage. Wash them down with water, because the pills are dry, and they taste horrible. And tell the patient to *keep taking them*, even if the infection seems to clear up. That last bit is very important." As Anna talked, Phaia looked at her so intently that it was making her nervous, but she plowed ahead regardless.

"The second pouch is powdered spores," Anna said. "To grow more, pour a thin layer of olive oil into a shallow pan, then sprinkle a pinch of these spores evenly on top. Um, and you need to dust a bit of dried, ground-up olive pit over the whole thing." Anna cleared her throat, as Phaia was looking almost angry by this point. "Keep it moist and warm, and in a few days you'll have a panful of fungus that you can dry out and grind up. Then you can make the pills any way you want, as long as they weigh the same as ours."

Phaia stood quietly for a long moment, staring.

"Um. Do you have any questions?" Anna asked.

"Why?" Phaia asked.

"Why what?"

Uh oh, Indy said.

"Why would you just give me something like this? Especially if it does what you say it does." Phaia looked back and forth from Anna to Indy. "Things don't work like that. I do things, I prove my worth, I get paid." She glared at Anna. "Nobody helps a slave for free."

Anna groaned mentally. *I'm the worst liar ever! Why do I always have to be the explainer?* Indy snorted over their link, but stayed silent.

"Well, so… back where we come from—" Anna stopped. "I mean, me. Back where *I* come from." Indy laughed again, soundlessly. "Slavery's something you only read about in books about how bad things used to be. And now that I live here, and I can't ever go back home…" She took a breath to forestall the sadness that clutched at her heart. "I like a lot of things about this place, and there's other stuff I can get used to. But I'm never just going to *get used to* what they do to you guys." Anna ran her hands through her sweaty hair. "The only thing I could think to do was to give you something that's common back home, but valuable here. Something that might help make your life better."

Phaia regarded Anna narrowly for another long moment. Then her expression softened, fractionally. "I'll try out this medicine of yours. But if it works, I pay you what I think it's worth. Nobody in this town is ever going to say that I cheated them, or that I didn't earn everything I have."

"I don't need the money," Anna said. "You should use it to help out your friends the same way we're helping you. Pay it forward."

"I'd be doing that anyway!" Phaia's eyes flashed defiance. "But that's not the point. A gift would be a claim on me, a debt. But since I'll be paying you, this will be a business transaction." She tossed the pouches on her table and sat down. "I'll try out your product, and let you know in two weeks what I'm willing to pay. At that point, you can either accept payment, or I'll give the rest of it back to you. *That's* fair enough."

You had better take the offer, Indy said lightly. *I think you're outmatched.*

"Done." Anna nodded in agreement as she reached out to shake Phaia's proffered hand. "And I'm sorry if that came across wrong somehow. I just want to—"

"Don't worry about it," Phaia said gruffly. "Let's let your product do the talking." She picked up a packet of dried plants and began carefully plucking off the leaves and setting them into a pile. She looked at Anna pointedly, then turned her eyes back to her work. "I'll see you in two weeks."

"Oh! Right." Anna took the barely concealed hint. "See you then." She turned to leave, followed by Indy, who Anna could swear was shaking her head.

43

Back out on the streets of Athens, Anna let out a pent-up breath as they headed for home.

That could've gone smoother. Indy snorted with amusement.

How could I know she'd be so prickly? Anna rubbed at the flop sweat beading her forehead. *We're just trying to help!*

I didn't think she'd react that way either, for what it's worth, Indy said. *But it makes sense in the context of slavery. It seems like it's just barely possible to buy your way to freedom here, with a lot of luck and hard work. So I can imagine that enslaved people would be very leery of letting it seem like anyone has any sort of claim on them that could call their status into question.*

I guess it makes a twisted kind of sense, Anna said. *And at least she's going to try it out. Once she sees how well penicillin works, she's bound to get excited about it.* Anna smiled. *Then* she *can be the one who explains it next time.*

Outside the normal round of errands for Oresus, Anna and Indy spent the next two weeks touring around the safer parts of the city, trying to get a better sense of how day-to-day life worked. For that, what little historical knowledge they had in their nets was almost completely worthless. Since most of what anyone knew about ancient Greece had been written down by elites, the lives of normal citizens seemed to have been mostly undocumented, especially the lives of the middle class of traders, crafters, and businesspeople. They were learning a lot, though they still felt keenly out of place at times. And though there'd still been no sign of the Thebans who'd almost kidnapped them weeks before, they didn't let their guard down, keeping to crowded streets and bolting themselves securely behind their gates at night.

Finally, the day came for them to visit Phaia again, to check the status of their first small attempt to improve the society they had found themselves trapped in. They went in the afternoon, after the morning's press of business was done, to take advantage of the lighter traffic. People with the option stayed inside to avoid the sun's heat at this time of day, saving any further errands until the shade began to return to the streets.

Anna knocked on the door frame to announce them as she walked in. Phaia was at the back of the room working on something, so Anna and Indy followed the usual trail through the stacked materials to reach the worktable.

As they walked up, Phaia reached into a drawer and picked up a small bag that clinked metallically. She tossed it to Anna, who caught it by reflex. It was surprisingly heavy.

"That's your share. Count it and see if you think that's reasonable for six treatments' worth of your drug."

"I'm sure it's fi—" Anna started to say. Then she reconsidered, opened the bag, and counted, the process coming easier to her now that they'd been in the city and working with coins for a while.

"There are sixty drachmae here," Anna said. "Isn't that a lot, though? That's like six months' rent!"

Goodbye, tight budget. Indy sounded exuberant. *And hello, frog legs!*

"Well, I charged twenty drachmae per treatment, and believe me, they took it as a bargain," Phaia said. "I had to get Oresus to authorize it, since slaves aren't allowed to make single transactions that large. And I probably could have tripled the price. I figured your share should be worth half."

"I don't understand, though," Anna said. "Why would they pay so much?"

"Where *are* you from?" Phaia shook her head. "No, don't answer that. You already told me, *Iberia*." She tapped a finger on her table, thinking. "Look at it this way. Say someone you barely know, with an unlikely and potentially dangerous motive—" she pierced Anna with her eyes "—hands you the recipe to an unknown drug. You've never heard of it, never seen it tested. It could be poison for all you know. How can you try it out without risking your patients' lives?"

Realization dawned on Anna. "You gave it to people who were about to die!"

"I made them a deal," Phaia said. "I've got a new medicine, but it might be dangerous. You could die even faster, or grow a third eyeball. Or it might do nothing. If it doesn't work, you don't pay me. If it does, it's twenty drachmae. Atropos is about to clip you off anyway. What would *you* do?"

"How did you even find patients like that?" Anna asked.

"I know a doctor at a temple of Asklepios near here. One of the good guys, not one of those idiots who drains perfectly good blood out of men because he thinks menstruation's so great for women. I had him pick me out seven patients with badly infected wounds. All of them already treated by other doctors, without success, so my guy was just treating their pain, waiting for the inevitable." Phaia frowned. "Most of these wounds were in bad shape. Swollen, draining yellow pus, red streaks coming off them and into the good flesh. Those are very bad signs," she added at Anna's quizzical look.

We would never have seen that kind of infection, Indy said. *Our genetic enhancements and medical treatments wouldn't let it get that far.*

"I started each of them on your drug, and most saw improvement immediately. One of them still lost his hand, but the surgeon could at least amputate it without his arm rotting off. One woman died anyway, but her case was the worst of the bunch." She looked at Anna, incredulous. "You don't even understand the significance of this, do you?"

"What's to understand?" Anna said. "You give sick people drugs, then they get well. That's what drugs are for!"

"Drugs don't work this well!" Phaia stood, shoving her stool back. "I've never heard of a drug that could have saved even *one* out of those seven cases." She paced as she talked. "This is going to attract attention. Pilgrims tell their families when they go home healed. Priests inscribe stories like this outside the temple as advertisements. If your drug works this well on other patients, it's going to be worth gold, not silver."

Phaia seemed to come to a decision. "Let me explain this so you'll understand me." Her mouth set with distaste. "I'm worth five minae and sixty drachmae. That's my entire value as a human being, here in Greece. That's about what some of these rich idiots in Athens might pay for five nights with a high-priced courtesan. Five hundred and sixty drachmae, or one hundred and forty good Athenian owls. That's how much it will take to buy my freedom from Oresus, gods willing."

"I've saved for over ten years to collect five hundred drachmae. I've starved myself!" She walked forward and glared at Anna and Indy. "Do you have any idea what it's like to be a slave for *ten years?*" She clenched her jaw and lowered her voice from a near-shout. "I'm lucky this stupid slave haircut looks terrible on me, and I'm too ugly and mouthy to be a brothel slave." She looked like she wanted to spit. "Some women have it much worse. But I can't say my life's been pleasant."

Phaia sat down at her little table again, deflated. "And then you walk in here and hand me something, just on a whim, that earns me sixty drachmae in *two weeks!*" A tear welled in the corner of her eye, but she wiped it away irritably before it could fall. "I'm going to walk into Oresus' house tomorrow and buy my freedom." She fell silent.

Anna walked forward and put her hand on Phaia's shoulder, and Indy came up to lean against her from the other side. They stood that way for a long moment, Phaia unconsciously stroking Indy's fur. Then she pushed them firmly aside, let out a breath and straightened her back again.

"Go on then," she said. "I'll see you back here in a week for your next payment."

44

The next week went by in a happy glow. Anna felt like they were finally making some tangible progress, like every moment they spent researching or working remotely in their lab back in Lebadeia was helping to move their project forward. Even her and Indy's errands for Oresus seemed more productive somehow. And spending some of their newfound income on a few small luxuries didn't hurt, either.

Anna rose early on the day they were scheduled to meet Phaia again, and jittered all through her new favorite breakfast of oxygala, which was some kind of Greek yogurt sweetened with honey. "I wonder if she got a good batch of patients this week?"

"I can hardly see how she wouldn't," Indy said. "She's got a blockbuster new drug on her hands. She'll have a monopoly for a while, at least until she can start training her friends to make penicillin too."

"I'm glad she was onboard with that part of the plan," Anna said. "If we had to come up with a new drug for every person we wanted to help, this whole thing would never work."

Indy made an affirmative noise as she wolfed down the last of her own breakfast and licked the bowl, then smacked her lips contentedly. "Renting this house was such a good idea. It's so nice to speak out loud again, and eat like a civilized being without worrying that someone will get suspicious."

Anna smiled fondly at her friend as they rose from the kitchen table. They left the house and closed the courtyard gates behind them, walking side by side along the now-familiar route to Phaia's shop and talking over their link about what their next steps should be. Yet another of Athens' seemingly endless calendar of festivals was taking place, this one called the Panathenaea, which involved a great number of cultural and athletic contests all over the city. But even the crowds that were beginning to build in the streets did little to dampen their spirits.

Anna knew something was wrong the moment she saw Phaia's shop. The door off the inner hallway was closed, which they'd never seen before. Normally Phaia opened at dawn, and closed only when she was gone on an errand, which shouldn't be the case this early.

Maybe she's gone to the agora, Indy said. *This is the best time to get the freshest meat. As a free woman now, she won't have to economize so much.*

Hang on. Anna examined the shop front more closely. *I don't like this.* She pointed to the window that opened onto Phaia's room. It was shuttered, but there was a sizeable gap between them, and the room inside looked empty, without even window hangings to block the view.

She wouldn't have moved out without mentioning it, Anna said. *Would she?*

I don't like this either, Indy said. *It smells like no one's lived in there for days. But why don't you knock, just to be sure?*

Anna knocked. It echoed hollowly. She knocked again. Still nothing.

Let's go ask Oresus, Anna said. *Maybe he's heard from her.* She felt dread beginning to well up in her stomach. *I hope we didn't get her in some kind of trouble. Maybe she moved to a nicer place, and sent us a message but it got lost in transit. She could be waiting for us somewhere else right now.*

Just as they turned to leave, a tenant across the hallway from Phaia stuck her head out of her door and looked around. Anna had seen her there before. She was some sort of metalworker and a friend of Phaia's, but they hadn't been introduced.

"Hey, come here a sec, would you?" She beckoned to Anna with quick movements. "You're the one who's been working with Phaia on that new drug of hers, right?"

"Yes! Do you know where she went?"

"Damn. I was hoping *you* knew." The woman looked down the hall toward the front door, then retreated back into her room a step, forcing Anna to come closer. "I'm Themis, by the way. Friend of Phaia's from way back." She extended her hand for a quick shake. The walls of her room were hung with fascinating geared mechanisms, and the workbenches held neat racks of small hand tools. "My girl walks out of here a week ago. Off to buy herself out, she says. But she doesn't come back. The next day, these suspicious characters show up without her. They load all her stuff onto a wagon, right down to the chamber pot, and haul it off. None of them would say a word about where they were taking it all, or where the hell Phaia might be."

Themis backed up even further. "I mean, I've seen some metics or other foreigners get kicked out of a rental before, if they got short on cash or their sponsor dropped them. But this seems like something else. I've known Phaia a long time, and she's not the type." She gave Anna a worried look. "You're sure you don't know anything?"

"I'm sure," Anna said. "But I'm going to find out."

Themis leaned closer, intent eyes flicking over Indy's harness and its fittings. Her hands twitched as if she wanted a closer look, but she held back with a visible effort. "Whatever you're thinking of doing, you might not want to be seen poking around here. The guys who packed up all her stuff looked more like criminals than movers to me." She popped her head out the door and took a look down the hallway. "Which isn't like Phaia either. I don't know what to make of it."

Could this be connected to those guys who tried to trap us in the alleyway? Anna felt queasy even thinking it.

I'm sure it's just a coincidence, Indy said. *Crime seems to be common here. Let's start with Oresus and see if he knows anything.*

"I've been asking around our mutual friends," Themis continued. "So far I've got nothing, but someone must know where she went. Eventually, I'll get a hit." She ushered them out into the hallway. "In the meantime, stay safe. Try back in a few days, and I'll let you know if I find anything." She closed the door in their faces with an apologetic look.

Anna and Indy left the building and walked swiftly through the growing festival traffic to Oresus' house, silent the whole way with worry and fear. When they arrived, they entered the open courtyard and called out to announce themselves. The side door creaked open, and the steward Kepthos looked out into the courtyard. When he saw Anna, his face became carefully impassive. "I'll inform master Oresus you're here. I imagine you wish to speak with him?" At Anna's nod, Kepthos walked to the rear door and spoke, too low for them to hear. Then he opened the door and ushered Anna and Indy inside, closing it behind them as he went back out into the courtyard.

Oresus rose from behind a cluttered desk. "Welcome, my friend, welcome! I trust your new house is still serving you well? It's been too long since your last visit, and Indy as well. Please, take a seat and make yourself comfortable." He indicated a chair in front of the desk, then re-seated himself.

"We just got back from Phaia's house." Anna remained standing, tense with worry. "We couldn't find her, and none of her neighbors knows where she is, either. We're really concerned. Do you know where she's gone?"

"Of course, my dear. Of course I do!" Oresus settled back in his chair. "There's nothing at all to worry about. I helped her to change households last week." He rubbed the back of his neck with one hand as he spoke. "She came to me a few weeks ago, asking if I would assist her by authorizing a few transactions for a new business venture of hers. Which I understand you had some hand in?" He raised an eyebrow. "And I was glad to do so. Then last week, she came back and inquired if I'd be interested in restructuring our current arrangement to feed into this new business. A business very different from her previous work with me, I was surprised to learn."

Oresus rose and walked back and forth behind his desk. "I was sorry to see her go, but I had to recommend that she re-situate." He paced faster as he spoke. "Honestly, this venture of hers was somewhat out of my league! Fortunately, I was able to find her a wonderful placement with quite a well-off family. They were very interested in helping her pursue her business, and they have more than ample means, so it seemed like a good thing all around."

That smells like a lie to me, Indy said.

"I assure you, it's for the best this way," Oresus continued, as if he had heard Indy speak somehow. "I didn't have the resources to help her, and she could have ended up in a bad situation by trying to go it alone."

"Last week, she said she was coming to you to buy her freedom," Anna said. "She'd finally saved up the money."

"Well, she did mention something about that at first," Oresus said. "Thankfully, I was able to talk her out of it! This idea of hers was attracting the wrong sort of attention, and she would have been completely unprotected on her own. There's nothing I could have done to help her in that case."

"She seemed pretty set on freedom when I talked to her." Anna looked intently at Oresus. "And why would she drop everything and let other people pack up all her stuff? We heard she never even went back to her place."

Oresus stopped his pacing. "According to the law, for a slave to be manumitted, the master must give his consent." He didn't meet Anna's eyes. "It has to be that way. Otherwise unscrupulous speculators could simply loan gullible slaves the money to buy themselves out, at usurious interest, then re-enslave them and send them straight to the silver mines when they can't pay! Believe me, there are predators out there, very bad people." He looked up again. "A family I know made a very generous offer for her, in light of her newly acquired skills. No one would pay that much for a slave who intended to abuse her."

"So you just… sold her?" Anna couldn't believe what she was hearing.

"As her master, it was my responsibility to look after Phaia's best interests for her. To make sure she didn't get herself in over her head." Oresus mustered up an indignant look. "If you had only come to me first, this entire unpleasantness could have been avoided. But once bigger players got wind of what was happening, there was no way I could protect her."

Anna felt like she should be angry. But all she could feel was a terrible cold hollowness in her chest, and a burning in her cheeks. Indy had been right about unforeseen consequences. They should have known that Oresus wouldn't honor Phaia's original buyout price if he realized there was more money to be made. Now, instead of buying her own freedom and helping other enslaved people win theirs, Phaia was even worse off than before.

And it was all Anna's fault.

"How much did they pay you?" she finally choked out.

"That's a private matter." Oresus sat back down at his desk, his forced air of friendliness dissipating. "Now, was there anything else? I have pressing business, otherwise."

"Just one more question." Anna had finally found her anger, and Indy's ruff bristled beside her. "Where is she?"

45

Anna and Indy walked side by side out into the country, on a mission to buy back the woman whose life they'd ruined by trying to make it better.

Oresus had finally parted with the name of Phaia's buyer, a man named Hylas from some aristocratic family called the Peisistratids. Along with the name had come a warning that Hylas was likely to react very poorly to any inquiry. But that seemed unlikely to Anna. After all, they were planning to pay him a lot of money.

A few discreet questions around the agora had yielded a surprising amount of information about the Peisistratid family, who seemed to be infamous in Athens. This Hylas guy turned out to be the great-grandson of the same Peisistratos who'd planted the olive grove they'd seen on the way into Athens with Thrasius many weeks ago, and he came from a long line of Persian sympathizers. His grandfather Hippias had died in exile after fighting on the wrong side of the Battle of Marathon, his grand-uncle Hipparchus had been killed by the Tyrannicides whose statues they'd seen in the agora, and his father Peisistratos the Younger was currently in exile in Persia or Asia Minor for treason while Hylas minded the family estate in his absence.

All of which was hard for them to fully digest, given their limited information about this time period. But most importantly, they'd been told that the Peisistratid family compound was out near Mount Parnitha, to the north of Athens, about a three hour walk away. Not much of a journey, for this era, though it was much further than Anna cared to walk in the heat of the Greek summer.

Indy had wisely insisted that they return to their house and prepare themselves before racing off to confront an unknown situation, no matter how guilty they felt or how desperate they were to try to fix it. But there wasn't a lot they could do to prepare beyond what they already did as a matter of course. Since their encounter with Nicon back in Lebadeia, they had worn their shield projectors almost everywhere, just in case. Anna's new, larger unit was hidden beneath her chiton at the small of her back, and Indy's was disguised and attached to her harness, which today held a single flat mini-bag instead of the usual pair of saddlebags they used for longer trips or shopping. They also had their stun-batons, Indy's in its holster and Anna's hidden beneath her wide belt, though it was uncertain how much use they'd be if they got into real trouble. Their real weapons on this mission were their small sacks of Greek silver and a few gold coins, tucked away in Indy's mini-bag.

The road north took them further across the plains than they had ventured before. All around them stretched fields that supplied food for Athens' many mouths, and the whirring buzz of summer cicadas filled the air. The fig harvest was ongoing, and Anna guessed by the field workers' clothing that farmers had paid some of the poorer city folk to come out into the orchards as extra labor. Normally Anna would have enjoyed their walk. But her thoughts kept circling back to how it was all her fault that Phaia was gone.

"I can't believe I was so reckless." Anna spoke out loud to Indy, since the long roads dividing the fields here were thinly traveled at midday, and they could see approaching traffic from quite a distance. "If we had just started with something smaller, Phaia could've kept it a secret, and Oresus wouldn't have gotten greedy."

"Or we could have given out our spores to many people at once, so no one could corner the market with a single kidnapping." Indy walked steadily, paws leaving tracks in the dust of the unpaved road. "But there's no way to predict this kind of outcome. Evil people are endlessly inventive. They can find a way to profit from any good deed."

"Too true." Anna's stomach clenched with worry, and she unconsciously hurried her steps.

"Take it easy," Indy said. The pace was no challenge for her four long legs, but she could see that Anna was pushing herself. "There's no point showing up worn-out and sweaty to a negotiation."

Which may have been good advice, but it was hard to follow. Hours later, when the Peisistratid compound began to come into view, Anna was a mess, long dark hair plastered to her neck with sweat, and dust covering her sandals.

The pair stopped before getting too close and took a couple of minutes to refresh themselves. Anna quickly brushed out Indy's coat, then dusted off her sandals and wiped her face. After a moment's thought, she also made sure that Indy's stun-baton was loose in its holster, and that her own was ready to be drawn from under her belt, without getting tangled in the folds of her chiton. Then they resumed walking.

As they drew closer, Anna could clearly see the front gate of a compound that included a large, stately home built of shining white limestone, as well as a variety of other buildings. The ornately decorated gate stood open, and a small but steady stream of slaves and citizens flowed in and out. A few of them watched Anna and Indy approach with interest.

Okay. Anna blew out a breath. *We go in, we buy Phaia's freedom, and we get out of here. Right?* She spoke over their link now, since the passers-by would hear her otherwise.

What if this Hylas person refuses to sell? Indy asked.

I'm pretty sure we're packing a lot more here than what he paid Oresus. Anna patted their money through the leather of Indy's mini-bag. *And he's old money, it sounds like. It was probably just a business transaction to him. With what we can offer, this ought to be an easy sale.*

But what if it isn't? Indy asked. *What kind of man would buy a slave who was trying to buy her own freedom?*

We'll promise him more drugs like we gave Phaia, then. Anna's mental voice sounded uneasy. *That's sure to be worth more than her. We can always renege on it later. But we have to fix this.*

They drew up at the gates, the focus of curious looks. An old man stepped forward to greet them.

I really hope this works, Indy said.

46

"I'm here to speak to your boss." Anna addressed the old man respectfully, but directly, and tried not to look as nervous as she felt. "About a business matter. Hylas is his name?"

"Yes, that's him." The old man looked at her oddly. "He's just come back from the city himself a few days past. He left word that he was expecting a young lady visitor. I'll take you to him." He turned and walked into the compound, gesturing for Anna to follow.

He's expecting us? Indy said. *I'm not sure I like the sound of that.*

Me either, Anna said. *But stay cool. Maybe Phaia told him that we might be coming.*

They followed the old man across the broad courtyard in the center of the compound, and into the main house. It was old, but its size and quality spoke of inherited wealth. The walls were lavishly painted with scenes both idyllic and warlike, and expensive-looking statuary, urns, and other pieces of art decorated every alcove.

Dang, this place is like a museum! How much money do these Peisistratids have, anyway? Anna craned her neck around as they walked, but saw no sign of Phaia.

My guess is that by the time a dynasty is named after you, we're talking about serious wealth. Indy's mental voice was bone-dry.

Finally, the old man stopped outside a closed door and tapped it with a knuckle. "Your young lady guest from the city is here, sir." There was a muffled reply that Anna couldn't make out, but the old man opened the door and ushered them through, closing it behind them.

Inside, a man rose from behind an intricately carved but tasteful wooden desk as they entered, dismissing a secretary carrying a stack of wax tablets. As the secretary let himself out, the man walked around the desk, eyes fixed upon them. He was darkly handsome, perhaps thirty years old, sporting a short, curled beard, and powerfully built in a way that only the rich and well-fed could be in this era.

"You must be Anna." He shook her hand with just a shade too much warmth. "And this must be Indy! Just as impressive as I was told. I am Hylas, as you are no doubt aware." He walked over to a pair of couches and sat, gesturing for Anna to sit on the one opposite. She perched on its edge self-consciously, and Indy sat on the floor beside her, their heads at almost the same height.

"So. It seems that we have a common interest." Hylas' voice was well-modulated, the voice of a man used to public speaking. "A new member of my household informs me that you are quite knowledgeable about innovative new medicines. I was hoping that you might pay us a call, so that we could discuss a mutually beneficial arrangement." His smile was very white.

Anna gathered her nerve. "I've come with a proposal for you." She cleared her suddenly tight throat, and tried to keep her voice from shaking. "My, um, project, in Athens could use the services of a talented compounder like Phaia. I was about to make her an offer when I heard that she left." Anna squirmed in her seat, then forced herself to stop. Hylas' smile widened.

Anna squared her shoulders. "I'd like to talk to you about buying her out. I'm ready to make a very reasonable offer."

"I have no doubt of it." Hylas leaned forward attentively on his couch. "But permit me to preempt you with a counteroffer. Suppose you were to come and work for me?" He spoke over Anna's shocked expression. "Hear me out. As you can see, my resources, and those of my family, are substantial. I could give you support well beyond your current means. Support that could be very helpful."

That seems unlikely, Indy said. *But he can't know that.*

"Well, thank you for your kind offer," Anna said, "but I'm not looking for a job. Mostly I just want to help my friend do what she loves. And make some money for myself in the process, of course," she added. *Hopefully that sounds like a more business-y motivation.*

"Oh, don't misunderstand me," Hylas said. "I'm not offering you mere employment. I would like to make you a member of our household. We would take all the burdens of raising capital, purchasing materials, and such, off your shoulders. You would be completely free to do what you do best, right alongside your friend Phaia."

"I'm sorry, but that's not really what I'm looking for," Anna said. "Maybe we could discuss my offer instead?"

Hylas leaned further forward and looked at Anna intently. She edged away slightly despite her best efforts. Up close, Hylas' dark beard gleamed with some sort of perfumed oil, and she could see thick muscle bulging at the shoulders of his embroidered chiton. Indy wrinkled her nose as the smell of his beard-oil wafted over them.

"Do you have a father?" His voice was oh-so-reasonable. "Brothers, perhaps? Where is your family?"

"I'm from far away." Anna was taken slightly aback by the change of subject. "My family... were all left behind." She could still taste bitter regret at the back of her throat as she said it out loud.

"Then you should consider my offer very seriously." Hylas' voice was quiet in the richly appointed office. "Many things can happen to a young woman alone. You're in a strange land, with no one to vouch for you. You speak oddly, and you cannot prove your citizenship here. What's to prevent some unscrupulous character from simply claiming that you are a runaway slave?" Hylas settled back comfortably on his couch. "There is no one who would say otherwise." He raised an eyebrow. "And you are not as anonymous as you may believe. An influential friend sent me a message some months ago, asking me to inform him if someone matching your description arrived in Athens. He would not tell me why, though I think I now have some idea. And he offered me considerable favors in return." He met her eyes, voice full of entreaty. "You need someone to protect you. This country is no place for those without kin."

He's not offering you a job. Indy's mental voice was outraged. *He's talking about making you a slave!*

Anna felt dread take hold deep in her guts. Hylas was right. There was no one here to back them up. *How did I ever think this was going to work?* Her feet felt stuck to the floor, and she couldn't open her mouth to speak.

Hylas picked up a small bell from beside his couch and rang it. Immediately a burly young man in leather armor wearing a short sword opened the door. "Please escort this young lady to the associates' quarters," Hylas said. "She is to be given the run of the house, but is not to leave until I am confident of her loyalties."

"Yes, sir." The young man hesitated as he saw Indy's size and fierce expression, but then pushed on into the room, right hand resting on his sword hilt. He was followed by two more men, both armed with thick staves bound in bronze. The first man raised his left hand toward Anna in a leading gesture. "Come with me, girl."

47

"No." Indy's voice rang out loudly from her collar, impossible to ignore.

Hylas and his three guards turned to look at the giant canine, confused expressions on their faces.

"You misunderstand your position," Indy continued. "Our offer is not a negotiation. We will take our friend and leave. You may choose to receive payment, or not."

Hylas' confusion wore off first. He looked back to Anna. "Your dog can speak?"

"Yes, she can speak." Indy's voice was mocking. "Now decide." She shrugged her mini-pack to jingle the coins inside. Reflexively, Anna opened it and pulled out one of the coin sacks, hefting it for Hylas to see before setting it heavily on his desk.

"As strange as this situation is becoming, I don't see how it changes matters." Hylas considered for a long moment. "Except that now I will also have a talking dog among my household." He addressed his men. "Take both of them to quarters and confine them there for now. Try not to kill the dog, but do whatever you must, and report back when it is done."

The first guard reached out to grab Anna's hand.

This time Anna didn't freeze. She mentally commanded her shield to pin the man's ankles and wrists in place with invisible extensions of its force. He wrenched to a stop, his body pulling hard against his limbs as his momentum was painfully cancelled out.

"I can't move!" He struggled against invisible bonds. "Get me loose!" The second guard moved to help him while the third advanced on Anna. She pinned them both the same way. They struggled, purpling with effort, but their bonds were as immovable as the floor beneath their feet.

Anna could already feel the shield projector heating up at the small of her back. Holding three strong men at once was taxing it. Even though its battery was the best they could make, she wasn't sure how long it could keep this up.

Hylas finally rose from his couch. "Fascinating." He seemed unafraid. "How are you doing that?"

Let me hold them all, Indy said. *My shield is more powerful than yours.* Anna gratefully relinquished their bonds after she saw Hylas similarly jerk to a halt. He and two of the guards struggled briefly, but relented when Indy tightened her hold on them. The last of the guards started to panic, chest heaving as he jerked at his bonds and looked around frantically, but Indy stepped forward, raised herself on her hind legs and put a paw on his chest. "Stop fighting it." Her huge muzzle loomed close to his face. "I won't be responsible if you injure yourself." The man stared at Indy with fresh horror, but stopped his struggle and sagged weakly in place.

I've got an idea. Anna walked up to one of the immobile guards and gripped his staff. Indy took the hint and forced the man's hands open with her shield so Anna could pull the weapon from his grasp.

Anna turned back to Hylas. "I'm really sorry it's come to this." She walked closer to him, and despite his efforts to put on a brave face, he flinched away.

Anna raised the staff over her head, her hands as far apart on its length as she could reach. Then she engaged her shield's force again, this time to amplify her strength.

The wrist-thick wood creaked as it began to bend. Hylas' handsome features slackened with surprise as the staff bowed further and further, the dense wood groaning with the strain. Anna could feel her shield projector heating up again. This time it was buzzing worryingly. It had to be close to failure.

With a terrifying *crack!* the center of the staff burst apart. A large, jagged chunk of wood hit the ceiling hard enough to crack the plaster, and shards rattled off the walls and floor. One razor-sharp piece grazed Hylas' cheek, leaving a drop of blood oozing in its wake. His mouth gaped in shock. One of the guards swore in disbelief.

Anna held up the two heavy ends of the staff, still bound in their bronze collars, then dropped them to the floor. One of Hylas' men jerked at the sound.

Anna pulled a smaller sack of coins from Indy's pack and set it on Hylas' desk beside the first. "This is our final offer." She pulled the sack open to show the glint of silver, and forced steel into her voice. "Now. Where. Is. Phaia."

The moment stretched.

Entering thermal shutdown, Anna's shield announced over her link. The shield casing was burning against her back now, almost too hot to tolerate, but she kept the pain off her face with an effort as she looked steadily at Hylas.

Anna was acutely conscious that she had no defenses left. Sweat trickled down her seared back as she tried to avoid looking down at the belt that hid her stun-baton. If Indy's shield ran out now, even both of their stun-batons wouldn't be enough to protect them. Not against four big men at close quarters.

Hylas swallowed, then came to a decision. "She's outside in the hallway." At Anna's surprised look he added, "I was going to call her in to help seal the deal, if it came to that."

"Call for her." Indy walked forward, still holding all four men immobile with her shield. "Then tell anyone with her that we're leaving, and are not to be molested." Indy bared her teeth at Hylas briefly. "After that, you may consider our business concluded. I would prefer never to catch sight of you again." The implicit threat hung in the air.

Hylas' face darkened with anger at this, but he schooled his expression to stillness after a few moments. He struggled momentarily. "Release us. I need to ring the bell to call them in."

"Very well. But mind yourselves, or I'll restrain you again." Indy released the force bonds from the four men. One of the guards staggered as he regained his balance, and another rubbed his wrists. Hylas walked back to his desk, lifted his bell, and rang it.

The old man who had first met them at the gate opened the door. "Bring in the new one," Hylas told him. The man disappeared briefly, then returned with Phaia in tow.

Phaia looked miserable when she saw Anna. "I was hoping you were smarter than this." She glanced fearfully at Hylas. "Now look what you've got yourself into." She sounded resigned.

"We're leaving," Anna said. "We bought you from Hylas."

Phaia stared, nonplussed.

"Hylas, tell her," Indy said. Phaia swung her head toward Indy, mouth opening slightly in surprise.

"Your friends have presented me with little choice," Hylas said. "I am afraid you will not be joining our family after all." He glowered, but said no more.

Phaia looked around, taking in Hylas' angry restraint, the pieces of a broken staff on the floor and the fearful looks on the faces of the three guards, who hung well back from Indy. She looked at Anna, and then at Indy. "What did you do?"

"Something that they may come to regret," Hylas said darkly. "Now leave us. Take them to the gates, and then return," he told the old man.

Anna thought about saying something, but thought better of it. She took Phaia's arm and walked out without a backward glance.

Indy followed, but turned at the door and faced the four men left behind. "Do not mistake our restraint for weakness, Hylas. Consider what our strength could do to a man's fragile body. Do not force our hand."

Hylas stayed silent, and kept still. But his eyes followed them until they were out of sight.

48

The old gatekeeper was as good as Hylas' word, escorting them out past the curious looks of the rest of the household, back across the wide courtyard again and through the gate. The short walk seemed to take an hour, and Anna's back expected an arrow at every step.

"I don't know what happened back there." The gatekeeper looked back at the house briefly before turning to the three of them. "But I've never seen the master so angry. I'd show my heels, if I were you." He turned and walked back toward the house as the three of them hurriedly set out along the road.

Anna realized that she was still holding Phaia's arm. She loosened her grip at the same time as urging her to walk faster. "I'll feel a lot better once we're out of sight of that place. I swear I can still feel Hylas' eyes on me." Phaia glanced nervously back at the windows of the house, and quickened her pace.

They walked quickly and in silence for a while, until the Peisistratid compound was hidden by trees and distance. Anna slowed, then stopped. She leaned forward and rested her hands on her knees, shaking and breathing quickly.

Indy turned back. "Anna, are you all right?"

"I'm fine." Anna worked her dry mouth and fought down the queasy feeling in her gut. Then she stood upright again. "I'm sorry for freezing up back there. I just couldn't seem to think."

"It's all right. I was ready to jump in." Indy nudged Anna's side with her flank. "I had a feeling it wasn't going to be an easy payoff."

"Sure." Anna started walking again, still a bit unsteady. "But I never thought he'd try to straight-up enslave the both of us."

"Just shows how naïve you are," Phaia said. "Not that I'm not grateful for you getting me out of there, however you managed it. But that Hylas is a frightening character. Talks like a gentleman, but he didn't blink an eye at buying me off Oresus to keep me from getting my freedom, then dragging me out to the middle of nowhere to try to make him some money." She turned her head and spat as she walked along. "He bragged about some of his plans. He was going to use your drug for political leverage. Sell it to allies, withhold it from enemies." She blew out a breath. "And he could never let me go, since I know the secret of how it's made. I got the feeling that once he knew everything I knew, I'd be dead in a ditch somewhere."

"And you!" Phaia suddenly turned to Indy. "When did you start talking?"

"I've always been able to speak," Indy said. "It's common where we come from. But here I usually stay silent, unless we're among friends."

Phaia looked skeptical at this, but then shrugged. "I guess if there's medicine that can cure walking dead men, there can be talking dogs with magic collars too. Not like I'm not hearing you with my own ears."

Indy's voice was wry. "People here have been far less surprised by it than I would have thought."

"You two aren't exactly masters of deception," Phaia said with a small smile. "Anna must've said 'we' instead of 'I' dozens of times in front of me by now."

"And I was trying to be careful, even." Anna colored with embarrassment. "I'm glad we can talk in front of you now." She twisted uncomfortably in her sweaty chiton. She badly wanted to remove the shield projector from her back and check herself for burns, but didn't want to explain it to Phaia, so she just kept walking and tried not to think about how much the hot metal stung her skin.

"So how *did* you get Hylas to sell me to you?" Phaia asked. "He offered triple my buyout price to Oresus, and that old bastard sold me out in a hot second." She looked angry and a little hurt. "I should have known he would. But after all the years I worked for him, I'd hoped for better."

"We paid Hylas well, and we'd planned to bribe him with more medical knowledge if we needed to," Indy said. "We were trying to play to his greed, but we hadn't planned for his kind of audacity."

"He said he was 'adding me to the household.'" Anna's outrage was beginning to crowd out the shock of their experience. "Like I didn't even have a choice!"

"So then we had to use threats to close the deal," Indy said. "I'm uneasy about it, though. Not because Hylas doesn't deserve it. But he looks like the type to hold a grudge."

"Too right." Phaia spoke with absolute certainty. "I don't know what you threatened him with, but you'd better hope it sticks."

"And the worst part was that he was kind of handsome." Revulsion curdled in Anna's stomach. "I can't believe I even thought that about someone who was going to try to enslave me."

"The good-looking ones are the worst." Phaia's face held no expression. "They think they're doing you a favor. Female slaves learn the hard way to avoid them."

And we came very close to getting captured back there, Indy added over their link. *My shield's at five percent, and yours will probably need to be reconditioned after running so hot.*

Anna felt sick at the thought of being in the power of a man like Hylas, and quickened her step again. She filled Phaia in on the events leading up to her rescue as they walked the rest of the long way back to Athens in the sticky heat, worrying and looking behind them for pursuit the whole way.

49

At last, the late afternoon saw them winding through the streets of Athens toward home. Phaia gratefully accepted Anna's and Indy's offer to stay with them for the time being. She had left what remained of her belongings back at Hylas', and since he had closed out the lease on her room in Athens, she had nowhere to stay and nothing to sleep on.

When they finally arrived, road-weary, at the courtyard of their modest rented house, they found Thrasius there waiting for them, dozing against the wall with his hat lying beside him. The older man got to his feet and embraced Anna, then patted Indy fondly on her furry shoulder.

"I'm so glad you all made it back safely." His face was drawn with worry. "After I talked to my brother today, I had no idea what to expect. What happened?"

"It's a long story. Come on inside and we'll tell you." Anna wiped the sweat from her forehead. "I've just got to drink some water first. We walked for six hours today, and I must've sweated out half my weight from terror." She nodded toward Phaia. "Oh, and we're out to Phaia now, so no need to pretend about Indy anymore." Thrasius raised his eyebrows at this, but said nothing for the moment.

They closed the courtyard doors behind them and settled in the kitchen after laying aside their belongings. Anna poured a bowl of water for Indy first, then dipped cups for herself, Phaia, and Thrasius. She drank hers off in one long draft, then got another one and drained it the same way.

Thirst slaked for the moment, Anna addressed Thrasius. "So, you talked to Oresus?" Thrasius nodded as he drank the last of his own water.

"I figure I know what he told you," Anna said. "But the short version is, Phaia went to him to buy her freedom. He refused, and sold her to this guy Hylas who's the younger head of some rich family up north."

"The Peisistratids, yes. They're very well known in Athens." Thrasius looked uncomfortable. "Two days ago, I would have told you that my brother would never refuse to let a slave buy her freedom. But now I don't know what to think."

"We'd even agreed on the price!" Phaia's face hardened. "He *knew* I was saving up for it, we'd talked about it for years. We weren't best friends or anything, but we had a deal."

"He told me that Phaia's value had gone up, so her price had to be renegotiated," Thrasius said. "I've never heard of such a thing, though. Usually, slaves get cheaper as they get older, not more expensive. No offense," he added when Phaia shot him a look.

"That part is our fault." Indy finally sat up from her water bowl, drops running down her muzzle into the white fur of her chest. "We taught Phaia how to make and refine a powerful new drug, to help her and her friends out of slavery. But it proved to be more valuable than we thought, and attracted attention." She licked her chops to clear the water from her whiskers. "Hylas found out about it, and made Oresus an offer he couldn't refuse."

"A big offer is no excuse," Anna said. "It's bad enough, enslaving people in the first place. Then you cheat them too?" Phaia nodded in agreement at this, but Thrasius just looked sad.

"I've spent some time at the bottom of the heap," he said, "so I'm inclined against slavery these days. I've been closer to it myself than most citizens have. Seen what it really means, you know?" He rubbed his beard thoughtfully with one hand. "But everything here is built around it. *Everything.* Slave labor's only a third the cost of free. How do you get people to give that up? If one person does, but everyone else still uses slaves, they've got you underpriced and you starve."

"Where we came from, long ago, governments had to ban slavery all at once, for just that reason," Indy said.

"It's hard to see that happening here," Thrasius said. "All our silver is mined by slaves. Go down south to Laureion sometime. The only free men you'll see there are the overseers. Athens owns the mines, and rents out the mining concession at a huge profit. And if it wasn't for that money, Athens would have no navy to speak of." He sighed. "If the council voted out slavery, the government's finances would collapse, and we'd be defenseless. The Persians would be knocking on our door in no time."

Thrasius wilted at the hostile looks from the rest of the room. "I'm not trying to say slavery's a good thing. But it's like a disease that gets into your bones. It's hard to get rid of." He sat back on his couch. "Leaving that aside though, how did you get Hylas to sell Phaia back to you? From what I've heard, he doesn't seem like the kind of person to give up something he's taken a liking to."

"You're right about that," Anna said. "We had to lean on him a little, as well as pay him off." Indy snorted at this.

"I'm surprised it worked, whatever you did," Thrasius said. "His family's in disgrace for supporting Persia, so they're not welcome here in the city. But they're still rich as Croesus, and any influence they've lost here, they've gained in Thebes. You should watch yourselves." He looked around. "In fact, it couldn't hurt to have more people here in this house with you."

"They seem very unaware of things like that, don't they?" Phaia said to Thrasius. "I don't know how they've survived this long. But I'll be staying here now, for what it's worth."

"I should stay here too, at least for a while," Thrasius said. "Assuming you'll have me, of course. And also," he added, "there were some words spoken between me and my brother when I found out you were gone and read between the lines. I may not be as welcome at the family home as I was yesterday." He looked down. "It's a shame. Things were going so well between us."

"Of course, you're welcome to stay with us for as long as you like," Indy said. "There's plenty of room." *And maybe he knows a good cook*, she said over the link to Anna. *We could use something new in our rotation.*

It's always about food with you, isn't it? Anna smiled mentally. Out loud she said, "We would love to have you, Thrasius. And I'm sorry that we're responsible for what happened between you and Oresus. I should've thought things through more carefully." She frowned. "Seems like I've been saying that a lot lately."

"Don't worry about Oresus," Thrasius said. "He's hot about this right now, but he's a good man at heart, he'll come around. He just needs some time to think about it without me there making him angry."

"Oh, and there was something I meant to ask you." Anna tilted her head in thought. "Hylas said that some 'influential friend' of his from out of town was looking for me and Indy. I thought maybe he was just trying to spook us into signing on with him. But does that mean anything to you?"

"There's only one thing it *can* mean." Thrasius' face fell. "Hylas and his family have many connections in Thebes, due to their shared sympathies with the Persians. And who do you know in Thebes who would have your description?"

"Nicon." Indy's growl emphasized her disgust.

"Back when we robbed together, we had to pay out a percentage to our boss." Thrasius looked pained. "In return for protection. But our *real* boss, all the way at the top, never came around in person, and low-grade thieves like us didn't even know his name. It was clear he had to be someone politically connected." He shook his head. "I wouldn't be surprised at all if Hylas knows him. Nicon must have talked, and gotten his bosses to believe him."

"Of course." Anna felt sick as the realization sank in. "It all fits together. When those thieves almost cornered us in that alley a while back, one of them said his boss had questions for us." She looked at Indy, chagrined. "We knew Nicon must have been behind them, but we thought they'd decided we weren't worth the trouble. But maybe they were just trying out their Athens connections first, before trying to grab us again."

"All the more reason for me to stay here too, then." Thrasius looked around at their house's sturdy walls. "I'll check over your gates and windows right now, to make sure everything's secure." He smiled grimly. "I never did break-ins, but I know what criminals look for."

"We'll give you any help you need." Anna rose. "And after that, we'll get you two settled in for the night. We're not quite set up for visitors yet, but we have a couple of cots downstairs that'll do for now." She stifled a yawn. "And then I'm hitting the sack. I don't think I've ever been this tired in my whole life."

50

ver the following weeks, their lives began to settle into a routine again. To reduce her value as a kidnapping target, Phaia spread the knowledge of their new drug among several friends and acquaintances in the apothecary business, mainly slaves but also a few resident foreigner metics, and Anna spent a good bit of time working with them and Phaia to help them make the most of it. Even though their engineered variety of penicillium spores was much easier to work with than the original, it still required care to get the greatest potency. And it took some creativity to explain the proper use of the drug to people who were still unfamiliar with the germ theory of disease.

They also did everything they could think of to step up their security. As in most Greek houses, their outside windows were too small and set too high up to admit intruders, and Thrasius pronounced their walls and inner doors to be sound. He did arrange for new metal hinges and fittings to be added to the courtyard doors, reinforcing the weakest spot on the house's perimeter. And with Anna's help, Indy placed tiny spy-drones up under the eaves facing down into their courtyard and out into the street, programmed to warn them if anyone suspicious lingered nearby or tried to scale the courtyard wall. But after a few weeks with no trace of their Theban ambushers and no sign of a response from Hylas, it seemed like their rescue of Phaia, as hasty and ill-considered as it might have been, was going to stick.

For his part, Thrasius had persuaded his brother to come to the city clerk's office and formally attest that Phaia was now freed. It turned out that Oresus had planned to do that anyway, so he could claim that Phaia had voluntarily indentured herself to Hylas, leaving his hands clean. But Oresus had stalked out of the clerk's office immediately afterward, and the two hadn't spoken since. After that, Thrasius had taken on an unofficial role as Anna and Indy's majordomo, working with their landlord to arrange repairs and upgrades to their home as they earned new income, and bringing in food from various sources he had around town. He'd also supervised the construction of a few new interior walls that gave their house enough bedrooms to accommodate all its occupants. But even with that and a few other odd jobs, Thrasius was somewhat at loose ends.

We just may not have enough work to keep Thrasius busy, Indy said over their link one night. It was quiet in their little house, but Indy was restless in the stifling heat of the summer evening. She had set up a blanket on the floor in the big upstairs room she shared with Anna, and now she sat up from its bunched fabric, trying to push it out smooth again with her paws. She lay back down again with a grunt.

I've been thinking the same thing, Anna said. *And he seems quieter since things went wrong with Oresus. I think he misses his brother.*

Well, his brother shouldn't have sold our friend and then tried to cover it up. Indy shifted around irritably before finally lying still. *What do* you *think we should do? I can tell that you feel partly responsible for this situation.*

I know you were suspicious of his change of heart, back in Lebadeia. Anna considered for a long moment. *And I was too, for a while. But he didn't have to come back and warn us about Nicon, and I feel like he's been a good friend to us since then. I'd like to do what we can to help him.* She shifted on her low bed, trying to find a cooler spot. *Assuming he even needs it. With his citizenship back in good standing, he might already have plans of his own.*

You're a nicer person than I am, that's for sure, Indy said. *But I can get behind that. I think Thrasius has earned my trust at this point. Though if we're going to keep a household this large, we'll need a bigger house.*

Give it a few more weeks. Anna smiled in the darkness. *If our income keeps picking up, maybe we can afford someplace with better ventilation.* She drifted off to sleep, and Indy followed soon after.

57

Deep in the night, Indy awoke with a start. She scented the air, then put a paw on Anna's shoulder to awaken her.

"Mmm. What?" Anna sat up and blinked in the warm darkness, then pulled out her phone to give a little light.

Indy sat with her nose held high, inhaling deeply. "I smell tar, close by. And I thought I heard something."

"Tar?" Anna asked. "That's weird. And I didn't hear anything."

Just then, there was a great *whoomp!* of displaced air from outside, and a crackling noise began to filter into their bedroom.

Indy stood up and began to bark, loudly and at even intervals. "Clothes on," she said between barks. "We need to get out of here!"

Anna quickly dressed and tied on her sandals, then cursed when she remembered her shield projector, which she shoved under her belt in the back. It wasn't as secure there, but it would take too long to get it properly situated under her chiton. She slipped Indy's harness on too, the shield projector already attached.

Moments later, they burst from their bedroom out into the second-floor main room. Anna could see flickering orange light coming in through the high front window, seemingly reflected off the white walls of the house across the street. Further up, smoke curled at the underside of their thatched roof, the thick material already hot enough to smolder. "It's on the roof!"

Indy flicked a glance upward without breaking stride. "Keep moving!"

The two of them ran to the door that opened onto the courtyard stairs. Anna grabbed the handle and yanked it open, then recoiled from what she saw. The roof across the courtyard was alight in half a dozen places, and smoke streamed up from somewhere below as well.

Indy stepped forward, but Anna held up a hand. "Wait! Shields up. That roof didn't catch fire by itself." She activated her shield with a thought, and Indy nodded in grim agreement as she did the same. "Let's go!"

They pounded down the stairs into their tiny courtyard. Bits of flaming thatch fell around them from the eaves as they ran to the thick courtyard doors, unbarred them, and pulled, Anna with her hands, Indy with her teeth.

The doors didn't budge.

They pulled again, frantically, with no better result.

"Son of a *bitch!* Look!" Indy jabbed her paw toward the bottom of the doors. Thin wooden shingles had been driven in beneath them, wedging them tightly in place against the stone lintel above.

"Someone's shimmed them closed from the outside." Indy backed up a step, cursing. "And Thrasius just reinforced them! If we pull that hard with our shields, the doors will smash us flat when they finally pop open." She looked at Anna. "They weren't meant to swing outward, but if we push together, maybe we can break them through." She faced the gates again. "Shields ready, push out on my count!"

"Wait!" Anna looked around the courtyard frantically. "Where *is* Thrasius? And Phaia!"

Just then, Phaia burst out through one of the downstairs bedroom doors, smoke billowing around her. She fell to her knees, coughing fiercely, hair hanging lower now where she'd started growing it out after gaining her freedom. Still fighting for breath, she pointed across the courtyard at Thrasius' bedroom door.

Anna ran to the door and pulled the handle sharply. The door jerked but didn't open. Thrasius must have barred it from the inside for the night.

Anna engaged her shield's strength and pulled again. This time the door handle came away in her hand, and she staggered back, off balance. She recovered with a snarl, then planted her feet and slammed both hands against the door with the full power of her shield behind them.

The door split vertically, one half crashing into the room, the other half falling twisted on one hinge. Dense smoke rolled out of the room from the floor up, which made no sense. How would a fire that started on the roof get downstairs so quickly?

Anna was forced to wait a few precious seconds for the smoke to lift, then she crawled inside, keeping her head in the clearer air near the floor. She saw the indistinct figure of Thrasius on his low cot, grabbed him by both feet with her shield-enhanced strength, and dragged him out the door, wincing when his head bumped along the ground as she pulled him out into the courtyard.

Phaia looked from Anna to the wreckage of the door, wide-eyed.

Anna froze. *Oops. I guess that secret's out now, too.* She gave Phaia a tight nod instead of an explanation, then ran back to Indy, who still stood by the courtyard doors.

"Push out on three!" Indy crouched low as Anna readied her shield again. "One! Two! *Three!*"

The courtyard doors crashed open, bursting through the surrounding masonry and sending chunks of stone and mortar tumbling out into the street. Two surprised figures ducked out of the way, one of them carrying a bucket of water.

"Bring them out!" Indy ran out into the street before them, facing this way and that, alert for any possible threat.

Anna turned back to Thrasius. Phaia had knelt to check the older man's breathing, but she stood up when she saw Anna, and they each took an arm to drag him out into the cooler air of the street.

Outside, it was chaos. The neighbors had come boiling out of their front doors, and a few stood gaping at the fire. The majority ran back and forth with tightly woven reed buckets, throwing water up onto their own roofs to try to prevent sparks from igniting them too, and burning the whole neighborhood down. Anna could hear the alarm cry echoing in the streets beyond their own.

Anna turned back to their house. The roof was ablaze from one side to the other. Smoke streamed from the high, small windows and curled out from under the eaves. Indy trotted over to join her, satisfied that there was no immediate threat.

Phaia had taken a knee beside Thrasius' unmoving form, but after a few seconds she looked up and shook her head. "Smoke inhalation." The former slave's face was grim, her voice still rough from coughing. "He was probably gone before you broke him out of his room."

Anna struggled with her churning emotions. She'd never seen anyone dead before, much less someone she knew. Could she have done something more to save him? And it just looked so wrong, the way he lay there in the dust. She reached down, thinking to arrange him in a more dignified way somehow.

"He's beyond our care now." Phaia gently caught Anna's hands as she rose to her feet. She nodded toward the fire, where the neighbors had begun to organize a bucket brigade to the well down the street. "And he'd want us to help the living."

Anna turned to Indy, torn. "Maybe you could… keep watch over him?"

Indy looked at her friend's face with concern. Then she silently moved to stand beside Thrasius' body, and Anna and Phaia went to help their neighbors fight to save their homes.

Two hours later, Anna stood on shaky legs as the first weak rays of dawn lit the sky. Her arms ached from the effort of passing water buckets, and she rubbed at a scrape on one forearm that she couldn't remember getting. Beside her, Phaia sank to the ground with a groan and lay exhausted.

The destruction was not as bad as it might have been. The night had been hot but windless, so the fire hadn't spread aggressively. Their right-side neighbor had been burned out, but he'd had time to rescue his family and most of his valuables. On their left side, the stout tile roof of their more affluent neighbor had spared them the worst of it, though the tiles nearest Anna and Indy's house had blackened in the flames.

Their own house was gutted. The thatch roof had burned down to the poles, which were charcoal where they still stood at all. The wooden ceiling of the first floor had burned and fallen in, leaving black stubs protruding from the inner walls. The walls themselves looked surprisingly intact, though the mud brick showed trails of black smoke above the windows.

The city guard had turned out to help fight the fire, but they'd left without asking any questions of Anna or Phaia, which Anna thought was very unusual. *Or maybe not so unusual,* she said to Indy. *Somebody's not surprised by what happened here.*

We'll see what the spy-drone footage shows, but this is probably the work of only two or three men, Indy said. *All you would need is a bundle of shims and a few balls of tarred cloth, nothing that would have triggered our alarm.* She sat on her haunches in the street, regarding their burned-out home clinically. *Two men cooperate to press the shims into place under the courtyard doors, using some sort of push-bar to avoid the noise of hammering them in. Another man throws tar balls onto the roof. Throw a torch up there and walk away, and the whole thing catches in a moment.* She rubbed at the soot on her white forehead with the crook of one paw. *That's what must have made the noise we heard.*

They must've thrown more of them through the vent window downstairs, Anna said. *Thrasius' room was on fire from the inside even before I got there.* She looked down, blinking dry eyes to try to clear them of grit and ash. *He never had a chance. Probably didn't even wake up.* She felt sick with guilt and rage. *I should've seen this coming. Hylas was never going to just let it go.*

Phaia looked at the two of them consideringly, but didn't comment on their long silence. There were still a few people about who might overhear. "What happens now?"

Anna dusted off Thrasius' scorched, floppy hat, which she'd recovered from a sheltered corner of his downstairs room. She placed it gently over his slack face, then turned to Phaia. "Do you have somewhere you can stay for a few hours?"

"I've got a couple of friends I think I can count on," Phaia spat from a parched mouth. "Though they might think twice if they find out what happened here. This wasn't an accident," she said flatly.

"We know," Anna said. Indy rose to stand beside her. "There's something we need to go and do. And when we get back, we'll need to get far away from here."

53

The long road out to Hylas' family compound seemed very different in the early morning light than it had in the afternoon a few weeks before. Anna and Indy stalked along, saying little, avoiding the eyes of the locals on their way to and from the morning market in Athens. All around them the dawn birds sang as the summer cicadas slept.

Anna was still wearing her soot-stained chiton from the night before, and she got a few curious or concerned looks from passers-by, but paid them no heed. Indy moved with a hunting gait completely different from her usual trot, her head level with her shoulders, smoothly tracing out a path that the rest of her body followed.

I was afraid Hylas might try something to get Phaia back, Indy said. *I hadn't anticipated this vicious sort of cleverness, though.* She glanced aside at Anna. *Hylas learned from our encounter. He noted our strengths, and chose an attack that could kill the strong just as easily as the weak.*

Thrasius is dead because of me, Anna said. *Me, always wanting to believe that everyone's basically a good person somehow, deep down.* She gave a wordless cry of rage. *I'm so stupid! I should have known we could never trust someone like Hylas.* Her gaze grew steely. *Now it's time for him to face the consequences of what he's done.*

We can still turn back. Indy gave her friend a measured look. *We could even leave this whole country, and take Phaia along with us. Are you sure you want to do this?*

We can't leave someone this dangerous behind us, Anna said. *And he won't expect us this quickly. If we take him by surprise, we can probably get clear before anyone else figures out what's happening.*

That smells like wishful thinking. Indy gave her a skeptical look. *We have to allow for the possibility of collateral damage. And there's a real chance we may not walk out of this in one piece ourselves.* She turned her gaze back to the road. *But I'm with you, regardless. Hylas needs to pay.* Indy's mental voice sounded sad. *I'm just sorry you had to learn like this.*

Anna pulled the phone from under her belt and checked the charging cable connecting it to her shield, which she'd once again concealed at her back, underneath her chiton. The phone's display told her that the shield would still take two more hours to reach full charge, though it would never be as strong as it had been before she overheated it. Another cable snaked from Indy's collar to the shield projector hidden under her pack. They'd only used their shields for a few moments last night, but even charging all night and into the morning, it was going to be close.

They kept moving.

It was still well before noon when they arrived at the Peisistratid family seat. Like last time, the gates stood wide open. But this time there wasn't a soul to be seen.

By silent agreement, Anna and Indy walked up to the walls on either side of the gates, staying out of the line of fire from the grounds inside. They looked at each other across the open entrance.

On three, Indy said silently. *One. Two.* Three!

They both surged through the open gate, eyes darting, shields at the ready.

Nothing happened. Anna stopped, nonplussed.

Perhaps they're planning to defend the house instead, Indy said. Her mental voice sounded uncertain.

Anna and Indy walked directly across the compound to the main house, looking around warily as they did. But there were no defenders anywhere. Anna drew up to the grand double doors and raised a shield-reinforced hand to batter them down. But then she noticed they stood slightly ajar.

She looked around again. Every other door she could see was likewise ajar.

I smell a trap, Indy said. *He's expecting us.* She almost sounded impressed. *There were no scent trails to any of the other buildings. He sent his people away and opened the doors to minimize the damage we'd cause.*

I don't see how he thinks he can trap us. Anna paused. *But at least this means no one else will get hurt. And we still need to keep alert.* She pushed the elaborately carved right-hand door inward cautiously, expecting an arrow to smash into her shield at any moment. The door opened with a faint creak.

Still nothing.

They walked down the wide front hallway, seeking out Hylas. The house seemed deserted, though the smell of food was every-where. Indy led the way, tracking the scent to its source.

Ahead, Anna could see an open archway painted to look like two trees intertwining, with a table and couches in the room beyond. She and Indy ran forward along the sides of the hallway, staying in cover as best they could. Then they burst through the archway together.

They arrived in the middle of an elegant lunch. Hylas reclined on a low couch, a half-eaten plate of food close by. As he saw them enter, he raised his shallow, two-handled wine cup to toast them mockingly, then took a sip.

To Hylas' left was a younger but strong-looking woman, dark hair tied back from her forehead with a leather band adorned with gold, coiled braids held in place with golden netting. And beside her were three young girls, the youngest perhaps six years of age, the oldest not far into her teens.

Anna and Indy stood silently as everyone in the room regarded them. The brightly patterned walls were lined with ornamental vases on gleaming marble pedestals. The liveried servants responsible for serving lunch had been stationed between the pedestals, but now they all filed out at once, leaving Anna and Indy staring at Hylas and his young family where they sat.

"I received word earlier this morning that my operation did not work out quite as I had hoped." Hylas spoke quietly, setting his cup aside. "So now, I await your response."

"What do you mean, our response?" Anna shouted. "You killed our friend!"

"Which was unfortunate," Hylas said. "I instructed the men to target only the two of you, and to take all reasonable care not to harm any others. But it seems that their first loyalty was to their organization in Thebes, who wished to make an example of him for some reason. I expect that as a result of this, my prior arrangement with Oresus is now at an end." Hylas' bearded face was calm as he spoke. "But when you issue threats of violence, you all but ensure that violence will be employed against you." He looked Anna in the eye. "If you are not prepared for the consequences of your actions, perhaps you should consider them more carefully."

"We're taking you back to Athens," Anna said. Indy's ears pricked up in surprise at this, but she stayed silent. "Thrasius' family are citizens. You can't just kill one of them and expect to get away with it." She looked down, ashamed. "Maybe it's an unfair system, where only citizens can get justice. But it'll still work well enough to get rid of *you*."

Hylas looked at her in disbelief for a long moment. Then he laughed, long and uproariously. And as he saw the outraged expression grow on Anna's face, his laugh grew even louder and more derisive.

"This is strangely disappointing," he finally said. "I had been steeling myself all morning to be torn apart by your eldritch strength if I misjudged the situation." He looked at Indy with an odd expression. "Your plan is to bring me before the Areopagus for murder? It is true, their authority is still supreme in capital cases, though their autonomy is less than it once was. But I think you will find that the majority of the council can see quite well which way the tide of history is flowing." He took another sip of his wine. "Precious few of them will want to make a ruling that could land them in trouble if certain events go in Persia's favor."

Can he really get away with this? Anna looked at Indy, uncertain. *I thought Athens was a democracy!*

We haven't exactly made a study of their justice system yet. Indy kept her eyes focused on Hylas, alert for treachery. *But it sounds all too plausible to me.*

"And finally," Hylas said, eyes aglitter, "a bit of further context. If I were to be convicted of murder, the punishment for that in Athens is exile. And to where would I be exiled?" he asked rhetorically. "To Asia Minor, where my father currently serves the Persian emperor, blessed be his name." He spread an arm, indicating his wife and children. "I would simply appoint a caretaker for this estate, as my father appointed me, then wait for our master's inevitable triumph before I return."

He stood, setting his cup aside. "So. Given that you have survived, I will reinstate my original offer. I wish you and your associates—" he glanced at Indy "—to join my household." He smiled and spread his hands. "And I think you will find my terms more than reasonable, given your lack of other options."

Anna roared and ran forward, right hand extended. Hylas flinched briefly, but then straightened and stood in place. Anna's hand slammed into his neck and pinned him to the stuccoed wall. Her shield hummed against her lower back as she lifted him until his toes barely touched the floor.

Hylas' wife gasped, but she made no move to interfere. His oldest daughter glared at Anna with hate in her eyes, but the youngest began to cry as her father's face swelled and reddened. Indy stalked closer and growled, and the little girl froze in fear. Tears tracked down her face.

Anna hesitated. Hylas croaked, but couldn't speak until Anna relaxed her grip slightly.

"Do not concern yourself with them." Hylas took a rasping breath. "They know that as the head of the family, it is my duty to risk everything I have to advance our house." He tried to clear his throat, but failed; Anna's hand was too tight. "Presumably, this means that my terms do not appeal. But before you make your decision final, consider this.

"If I die here today, who suffers?" He wheezed in another breath. "Whatever you may think of me, I support a family. A household of many dozens. Without me, what will become of them?" He worked his mouth to moisten it. His speech was not much above a whisper. "The slaves will be sold off haphazardly, their families sundered. My wife will swear vengeance upon you. Perhaps she will also die at your hands. And I'm sure you know what can happen to young girls such as mine." He took another pained breath. "With no family to protect them, they'll be fortunate not to end as slaves themselves."

Anna's face hardened. "This whole place is rotten with slaves anyway," she hissed. "And having a family can't protect you from justice." She glared at Hylas as Indy walked up to stand beside her. "You brought this on yourself, and on them too. Your men tried to roast us all alive in our beds! Just because we wouldn't let you enslave our friend." Tears of rage began to run down Anna's cheeks. "We were trying to help her!

"And Thrasius." Anna's voice rose. "You killed him. He never woke up, never even knew what happened to him. He never did anything to you!" She began to lift Hylas by the neck again, eyes slitted with hate. "You deserve to *die!*"

Hylas struggled as his toes lifted from the floor. His bearded lips worked without sound, hands clawing uselessly against Anna's shield, sandaled feet kicking the wall behind him. Hylas' wife took her youngest daughter in her arms and covered the girl's eyes. Her own eyes remained fixed on Anna, face rigid.

Hylas gurgled, and spittle began to run from the corner of his mouth.

Anna's enhanced strength held him as mercilessly as an iron

bar. For long moments, the room was silent except for the sound of a child sobbing.

Then Indy set one huge paw gently on Anna's shoulder. "This isn't how we do it."

Hylas' wife started back, composure broken as Indy's voice sounded from her collar.

Anna's tears flowed more freely now, but she still held Hylas fast.

"You taught me something, when we dealt with Nicon," Indy said. Hylas' daughters looked at her wonderingly now as she spoke. "I wasn't ready to hear it, then. But you were right." Indy moved closer. "*We can't kill our way to a better world.*"

Anna's face slowly tilted forward. Tears fell from her chin and pattered onto the floor.

Then she set Hylas back on his feet and released him. He sucked air back into his lungs and bent over, eyes dripping. She turned away, leaving him wheezing.

Anna turned to Indy. "You're right." She blew out a shaky breath. "This isn't who I am. Not who *we* are. We'll find another way." She turned away from Hylas to leave, Indy falling into step beside her.

"I'm a very good judge of character." Behind them, Hylas found words again, his voice was rough with abuse. "And you didn't disappoint me. The kind of person who'd give the breakthrough of the ages to a slave out of kindness isn't the kind of person with the strength to kill a man in front of his wife and daughters."

Indy froze and turned, teeth bared in a rictus. Anna gasped and reached out to hold her back, but Indy shrugged her aside.

"We underestimated you, Hylas." Indy stalked over to a row of museum-quality vases that held pride of place against a wall, her tail held high and rigid. "But we won't do it again. You may have all the trappings of wealth, but your father still holds the power." She deliberately swung her heavy tail, sending a fine example of black-figure pottery crashing to shards on the stone floor. "What would he do if everything he'd worked to build was reduced to ash while he was away in exile? Your house can burn as easily as ours did."

Hylas grimaced slightly, but stayed put. Indy took two deliberate steps to the next vase, this one showing warriors clashing with spears and shields on a red background. She swished her tail again, and the vase joined its neighbor in destruction.

"My condolences. Those looked very expensive, and in excellent taste." Indy looked at Hylas from under lowered lashes. "I'm guessing they were Daddy's?"

Hylas twitched, but didn't move. He glared hatefully at Indy, who took two more steps and stopped again.

"I really must apologize." She dropped her jaw in a mocking smile. "Sometimes this thing has a mind of its own." Indy lashed out with her tail again, demolishing a third vase. And this time she squatted and urinated on the broken pieces, looking Hylas directly in the eye as she did so. Then she turned and raked her hind paws through the wreckage, sending wet shards bouncing under the family's couches and rattling across the tile floor.

Indy shook out her coat, then rejoined Anna. "We can go now."

Anna shook her head, but couldn't suppress the barest hint of a smile. They turned and left together, Hylas seething but silent behind them.

54

Twenty minutes later, Anna and Indy had passed out of sight of Hylas' eerily empty compound, with no pursuit as far as they could see. Anna felt drained. Her clothes were grubby, her hair was a tangled, smoky mess, and every muscle ached after spending half the night fighting the fire back in Athens, and then half the morning walking. It felt like she'd been awake for days.

"I feel so stupid," Anna said. "I can't believe I thought we could drag Hylas back to Athens and have him thrown in jail." Sweat ran down the small of her back as they trudged in the midday sun. "But I was just so mad! And scared," she added. "He tried to kill us, and it almost worked. We had to do something."

Anna looked down as she walked. "Thank you for being there." She swallowed. "If you hadn't, I'd be a killer right now. Just like Hylas." She looked over at Indy. "I don't think that my father and mother and everyone else in the world died for that."

"I have a confession to make," Indy said. "I thought we were coming out here to kill Hylas." At Anna's shocked expression, she continued. "That's what I thought you meant by 'it's time for him to face the consequences.' Remember, I asked you if you were sure about this?"

"Whoa." Anna's walk slowed. "So you were ready to back me up to go and murder someone?"

"I couldn't very well let you do it alone," Indy said. "We're in this together, all the way. And right up until the end, I probably could've snapped his neck myself." She snorted wearily. "Using his own family as a shield? Every time that kind of person gets away with something like that, they just get worse." She looked back at Anna. "But seeing that expression on your face, when you were about to choke Hylas out? You shouldn't have to live with doing something like that."

They walked along in silence for a few moments.

"Plus, I figured it wasn't fair, you always having to be the bigger person," Indy said. "Especially since you're so much smaller than me," she added with a doggy grin. "It was about time for me to step up."

Anna stopped and held out her hand to Indy. "So. From now on, the right way?"

Indy stretched out her foreleg and set it pad-to-palm with her friend. "Damn right. Though I reserve the right to apply beatdowns where necessary and deserved."

Anna cocked an eyebrow at this. "What?" Indy said. "We can't *both* be pushovers."

Anna shoved Indy's shoulder playfully, and they continued the long walk back into Athens.

When they got back to the burned-out ruin of their house, they found that Phaia was still there and had taken charge in their absence. "I took a few liberties while you were gone," she said after they exchanged greetings. "I picked through the ashes as soon as they were cool enough, and recovered your money. It was melted into a solid mass, but I sold it to a silversmith at a tolerable discount in exchange for new coins." Phaia handed over a small bag, which Anna held awkwardly, since her own pack and Indy's saddlebags had been lost in the fire.

"My own money was under a tile in my room," Phaia said. "Slave habit, but saved it getting melted. Hylas' goons didn't find it at my old place, either." She patted her belt, satisfied. "We'll just need to make arrangements with the landlord for the damages. He's already come by, but I put him off for now. I guess that means my hair's finally grown out long enough to look respectable." She paused and looked at the wreckage. "And it's a good thing one of us was here to stand guard. Otherwise, we'd have been stripped bare by thieves before you two got back."

"Sorry about that." Anna looked chagrined. "I suppose we should tell you what happened with Hylas." Anna quickly filled in the story while Phaia listened, with Indy interjecting the odd detail since no one was nearby.

When they were finished, Phaia shook her head. "Sending everyone away, leaving all the doors cracked?" She tapped the side of her head with a finger. "Hylas had your number, all right."

Anna exhaled, looking rueful. "What kind of person would even think like that?"

"You two need to understand," Phaia said. "Power justifies itself. Your master not only *can* beat you, he thinks he's *right* to beat you."

Anna bridled at that, but Indy simply said, "You're right. Their believing it doesn't make it true, but it's an accurate description of the way things work here. We need to recognize it."

"Damn right I'm right," Phaia said. "Glad it's finally sinking in."

Anna suddenly realized what was missing from the scene. "What happened to Thrasius' body?"

"I had him delivered to Oresus' house." Phaia looked down. "Along with a few bits of his stuff that didn't get burned," she said. "I added a note, and I'm sure Oresus can read between the lines and figure out who did this. Still, I wouldn't mind getting some distance, in case he's looking for someone else to blame." She looked at Anna. "Didn't you say you were clearing out?"

"Yeah," Anna said. "Once they find out we survived, those Thebans will probably come looking for us again on their own, even with Thrasius gone and without Hylas' paycheck. And we couldn't sign another lease here anyway, not without a citizen to vouch for us. We've got more resources back in Lebadeia. And some folks who're on our side, though I wish we could warn them we're coming." Anna felt a surge of guilt at the possibility that their return might endanger Leitus, Helene, and the rest, but they literally had nowhere else to go. "You're welcome to come with us."

"Sounds good to me," Phaia said. "Now that I'm free, I can't wait to see the back side of this place. Athens just smells like slavery to me." She looked at Indy thoughtfully. "And I want to see how this whole situation plays out. I've got a feeling you two haven't told me the whole story yet."

Anna looked guiltily at Indy, then flushed when she saw Phaia notice.

"Give us a little more time, Phaia." Indy looked over at Anna, humor in the tilt of her head. "As you can tell, our strategy until now hasn't been as well considered as it might have been." Then more seriously, she said, "We can't promise anything, but we will do as right by you as we can."

"Good enough for me." Phaia jerked a thumb toward the street. "Let's get the hell out of here."

55

ithout Thrasius to guide them, the trip back to Lebadeia was very different. As before, they made the trip over two nights. But this time, Anna and Indy had to plan ahead to find their previous campsites, without letting Phaia see them consult the map on Anna's phone. As for Phaia, she walked along with a satisfied expression, swinging her arms and generally enjoying herself.

At least someone's happy. Indy slid a discreet glance toward Phaia.

I would be too, if I were her, Anna thought back. *Slaves in Athens probably don't get many hikes in the country.* She paused. *Gotta admit though. I'm feeling pretty low, myself. I really thought our plan was going to make a difference for people.* She looked aside at the passing trees. *Did it ever make sense? Or were we just fooling ourselves?*

It seemed like a good idea at the time. Indy shook out her fur briefly as she walked. *Ask me again after I've had a few good meals and some rest.*

The first night of the journey, they weren't nearly as comfortable as they had been the last time. They had bought some dry provisions on the way out of Athens, but Anna still felt strange in a new chiton she'd bought to replace her soot-stained one, and Indy keenly felt the loss of her fashionable saddlebags. They could've had the carrier-drone visit them and drop off a new set, but there would be no way to explain that to Phaia. So for the time being, they soldiered on in discomfort.

On their second day of traveling they swung wide to the south around Thebes again, mindful of the fact that Nicon still lived there somewhere. Though compared to their new enemy Hylas, he seemed distinctly less frightening now.

"Wouldn't it be better to go through Thebes?" Phaia was curious about their path. "I've never been, but I've heard it's worth a visit. Plus, a *free woman* could use a bit of refreshment." She dusted her clothes with her hands theatrically.

"Well, there's a little problem with this guy Nicon that we ran across," Anna began.

"Athena's sake, don't tell me you somehow made enemies in Thebes too?" Phaia was incredulous. "On your way to Athens? Just passing through?"

"No, this happened before we left Lebadeia." Anna fought down embarrassment as Phaia barked out a laugh. "Compared to Hylas, he's minor-league, but he's still plenty dangerous face-to-face. He was…" She stopped, sorrowful. "I guess it doesn't matter anymore if people know. He was Thrasius' old robbery partner a while back."

"I'd heard some rumors," Phaia said. "But Thrasius was already gone when I showed up."

"He got in with some bad people in Thebes, and his family disowned him." Anna swallowed a lump in her throat. "We met him when he and Nicon tried to rob us. We… well, Indy defended us, and we let them go. Thrasius turned his life around afterward, but Nicon got hurt pretty bad, and he came back later to kill us for it. Thrasius' warning probably saved both our lives. And our friends in Lebadeia too." She looked at the ground as they walked.

"It's not just Nicon we're avoiding in Thebes," Indy said. "There's also the criminal gang he's part of, who he must have set on us after we let him go. Three of them even tried to kidnap us back in Athens." She looked at Anna. "Hylas didn't say it in so many words, but I think he hired those same three to burn our house down. I guess since they couldn't grab us, they decided to skip straight to getting revenge for one of their own." She panted in the midday heat as she padded along. "Thrasius told us a long time ago that if his old bosses found out he was helping us, he'd be in deadly trouble. So from the gang's point of view, Hylas paid them to do two jobs they would've done for free."

"Don't worry about skipping Thebes, though." Anna brightened somewhat. "We've got a stop planned for some of the best grilled lamb you've ever tasted." At this, a string of saliva began to hang from Indy's muzzle, and Anna pointed with a smile. "That's how you know it's good."

"After walking this far, anything sounds good." Phaia cracked a rare smile. "And Indy's always hungry."

Anna looked ahead hopefully as they approached Haliartos again. She wasn't entirely sure that Doros would still be open for business. *Maybe the summer is too hot for travelers? He might not be able to make money if there aren't enough of them.*

The heat didn't seem to stop farm labor, at least. All around them, the almond harvest was ongoing, slaves knocking the ripened nuts down out of trees with long poles and collecting them in baskets to remove the husks for drying.

As the road finally began to run alongside Doros' fence, Anna heard a joyous bark in the distance. She looked around in surprise and saw Argos, Doros' great shaggy herding dog, running toward them at top speed. His sheep were left far behind him, contentedly spreading out to graze on their own.

When Argos got within fifty yards of the fence, he slowed, seeming to remember his composure, and approached at a slower trot. He walked up and sat behind the fence, tongue hanging in a pant, just as Anna, Indy, and Phaia walked past.

"Ha! Who's this, then?" Phaia sounded amused. "A boyfriend?"

If Indy had exposed skin, it would've colored pink. "Just someone we met on the way to Athens." But her actions belied her words. She walked up to the fence opposite Argos, tail waving, and poked her muzzle though to place it alongside his for a long moment. Argos stood, then spread his forelegs and dipped his head in a brief play-bow, eyes shining. Then they both backed up a step and trotted along on opposite sides of the fence, keeping pace with Anna and Phaia as they walked.

Phaia raised an eyebrow at Anna, who giggled, but stifled it when she saw Indy's ear flick back toward them. The two canines walked like that for the rest of the way to Doros' compound, Argos occasionally favoring Indy with an adoring look when he thought she wasn't looking.

Thankfully, Doros' grill was open for business. If anything, it was busier than it had been last time, with a line of sweaty travelers ahead of them awaiting their turn. Doros acknowledged them with an up-nod when he recognized them, but he worked through his line of customers in order, favoring each one with a greeting or a slap on the back before handing over their food and taking his payment.

Finally, they reached Doros' serving table. He laughed when he saw Argos in line with the three of them, but he didn't seem surprised. "Argos is a free man," Doros said at Anna's look, "and he does as he pleases. We've got a gentleman's agreement about him taking care of my sheep. But aside from that, anything goes!"

"I'd like two of the roasted vegetable, please," Anna said. "And two of the lamb with garlic sauce for this one," she said indicating Indy. "Turns out she likes garlic better than we thought." Doros laughed as he reached for his implements.

"Actually, make that four lamb and garlic," Anna said after Indy murmured to her over their link. "It looks like Argos is joining us for lunch." Doros laughed even harder at this, until Anna thought he'd turn red as a tomato.

Phaia had viewed the proceedings with skepticism, but after quizzing Doros quickly about his offerings, she decided on the pork with pureed artichoke sauce, which sounded delicious to Anna.

Doros quickly handed over their food. Indy was missing her saddlebags, and her collapsible bowl had burned up in the fire with everything else, but thankfully Doros had an extra serving platter they could use. Anna arranged four pitas on it and placed it on the ground for Indy and Argos, who walked up and began eating hungrily. Doros smiled fondly as he turned back to Anna.

"Any news of my friend Thrasius?" he asked. "I haven't seen him these last few months since I saw you together."

The guilt and sadness that Anna felt at those words must have showed on her face. "What happened? What have you heard?" Doros' voice was anxious.

Anna briefly told Doros a heavily edited version of the tale, including how responsible she felt for the outcome. Afterward, she fell silent.

"I didn't know Thrasius… before," Phaia said, having drawn closer during Anna's explanation. "But he seemed like a good man. He was ready to break with his own brother over a matter of honor. A promise made to a slave."

"Thrasius and I shared many confidences over the years that he passed back and forth along this road." Doros looked sorrowful. "I know he was a man who had seen more sides of life than most. I think that gave him more sympathy for those who were born without advantages, or who lost the ones they had." His voice roughened. "I'm glad he found his good side again."

Doros turned away for a moment to recover his composure. Then he opened a wooden chest that stood under his serving table and took out a small narrow amphora. "Hyrcanian, from Persia. Traders come through here on the way to Thebes. I don't much like their emperor, but their wine's something else." He poured wine into rough cups he had handy, diluting it with water from another small vessel.

He handed one cup to Anna, and placed another in front of a somberly sitting Indy. Argos sat beside her with eyes for no one else. A third cup went to Phaia, then he took the last for himself and raised it.

"To a man who took a twisted path, but found the right way before the end." Doros poured out a few drops on the ground before sipping from his cup. Anna and Phaia did likewise. Indy dipped a toenail into hers and flicked it on the ground before a mystified Argos. She then lapped a bit of it up, followed by Argos, who Indy gently nudged aside before he could drink it all straight down. Argos bore this rebuke peaceably, sitting back down beside Indy and licking his lips.

"To a man who changed from a robber to a friend." Anna raised her own cup for another sip. The others echoed her gesture, Argos this time needing no prompting to take only a single lap.

All eyes turned to Indy. She didn't say anything, she merely dipped her head in acknowledgement, then bent to lap up the last of the wine, joined heartily by Argos. Phaia, Anna, and Doros followed suit, draining their cups and setting them back on the serving table.

"I'm sorry this was the news I brought." Anna looked down. "I wish it could have been a happy story about Thrasius and his brother working together again. Instead of one being dead and the other probably holding us responsible."

"This moment comes for all of us." Doros' voice was regretful, but firm. "I hope that when the news of my death arrives, there are people there to remember me and drink to my name." He gripped Anna's shoulder. "We'll talk more about this another day, I hope. Right now, I can see more customers coming." He smiled sorrowfully. "And I know Thrasius wouldn't have wanted me to lose any money over him."

"We'll come this way again," Anna said. "We're just going back to Lebadeia, so we'll be close by."

"If you're not careful," Doros said, "you may have a companion all the way there." He winked and nodded toward Argos, who still sat side by side with Indy, his sturdy, shaggy frame a contrast with her elegant long limbs.

Anna laughed and waved goodbye as they set off again ahead of Doros' incoming customers. Argos walked along with Indy for several minutes, but eventually laid his muzzle beside hers again and turned to leave. Indy watched his retreating form for a long moment before rejoining Anna and Phaia. They walked along in silence for a few minutes, each lost in thought.

"I suppose he's growing on me," Indy said. "But I'll have to work on his table manners."

Anna and Phaia burst into laughter.

56

The travelers bypassed Lebadeia proper, eager to see Leitus and Helene again after months away, and hopeful that they'd still be welcome even when arriving unannounced, with trouble somewhere behind them. They wound past trees and over hills, until at last, as the sun was beginning to set, they saw Leitus and Helene's humble cottage appear above them on the mountain.

At least, it *had* been a humble cottage. Anna could see where a large new room had been added to the right side, presumably so Neleos and Iole could sleep in comfort while leaving the old couple in their accustomed back bedroom. The stone walls of the new room were freshly cut and brighter than the rest, but well-laid and of high quality.

Indy surveyed the new addition with approval. "It looks like Neleos is doing his duty well."

As they approached, Iole came around the side of the house. The young woman dropped her basket of chicken feed and ran out to greet the returnees.

Before she got within earshot, Indy said, "Shall we bring Iole and Neleos in on our little secret?"

Phaia smirked. "How much do you want to bet that Anna already tipped them off accidentally?"

Anna pulled a mocking face. "Ha ha, very funny." She looked at Indy. "I think we're done hiding. But let's give her a moment," she added. "We'll fill her in once we're inside."

Iole hugged Anna like a long-lost sister, gave Indy a fond pat on the head and rub on the jowls, then turned to Phaia. Anna could see a little of her old shyness re-emerge as she introduced herself. "Hello, mistress. My name's Iole."

"Don't bother with 'mistress.'" Phaia spoke gruffly, but not without humor. "I'm just Phaia. I met these two characters in Athens. Figured I'd come out and see the country life they keep talking about."

They shook hands warmly, then Iole turned and rushed to the cottage door, throwing it open. "Uncle! Auntie! They're back!"

Voices sounded from within the cottage, and in a few moments Iole's husband Neleos appeared in the doorway. He looked like marriage had settled him nicely, lending him a bit more gravitas than he'd had as Iole's illicit suitor. He greeted Anna and Indy with the seriousness appropriate to the master of the house. Then he spoiled it by grinning widely.

"I half-thought we'd never see you two again," Neleos said. "You're welcome to guest with us here, of course, and your friend too. For however long. We owe you more than we could ever repay."

Relief surged through Anna at this, but before she could reply, Leitus and Helene were there, rushing around Neleos to embrace Anna and rub Indy's shoulders. Indy barked happily and pranced about in delight.

"You two are looking great!" Anna said. And indeed, while still clearly elderly, the pair of them looked markedly sharper and healthier than the last time she'd seen them.

"All thanks to you." Leitus smiled and flexed one wiry arm. "I haven't felt this good since I don't know when. And my wife! Zeus only knows where she gets her energy from now. She spends all her time cracking the whip over the rest of us."

Helene laughed at this, but then her eyes fastened on Phaia. "Who have you brought to us, Anna? A new friend?"

Anna stepped forward. "Let me introduce Phaia, a friend and, um, business partner we met in Athens." Phaia rolled her eyes at "business partner," but kept silent. "Phaia, this is Helene and Leitus, who took care of us for many months when we first got here." She smiled mischievously. "Leitus taught Indy how to herd sheep."

"I'm afraid I must object." Neleos and Iole gaped as Indy spoke aloud in an affectedly formal tone. "We canines are *born* with the herding instinct. I'll grant that he helped me refine my skills, though," she allowed graciously.

At Iole's and Neleos' shocked expressions, Anna said, "Sorry guys, we knew we had to tell you at some point. But the right moment never seemed to come."

"Surprised you didn't already know," Phaia said. "They managed to keep their secret for about two whole days after they got to Athens."

"I blame Anna." Indy's mouth dropped open in a grin. "She just doesn't have the temperament for deception." Anna glared at her friend in mock betrayal, but didn't contest the statement. "We'll tell you the whole story in a moment," Indy continued. "Let us get a drink first, though. It's been a long walk from Haliartos."

"I'm so embarrassed!" Iole put a hand to her mouth as Indy spoke. "I can't believe I just rubbed your jowls when we met, like you were a pet. I'm so sorry!"

"No need to be," Indy said. "Everyone likes a good jowl rub. Though human jowls are an inconveniently high reach," she added.

"This is going to take some getting used to." Neleos still looked a little dazed, but he gamely gestured the three travelers to come in, and they settled in around the same old dining table, more crowded now for seven than it had been for five.

A wiry young black-and-brown dog trotted in through the open door. He saw Indy's huge black-and-white form and froze, then ran behind Leitus' legs to bark at the intruder.

"Easy, Brygos, easy!" Leitus laughed. "Indy's a friend. She used to have *your* job!"

"He's welcome to it," Indy said to general laughter. "Though we did have some great days up there on the mountain," she said wistfully. Iole and Neleos still goggled as she spoke, but seemed to be getting used to the idea of a talking dog.

"He's a fine little herder," Leitus said. "About forty pounds, so he's big enough to move a ram. Good eye, doesn't push too hard. I've been at loose ends a bit, since Neleos here showed up to take over all the hard work." He glanced fondly at his grand-nephew-in-law. "I finally had time to do some looking around. Bought this pup off some folks down past Lebadeia, since our neighbors never seemed to have one for us." Brygos had stopped barking, but still regarded Indy with mixed awe and terror from beside Leitus.

"He's been a great addition to the household," Neleos said. "He saves father Leitus plenty of walking, that's for sure." He rose and served out cups of water, hesitating before putting Indy's on the floor instead of the table. Then waited for everyone to refresh themselves before turning to Anna and Indy. "Tell us everything."

"Yes, everything!" Helene said. "I'm about to burst with curiosity!" Leitus laughed and looked at his wife fondly.

The story took a while. Indy started the tale, first explaining that her ability to speak was common where they came from, which had the benefit of being true. Then she briefly described the first part of their journey to Athens.

Anna took over the story at the point where they had decided to try to make the world a better place by giving away medical secrets to the slaves of Athens. Phaia snorted at their naïveté but didn't comment, other than to confirm that that's where she had come into the picture. And all four of their human hosts and one young herding dog were rapt as Anna told an edited version of Phaia's abduction and rescue, and the sad events that had happened afterward.

When the whole story was done, there was a long moment of silence around the table. "So leaving Athens was really our only option," Anna concluded. "The Thebans are still out there somewhere, and there's no telling what that maniac Hylas might do next, even after our warning. Something tells me he's not going to just forget about us."

"Too right," Phaia said. "The more miles between me and him, the safer I feel."

"Maybe the whole idea was naïve." Anna looked over at Indy. "You tried to tell me the risks, but I didn't listen." Her shoulders slumped. "I was so sure that I was doing the right thing. Helping people! But I was really just feeding my own ego."

"Nonsense!" Helene rose from her seat as she spoke, with a flexibility that wouldn't have been possible before Anna and Indy's healing treatment. "You and Indy saved my life." Her breath caught in her throat. "And it sounds like plenty of people in Athens can say the same, now. You can't blame yourself if someone answers your good deeds with evil ones. You can't let them snuff out your spark." Her voice crackled with emotion. "You should think even bigger!"

Leitus shot her a surprised look, but Helene persisted. "It's clear that you two are privy to knowledge and skills that the rest of us aren't. Right?" She looked Anna and Indy both in the eye. "So think about this: what do you do with knowledge?"

"Um," Anna said, looking around. "Is this some kind of philosophical riddle?"

When no answer was forthcoming after a moment, Helene continued. "When you have knowledge, you pass it on to others. You multiply it, so no one can stamp it out. What you need to do is start a school."

Anna was transfixed. "A school!" Her mind began to run through the possibilities.

"An intriguing idea," Indy said slowly. "Spreading some of our knowledge more widely *would* make us less of a target." She paused. "And doing it through students is more gradual than what we tried before. Perhaps it's less likely to cause trouble."

"There's even a precedent," Neleos said suddenly. "Remember the story of Asclepius?" The other Greeks nodded, but he went on when he saw Anna's questioning look. "He was one of the sons of Apollo. After his mother died, they gave him as a baby to the centaur Chiron, who taught him the arts of medicine. So it's not like no one's ever heard of learning from a talking animal."

Iole smacked Neleos' shoulder in wifely chagrin. "No offense meant, of course," he said to Indy with an apologetic gesture. "Everyone can see you're not just a dog."

"None taken," Indy said. "After all, humans are essentially hairless monkeys, and I learned most of what I know from them," she said to Leitus' bray of laughter. "It's only polite for me to help return the favor." Neleos raised his water cup to Indy with a smile.

"I can help too," Phaia said. "I know plenty of other freedmen and slaves in Athens, and most of them have useful skills like smithing or glassmaking. I suspect these two could teach them something new. Then we'd have more hands to help teach more students."

"Adjunct faculty!" Indy said with a laugh. "Sorry, a joke from our homeland," she said at Phaia's puzzled look. "I agree, it's a very good idea. Truly," she added before Phaia's frown could deepen. "It will be very helpful."

Mollified, Phaia continued. "I've seen how it's done in Athens at schools of medicine. You have a few senior instructors who own shares of the business. Then you have the juniors who get paid a wage to teach the basics, and maybe move up to senior one day."

"There are similar arrangements where we come from," Indy said. "And I think that any Greek adjunct faculty will have things to teach us as well."

Leitus cleared his throat. "I might even have a thought about where you could put a school."

Helene looked up with interest. "Are you thinking what I think you're thinking?"

"Probably?" Leitus spoke with the smile of a man whose wife knows all his thoughts before he does.

"The neighbors," Helene said. "They've been irritating us for years. Never anything serious, so we don't have any real ill will toward them. Despite the fact that they never would sell Leitus a puppy," she added with a smile. "But over the last dozen years or so, they've been overgrazing—"

"Out of sheer foolishness, as far as I can tell," Leitus broke in. "Just trying to make more money. But now their returns are way down. I've heard talk around town that they're thinking of upping sticks back to Thessaly and moving in with their children."

"So, to avoid a long story," continued Helene, "they may be looking to sell. In case you have another box full of money lying around," she said wryly.

"Box full of money?" Phaia perked up. "Now you're speaking my language."

Helene laughed. "Many people speak that language. You may not know, but Anna and Indy helped out with Iole's dowry. Made her this great match here," she said, patting Neleos' meaty shoulder fondly with a thin hand. Neleos rolled his eyes in embarrassment.

"Sounds like I latched onto the right two people." Phaia eyed Anna and Indy shrewdly. "You might want to let me come along and help you get a good deal on that land, though."

"My father Timais could be helpful too," Neleos said. "He's a merchant, and our family is well informed about the value of the land around here." He smiled at Anna and Indy. "Hopefully, between all of us, we can ensure that Anna doesn't get taken advantage of."

Anna reddened as the others around the table laughed. But Indy spoke seriously. "Go easy on my little sister here. She has a pure heart, and that's worth more than gold."

"Thanks, Indy. That means a lot to me. Really." Anna leaned over and hugged her friend close, then released her and sat back up. "It's been a lot harder to do the right thing here than I ever thought it would be." Regret tugged at her features. "And I've made some pretty big mistakes."

"That may be," Phaia said. "And I know I can be sharp sometimes. But I know a good person when I see her." There was a murmur of assent from the others.

Neleos' stomach broke the silence with a growl, and everyone laughed. "Sorry," Iole said, "It's after dinner time, and we were so wrapped up in your story I haven't even started cooking!"

"Just tell me how I can help," Phaia said.

"Me too," Anna said. "Suddenly I'm starving!"

57

It turned out that starting a school was much easier said than done.

The first step was to buy land to build it on. But as they should've guessed from their experience renting a house in Athens, non-citizens like Anna weren't allowed to own land, not to mention non-humans like Indy.

Here, Timais' legal advice proved invaluable. The first difficulty was that Anna needed a citizen sponsor. Leitus leapt to volunteer, even after Timais cautioned him that he could be making himself liable for anything that might go wrong in the future. "It's the least I can do after all Anna and Indy have done for us," he insisted. "Besides, with Neleos managing more of the household these days, I could do with something to keep me busy."

After Leitus' sponsorship was approved and recorded, Anna became an officially registered immigrant. This allowed her to legally gift a large sum of money to Leitus, which he used to purchase the distressed land from his neighbor. The land came to nearly a hundred acres, but much of it was mountainous, and all of it had been poorly managed. Parts of it were seriously eroded, and it was obviously unfit for sheep or even goats, at least not anytime soon. The owners closed the deal with unseemly haste, obviously wanting to sell before Leitus realized he was making a mistake. All it took was a handshake and a witnessed oath down in Lebadeia, and the deal was done. Then Leitus simply rented the property to Anna. She tried to make the fee a generous one to compensate him for the trouble and risk, but Leitus and Helene refused to accept more than a nominal payment, and finally she acquiesced.

At the end of the process, Leitus and Helene were now Anna and Indy's landlords, and all it had cost them was a box of silver holding twice as much as what they'd given away for Iole's dowry. Fortunately, their mining-drones had dug deep while they were in Athens, sifting out tiny bits of silver and other easily transmutable metals and replacing the rock behind them as they traced narrow deposits down into the earth. They were flush with cash again, at least for the moment.

Building the school itself was another challenge. They still couldn't make proper power supplies, so even if they'd had a fab big enough, they couldn't create any large-scale construction equipment. Which was just as well, since there was no way to keep such equipment concealed during use. And even smaller tools like rock molders or joiners would certainly be found out, since they couldn't very well build the whole school by themselves in secret.

So they took their small stock of gold, painstakingly scraped together by their mining-drones over the whole ten months or so that they'd been in ancient Greece, and went to talk to Timais again. It turned out that he was more than willing to act as lead contractor for them, hiring laborers and stonemasons to come and camp out on their land for the months it would take to build a modest but attractive school from the local limestone.

Meanwhile, Phaia had gone warily back to Athens to find them some suitable assistant instructors, careful to keep a low profile even though her lengthening hair no longer marked her as someone else's property. In late September, as the grape harvest wound down and construction of their school neared completion, she returned to their construction site one afternoon with a pair of Greek candidates in tow.

"This is Themis, who I think you've already met." Phaia gestured to the first of her companions, a slender woman with intense, dark eyes. "She was my across-the-hall neighbor in Athens, and the best freaking designer and metalworker I've ever known." Themis tilted her head in ironic acknowledgement. "And this—"

"Wait!" Anna looked at the second of Phaia's companions, a huge square of a man in early middle age, burn-scars stippling his knuckles and forearms. "Don't we know you from somewhere?"

"You do indeed, young lady." The man smiled, inclining his head toward her and Indy. "Though we were never formally introduced, due to the brevity of our meeting. My name is Melas."

The smith who let us escape the Thebans by going through his shop, Indy said.

I knew I recognized him! "I'm Anna," she said out loud, offering her hand. "And I'm sorry. We didn't mean to bring trouble to your door."

Melas made a dismissive gesture. "My nephew and I saw them off with just a hard look, once you had slipped away." He smiled. "I am glad they did not find you again after that. They had a persistent look about them, somehow. I was surprised to hear from Themis that her friend Phaia was looking for instructors to work out here in the country, and was even more surprised to recognize your description from her."

"I've known the big guy here professionally for donkey's years," Themis said, her words tumbling out in a rapid-fire cadence. "I worked for him back in the day, before I struck out on my own. I figured this would be right up his street."

"I have always wanted to teach, and to learn." Melas' demeanor was surprisingly calm and intellectual, incongruous against his imposing physique. "Phaia has withheld some details of the situation, pending this meeting, but it seemed like an intriguing opportunity. There is always plenty of paying work to be done, but after a while, a man can't help but wish for something more." As he talked, he effortlessly lifted a fifty-pound limestone block from a stack waiting to be laid, muscles rippling in his thick arms as he turned the block this way and that to inspect the chisel marks. "My nephew has been a journeyman for some time now. If the position here proves compelling, I may elevate him to master sooner than he was expecting."

"Knowing the big guy here, he's got a ton of deep questions he's about to hit you with," Themis said. "So let me go first." Her eyes shifted from Anna to Indy as she spoke. "I only need to see one thing to make up my mind."

Quick as a snake, Themis' arm darted out and took hold of one of the spring clips attaching Indy's mini-pack to her harness. "Mind if I check out the hardware?" She bent and examined the clip minutely before Anna could reply, running a thumb over its curvature, tapping first with a fingernail, then a knuckle to test its stiffness, clipping and unclipping it a few times quickly as Indy stood still, nonplussed.

"You called it, P." Themis straightened back up as she spoke to Phaia. "Whoever made this, I want to know what they know." She gave Anna an up-nod. "Count me in, chief."

"I'm not sure what you mean." Anna put on her best fake-serious expression. "It's just a dog harness."

"Please." Themis made a rude noise. "If you'd said it was hand-crafted by the smith-god's buxom golden fembots, that would've been more believable."

"Golden… fembots?" Anna awkwardly echoed her translator's rendering of Themis' slangy speech.

"The smith-god Hephaestus is said to have created golden automatons in the form of young maidens to assist him in his work," Melas said. "I have always liked that story. Though the creation of thinking beings would be morally problematic."

"Don't get him started," Themis said. "These buckles, though!" She jerked her chin toward Indy's harness. "I've seen steel from India of this quality, but nobody can hammer out a sheet of steel this thin and smooth. And then cut it, fold it up into a buckle, temper it to give it back its spring, solder the cut edges together, sand it down, and somehow give it a matte black finish that isn't paint." She snorted. "All that to make dog harness buckles? Put me down as doubtful." She gave Anna a direct look. "So I'm in," she repeated, "as long as you teach me how to do this."

I think this one is going to work out well, Indy said.

"Okay, so here's the deal," Anna said out loud to Themis and Melas. "We came here from a place far away to the west."

You said 'we' again, Indy said.

"*Our* homeland," Anna continued, "knows some things about metals, medicines, and other stuff that might be helpful here. We'll teach it to you, and pay you to help teach other people. There's one small twist, though."

"You are smiling," Melas said, "but in my experience, a 'twist' is seldom the good part of the deal." Themis nodded agreement, eyeing Anna speculatively.

"The twist," Anna said, "is that you haven't met our most senior faculty member yet."

You're sure about this? Indy said. *Once we let this cat all the way out of the bag, it'll never go back in.*

You've already had to stay quiet for way too long, Anna said. *Plus, I'm not scary enough to be headmaster of a school!*

Good point. Though now that it's finally time to do this, I'm the one who's scared.

Indy planted all four feet and fixed her gaze on Melas and Themis with human directness before speaking aloud. "Welcome, new instructors!"

Then she paused, since Themis had frozen with her mouth open in surprise. The more phlegmatic Melas looked to Phaia, who gave him a short nod to indicate that this was really happening. Then he returned his gaze to Indy, seemingly unperturbed.

"Here's our offer," Indy said. "We will teach you how to make a variety of useful and valuable products, along with whatever supporting knowledge turns out to be necessary. In turn, you will teach those same things to our students, and help us refine our curriculum. You'll get paid in silver once every two weeks, plus free food and housing. Any questions?"

Melas raised his hand and spoke mildly. "How is it that you can talk, Indy? Or should I call you 'mistress Indy'?"

"Call me whatever makes sense here," Indy said. "Back home, people with my degree could choose to be called 'doctor,' but we usually didn't bother."

As Indy talked, Themis had crept forward and was now holding her ear to one side of Indy's collar and then the other, trying to figure out where the sound came out, and tapping it to try to determine its composition. At a long-suffering look from Indy, she reluctantly stepped back to a normal distance, though she kept moving around to view the collar from as many different angles as she could.

"And as for my ability to talk," Indy said, "one of your fellow Greeks told us recently that a centaur named Chiron taught the medical arts to a doctor named Asclepius. And a centaur is just a talking horse, more or less. So I don't see why this is so unusual."

"Well, yes," Melas said, "but that is a tale out of legend, and this is real life. I have never seen a talking horse *or* a talking dog." Beside him, Themis nodded vigorously. "Though Hesiod did speak of a race of dog-headed men who lived in far Libue. And I have heard it said that Asclepius' statue in Epidaurus includes a dog lying by his side," Melas added. "But that is symbolic of the reputed curative power of dog saliva, rather than a teaching relationship."

"I've never tried using it on a human." Indy barked out a laugh. "It probably couldn't hurt, though." She raised an eyebrow. "My boyfriends always seemed to enjoy it."

"First of all, ew." Anna made a face. "And second of all, let me try explaining this. We can't tell you guys the whole story now, because… of some reasons. But I promise everything I say will be true."

"Go on…" Themis made a drawing-out motion with her hands.

"Yes, go on." Phaia smirked as she leaned back against the stack of limestone blocks that Melas had been inspecting earlier. "I've been waiting to hear more about this myself."

"Okay." Anna took a breath. "So I already mentioned how we're from a distant land. It's far off to the west of here, and a little way to the south."

"Our girl P told me it's Iberia," Themis said to Melas in a stage whisper.

"That seems unlikely," Melas said. "The Iberians are barely more than herdsmen." He looked at Anna keenly. "Though she does bear some resemblance to them in the facial features, at least."

"Not important right now," Anna said. "So. Where we're from, a long time ago, we found out how to make animals intelligent. Well, they were already intelligent, I guess. But we figured out how to make them even smarter." She paused, squirming as she considered what to say. "Some mistakes got made. But eventually, they became full citizens, with the same rights as everyone else."

"Sounds like there's more to that tale," Phaia said.

"Of course there is," Indy broke in. "But it's our story, and we'll tell the rest of it when we think it's time." She softened her tone. "Plus, she'll never finish if you keep interrupting her. Anna, please continue."

"Thanks, Indy." Anna considered for a moment. "Anyway, long story short is that we changed them, the dogs I mean, in our own image. And when we did that, it made us responsible for them, though people didn't think it all the way through. At least not at first." She paced, trying to think of a good analogy. "It's like when you have a child. You created them, so you have to do everything you can to care for them. But animals aren't children, they're already adults in their own way, so they have to have some choice in what happens to them. They have to consent." She stopped and looked at Indy. "Okay, maybe this is harder to explain than I thought."

Indy stepped forward and continued the story. "My earliest ancestors had no say in what happened to them. And after a time, they were at an uncomfortable middle ground, between canine intelligence and human intelligence. And once a being is sufficiently intelligent and self-aware, as Anna said, they must consent to what is done to them. Or the one doing it becomes a monster." She curled her lip in a snarl without seeming to realize it.

"There were more than a few monsters. But eventually, decency prevailed." She sat and faced Phaia, Melas, and Themis. "Those of my ancestors who chose for themselves to continue, were raised up until they became like me. The rest chose to return to their original state of nature, over the generations."

Indy brushed her collar with a thick claw, making the metal ring. Themis raised a hand unconsciously as though to tap the material herself, but held back with a visible effort.

"Even with our arts, there's only so much you can change a dog before she is no longer a dog," Indy said. "So they left us as close as they could to our original selves. That's why I speak through a collar and not through my mouth. Our jaws and lips could never produce human speech, not without disfiguring us into freaks." She raised a paw and flexed its independent pads, showing off their dexterity. "Many things *can* be changed, though." She stood up on her long hind legs, balancing effortlessly upright with her head nearly six feet above the ground and front legs spread wide, before settling smoothly back onto her haunches.

"So, in our land, there are those like me." She considered a moment. "We're relatively few in number, but we live close together, so in the cities we're not uncommon. We go to school, and live and work just like anyone else does. Back home, I was training to become a researcher and teacher, but my training was cut short when we came here."

Anna laid her hand on Indy's shoulder. "My father was a great teacher, and Indy was his best student." Anna's throat closed up with emotion, and she had to pause before continuing. "That makes her the closest thing to a big sister I have." Indy laid her muzzle along Anna's arm and pouched her whiskers in a smile.

Themis opened her mouth to ask what looked to be the first of a million questions, but Melas spoke first. "Thank you for sharing part of your story with us." His mouth bent in a half-smile. "You must realize that your words raise many questions in my mind."

"Mine t—" Themis began, before Melas cut her off. "Of course, we both would like to know more." Melas regarded Anna and Indy with sympathy. "But as they said, their story is theirs to tell. We are here, and we have work that we love waiting for us. The rest can wait for another day, surely."

"By the goat-god's hairy hindquarters, Melas." Themis rolled her eyes. "Has anyone ever told you there's such a thing as being *too* patient?"

"Indeed they have," he agreed calmly. "You prominent among them." He smiled. "But this is an agreement between free people. Free *beings*," he amended, looking at Indy. "They have offered us terms of employment, and we decide if we wish to accept. I *do* accept, by the way," he added. "And don't worry, Themis. I'm sure we will get more out of them in due course."

"I'm already signed up," Themis said with a snap. "That doesn't mean I'm as incurious as a stone."

Melas smiled at her kindly, which made Themis grit her teeth. Then she gave it up and turned back to Anna and Indy. "So, about that free housing," she said. "Where do I sling my gear?" She jerked a thumb toward Melas. "And because I know he's gonna ask, where can a free being get a beer around here?"

58

later that evening, not far away but safely underground in their hidden lab, Indy stood up from her workstation and heaved a sigh. "I still have no idea how we're going to make this work."

Anna looked up from her own screen. "How we're going to make what work?" She was busy programming their mining-drones to dig a tunnel that would eventually connect their underground lair to the school, so they could come and go without fear of discovery. Ready for a break herself, she stood up and joined Indy as her friend paced out into the hallway. It and the growing cluster of rooms beyond their original cave were new, excavated by their industrious mining drones during their time in Athens.

"Our curriculum, what else?" Indy walked down the long hallway toward the recently finished kitchen. "Our school will be done in another few weeks, and we still don't know exactly what we're going to teach our new teachers." She sighed. "They're both already on the payroll, since we wanted them out there finding students for us. But who's going to sign up for a school without knowing what the classes are about?" She snorted in amusement. "Though Melas is having a grand old time wandering around Lebadeia and Haliartos, sampling the local cuisine and complaining how they don't make good beer in this part of Greece. And Themis is driving all our stonemasons crazy, asking questions and making suggestions about every little detail of the construction."

"Why not just teach them whatever they would've found out next in our original history?" Anna flashed a self-deprecating smile. "I'm not a math genius like you, but I'm pretty solid up through calculus, which has gotta be like magic compared to ancient geometry! We print up a few books and we're done, right?"

"Hold that thought." Indy turned into the kitchen and ordered a drink via her collar. Its lights flashed, their new kitchen fab buzzed to life, and a few moments later its bell chimed. Indy reached up with one paw and popped the door release, then retrieved a small bowl of chilled orange drink from inside, balancing herself delicately upright. She placed the bowl on the low kitchen table and sat on the floor beside it, lapping noisily.

After a moment she leaned back and smacked her lips. "Ah! It's so nice to drink something other than water or wine. And to finally have a real kitchen fab, so our food's at the right temperature! I can't wait until our tunnel to the school is done, so we can sneak back here every night and live in modern quarters." She took a breath. "But back to your question."

Indy rose and walked back and forth as she talked, tail low and steady. "The problem with just taking Greece through our technological evolution all over again is that it almost destroyed the planet when *we* did it. Imagine if we teach Melas a new method of smelting iron ore, say. There aren't enough trees in all of Greece to make enough charcoal to do something like that on a large scale. And once we release that knowledge into the world, people are going to use it. It will spread."

"But we *want* it to spread," Anna said. "We're trying to make the world better, remember?"

"True," Indy said. "But most of the next things we invented in our timeline would end up throwing them into an accelerated version of the Industrial Revolution of the 1800s. Think about all the social change! What happens when all these subsistence farmers race forward through two thousand years of progress, with us guiding them around all the dead ends?"

"Okay, I see what you're saying." Anna leaned back against the counter, musing. "We want to get them up to our modern world, where things are nice again, but without them plowing through all the horrible mistakes we made the first time."

"Exactly!" Indy walked back to the table and took another lap of her drink. Anna sat down at the table across from her.

"Ooo! I've got an idea!" Anna sat up straighter, then paused. "No, wait, it wouldn't work." She slumped back down in her chair.

"What was the idea?" Indy asked. "At this point, I'll consider anything."

"Well, I remember back in school—" Anna stopped and swallowed. Thinking back to that time still brought up painful memories, though they were much less sharp than they used to be. "Back in school, we learned about the cleanups they started in 2100 or whenever, after people finally stopped being so crazy. And I remember they used some kind of special plants." She stood up and walked around to help the memory come back more freely. "They made these plants that they could grow on the tops of old landfills and factories and things, and the roots would dig down into the ground—"

"That's brilliant!" Indy said.

"It is?" Anna sounded skeptical. "I figured it wouldn't work, because we don't have huge amounts of tech garbage here to dig into. Back then, they had tons of stuff buried *everywhere*."

"No, it's perfect!" Indy leapt back to her paws to join Anna. "Those plants didn't *need* such a rich source of material. But back then, they were trying to do environmental remediation, so that's what they used them for." She looked at Anna, eyes flashing. "In our case, we could just as easily engineer plants to mine ore out of the ground with their roots, or create designer drugs, or do whatever else we want." Her tail rose and waved faster, the white tassel at the end flipping. "We can't give the Greeks fabs yet, because they could destroy the whole world with that kind of power. And we can't evolve them along our technological path, because we barely survived it ourselves. But special-purpose plants solve many problems at once!"

The big hybrid sat back down, trying to control her excitement. "Plants can be grown from seeds, and they make new seeds on their own. So we can spread technological abilities, but without spreading something as dangerous and obviously unnatural as a fab. And plants are naturally limited to using only as much energy as falls on them from the sun, so they can't be used to develop an economy that requires more energy than they can get renewably." She frowned. "Though you could still over-cultivate and destroy the natural environment that way. So I guess it's not totally foolproof."

Anna tapped at her phone. "Our catalog says we've got the plans for hundreds of kinds of bioengineered plants here. We might not have to do much work ourselves, even."

"I just never thought to look for them," Indy said. "The credit goes to your father, of course. I still wish he'd known to send us more historical data about this time period. But he did an unbelievable job of pulling together all the data we need to essentially re-start our whole technological infrastructure. If it weren't for him, we'd have been dumped straight into the Iron Age to fend for ourselves." She fell silent, looking at Anna sorrowfully.

"No, it's okay," Anna said. "I've had a lot of time to think about it over the last year. I can appreciate what he did for us now, without getting so caught up thinking about the past." She waved around at their new kitchen, extending the gesture to include everything else they'd built over the past twelve months. "Kind of ironic that the whole reason I'm here is because I'd decided I didn't want to follow in my dad's footsteps anymore. But now here we are, starting a school and trying to do research for the whole world at once."

"Well, I think your idea deserves a celebration dinner!" Indy said. "And you're right. I'd totally forgotten we've been here almost exactly a year now, so it's an anniversary dinner too." Her face grew serious again. "You ready for our ceremonial quarterly landing-site check?"

Anna's smile was bittersweet. "Sure." She pulled up an image on her phone from the spy-drone they had permanently stationed near where they'd first appeared in ancient Greece, one year ago now. "Status, still negative." She turned the phone around so Indy could see.

"Agreed," Indy said. "Maybe someday, though." She finished the last bit of her orange drink, tongue licking the bowl dry.

"Back when we first got here, I must have checked that spot every day for months, even though I know our drones would've told us if anything changed." Anna replaced her phone on the table. "And every time I checked, I'd get a knot in my stomach, hoping this would be the time I'd see my dad stepping through a portal, here to save us." She made a rueful little laugh. "Now it's more like a compulsive habit. Like checking my alarm to make sure it's set before I go to sleep."

"But back to our celebration dinner!" Indy pushed back her empty drink bowl, eyes twinkling. "I already told Helene that we wouldn't be coming home again this evening. The poor woman thinks we're spending our nights out in the open, keeping watch on our construction site." She dropped her jaw in a doggy smile, and Anna grinned back.

Indy's collar lights winked blue as she programmed the kitchen fab with their old favorites. Mini-cheeseburgers for her, this time with a dollop of chili on each one, and crunchy tacos Tex-Mex style for Anna, complete with the traditional bright-yellow cheddar cheese grated on top. Indy completed the menu with a celebratory margarita for Anna, and a dark beer for herself.

"I got the idea from hearing Melas drone on about his Greek beer," Indy said, indicating her bowl. "I never drank beer back in Texas, but I get a lot more exercise here, so I can afford it."

She stood. "Here's to keeping the old world alive in our hearts, and making the best of the new." She took a lap from her bowl.

"To the old and the new," Anna agreed. She raised her margarita glass and sipped, then made a face.

"Oof! Okay, that's way too strong. These hit a lot harder than watered wine." Anna took a bite of a taco to banish the tequila flavor from her mouth. "I'm so glad to finally be back on clean food from the fab, though. I was not loving life as a vegetarian." She put her margarita back in the fab, quickly programming it to halve the alcohol content.

"Gotta admit, I'm getting used to living here." Anna finished her first taco, then removed the remade margarita from the fab at the *ding!* She took a tentative sip. "Ah, much better." She set the glass down. "It still feels weird drinking these on my own. My parents only ever let me try a taste here and there before college." She picked up another taco and paused to recover her train of thought. "Oh yeah, living here. At first it seemed so strange, but now it feels like someone else's life when I look back at my old videos and pictures. Like this life is starting to be the real one."

"I know just what you mean," Indy said. "I went through a phase in graduate school, where I was starting to realize that my life wasn't a dress rehearsal, and that I needed to buckle down and live like it mattered." She paused to down the last swallow of one of her mini-burgers. "And now I'm going through that feeling all over again. It *is* sort of like starting a new life." She looked pensive, then lapped up the last of her beer from the bowl. "Another round?" she asked, looking at Anna's mostly empty glass.

"Sure." Anna sucked up the last bit of margarita with her straw and smiled. "We can sleep in tomorrow. Give our construction crew a break."

Indy's collar flashed as she programmed two more drinks. After the fab dinged, she took out her own bowl, but left the new margarita glass behind for Anna. "Those stemmed glasses are impossible with paws. What kind of monster would think up such a container?"

Anna laughed as she took out her full glass, then set the empty glass and bowl back inside the fab for recycling. She sat back in her chair with a contented sigh.

"So…" Indy looked sheepish. "There is one more little thing I'd like to mention." Anna perked up while Indy took the first lap of her beer.

"I want to start a family," Indy said.

Anna was stunned silent for a moment. Then she hesitated for another, longer moment. Her friend obviously felt deeply about this, and Anna didn't want to mess it up. "Go on."

"Like I was saying, this life that we have here now is not a rehearsal." Indy exhaled. "We have to start living it. I want to have a normal life, with all the things I would have had back in our world." She took another lap of her beer, eyes defiant. "And that includes puppies. I'm almost thirty! I was a postdoc for a long time, and we develop faster than you simians."

"Well, um," Anna fumbled for words, not knowing what to say. "Congratulations? And who's the lucky guy?"

"Argos, obviously!" Indy managed to look a little embarrassed. "Though he doesn't quite know it yet." Indy hesitated before continuing. "Actually, I *would* like to ask for your help with something."

"Um, I'm not sure how much I can contribute there, advice-wise." Anna took another sip of margarita. "I only ever had the one boyfriend in high school, and we weren't really that serious."

Indy snorted in exasperation. "Not that sort of help! I know my way around the opposite sex." Her voice was so smug that Anna choked on her drink, and Indy laughed. "No, there's a matter of tradition that I'd like you to help with. In a week or so, I'll let you know what to do."

"Ooo, that's not scary-sounding at *all.*" Anna stirred her drink with her straw.

"Don't worry." Indy smiled and lapped at her beer. "You might even learn something."

59

The next week was a stressful one for Anna. Indy was busy at odd hours in the lab preparing for something she called "the choosing ceremony," which she refused to explain further. And they were both distracted by the effort of getting their genetically engineered plants ready to go so they could start teaching their new faculty how to grow and use them. There were only two weeks left until the school building would be finished, and a few weeks after that, students should arrive after the winter harvest, though they had no idea how many or what kind they'd turn out to be.

Finally, one morning a week after their getting-thrown-back-to-ancient-Greece anniversary dinner, Indy tapped Anna on the shoulder as she sat at her workstation in the lab. "Today is the day I need your help." The big canine looked as nervous as Anna had ever seen her, shifting back and forth on her front paws slightly as she stood. "We'll walk for a few hours down toward Haliartos. I'll bring everything we need."

"Sure. Do I need to look good, though? I can put on a cleaner chiton." Anna patted ineffectually at the white limestone dust on the hem of her garment she'd trailed in from their construction site.

"Don't worry. You'll be there as a representative of your species, so the details of your clothing don't matter much. Just bring your monkey genes," Indy said with a hint of her usual humor.

"Um. When you say it like that, it kinda makes me want to put on cleaner clothes," Anna said.

"If it makes you more comfortable," Indy said. "And could you stop by Leitus and Helene's cottage and bring their new dog Brygos back with you on his leash? He has a part to play, too."

Anna stifled the urge to ask more questions, and ran off to change into a different chiton and collect Brygos. Fortunately, she found Leitus' new herding dog relaxing in the shade near the family's cottage, so she didn't have to send drones hunting for him all over the mountainside. After explaining things briefly to Leitus, she returned to Indy a few minutes later, Brygos in tow.

"Excellent," Indy said when she saw the two of them. She had loaded up her mini-pack with something, but otherwise looked the same as usual. "Let's get going."

The path to Haliartos was familiar by now, and Anna and Indy walked it companionably. Brygos ranged back and forth on his lead, sniffing each tree and marking the worthier specimens, still lifting his leg perfunctorily even after he ran out of urine. Between trees he simply trotted beside the two of them, enjoying the sunny but cool early-winter day.

For a while, they just strolled along in companionable silence. But eventually, Anna couldn't suppress her curiosity any longer.

"So, can you finally tell me what this 'choosing ceremony' is about? What are we doing out here?"

Indy flicked a glance at Anna. "All you need to know is one three-word phrase: 'And choose wisely.' Say only that, *exactly* like that, when I prompt you. You'll find out the rest soon enough." Indy still looked nervous, though she was hiding it well. "And try not to think about it beforehand. It can spoil the results." Her brow furrowed. "And I really, *really* want this to work."

They walked for a few more hours, discussing safe topics like the school's construction and their plans for the future, and approached Haliartos as the sun was halfway past its zenith. Anna thought they might stop by and say hello to Doros, but this time Indy led them off the road and over the hills, searching out Doros' sheep where she could smell them in the distance.

"Where there are sheep, there'll be a herder," Indy said. Brygos tugged at his lead as he caught the scent himself, and he barked in frustration.

Anna laughed. "He wants to go to work!"

"Hush, little brother." Indy nudged Brygos with her foreleg. "We'll return you to your own flock shortly. But first I have a favor to ask you." Brygos looked at Indy, then longingly at the sheep, but he stayed silent and walked along beside them as they approached.

Up ahead, Anna could see Argos come into view, heading off the sheep to stop the flock from its drifting path. His shaggy figure stayed in place for a few moments until the sheep began to spread out and graze again, then he trotted eagerly over to their party.

Indy walked out to meet him, and they touched muzzles in their usual greeting. Indy looked back at Brygos and gestured him forward with a slight dip and turn of her stance. The smaller dog came up hesitantly and greeted the much larger Argos with tail tucked. Argos gently sniffed Brygos, who raised his tail hesitantly, but then hung back beside Anna.

"Now for the choosing ceremony." Indy licked her nose once, clearly anxious, but then schooled her features back to stillness. "Do exactly what I say, and try not to make any extra movements or facial expressions once we get started. Just act natural."

Indy took a deep breath and released it. Then she sat, popped the chest clips of her harness with practiced motions and shrugged out of it. She opened her mini-pack with deft paws and brought out two small covered bowls. She peeled the covers off the bowls, and both Argos and Brygos scented the air with interest.

Indy motioned Anna over. "Take the right-hand bowl. Show it to Argos, but don't let him eat it."

Anna could see that the bowl contained half of a medium-rare steak, glistening with juices. Her own stomach growled. "Smells delicious," Anna said softly. "What're *we* having for dinner?" Indy shushed her with a look.

Anna carefully showed the steak to Argos, keeping a neutral expression. Then at Indy's motion she withdrew a few paces with Brygos and gestured for the smaller dog to sit beside her.

"Good! Now wait for a moment." Indy picked up the bowl containing the other half of the steak and showed it to Argos, who sniffed it with great interest, but refrained from taking a bite after Indy's admonishing look. Then Indy withdrew until she was at the same distance from Argos that Anna was. She sat down and held up the bowl in one paw.

"Hold your bowl up like this," Indy said. Anna did so. Brygos kept his seat, barely, but his eyes stayed locked on Anna's bowl.

Argos looked between Anna and Indy, seemingly confused.

"Choose freely," Indy said. Then she gave Anna a prompting look.

"And choose wisely," Anna said, completing the formula that Indy had taught her on the walk.

They waited, the silence broken only by Brygos' panting and the occasional bleat of a sheep. Argos looked from Indy to Anna in bemusement for a few more moments. But then he stilled. He looked behind him to where the sheep were still spreading out, unsupervised. He looked at Brygos where he sat beside Anna, his whole body intent on the steak bowl. Then finally Argos looked at Indy's seated form. Indy looked back at him, still holding up her bowl to match Anna's.

Argos rose to his feet, and without hesitation walked over to Indy, laying his muzzle beside hers again. Indy laid the bowl down, and Argos seized the half-steak inside, devouring it in one swift gulp. Indy's eyes shone as she looked over to Anna.

"You can give the other one to Brygos now," Indy said. "Just hold it and let him tear pieces off. I scored it earlier, so it should be easy."

Anna did as she was told, holding the steak by one end as an ecstatic Brygos ripped bites from the other side. Finally, she threw him the remaining piece to save her fingers, and looked around for something to wipe her hands on.

"Sorry," Indy said. "I'm afraid I didn't think to bring napkins."

"That's okay," Anna sighed, wiping her fingers on the hem of her clean chiton. "I can change again when we get back." Brygos sniffed at her chiton with interest, then ranged out on his lead again, edging toward the sheep.

"Come on, Brygos!" Anna tugged the lead. "We're going home. Home!" Brygos turned away from the sheep reluctantly and followed Anna as she withdrew.

Indy stayed behind for a moment with Argos, who was still licking his chops and appearing mightily satisfied with himself. She whispered something in Argos' ear that Anna couldn't hear, then laid her muzzle beside his in parting, and turned to go.

Argos barked once, then stood up and turned back to his sheep. But as he began to gather them in again, he looked off toward Indy's retreating form, pausing for a long moment before he went back to his flock.

Anna, Indy and Brygos walked for a few minutes, this time heading back to the road by the most direct route. Anna took off Brygos' lead to let him sniff around as they walked, then unclipped Indy's mini-pack from her harness and rummaged around inside. "Got anything to eat in here?"

Just then Brygos sneezed and tentatively play-bowed to Indy, who bowed back, then launched after the smaller dog in a romping game of chase. The two tore back and forth across the path as Anna walked, alternating who chased who, clods of dirt and grass flying.

Anna's face lit as she found something in the mini-pack. Then her expression fell as she pulled out two bent, paper-wrapped protein bars. She sighed, then opened one and bit into it, munching as she watched Indy and Brygos play. A minute later, the two canines rejoined Anna, panting and happy.

"I think Argos and Brygos got a better deal than us." Anna took the last bite of her snack and chewed it without much enthusiasm, since she could still smell perfectly cooked steak on her fingers. She unwrapped the other protein bar and offered it to Indy.

"Sorry about that." Indy gulped her own bar down in one bite and started panting again. "I was so caught up preparing for the ceremony that I forgot about the little details like what *we* would eat for dinner." The big hybrid looked down at Brygos, who trotted along beside them happily, ear tips bobbing. "He looks happy, at least."

"Of course *he's* happy," Anna groused. "He got a steak dinner and playtime." She paused. "And hey, since you're starving me, I figure that gives me license to pry. What just happened back there? What's a choosing ceremony?"

"It's an old tradition, from after the bad times ended." Indy laughed, the sound more carefree than Anna had ever heard from her before. "Way back, hundreds of years ago, there were science fiction stories about 'uplift,' where aliens or humans would raise animals up to higher intelligence. Sometimes the uplifted animals would become equal partners, other times they were essentially slaves." Indy scowled, though she still looked happy. "But a common feature of most of those stories was that no one ever asked the animals involved what *they* wanted."

"So in the ceremony, we tried to give Argos a choice he could understand." Indy nodded toward Anna and Brygos. "On one side, there is a human, looking familiar, with a dog by her side, leashed. On the other side there is me, looking fabulous—" she tossed her ruff "—representing his other choice. Both sides hold rewards, and he gets to choose between them. A dog who doesn't like the look of us hybrids, or who's drawn more toward the things he's always known, will pick the human side."

"What happens when they pick the hybrid side?" Anna put Brygos back on his lead, since he seemed content now to walk beside them.

"My steak contained a dose of the nanoformula that will begin the awakening process. Yours was just a normal steak. Though to look at Brygos' face, it was the most delicious thing ever," Indy added with a trace of envy.

"So how long does the uplifting take? And what if he changes his mind?"

"It takes about eight months," Indy said. "He'll eat and sleep more than usual. And we'll redo this ceremony every month or so. As his mind gradually swims upward toward full awareness, he'll gain a better understanding of what's happening to him, and he'll have the opportunity to change his decision. It happens, though not very often. Usually, a dog who chooses a strange hybrid over a familiar human is already drawn to us for one reason or the other."

Anna laughed. "Hmm, can't think why Argos might be drawn to your side."

Indy coughed and looked down, but smiled to herself. "In any case, he's set things in motion. All we have to do is guide the process, and make sure Argos' rights are respected." Indy looked up at Anna. "That, we treat with the utmost seriousness. I'd be very disappointed if he chose not to go forward, but I would respect his decision. His fate is his own to decide."

"I don't think you've got anything to worry about, big sis." Anna smirked. "I think he's way ahead of you."

60

The next day, Anna awoke tired and footsore. They'd walked eight hours yesterday, most of the way to Haliartos and back at a brisk pace, and she could've used more sleep. But they'd already told Themis and Melas last week that they would explain the first parts of their new curriculum this morning, and she didn't want to put it off any longer.

She and Indy had slept in their quarters in the almost-completed school, so at least they didn't have far to walk. The tunnel to their secret base had broken through three days before, at the back wall of a small storage room, so they had been able to move a few of their new engineered plants out onto the school's spacious rear lawn. Which was currently just a smoothed expanse of dirt, but eventually it would be nicely grassed over.

A fountain stood incongruously alone in the center of the bare yard, water trickling from its basin and away along a winding bed landscaped with rocks. Indy and Anna had shoved an empty pipe into the ground before construction and told their workers to build a fountain over this "seasonal spring," then had their mining-drones tunnel to it from below and connect it to their cave's water supply. They couldn't very well have their Greek builders install modern showers and toilets, but at least they wouldn't have to haul water for a mile.

Their plants sat in two rows of clay pots, carefully fabbed to look like authentic Greek workmanship. Anna checked them over again nervously, then looked back at the school to see Melas emerge, still chewing something from breakfast. They didn't have any support staff at the school yet, but the builders usually set up a communal breakfast which Melas and Themis contributed to.

Themis and Phaia followed closely behind Melas, and a few moments later Indy joined them. The doors weren't hung yet on the back side of the school, so for now they were walking in and out of open portals. But in the mild Greek climate this had worked out well enough so far, even in early winter.

Phaia was reading something on a battered, much-reused parchment scroll as she walked, but she closed it self-consciously as Anna approached. "Trader brought me a message this morning from Oresus, of all people. He's got some story how he didn't want to do what he did to me, but financial trouble pushed him into it. Guilty conscience, sounds like." She looked bitter. "Not my problem anymore, though. And nothing you all need to worry about. Let's just get started."

Anna and Indy exchanged a look, but stayed silent as Indy took up the instructor's spot behind one end of the row of plants. Anna, Themis, Phaia, and Melas formed up on the other side to listen.

"Let's begin." Indy indicated the plant in front of her with a raised paw. "All the technology I'll demonstrate today has a common feature. It uses the power of the sun to gather and shape substances from the earth." She lifted the leaves of the little plant to show heavy seed pods dangling below them. "Melas, please pluck one of these pods and tell me what you find inside. A yellow one please," she added as Melas reached toward one of the greener ones. "Those are the ripest."

Melas detached a pod gingerly, his callused hands careful not to pull the stem from the plant. Then he shredded the pod's outer casing away. "I see a thin layer of white fluff inside. And then—"

"And then what?" There was a hint of a smile in Indy's voice as Themis and Phaia leaned in to see.

Melas held up a smooth globule of shining, silvery-white metal, about the size of a grape. "I see what appears to be a bulb of pure iron."

"And how do you know it's pure?" Indy asked.

"Well, I have never seen pure iron before, so that is only a guess." Melas bent and picked up a sharp bit of stone from the unfinished yard, then used it to score the surface of the globule. "But see how soft it is! I've never managed to smelt anything nearly this pure."

"Not a spot of rust on it." Themis took the globule and eyed it closely. "Never seen that before, either. And it's not spongy at all." She gave Melas a puckish look. "Not like the locally-smelted iron from some of my previous employers." Melas smiled self-deprecatingly at this, seeming to take no offense.

"This will be the first half of your production process." Indy nodded toward the first few plants. "We call these plants 'miners.' Each variety of plant produces pods that contain a different substance." She walked a few plants down the row, nosing at the leaves. "You can tell from the leaf shape and color which is which." She looked up. "The roots of the plants gather impure or rare materials from underground, potentially very deep underground." Indy opened her mouth in a smile. "We cheated for this demonstration by putting those materials into the pots for the plants to find."

She gestured to Anna, who poked a finger into one pot and carefully pried a root out of the soft soil. Small bits of scrap iron hung from the root by tiny hairlike rootlets. Anna plucked one of the iron scraps loose and crumbled it between her fingers, showing that the rootlets had permeated it completely and were in the process of breaking it down. Then she buried the root again, gently patting the soil back into place.

"The pods grow as they collect the purified materials," Indy continued. "If the pure form is dangerous to handle, the material is stored as a safe compound instead." Melas looked keenly interested in that part, but stayed silent, unable to formulate a question yet.

Indy walked further down the row, where the character of the plants changed. These looked more like giant Venus flytraps, with broad vegetable mouths above and dangling pods below. Indy stopped in front of one plant with a closed mouth and a set of several dangling pods.

"These are the second half of the process, the 'formers.'" Indy held up a small wooden buckle, a carefully carved replica of the ones on her harness, and handed it to Themis. "You place a model in the plant's mouth, together with globules of refined materials from the miners. The mouth closes, and the pods start to grow. Eventually, they're ready to harvest." She tapped one of the ripe pods with a dexterous claw. "Would you open one of these pods?"

Themis popped a dried yellow pod loose from its stalk and cracked it. Inside was a perfect replica of the wooden buckle, but wrought of a shining alloy.

"This alloy is called 'spring steel,'" Indy said as Themis turned it about, then handed it off to Melas. "It is composed of iron, chromium, manganese, and carbon, in ratios which we will teach you." Indy paused. "Any questions so far?"

"Not a question, but more of a comment, perhaps." Melas eyed his corded forearms ruefully. "It seems as though I've invested a great deal of effort building up a skill which may no longer be required."

"That's up to you," Indy said. "If you choose, you can use the miners and formers merely to produce exotic bar or flat stock, which you can work using traditional, muscle-based techniques." Themis laughed, then stifled it at Indy's reproving look. "Think of what you could make, with inputs of any substance or alloy you can think of." Melas looked pensive at this.

"Hey, boss." Themis raised her hand. "I have an *actual* question that's not about my bulging man-steaks," she said with an amused glance at Melas. "How do we 'form' something with any kind of precision if we have to carve it out of wood?" She held up the new spring steel buckle. "Look, you can still see the wood grain on this thing."

"You use multi-step forming." Indy held up the wooden buckle again. "You start with a wooden model. Then you form a mild steel version, say. Then you sand and finish that part. Then that piece becomes the model for the next step." Indy moved closer to the end of the row of plants, then tugged a pod free and threw it to Phaia. "Here is a more refined version."

Phaia cracked the pod open and pulled out another version of the buckle, this one dark gray and wondrously light. "Aha! Now we're talking! What's this one made of?"

"It's an alloy of a metal called 'titanium,'" Indy said.

"Named after the fathers of the gods?" asked Phaia.

"Yes, those same Titans." Indy smiled. "But it doesn't have any supernatural qualities, it's merely a very light, strong metal."

Indy walked to the very end of the row, nipped another pod free with her front teeth, and tossed it to Melas. He cracked it with one massive hand, then almost dropped the translucent white blob that was revealed. "So light!" He rubbed it between his fingers. "What is it?"

"We call it 'plastic,'" Indy said.

Themis had taken the plastic blob from Melas and was holding it up to the sun, trying to see through it. "You sure about that, chief? Back where I'm from, 'plastic' means 'moldable.' And this thing feels pretty stiff to me. Said the priestess to the politician."

Indy looked embarrassed. "Yes, well, sometimes our nomenclature has historical quirks. The inventors called it 'plastic' because it's easy to mold while it's hot. But in our case, it will be easier to work with in the formers instead of by hand." She stopped at the last former in the row, and tugged free another pod, tossing it to Themis this time. When split, it revealed a white plastic version of the buckle, which Themis flexed with interest before passing it to Melas.

Indy came around to the other side of the row of plants to join Anna and the three Greeks. "We will teach you about many more substances over time. Elements, alloys and compounds. Where to plant your miners to gather the ingredients, how to create new mixtures with new properties, and much more. But for now, that's the outline. Anna will teach mathematics, Phaia medicine, you two crafting and metalworking, and I will oversee our program." She sat, looking very pleased with herself. "So, are there any questions?"

"What's the catch?" Phaia asked immediately.

"Why would there be a catch?" Anna looked mildly affronted.

"May not be." Phaia smiled. "But whenever I ask that question, I usually find out something I really should know." She gave Anna a speculative look. "Maybe something like with the penicillin? Where I had to add olive pits to keep the culture alive?" She raised an eyebrow expectantly.

Indy opened her mouth in a wide smile. "Already an expert!" She got up and nosed at the plants idly as she spoke. "But you're correct. Each of the plants here requires a human or canine touch to keep it viable. Too long without contact, and they will wither."

"How could such a plant come to exist?" Melas looked thoughtful. "The vast majority of plants in the world are probably never touched by man or dog. How could they propagate themselves without—" He stopped.

"Without what?" Themis asked.

Melas looked at Indy and Anna forthrightly. "These plants are outside of normal creation. They were bred somehow by man, and the touch of man is required as a safeguard, to prevent them overturning the natural order if anything were to go wrong."

Crap, Anna said to Indy over their link.

I'll let you explain this one. Indy gave a silently mocking grin.

"Even with a safeguard like that, there's plenty of ways for things to go wrong. It's happened to me once already." Phaia frowned with the memory. "Things like this could travel faster than we can know or control. Faster than people can figure out how to deal with it. And if it turns out badly, even in some way we didn't think of, we're still responsible."

Phaia looked unhappy at the thought, but Melas was nodding along. "Of course." He looked over the row of plants. "I would suggest that we hold back this part of the curriculum from the students for a while, at least until the three of us have had more time to think through the implications." He looked at Phaia and Themis. "Pandora's jar is hard to close up again."

"Pure knowledge seems like a safer starting place," Phaia looked a question at Themis. "Like that germ theory of disease I told you about back in Athens?"

"Fine, fine, if it'll make you two feel better." Themis rolled her eyes, but without rancor. "As long as *I* get to work on the fun stuff, we can teach the students whatever you want." She looked at Anna and Indy. "As long as the bosses sign off on this change of plan?"

"Um, sure?" Anna said, with a glance at Indy to confirm. "I'm a little surprised though. I thought you guys would be totally up for this."

"Let us consider it for a while," Melas said. "I am no great believer in gods or demigods. But even for me, these plants are uncomfortably close to magic." He frowned. "When I teach something, I first want to understand it myself, all the way from the roots." He gestured ironically at the plants. "So to speak."

"The big guy's got jokes now," Themis said with a laugh. "But I'm way too sober for this much philosophizing right after breakfast." She turned to Indy. "For now, show me more!"

67

Three weeks of curriculum revision and hard training later, Anna and Indy stood in front of their newly completed school after delivering their welcoming speech, watching the first incoming class being ushered in through the front doors by Themis, Melas, and Phaia.

There were only eight students, all aged between fifteen and twenty or so. Most were locals, one of whom had brought a welcome bundle of fresh leafy greens from the winter harvest as a gift, since they weren't charging tuition. Another one had come all the way from Thebes, and had almost left again when they'd told him that his accompanying slave would have to be allowed to learn alongside him.

We'll see how many of these last the full three months, even with free room and board, Anna said over their link.

"Even so," Indy said as they closed the front doors behind them. The small group of students babbled away excitedly as they walked off after the teachers to be shown to their rooms. "I feel like this is the start of something larger, now."

Definitely. Then Anna laughed. "Sorry, I forgot you already talked out loud in front of the students. Just habit to use the link, I guess."

"It took you long enough to develop that habit." Indy smiled. "I halfway think we should keep it going. I'm sure there will be places and times where we can't be fully open."

"Nope, we're committed now." Anna put a hand on her friend's shoulder. "It's not fair for you to live in silence just because it might be inconvenient if the wrong person heard you talk." She looked around, proud but disbelieving. "This feels so weird! A year ago I thought *I* was going to be the one going off to college, and now here we are running one. Even though it's really small."

"On the good side," Indy said, "We're both tenured faculty already, which probably would have taken me at least five or six more years back in Austin."

Anna laughed. "Way to look on the bright side, Professor Fuller!"

Indy sat up with mock dignity. "I like the sound of that, Professor Reyes. The Younger."

There was a knock at the front door behind them. Indy looked back. "Are we expecting anyone else?" Anna shrugged and went to answer it.

When she opened the door, Oresus stood on the other side. His tall figure looked grayer and more worn than Anna remembered him, and he stood in an uncharacteristic attitude of humility.

Anna opened her mouth, but Oresus spoke first. "I'm sorry to visit unannounced. But there are a few things I'd like to say to you, if you're willing to listen. And to Phaia too, though her lack of reply to my messages probably means she won't be receptive."

Anna paused, then opened the door wider. Indy came up and stood beside her in the entrance, hackles rising slightly, posture stiff.

"How did you find us?" Anna asked.

"It wasn't difficult." Oresus spoke with a flicker of his old assertiveness. "Phaia seems to have been very cautious when she returned to Athens, but she is widely known in our circles. There were people I could ask to find out where she had gone. And Thrasius..." Oresus paused to collect himself. "My brother mentioned to me that he had met you here."

"*Why* did you find us?" Indy asked out loud.

Oresus started at that, but didn't look terribly surprised, though he took a moment to recover. He had probably heard about Indy's unusual nature from someone local while asking directions out here.

"I've done wrong, and I want to make amends." Oresus gathered his dignity. "The way I treated Phaia was not the way an honorable man should act. My actions, my greed, resulted in great danger to you both, and led to my own brother's death." He swallowed. "I'm not so proud that I can't recognize when I'm on the wrong side. And I learned from Thrasius that it's never too late for a man to make a change." He spread his hands. "So I left Kepthos in charge back in Athens, and here I am."

Anna and Indy looked at each other. Then Indy turned back to Oresus with eyes flashing. "You almost got both of us killed! We ran off to rescue Phaia, and barely escaped with our skins intact. Then that maniac Hylas sent his hired thugs to wedge our doors shut and burn our house down around us!"

"You're right," Oresus said simply. "You're right. I could have been happy for Phaia's enrichment, and set her free with my best wishes. But instead, I only saw how it could rescue me from my own financial misfortune. And given Hylas' fearsome reputation, I thought my mention of his name would put an end to any questions." Oresus looked pensive. "I couldn't have known that you two would go off and somehow get Phaia back from him. I'm still not sure how you managed it, though I've heard some strange stories. But I'm still to blame. If I had done the right thing, you would have been safe, my honor would still be intact, and my brother would still be alive."

"So, what do you want, then?" Anna asked.

"Well, I'd still like to talk to Phaia. Beyond that, it depends on you." Oresus looked around at the front of the school building with appreciation. "I've heard a bit about what you're doing here, and there may be things I could do to help. I have connections. I know how things work."

Indy gave him a skeptical look. Oresus raised a hand to forestall any objection. "I can understand if you don't want anything further to do with me. If that's the case, I will simply leave after I've spoken to Phaia." He looked between Indy and Anna. "But my offer to help is sincere. It can't hurt to consider it."

Indy looked like she wanted to object, but deflated herself after a moment. "No one can say that you don't know how to apologize, Oresus." She backed grudgingly away from the door, making space for Oresus to enter. "Come in then, and we'll take you to Phaia. After that, we'll see."

Anna closed the door behind Oresus, then followed as Indy led the way left, to the teacher's wing of the building. Oresus looked around with interest, especially at the open and unfinished rooms, where there was still space for perhaps five more teachers to live, and sniffed appreciatively at the aroma of dinner preparations coming from the kitchen in the other wing.

They stopped outside Phaia's quarters, and Anna knocked on the door. "Phaia, you have a visitor!"

A muffled reply came from inside, then the door opened. Phaia saw Anna first. "I thought dinner's not for another—" She broke off when she saw Oresus standing beside Indy. Her face hardened, but she said nothing. Her fists clenched at her side, then she relaxed her hands.

"Oresus asked to speak to you," Indy said. "But if you like, we'll see him back out."

Phaia glared for another moment, but came out of her room and closed the door behind her. "I'll show him out myself. We can talk outside."

Oresus nodded soberly at this, and followed Phaia back down the hallway toward the front door. As he exited, he said to Anna and Indy, "It was good to see you again."

Phaia gave Anna a look that clearly said to leave her and Oresus alone for a few minutes. Anna nodded her understanding and closed the front door behind them. Then she and Indy settled in the atrium, in case Phaia should call out. They could hear raised voices outside the door, but couldn't make out the words.

Indy's stomach rumbled. "I hope this doesn't take too long. It's almost time for dinner, and we're having one of my favorites." She settled onto the floor reluctantly.

"Don't worry," Anna said with a smile. "No one's going to eat your share of the lamb. I fabbed it just like you like it, then had it delivered it to the cooks like we'd bought it in town. I even threw in some of those fig cakes you like for dessert."

"They're braising the shanks, right?" Indy rubbed the drool off one side of her muzzle with a forepaw. "They know I like the shanks."

Themis walked up a few moments later. "Students are all settled in, boss-babes." Anna's translator hiccupped at this, even though it had much improved its handling of Themis' unusual phrasings. "But I thought I heard a man's voice out here?"

"Oresus came for a talk." Anna pointed at the door. "Phaia's outside with him."

"*That* might not go well. My girl P's not exactly the forgiving type." Themis got a calculating look. "He's probably here because he wants more stuff like that drug you gave her."

"So, what do *you* think will happen?" Anna looked at Indy, then toward the front door.

"That's up to Phaia. I'm not the one who got sold off onto Hylas' plantation." Indy smacked her lips together. "Though I still wouldn't mind getting my teeth into him, for how close we came to getting ourselves enslaved or killed."

"I wish Thrasius were still here." Anna looked at Themis. "Oresus' brother. Phaia told you the story?" At Themis' nod, Anna looked back to Indy. "It's so sad. He'd become a real friend to us, and it seemed like his life was turning around. Now we'll never know how it might've come out." She heaved out a breath. "How many robbers would have come back to warn us about Nicon after what we did to him?"

"Thrasius' and Oresus' mother must have taught them well," Indy said. "They make many mistakes—"

"*Huge* understatement," Anna said.

"—But they also seem to have a strong urge to try to make

things right afterward," Indy finished. She suddenly cocked an ear at the door. "Did you hear someone in pain out there just now?"

Anna leapt up and jerked open the door, then stopped in surprise.

Oresus stood stiffly, blood running from his nose. Phaia stood in front of him, hand raised as if to strike him again. She paused for a long moment, then stepped back and lowered her hand.

"No, you weren't the worst of them." The anger on Phaia's face changed to disgust. "But that's just a way for you to lie to yourself. What you took away from me..." She shook her head. "That's not something you can just apologize for." Her eyes flashed. "And it's not like you've freed all your slaves and set them up with pensions." She looked at him more closely. "Have you?"

Oresus pulled a cloth from his sash. "You know I haven't." He wiped the blood from his face. "I'm barely afloat as it is."

"Not my problem." Phaia backed away another step. "Pharmaceuticals are a profitable business. No idea how you're making such a bad job of it, but you should get it together. You have a household of *slaves* depending on you." She turned and walked past Anna and Indy back into the school. Themis joined her with a nod, and the two quickly disappeared down the hallway to the dining room.

"I'm sorry I brought this to your doorstep." Oresus looked at Anna and Indy sadly. "My earlier apology to you two still stands, of course. But perhaps Phaia is right. Some things may be beyond apology." He turned to go, then hesitated. "I wish the best of luck to your efforts here. If there's ever anything I can do to help honor my brother's memory, you know where to find me." He nodded to the two of them, then walked away toward Lebadeia.

Anna waited until Oresus was out of sight, then shook her head. "I wish..." Her voice trailed off. "Crap. I'm not sure what I wish."

"Me either." Indy's ears flicked back. "I suppose everyone has to live with the consequences of what they've done." She started toward the dining room.

"Yeah." Anna's mouth pulled into a frown as she followed her friend, closing the school's front doors behind her. "That's kinda what I'm afraid of."

The three-month school term passed in a blur for Anna. Their students picked up knowledge quickly, though Indy and Anna were starting them at a much more basic level than they had planned. Melas and the other Greek instructors had been right to delay introducing their plant-based mining and forming technology to students. The basics turned out to be plenty difficult for Iron Age farmers, and choosing the most engaging topics was unexpectedly challenging as well. Indy spent a huge amount of time with Phaia covering human anatomy before she could even start on diseases, and Anna found that her students were much more interested in bookkeeping using exotic Arabic numerals than they were in solving algebraic equations.

Another unforeseen problem was the dearth of teaching materials. They taught classes the same way as any other ancient Greek school, using stylus and slate, but students also needed something they could refer back to once they returned home. So Anna spent a while searching their library of plants, and finally came up with one that would produce paper pulp if you fed it a mulch of discarded plant husks and rags. Another plant could make pods full of an indelible black ink without any special feed requirements. Then

Anna worked with Themis to create a basic, single-sheet printing press, the movable type for which they created by first carving it from wood, then refining it using their former plants until they had boxes of shiny, rust-proof metal print for each of the Greek letters, including the lower case they'd introduced to make the printing more compact. Eventually, they'd teach printing to students too, but for now it was teachers-only while they figured out how to do it with plant-based technology.

Themis grinned unashamedly when she pulled the first printed sheet out of the press in the school's workshop and held it up to dry. "Okay, so I splotched this one up. I'm still working on my technique. Which for once is not an innuendo." She turned to Anna. "But it's beautiful! We could make a hundred of these weird flat books of yours in a month!"

Anna smiled. "Indy and I have been printing up copies of what we're teaching the students here, so they can take it with them after they graduate." She pulled a slim, wood-bound volume from her bag and handed it to Themis, who opened it and thumbed through the pages appreciatively. She and Indy had finally remembered to fab things that looked authentically home-made, so the pages had rough edges, the letters were uneven, and the binding looked hand sewn.

"This is going to make a *big* difference." Themis looked impressed. "Having flat pages instead of a roll of papyrus will add ten freaking years back onto my life. Have you ever cracked one of those stupid little strips and had to patch it?" She snorted in disgust. "And close to the end, you can't unroll it flat enough to read without destroying the damn thing. We're just lucky that boustrophedon went out of fashion a while back." Themis laughed. "If we still wrote backward on every other line, we'd need a whole second set of backward letters!" Anna laughed too, though she'd never even heard of boustrophedon before a month ago.

Indy trotted into the workshop with Melas beside her. "Ah, there you two are." She nodded at Themis. "I wanted to show one of our new textbooks to Melas."

Themis handed the book to Melas, who handled the pages carefully as he looked through it, pausing on a page full of illustrations. "This is especially nice, given the uncertain literacy of most of our students. Though it must have taken forever to carve the plates for these." He gave Anna and Indy an amused look that said he fully expected an explanation at some point. "This will definitely make teaching the next term easier."

"About that." Indy gave the kind of smile that made Melas close the book. "How many of the students do you think will want to continue?"

Melas considered. "I haven't asked them to make a formal commitment, but I believe perhaps only three. The others seem more eager to go out and put their new knowledge to use."

"I suppose we should have expected that." Indy sighed. "I can't blame them. Though it's going to be hard to build up to more advanced topics if most students leave after one term." She looked at Themis and Melas. "Are there any you think are especially promising? I'd like to make at least one or two of them teaching assistants next year, so that you two and Phaia can spend more time on learning and teaching our new additions to the curriculum."

"Ah, our rumored new curriculum," Themis said. "I'm eager to know what I'll be teaching next term." She gave a mock-pointed look. "Knowing it before the term starts would also be nice."

"I apologize for our irregular situation." Indy looked embarrassed. "But curriculum development has proven more difficult than we thought."

Anna smiled. "Come on, Themis, cut us some slack. None of us has ever started a school before."

"True enough." Themis pursed her lips. "It just makes me antsy. I'm used to being the one who's got the material nailed, not the one who's squeaking by."

"It does go against the grain." Melas looked uncomfortable. "I do not like feeling as if I know barely more than my students do."

"Nonetheless, you're essential to this process," Indy said. "If we didn't have the three of you, Anna and I would have a very difficult time figuring out what to teach, and how. You saw how many of our ideas we had to change or postpone after we talked to you."

Melas looked mollified at this, but before he could continue there was a knock at the doorframe. One of the staff stood there, a young local boy who they paid to run errands and do light work around the school.

"Ma'am?" He looked nervous to be addressing Indy directly. "Ma'am, you have two visitors here. I hope it's all right?" At Indy's nod, he motioned to someone back in the hallway, and a moment later Indy's would-be boyfriend Argos the herding dog appeared in the doorway, followed closely by his owner Doros.

"Indy! Anna!" Doros boomed in a voice more suited for wide lowland pastures than to the inside of a school. He strode forward and clasped hands with Anna, then did the same with Indy's giant paw. "I'm sorry for visiting without sending word, but my boy here—" he indicated Argos with a callused thumb "—gave me all kinds of hell this morning until I'd come here with him."

Argos exchanged a greeting sniff with Indy and seated himself calmly, not showing any guilt at all over dragging his owner several hours' walk away from his food business near Haliartos. Over the past few months since the choosing ceremony, Anna and Indy had brought Doros into their confidence and shared the outline of Argos' earlier choice with him. So he knew in general terms what might happen if Argos continued to choose uplift, though it had been impossible to tell him exactly when any particular step in the process might occur.

"He'd run down the road, then back and look at me, then down the road again, and wouldn't take 'no' for an answer." Doros patted the big beast's shoulder fondly. "I figured he knew what he was about." He looked uncertain. "I still say, like I always have, that Argos is his own man. I just don't like to see him agitated. I wish I knew what was going on with him." He paused. "I worry about him."

Indy gave Argos a long look, and Argos looked back at her, completely calm except for the tiniest wag of the tip of his tail against the floor.

"I think it's finally time to put your mind at ease, Doros. Would you and Anna come with me please?" Indy turned to Melas and Themis, who were clearly bursting with curiosity but trying not to show it. "Please excuse us." She swept out of the room toward her quarters, Doros and Argos close behind. Anna gave one last apologetic glance to Melas and Themis, then excused herself to follow them down the hallway.

Indy ushered the three of them into her quarters, motioning for Anna to close the door behind them. "Please, sit." She indicated a guest chair to Doros. "I'll just be a moment."

Doros settled uneasily into the chair. Argos sat beside him calmly, but his eyes followed Indy across the room as she reached under her wide, low bed and pulled out a flat wooden box, perhaps eight inches across and two inches deep.

Indy placed the box on the table in front of Doros, then flipped open the lid, revealing a metal collar gleaming on a black velvet pad. Its satiny finish shone with a color somewhere between brownish-gold and black, a perfect complement to Argos' coloration. Indy's collar lights flashed briefly blue and gold, and answering lights shone from the other collar as it clicked and separated into two halves.

"This collar will function for Argos the way mine does for me." Indy touched it with a paw. "It will give him a voice, and other ways to reach out to the world around him. Though for now, it will need to be charged every few days from my collar or Anna's phone." Indy grew more serious. "He must choose it for himself, and he can take it off again at any time, if he wishes." Indy indicated Doros with her nose. "Traditionally, the human closest to him makes the symbolic offering of the gift of speech."

"If you feel comfortable with that, Doros," Anna said after Doros didn't immediately reply.

Doros started a little. He'd been rubbing absently at the collar's smooth surface. "Sorry, just got to thinking there." He cleared his throat. "What do I need to do?"

"Pick up the two halves of the collar and hold them out to Argos," Indy said. "He will do the rest, if he agrees."

Doros picked up the collar hesitantly, hefting it. "It's lighter than it looks." Then he held it out before him.

Argos walked over without hesitation and thrust his head between the two half-circles of dark metal. Doros brought the ends together, and they fused with a soft *click*. The collar lights came on again, this time cycling through a range of colors and patterns that chased themselves across its surface.

"Calibration," Indy said at Doros' worried look. "That's normal. It will only take a minute or so."

Argos looked uncertain now. As the collar lights continued their cycle, he turned his head from one side to the other, as if hearing something inaudible to the rest of them. At one point he turned quickly to look behind him, turning back sheepishly when he saw that there was nothing there.

Indy laid a calming paw on Doros' knee. "Don't worry. We would never let any harm come to him."

Nevertheless, Doros squatted down in front of Argos and rubbed him on the shoulder. "You doing all right there, big man?"

The lights on Argos' collar went out. The shaggy brown-and-black shepherd looked around for a few seconds longer, ears swiveling, then regained his composure. He looked slowly at the three of them, first at Anna, then more lingeringly at Indy, and finally at Doros, who was still smoothing the fur of his shoulder.

He looked into Doros' eyes. "Father?" Argos' voice, lower and with more gravitas than Indy's, came clearly from the new collar. His ears twitched in reaction to his own voice. "Father?"

"Argos!" Doros' mouth twisted with emotion. "Is that really you?"

"Father." Argos stood straighter. "Father! I speak. I speak!" His tail began to wave, first tentatively, then more broadly.

Doros leaned forward and embraced his dog with both arms, his face against Argos' furry neck. A tear rolled down his cheek as he hugged Argos tight.

"I'm just glad you're all right." Doros pulled back and looked at Argos again. "I can't believe you can really talk!"

"I speak." Argos dropped his jaw in a grin. "I *talk!*" He barked over his own words in delight.

"His elocution will improve over time." Indy's voice was dry. "He must learn to use the collar, and his intelligence is not yet fully developed. Speaking and listening will help him advance to the next level, if he chooses to continue."

Argos turned to Indy. "I choose," he said clearly.

"Give yourself some time there, big guy," Anna said. "This might take a while to get used to."

"I choose, I choose!" Argos repeated. He sniffed noses with Indy briefly, then turned back to Doros and held up a paw.

Doros shook it gravely. "It's very nice to speak with you at last."

"Speak!" Argos barked again.

63

The next day, Indy and Anna accompanied Doros and Argos back to Haliartos. A delighted Argos practiced his halting speech all the way back, quieting only when he might be overheard. He seemed to instinctively want to keep his secret, for now at least.

They stayed for lunch at Doros' home, but they couldn't linger, as they were scheduled to stop by Lebadeia on the way back to leave a payment at Echetlus' shop for the school's next delivery of supplies.

Indy laid her muzzle beside Argos'. "I'll come back to visit soon."

"*I* visit!" Argos said.

"You can visit us too, if you want." Indy looked at Doros for confirmation. "But bring Doros if you do."

"Don't worry," Doros said, "I've got one of my people who can handle things here if I need to leave sometimes. I'll make sure Argos doesn't get into trouble."

"Just keep in mind that he may be unusually inquisitive for a while." Indy's voice was serious. "There's no harm in indulging him, but make sure to keep an eye on him until he steadies."

"We'll be working hard, training up a new herder to take his place one of these days when he's fully independent." Doros' voice was proud and sad together. "So that should help keep him grounded." His eyes twinkled. "And you heard him offer to help me find another wife, during lunch." He laughed. "No one can say my boy's not sure of himself!"

Anna and Indy took the lakeside road back, since they were heading to Lebadeia instead of straight back to the school. Off to their right, Lake Kopais had filled with the winter and spring rains, elevating the usually swampy shoreline. The road had been set back from the high-water line to avoid the marshy areas, but they had a good view of thousands of black cormorants wheeling over vast carpets of rushes, diving for fish. Long-legged ibises waded near the shore, probing for frogs with downcurved beaks, and fishermen plied the waters in reed boats. Indy walked along in silence, occasionally lifting her head to look out over the lake.

"Don't worry about Argos," Anna said. "He's going to be fine."

"Is it that obvious?"

"Yeah, kind of." Anna smiled. "But seriously, he's got Doros there, and he's got his sheep to keep him busy."

"I also set a monitor on his collar to alert us if he goes astray or if his vital signs show that he's frightened." Indy looked abashed when Anna laughed. "Well, you can't be too cautious."

"You're doing the right thing," Anna said. "Argos clearly wants to be with you. Doros is helping out. There's nothing to worry about."

"I know." Indy shook out her coat as she walked. "But it's hard not to get a little apprehensive sometimes."

"I know just the cure for that," Anna said.

"What?"

"I'll bet frog legs are in season now, with the lake so full." Anna gestured out to their right. "We can probably get some in Lebadeia, freshly grilled."

"What an excellent thought!" A few drops of saliva fell from Indy's jaws to patter on the dusty road.

Anna laughed. "We just ate lunch! No clue how you can be hungry already."

"A true canine is always ready to eat." Indy showed a toothy smile.

As they neared Lebadeia the road turned left to follow the Herkyna River toward the center of town. The tall plane trees along the river were leafing out for spring, and flowers dotted the land around them.

Anna looked around with interest as they entered the city proper. *Hey, what do you think's going on?* she said over their link.

What do you mean? Indy replied the same way. By this point, many of the locals had heard that Indy could talk, but not all of them took it with as much equanimity as their host family had. She usually stayed quiet on the streets to avoid drawing extra attention, though this didn't stop the occasional fearful glance or warding gesture in their direction.

Seems like lots of folks are hanging out gossiping about something. Anna nodded her head toward one such group, where four or five townspeople were talking excitedly together.

Well, I could walk over and ask them, Indy said dryly. *But that might not be the best way to find out.*

True. Anna smiled mentally. *Let's try asking when we drop off our payment.*

They walked the rest of the way to Echetlus' shop, finding it by the now-familiar sight of the old broken plow over the front door. Echetlus himself was out front, seeing off another customer, and waved as they approached.

Then he gave a hard look at something behind Anna and Indy. When Anna turned, she glimpsed her old harasser, the son of the town's previous archon, ducking out of view around a corner.

Ugh, that guy again. She shook her head in disgust as she turned back to greet Echetlus. *I hadn't seen him since we came back. I'd been hoping he found a job or something.*

It's never that easy, Indy said.

"Anna! Indy!" Echetlus greeted them warmly. "Come on inside, we'll get your payment taken care of." He ushered them back to his office, which was really more like a large closet that doubled as a storage area for a few of the more expensive items. He was used to speaking to the two of them together by now, since they'd continued to buy supplies from him as they established the school, and he had been glad of their growing business.

"By the way," he said, "it's none of my business, but if you want any help with the unwelcome attention out there, you might drop a word to Sarpedon, the new archon."

"I can handle him," Indy said. "He knows better than to come near us."

"He still talks crazy rumors about you two to anyone who'll listen," Echetlus said. "I'll butt out now, but consider it. The old archon's son is clearly a bad seed, your school is a growing local employer, and Sarpedon's very keen on expanding his tax base. You might have more clout with him than you think."

"Thanks, Echetlus," Anna said. "We'll definitely consider it." She dug out her purse and handed over the agreed-upon amount for their upcoming supply delivery, in the silver coin that they mined in increasing quantities from deep below the surrounding lands.

"Just a word to the wise," Echetlus said, as he presented the potshard receipt for her to sign.

"So, I—*we* noticed a lot of people talking as we walked through town." Anna tried not to sound too concerned. "Is there some news? What's going on?"

Now you're getting those pronouns wrong the other way around, Indy said with a mental smirk. *It's a good thing we already stopped keeping me a secret.*

"It's been all over town." Echetlus looked grave. "The news came this afternoon."

"Yes, but *what* news?" Anna tried to speak patiently.

"The Persians. They're finally coming to get revenge for Marathon."

"Um, Echetlus? You remember we're not from around here, right?"

"Ah, of course, of course." Echetlus' expression was apologetic. "Well, to shorten things a bit, ten years ago we smashed Darius' army at the battle of Marathon—"

"And Darius is...?"

"Darius *was* the ruler of the Persian Empire." Echetlus considered briefly. "Let me do the *really* short version, then." He gestured to punctuate his words. "Years back, some of our Ionian colonies across the sea revolted against the Persian pigs' rule. We supported them, because they're fellow Greeks and shouldn't have to be ruled by effete, pants-wearing foreigners. Darius found this irksome, so he crushed the Ionians and then invaded us to teach us a lesson. After a couple of tough years, we gave him a spanking at Marathon, and he slunk back to Persia, then died before he could try again. Huzzah!" His voice was sardonic.

"Why do I feel like there's a 'but' in here?" Anna asked.

"Because there is." Echetlus drew another breath. "Darius' son Xerxes swore vengeance, as dead emperors' sons do, and he's apparently spent the last five years or so building up a huge army over in Persia. He sent some clowns over last year asking for tribute, but we told him to stuff it. But the news is, he's brought a giant army across the Hellespont somehow, and is marching his way through Macedon right now, with that turncoat Alexander supplying him. The Persians must've been stockpiling food up there for years, to feed an army the size they're talking about."

This is bad news, Indy said over their link. *Uh oh. This is very bad.*

What is it? Anna tried to keep a straight face.

We should have been looking forward *in our sketchy, cobbled-together historical data instead of backward.* Indy sounded anxious. *It must be 480 BC! The year when the Persians win the battle of Thermopylae, then rampage right through here on their way to burn Athens to the ground.*

Anna blanched as much as her tanned skin would allow. *Oh no!*

"*Now* you're getting the idea," Echetlus said, unaware of the side discussion. "The Persians don't just send a few thousand troops. They send tens, *hundreds* of thousands. Nobody knows what we're going to do about it yet. Our Boeotian League delegates are going to another congress soon to discuss it." He paused and looked down. "We might end up sending our levies out to fight. But I'd rather my son didn't have to go through what I did."

At Anna's unspoken question, he went on. "I used to live in Plataea. We helped the Athenians beat the Persians at Marathon. And we won, but we didn't deserve to. We were so desperate and poor, I had to fight with a plowshare instead of a real sword." His face darkened with the memory. "I was much younger and stupider then. If the Persians hadn't been so overconfident, marching in like idiots right where we wanted them, they'd have killed us all. That's half of why I pulled up and moved here, to be further away from that sort of thing." He shook his head and sighed ruefully. "Though I was still vain enough to make my old plow into a shop-sign."

"Thanks for letting me know what's going on." Anna's voice was bleak. "And I hope it doesn't come to a war." But she knew that it already had.

64

Anna and Indy walked the rest of the way back to the school and through its halls with agonizing casualness, not wanting to make anyone curious enough that they'd be followed to the hidden door in the storage room. They had to wait until they were through their secret passage and secure in their underground quarters before they could pull up a map and see the full extent of the oncoming disaster.

"It looks like Echetlus is right to be worried." Indy studied the map on the big monitor in their shared workroom. "In our original history, after Xerxes beat the Spartans and Athenians at Thermopylae—look, that's only thirty miles from where we're sitting!—the Persians took over all of Boeotia and went on to destroy Athens." She scrolled around on the map to get a better view. "The Greeks finally kicked the Persians back out after a year or so of fighting. Then it sounds like there will be another war where the Greeks try to take the fight back to the Persians."

Anna glared at the map. "I can't believe we didn't figure this out before."

"Well, to be fair to us, we didn't know exactly what year it was on the future's calendar until just now." Indy scratched briefly at her ear with a front paw. "And our data on this time period is pretty thin. If the battle of Thermopylae hadn't been mentioned in so many little quotes embedded in later works, we wouldn't even have as much information about it as we do."

"I still feel like an idiot," Anna said. "We've been making up plans and bumbling along, but we should've put more thought into what was going to happen next." She blew out a breath. "I guess I'm just not used to thinking of the future as a known thing."

"Indeed. Our world certainly didn't work that way." Indy paused in thought. "And this world may not work that way either. At least not for much longer. If we *do* manage to change things, for the better or the worse, this new history will diverge from ours. It probably already has, to some extent, due to penicillin and our school. Soon we'll be flying blind again."

"Okay, so speaking of blind," Anna said. "Let's get some drones moving and see what's going on. What have we got available?"

Indy's collar lights flashed, and a list scrolled onto their shared screen. "Our long-range fleet is still tiny. The one large carrier-drone can only travel about five miles one-way without a recharge, and our recharging drones along the route to Athens are too weighed down with disguised solar cells to travel with any speed. Plus, they can't move with their cells unfolded." She scrolled further down the list. "We have three long-range drones that are solar-powered, but their solar cells had to be small to keep them inconspicuous, so they can only gather enough power to operate for part of each day. Right now, we've got them all out upgrading our maps in other parts of the country, but we can refocus them to the north."

"How long will it take to find Xerxes' army?" Anna asked.

"Ironically, now that we're looking for them, large armies and navies should be easy to spot." Indy's collar lights flashed as she looked something up. "Our best information says that the ancient Greeks and Persians have to pull their ships up on shore at night, so we can just trace the shorelines north until we find them."

Her collar lights twinkled again, and the icons representing their three long-range drones flashed to indicate their status. "Two of our drones are pretty far south, so it'll take them a few days to get back up here on their pre-programmed paths before they're close enough to receive new orders. But the third one is just north of here, and it's been charging all day." Indy flashed her teeth in a grin. "And these new spy-drones still may not have much power density, but they've got optics like you wouldn't believe. It's a clear day, so we'll wait until we're almost out of sunlight, then we'll send the drone straight up a few miles and scan the coast long-distance. It'll be poor quality, but worst-case we should see Xerxes in a couple of hours."

"Might as well get an early dinner then." Anna stepped back from their screen. "There's no point standing here watching until it's time." Anna tapped at her phone. "The drone'll send us a ping when it sees something."

The two friends adjourned to the kitchen for a tense dinner. Anna ordered a ham sandwich, but munched at it numbly, barely tasting it.

Indy stepped up to the fab and popped the door, revealing the usual plate of mini-burgers. "Are you sure you don't want some chips, at least?" she asked Anna. "There's never a point in a dull dinner."

"Sure." Anna brightened. "The jalapeño ranch ones, please."

Indy flashed her collar again, and the fab dinged a few moments later. Anna reached in and took out a bag of chips, pulled it open, and dumped them out on the plate with her sandwich. She looked thoughtful, then brought out her phone and entered another order. After another *ding!* she withdrew a small bowl of steaming queso.

"Ugh." Indy stuck out her tongue mockingly. "Queso on ranch-flavored chips?"

"I thought you said that true canines are always hungry!"

"That's true." Indy dropped her jaw in a grin. "But there are some limits of good taste, even for us. And why do you fab those chips in a bag, anyway? Why not just fab them right on the plate?"

"The bag is half the fun." Anna opened and closed the empty bag mockingly, sending ranch seasoning crumbs flying. "Maybe even three quarters." She grabbed a triangular chip, defiantly poked one corner into her queso, and crunched it down. Then she pulled her phone out again and ordered some iced tea. "The chips do need some washing down, though."

The two friends sat together eating, mostly lost in thought. They had dumped the dishes back into the fab for recycling and were pondering what to do next when Anna's phone buzzed. Indy's collar lit up at the same moment.

They ran back to the lab without a word, Indy's nails sliding as she went around the corner at speed. As they went, Indy sent commands ahead through her collar, so when they ran up to the big screen, a new picture was already in front of them.

It took Anna a few moments to make sense out of what was being displayed. Then she gasped involuntarily. "Xerxes' navy is *huge!*"

The image on the display was tinted subtly red in places, to mark where it was being enhanced to make up for the extreme distance and bad viewing conditions. But what it showed was clear enough. Dozens of narrow war galleys were pulled up onto a sandy beach, bristling with oars from multiple decks. Every one of them had another warship tied to its stern, and more were tied to *their* sterns, forming long lines out into the water, and keeping the mass of ships from colliding at close quarters. Icons on the screen showed where the drone had already surveyed many more landing sites in the last few minutes, with more coming into view as the drone swept its camera north along the coast. The drone's viewpoint was from miles aloft and was moving quickly, but the enormous number of men camped on shore was all too apparent. Campfires were being lit as the sun set, leaving a fiery trail for miles along the coast.

"Bringing up a summary." Indy's collar flashed, and numbers sprang up on the screen, showing an increasing total of ships and men that the drone had counted. "Four hundred ships so far."

"Four hundred!"

"Make that four hundred and fifty." Indy's voice was tense. "We're still counting. And that's just what we can see. There are mountains and hills blocking parts of the coast from our drone's point of view."

The two of them stood mutely as the totals increased. Within a few minutes the numbers stood at over seven hundred ships.

"Our estimate of their numbers is still uncertain," Indy said slowly. "But given what we know about this time period, there could be up to two hundred oarsmen and marines on each ship."

Anna thought for a moment. "That's a hundred and forty thousand men! And we haven't even seen the army yet!"

"They should be nearby." Indy searched the map. "Supposedly their army and navy advanced in parallel to support each other." As she spoke, another icon lit up on the map, this time inland of the others. "There, the drone has them." Her collar flashed, and a second inset window opened, showing the recorded video from the sweep of the inland site. The screen crawled with a confusion of men and beasts, each group seemingly wearing different clothing and weapons from the next.

"Look at all those maniacs," Anna breathed. "Marchers, camel-riders… oops, and camels don't seem to like those horse chariots at all." She paused, watching a near-collision on their screen. "Those poor animals didn't ask to get dragged into this." She moved her head, trying to get a better angle. "Ooo, those guys have helmets that look like foxes' heads. What *don't* they have in this army?" She took out her phone and poked at it. "Ah, they're from all over the Persian empire. That must be why they look so different from each other." She looked back at their screen. "Whoa! What's with the super-tall spear-guys, red on the left and white on the right? Best uniforms so far!"

"It looks like their bodies are painted that way, actually." Indy peered closer. "And those spears might be tipped with some kind of sharpened animal horn? But I'm hardly an expert on ancient militaries. And at this range, these images are highly interpolated by our nets, so some of the details may not be right until we get more data." She settled back on her haunches. "We might as well get comfortable. It could take a while to finish the survey, depending on how spread out they are."

"I know this sounds horrible," Anna said. "But a spectacle like this? I could use some popcorn."

Indy looked at her archly, then laughed. "I'm *always* hungry, remember? Bring a second bowl."

Anna walked off to the kitchen again, and returned to the lab a few minutes later with two steaming bowls of popcorn. The two friends sat and watched as their high-altitude drone tallied up their doom, crunching kernels as they looked up the odd bit of information on phone and collar. After another thirty minutes, the sun had set, and the totals finally stopped rising on the display.

"Well, that's all of them that we can see, anyway," Anna said. "A hundred and thirty thousand on land, and more than that on the boats. Er, galleys, whatever they're called. But that's almost a quarter of a million men! How do they even feed that many?"

Indy rose and nudged her empty popcorn bowl aside. "Remember what Echetlus told us back in town, about the Macedonian king Alexander supplying the Persians?" Her collar flashed, and their map pulled out to show a bigger picture. "From what we can tell, the Persian empire controls an enormous area, starting about one hundred miles north of here in Macedonia, and wrapping all the way around the Mediterranean clockwise, through Turkey and down past Egypt, ending to the south of us."

"It's like Greece is surrounded." Anna's after-dinner snack suddenly sat like a stone in her belly, and she set aside her popcorn bowl, guilty.

"All the land right up to Greece's doorstep is controlled by the Persians." Indy licked some leftover salt off her narrow black lips. "So they've had ample opportunity to ship non-perishable food and supplies ahead and stockpile them in friendly territory over the last several years."

"So *that's* what Echetlus meant," Anna said.

"Exactly," Indy said. "The Persians can field an army much bigger than you could supply by forage or pillage, because they've got the resources of a whole empire behind them, including Egypt, where much of the grain comes from." She stood up on all fours and began to pace around. "We'd better start preparing to hide. The safest option is probably to close down the school for a couple of years until the worst of the fighting has passed us by and the Greeks are back on the offensive." She looked at Anna sadly. "We may have to live shut up here in the tunnels for a while. It's probably best if people think we're gone, so we don't attract any more attention than we need to."

"But what about all the Greeks?" Anna asked.

Indy stopped pacing as she queried her collar. "It sounds like many of the Athenians evacuate and let their city get burned." Her voice was bleak. "Here in Boeotia, they'll probably just have to stand aside and let the Persians through, since otherwise they'd be crushed." She sighed. "I'm afraid the people here are in for a difficult few years. Even if their cities aren't burned, the countryside will be eaten bare, and they'll be forced to pay tribute to the invaders at the same time."

"There must be *something* we can do," Anna said.

"I wish there were," Indy said. "But look at how limited our resources are! We can build beetle-drones and small-scale toys like personal shields, but we're a long way from being able to make large defensive weapons." Her ears swiveled forward in thought. "Though there were some offensive weapons on our doomsday list that we could fab now if we wanted to. Biological weapons, nano-weapons, things like that."

"I don't want to *kill* the Persians." Anna spoke firmly. "I just don't want them to destroy our new home. Things were just starting to go right, for a change." She thought for a moment as she prodded her phone's screen. "What if we make a bunch of tiny drones, then sneak them into the Persians' food supply to spoil it? If they see that they're going to run short of food, they'll *have* to pull out, if Greece really can't feed them all."

"It's an interesting thought, though we still can't make tiny drones that can fly that far on their own," Indy said. "But think of the consequences of that many soldiers, trapped in a foreign land, when they suddenly realize their supplies are running short. They'll seize everything edible and leave, and the Greeks will starve behind them." Indy sat back down again. "It might kill fewer people overall if we hit the Persians with something terrible enough that they're forced to run for their lives." At Anna's shocked look, she added, "Not that I'm advocating that, mind you. Unleashing biological weapons against the Persians would put us into war-crimes territory. But even if we just hide out and do nothing, we'll still be letting many thousands of Greeks die in the invasion. Though at least we wouldn't be *directly* responsible for their deaths." Her ears lay back against her head. "It's unfortunate. But sometimes even with great power, there's nothing you can do that won't make things worse."

Anna stood and paced. "I can't accept that!" She slowed, looking at the map again. "But a quarter of a million Persians. That's…" Her face twisted with worry. "That's really a lot."

"It might be all we can do just to survive this." Indy's face mirrored her friend's concern. "But before we can decide anything, we need to know a lot more about how the Greeks are going to respond." Her ears swiveled forward confidently. "And I think I know how we can find out."

65

ndy's idea had been simply to ask Neleos' parents Timais and Nephele if they knew about any Greek plans for resisting the Persian invasion, since they seemed well-connected. But it paid off better than they could have hoped. Two days of hurried preparation later, Anna and Indy set off to Corinth with Timais, Nephele, and eight more Lebadeian delegates to an upcoming congress of allied city-states.

The first day of the trip was familiar, the same route through Haliartos and south of Thebes that they had passed along on their way to Athens. But on the second day they turned south instead of east, crossing from Boeotia into Attica near the fortified town of Eleutherai. They trekked along narrow footpaths through the low, wooded mountains of the Megaris region, where they camped for the night under spreading fir trees on the isthmus leading to the southern peninsula that the Greeks called the Peloponnesos.

The third day saw them down out of the mountains, skirting the capital city of Megara before joining the main road that ran down the east coast of the isthmus. They passed the Corinthian region-marker along a road hemmed in by rocky hills marching right down to the seashore. To their left, out in the waters of the gulf, cargo ships plied the waters, the voices of the crews and sounds of the oars coming to their ears intermittently on the sea breeze. At the end of the third day they camped early, retreating off the road and up into the wooded foothills of the mountains to find a bit of privacy from other travelers.

Anna laid her pack aside near Timais and Nephele. Then, as she had during the previous two nights of camping, she unclipped Indy's saddlebags and gave her coat a quick brushing.

"Ah, much better." Indy walked away a few steps before shaking out her coat briefly and rejoining them. "Saddlebags are convenient, but my sides start getting hot after a few hours."

Nephele started a little as Indy spoke, then relaxed with an apologetic smile. "Sorry, I keep forgetting you can talk." She laughed. "You'd think I'd be used to it by now!"

"I wish everyone was as accepting as you and Timais," Anna said more quietly. "A couple of these folks have been giving us the eye for the whole trip, it feels like." She tilted her head back slightly to indicate one of their party some yards away, a man with a thin, pinched expression wearing clothes inappropriately hot for their long journey.

Indy looked across at the man as she spoke, her voice clearly audible across the camp. "Not everyone has the mental flexibility to adapt to new things." The man looked away, busying himself with his bags and speaking under his breath to his companion. Indy panted a laugh as she turned back to Anna and Nephele. "Let them look."

"Camp rations again tonight, my dear?" Timais looked up from his pack, holding bread and cheese in one hand, and dried sausage in the other. His face held humorous resignation. "I suppose it's our only option, so I don't need to keep asking every time."

Nephele smiled. "One more day of travel, and then we can buy fresh food in Corinth," she said. "Until then, we'll just have to suffer."

"We still have some daylight left." Indy looked at the lowering sun, considering. "I might wander around for a bit and stretch my legs, see what there is to smell out there."

"I'll come too," Anna said. "I'm not quite hungry yet, anyway."

"Just don't wander too far," Timais said. "I know you two can take care of yourselves, but this is unfamiliar ground for you."

"We'll be careful," Anna said. "You guys have a nice dinner, and we'll be back in a while." She waved goodbye, nodding at the nearest of their group as she joined Indy on her way back toward the road.

"It's nice not having eyes on my tail for a change," Indy said once they were out of earshot of the camp.

"Most of them mean well. There's only one or two that keep giving you looks." Anna laughed. "Honestly, I'm surprised people didn't kick up more of a fuss."

"Who could resist all this?" Indy tossed her ruff, shooting Anna a mockingly smoldering look. "Any reasonable human is already predisposed to like my kind. The talking is just a bonus."

They picked their way back across the road and down a long slope toward the rocky shoreline off in the distance, Indy trotting from side to side and sniffing at the bushes. She raised her head and scented the sea breeze. "Smells like someone cooking down there." She nosed toward the ocean. "Grilled fish, maybe?"

"Remember what Timais said." Anna looked around as they walked, but couldn't see anyone amid the low shrubs. "We don't know who might be out there. Actually, hold on a sec." Indy stopped as Anna reached into her small day-bag and pulled out one of their tiny bee-drones. *Alixa, send this drone ahead to see who's cooking.* The fake insect flew up and out as Anna and Indy continued walking.

A few minutes later, Alixa's voice came over their link. *A cargo ship has beached for the night. The crew are ashore cooking dinner.* Her synthetic voice paused as the bee-drone fed back more information. *Several women and children have joined them from a nearby village, bringing food.*

Anna relaxed. "That sounds safe enough." Her stomach growled. "I'm getting tired of bread and cheese, too. I've got some coins on me. I'll bet we can buy something better off these guys. What do you say?"

Indy turned back toward Anna, drool hanging from her muzzle.

"It smells great from here. I'll let you do the talking, you know what I like."

The two of them kept walking, and soon they could see the cargo ship their bee-drone had reported. It was different from the warships they'd seen in their drone images of Xerxes' navy. Instead of being long and narrow with oars along its entire length, this ship was short and wide, with oars only at the front, and a square stern seemingly made to be pulled up on shore when a dock was not available. The square sail was furled for the evening, and the ship was secured by long ropes ending in shore anchors driven deep into the gravel a few dozen yards up the beach.

Anna stopped when she was close enough to be heard. "Ahoy, the ship!"

Ahoy? Indy's mental voice was amused. *Really?*

You're just mad because you don't know boat words, Anna said.

Several of the crew had looked up at her hail, and one of them, an older man, beckoned her to approach. She and Indy picked their way down the beach, gravel crunching under their feet, until they were near enough to talk easily.

Up close, the older man had a kindly face, though it was seamed from years on deck under the sun. A woman of similar age stood beside him, looking at Anna and Indy as they approached. Around them, the rest of the crew continued their preparations for dinner, hauling more fish down off the deck and cleaning them, or foraging off in the brush further along the shore for firewood. Many women worked among them, dressed as villagers rather than sailors, sorting vegetables from baskets. A few children ran about, playing as their parents worked.

"Hello, sir. I'm Anna." She extended a hand to shake as soon as she was close enough. "And this is my dog Indy." She tilted her head to where Indy had sat down calmly beside her.

"My name is Celeas." The man's voice was raspy from a lifetime of shouting orders at sea. "I'm the captain. This is my wife Perse. And this—" he smiled at a tall young man who joined them "—is my son Crathis, our first mate."

"I didn't know we were expecting anyone but family, Father." Crathis' voice was light as he smiled at Anna. "You're not from Krommyon too? I would've remembered you, surely."

"Krommyon?" Anna looked around, puzzled.

"Our village," Perse said, no-nonsense. "Can't see it, but it's off there a ways." She pointed down the shore. "When our men sail past, we come down here to meet them. Bring them some fresh greens for dinner, so all their teeth don't fall out. I'm a sailor's wife, but that doesn't mean I like 'em gummy."

"Best part of the Piraeus to Isthmia run," Celeas said. "We make a good profit shuttling back and forth, and get to see our families going both directions, plus the houses here are a lot cheaper than in Athens or Corinth. And it keeps the teeth in our heads." He bared his front teeth mockingly to his wife. "So, what brings you to our camp, young lady?"

"Well…" Now that they were actually here, Anna felt a little embarrassed. "We're traveling with friends down to Corinth. But we've never been this way before, and wanted to explore a little before dinner. And then Indy smelled your food, and we… I mean *I* figured I'd come down and see if we could buy something tasty to eat, instead of another night of travel food."

"We'd be glad to give you whatever you'd like!" Crathis, the handsome first mate, spoke up before his father could. He smiled broadly at Anna, prompting his father to roll his eyes in good-natured derision.

"Son, you're never going to be a trader if you bargain like that." Beside him, his wife Perse suppressed a smile. "At least wait for her to make an offer, for Poseidon's sake!"

Anna quickly worked out a reasonable price for her and Indy to sample the food the sailors and their wives were cooking, and handed it over to Perse for safekeeping. Then Crathis jumped to prepare her food, skewering bits of grilled fish on small slivers of wood that could be carried around without the need for heavy plates.

Nice. Indy smacked open-mouthed on a bit of fish from a skewer Anna held out for her. *Just olive oil and salt, but well done.* She licked her lips, and Anna held out another skewer. *Though you could've just batted your eyes at Crathis a few more times, and we'd be eating for free.*

Anna colored, glancing aside to where Crathis was returning with his own fish skewers and two more bearing what looked like roasted turnip chunks. He handed one to Anna, and she sampled it tentatively before passing it on to Indy.

"Would you like to see the ship?" Crathis asked. "It's nothing fancy, but I noticed you looking earlier."

"Sure." Anna looked up at the square stern. "How do you get on, though?"

Crathis laughed. "We're all sailors here." He pointed to a rope ladder dangling from one side. "The boarding plank's only for when we're docked." He juggled his two fish skewers into the same hand and swarmed up the eight-foot ladder with practiced ease, then turned and beckoned her up.

Anna put her last skewer between her teeth and climbed with both hands, waving Crathis back when she reached the top. She took the skewer out of her mouth and looked out over the railing, out to sea. "Nice view from up here."

Crathis was looking back down at the beach. "Will your dog be all right down—whoa!" He leapt aside as Indy appeared at the top of the ladder, having made the vertical leap with height to spare.

Please. Indy dropped her jaw in a smile at the surprised Crathis, then padded around the deck, sniffing at bundles and storage lockers. *Why climb if you can jump?*

"Well, welcome aboard then." Crathis grinned at Indy, then turned to Anna. "Not too much to see, but the breeze is nicer up on deck. I like to eat up here, myself." He gestured past the sail to the front of the ship, where a few of the crew lounged on the rowers' benches, eating their own dinners and passing around a wineskin. "Down below is all storage. Tomorrow we'll unload at Isthmia, and they'll cart it across to Corinth, then sail it through the gulf and across the sea, to Kroton and beyond. We don't see any of that, though. We just take on another load at Isthmia and haul it back to Piraeus for the Athenians."

He stripped the last bit of fish off his skewers with his teeth, then threw the thin slivers of wood overboard as he chewed. "You were heading to Corinth, you said?" He spread his hands in invitation. "You could always hitch a ride with us."

Indy laughed over their link. *This one is persistent.* She looked up from her investigation. *But at least he's polite. And handsome?*

Anna laughed, embarrassed. "I'm traveling with a group. We're going to a meeting of the Greek alliance, to hear about plans to try to fight off the Persian invasion."

Crathis' face grew grave. "I'd almost managed to forget we had that hanging over our heads. We heard the news a few weeks ago." He looked out to sea, letting the breeze blow his hair back over his shoulders. "Even if they don't get this far, it'll be terrible for trade. Piracy's always worst when there's a war." He looked back at Anna. "We might just pack up everyone's families and head south, further around the Peloponnesos for a while. It's better than worrying."

Anna stirred. "We should probably get back to our friends." She checked the sun, which was beginning to set. "I don't want them thinking we got lost somehow."

Crathis looked disappointed, but bore it gracefully. "Let me at least pack you a bit more food to take along. You've hardly—" He broke off, ear cocked to the wind. "Did you hear that?"

"What?" Anna looked north along the beach, but didn't see anything but a long, graveled expanse, breaking into shrubby trees a few dozen yards inland.

The other way! Indy was alerting the other direction along the beach. When Anna whipped around, she saw a group of perhaps a dozen men running on the packed ground above the high-water line, approaching fast with weapons in hand.

All around them the alarm went up from the sailors. On the beach, a few of the youngest scurried north with the women and children, disappearing quickly into the trees toward the unseen village of Krommyon. The others snatched up their gear and scrambled up the rope ladder into the ship, rushing around to retrieve weapons and push bags into their storage places.

"Raiders." Crathis' father Celeas spoke from a lookout at the rail, slightly winded from the hurried climb up onto the deck. "Probably hauled out on the other side of that spit south of us." He gestured along the beach at the running men. "Bastards know we can't sail off until morning, when the wind'll be with us." He gave the attackers an assessing look. "Not enough of them to board us, though. We just need to fend them off until the men from the village get here."

"Some of those kids run like deer." Crathis clapped his father on the shoulder. "They'll be there and back in no time." He turned to address the crew. "Be ready to take cover! I saw bows among them."

As if hearing his words, three of the attackers knelt, fitted arrows to strings, and began loosing them toward the ship. With so few bowmen, it was not withering fire, but it was enough that the ship's crew had to keep their heads down.

"Ready at the rails!" Celeas' harsh voice rang out. "Stay low, but be ready to repel boarders."

More problems. Indy's voice came tense over their link. *I sent our drone up to look. The boat that dropped this bunch is incoming from the south.*

"Crathis!" Anna called into the tense waiting. "Their boat's coming from the south!"

The young first mate chanced a peek over the rail, and dropped to the deck again, swearing. "Ten more in a longboat, father. They mean to swarm us."

"Hold steady." Celeas' voice was firm as if he'd done this many times before. "We don't need to beat them, just keep them at bay until we're relieved. They know it, too. If they don't overrun us in the first rush, they'll cut their losses and—"

A pair of iron hooks bit into the wood at the stern gunwale, opposite where the ship's own rope ladder had been pulled up after the crew. Two more solid clunks announced another pair of boarding ladders on the starboard side, facing the oncoming pirate longboat. The ship rocked at anchor as the ladders took the weight of their attackers.

Wait! Celeas mouthed the words silently to his crew.

Hands appeared at the top of one ladder, but the crewman nearest to it held his short sword at the ready instead of striking at the vulnerable fingers. When a raider's scowling face thrust up into view, he got a blade in the neck, and fell gurgling into the shallow water. The rest of the crew cheered, and Crathis flashed Anna a fierce grin.

A heavy *thud!* shook the vessel. Then arrows began sailing up from right beside their ship, arcing high into the sky to fall back, point-first, toward the deck. One of the ship's crew howled, his leg laid open by the slow but still dangerous missiles, and the rest tried to shrink under cover. Another boarding ladder clanked into place, and the deck tilted to starboard as more weight came onto the attackers' ropes.

"They've got another boat!" Anna spoke out loud, relaying Alixa's words as she slewed their bee-drone about invisibly high above them. "They're coming in from the other side!"

Celeas' tanned face slackened in despair, but his voice sounded as strong as ever. "Hold your blows until you're sure of a kill!" he called out loudly, seeking to undermine the attackers' morale. "We only need to hold them off for a few more minutes!"

We need to escape. Now. Indy's voice sounded tense over their link. *Our drone can see the village from here, and they don't have nearly enough men to take on these pirates.* She flashed Anna a look where she huddled up against a supply locker. *There are probably thirty more armed men in the second boat. We're about to be overrun.*

But how? The sun had just slipped below the mountains to the west, plunging them into sudden twilight. But even at noon, Anna wouldn't have been able to see anything from her position flat against the deck. *They're all around us!*

The starboard—the right side of the ship, as you face the sea, Indy said. *The pirates on that side have fewer men aboard, since half of them attacked from the land to distract us.* She belly-crawled across the deck toward Anna. *Their boats are narrow. Jump straight over them, into the sea, then use your shield to skim along the surface. It should be able to float you. Just don't try to stand up.* She gathered her haunches under her.

But what about—

Hup! Indy sprang aloft with a grunt, easily clearing the rail and soaring out into the air. A moment later Anna heard a splash. *Wait a few seconds, then follow.* Indy's voice sounded bubbly, her collar's software adding the sound effect to indicate that she was swimming below the surface. *It's the last thing they'll expect.*

Anna squirmed over to the gunwale on knees and elbows, then squeezed between Crathis and his father and braced herself under the rail with her feet on the deck, ready to jump. Ten feet below, a longboat full of pirates looked up at her.

One of them drew his bow in an instant and shot her in the throat.

66

The arrow bounced away from Anna's neck with a dull rasp, the shield generator at her back doing its work. But the shock of it made her body jerk involuntarily. She lost her grip on the rail and tumbled into the longboat full of pirates with a cry, Crathis' horrified face receding above her as she fell.

Her back slammed into one of the thwarts, shield engaging to muffle the impact and to keep her back from being broken across it. She rolled forward, sandaled feet splashing down onto the bottom boards. Rough-handed pirates grabbed her from every side, and she shrieked.

Indy!

What's happening? Indy's voice sounded breathless, but lacked the bubbling sound effect from before. *Are you behind me? Swim around behind the spit before you stand up, and they won't see you.*

They got me! Anna thrashed, but on a boat there were no walls for her shield to push against, no way for her to shove the men aside with pure strength. She was surrounded by the shield, but without any leverage it merely clung to her skin, preventing her from being stabbed or slashed.

I'm coming! Indy shouted. *Hold on!*

Anna sagged to the bottom of the boat, pirates piled atop her. She thrust her hands upward, but instead of launching the pirates into the air, her shielded arms just slid through their midst. The boat rocked from side to side, unable to apply any lateral force without a firm grounding.

Wait. Anna concentrated, subvocalizing a new command to Alixa. Her shield reshaped itself, smoothing any edges that might offer a hold, extending a thin wedge ahead of her along the bottom of the boat, allowing her to slip forward into the gap. She shoved forward, squeezing under and between the pirates like a watermelon seed, until she slipped over the gunwale and into the water.

Summer or not, the cold seawater hit her like a shock. She twisted around, submerged and disoriented, before she remembered Indy's earlier advice. She broke the surface, forming her shield into a shallow, invisible pan beneath her, and paddled as hard as she could away from the longboat. *I'm out! I'm coming!*

She shot forward over the darkening ocean, her shield offering much less resistance than a boat's hull would have. She could hear shouts behind her, and an arrow punched her low in the back and went skimming off in front of her. But the longboat was held fast to the merchant ship by its boarding ladders, and the attackers couldn't cut loose and row after her in the middle of the action. In moments, she was hidden intermittently in the troughs between swells as she paddled away, and soon she was out of earshot of the pirates.

I've got you on the drone feed. Indy's voice was calmer now. *Go forward for another minute, then cut to your right, and you'll see me on the beach.*

Anna splashed onward, out of breath now. Paddling up each long wave made her feel like she was going backward, but then slipping down the other side on her shield shot her ahead. She began to hear surf, and in a few more minutes her feet touched the pebbly bottom. She walked forward, then staggered to her hands and knees in the surf as a wave took her.

"Right here." Indy spoke aloud from just ahead, rising to her feet in the gloom. They were screened now from the pirates and merchants alike by the same narrow spit of land that the pirates had first attacked from. "Follow me."

They ran up the beach for the tree line, Anna crouching over, Indy running protectively beside her. When they reached cover, they turned to look back toward the merchant ship and its attackers.

On deck, Anna could see the crew silhouetted against the dark sky, hands raised. Pirates walked among them, a few holding lanterns, the rest either menacing the crew with their weapons, or tying up their newly taken prisoners. She gasped as one crew member was knocked to the deck by a cudgel's blow, his face unrecognizable in this light and from this distance. She hoped it wasn't Crathis, but there was no way to tell.

"They're restraining the crew." Indy growled low. "Hopefully that means they'll only be robbed or ransomed, and not killed."

"We've got to do something!" Anna fought to keep her voice at a whisper.

"What would you suggest?" Indy looked back at her. "There must be dozens of them, when you count the second longboat." She stared out at the beached merchant ship again. "They knew what they were doing. A distraction from the shore, then two boats close in on them."

"I could sneak back down there, sink those pirate boats." Anna struggled to think of something useful. "I didn't think of it before, but my shield could pull their planks apart and let the water in."

"Then we're facing forty angry pirates on land," Indy said. "We could use our shields to snip off their heads like dandelions, or break their limbs, at least for a few minutes until they run out of energy. But short of that, what options do we really have?"

Anna shook her head, sickened by the thought. "But—"

"And what about the rest of our party, at our campsite back across the road?" Indy sounded weary now. "If we attack these raiders and fail, and have to run away, we might lead them right to Timais and Nephele and the others. Even that idiot who keeps eyeballing me when he thinks I'm not looking." She sighed, eyes gleaming in the dim light. "We're not infallible, or invulnerable.

Remember what happened last time we used force on someone?" She looked down. "Maybe it's better for everyone if we don't get any more involved."

"Not for everyone." Anna's mouth twitched into a pained expression. "What happens to Crathis and the rest?"

"The same thing that would've happened if we'd never come here." Indy's voice softened. "We can't fix everything that's wrong about this world. We're already doing everything we can, with the school and everything else. If we push it too far…"

"We could make things even worse. Again." Anna mastered herself, slowly. "You're right." She looked away from the beach. "I just hate it."

"I do too," Indy said. "But let's get out of here. Before we change our minds."

67

They trudged back to camp, dripping and exhausted. Their drone, critically low on power after all the action, had to ground itself and wait for the next day's sunlight. But there was no hue and cry from behind them, and after a tense half hour or so, they seemed to have escaped without pursuit.

Timais, Nephele, and the rest had long since finished dinner, so Anna and Indy simply settled down with them to sleep, after reassuring everyone that Anna's wet clothes and Indy's damp fur were just the result of a late-afternoon swim at the beach. They left collar and phone on watch, with alarms set as usual. But their sleep was disturbed only by uneasy dreams of what they'd witnessed, and by their guilt over leaving the merchants to face whatever fate the pirates had planned for them.

The next morning dawned another fine Greek summer day.

Anna's first thought was to check on the merchants, but their drone wouldn't have enough power to fly again for hours yet. She twisted uncomfortably in her clothes, trying to break up the crust of salt that had dried into them the night before, but it didn't help much.

After a quick breakfast the party set out, rejoining the road and heading south. They took their time, since the meeting in Corinth wasn't due to start until tomorrow. Anna was fine with their slow pace, since the hike soon revealed bruises and stiffness developing after their misadventure of the previous day.

Around noon they came to the Diolkos, a four-mile-long stone trackway cutting all the way across the isthmus from west coast to east. It was crowded with wagons full of trade goods, and even a small ship being hauled overland to avoid sailing south around the Peloponnesos. To their left where the trackway met the sea a busy port bustled, loading and unloading cargo from ships similar to the one that had hosted them the afternoon before.

The drone just finished recharging enough to go and check. Indy spoke in answer to Anna's unasked question. *And the beach was empty. No ship, no merchants, and no pirates. The drone doesn't see them down there at the port, either.* Indy paused, an uneasy silence. *With any luck, the pirates just robbed the crew, then set them free to go back to their village. They probably took the ship off somewhere else to transfer the cargo.*

"We did the right thing." Anna looked down. "The smart thing."

"I hope so." Indy turned away from the port and Anna fell in beside her, following the rest of their party. The last part of their journey passed slowly, silently putting one foot in front of the other, since neither of them felt much like talking. Finally, that evening, they pitched camp outside the city of Corinth, and fell asleep warm under the stars.

Late that night, Anna stirred to wakefulness and looked up at the wide, dark sky. Beside her, Indy's ears twitched to the sounds of the ocean a mile distant.

It wouldn't have done anyone any good for us to get ourselves killed. Anna squeezed her eyes firmly shut again. *Right?*

There was no answer.

68

The next morning, Anna and Indy stood outside an open-air theater in Corinth, ready to hear the Greek alliance's plan to repel the massive Persian invasion.

Corinth was a coastal city, built at the narrow neck of land that connected central Greece to the large almost-island of the Peloponnesos to the south. The early-morning sun shone white from the arcs of stone benches rising in front of the circular stage. The mountainous bulk of the Acrocorinth loomed half a mile further inland, a peak of monolithic rock encircled by walls and crowned by temples, its sides girdled by groves of scrubby oak. And everywhere in the packed theater there was an enormous hubbub as hundreds of delegates to the congress of Greek city-states engaged in last-minute politicking before taking their seats.

I hope this trip is worth it, Indy said over their link. The two of them were well outside the theater, but they could hear every word clearly, thanks to the tiny flea-drone that Anna had planted on Timais' clothing earlier. *It sounded like a good way to get some first-hand information about what was going on. But I didn't realize it'd be so dangerous just to get here.*

You couldn't have known, Anna said. *And I'm glad you'd caught that Neleos' father is one of Lebadeia's delegates to that Boeotian League thing.* Anna craned her neck, trying to see the stage better. *Apparently that gets you into this congress too? Surprising that even little Lebadeia has a dozen people here.*

This is much bigger than Boeotia. Indy tried not to look around too obviously. *There are representatives here from all over Greece. Though I did overhear someone say that the Theban delegation is unusually small.* Her mental voice turned dry. *People seem to think they're secretly siding with the Persians.*

Can't blame them for thinking it. I'm not the biggest fan of Thebes myself, what with Nicon and his gang. And I've never even been there. Anna looked around their camp, reduced in size now that Timais and their other voting delegates had entered the theater. Nephele was sorting through the supplies the party had brought along, and she beckoned Anna over. Anna discreetly turned down the audio of the meeting as she approached, Indy a pace behind her.

Nephele greeted them with a smile. "I still don't know why you two volunteered to come all the way here for this. Political meetings are infamously tedious." She frowned. "Even when there's so much at stake, and so little time to decide."

"We could hardly just sit at home waiting to hear the outcome," Indy said. "History is being made here that will affect us all, for better or worse."

Nephele laughed. "I think you'll find that history-making is less exciting on an empty stomach. Would the two of you mind going to the market to get us some fresh food before it's stripped bare?" She indicated the field around them, which was crowded with the retinues of all the other delegates from all over Greece. "Fresh greens, bread, whatever seafood looks good, enough for say, twelve people. We can buy more travel food before we leave, but I'd like to eat something fresh at least once, after coming all this way."

"Sure, not a problem." Anna and Indy had already sampled fresh food with the ill-fated traders of Krommyon two days before, but they hadn't told the story to Nephele and Timais, so she tried not to let her expression show anything that would require explanation.

"I'll see if they have any frog legs, while we're there." Indy smacked her lips enthusiastically. "It smells like a good-sized town, so it should have a nice market." She paused as a thought struck her. "Wait. Are there such things as saltwater frogs?"

"Don't worry, we'll bring back more than just frog legs," Anna said to Nephele with amused reassurance.

"Go on then." Nephele turned back to the group's haphazard pile of bags. "We should be set up to cook by the time you get back."

Anna and Indy walked purposefully toward the center of Corinth, Anna not bothering to hide her rubbernecking since there were so many others here from out of town.

I've asked our nets to summarize the meeting, Indy said over their link. *In case something interesting happens while we shop.*

The delegates are all talking at once. Alixa's impersonal voice began a running commentary. *Summary will begin once a trend is detected.*

Huh. Anna smirked to herself. *Maybe it's less boring this way anyway.*

Politics seems to be the same in any time period. Indy stopped and peered down the street. *A lot of interminable yapping.* She sniffed the air carefully, waving her head from side to side. *This way!* She set off again, leading them deeper into the city.

They eventually emerged into the market and hurried up and down the aisles, trying to finish their mission as quickly as possible. Occasionally Alixa would say something like, *Unidentified delegate from Coroneia failed to negotiate better seating,* but mostly it sounded like nothing was happening yet.

They collected a good quantity of fresh vegetables, cucumbers and artichoke among them. They also found barley bread, end-of-season asparagus, and some freshly netted red mullet which they wrapped in a cloth Nephele had given them, once it passed Indy's smell test.

One final addition was some kind of fish sauce called garos by the locals, which was pungent enough that even Anna's nose could pick it out from yards away. By the time both their packs were filled, their stomachs were grumbling, so they returned to the market's edge for Indy's favorite treat.

Mmm, fennel-flavored. The giant canine took a dainty bite from one of the two skewers of frog legs Anna held for her. *These coastal Greeks seem to know a thing or two. And there's wilted beet greens between the pieces!*

Anna had opted for her usual vegetable skewers, and chewed contentedly as they walked back out toward the theater. *You and your frog legs. Good thing Lebadeia's near a giant lake, or I'd never hear the end of it.* She grinned as Indy took another bite from the frog leg skewer without deigning to comment. The sun was shining overhead, and even with the threat of the Persians in the air, it was still a beautiful early-summer morning.

Anna's smile faded into a thoughtful frown. *Hey, so... I know we'd kind of decided to try to avoid getting too involved in things. To make sure we don't mess them up worse. But...* She stopped, unsure of herself.

Indy looked at her friend, sympathy in her eyes. *I know that was hard on you, back at Krommyon.* She walked along, swallowing the last of her bite. *But it wouldn't have been worth the risk, us charging into a situation like that with no preparation and no backup.*

You're right. Anna nodded slowly, convinced but not agreeing. *But maybe we could come up with a plan ahead of time, to keep us out of danger?* Anna held the frog leg skewers out to Indy again. *Like, what if we could just make the Persian army sick, somehow? Like really bad diarrhea or something, where they couldn't fight? Eventually they'd have to give up and leave, right? And we'd just be watching from home.*

Indy looked thoughtful as she took another bite. *Well, we weren't lucky enough to get any textbooks on ancient military history from your dad's data dump.* She chewed and swallowed as she spoke through the collar. *But my impression was that in the old days, disease killed more soldiers than the enemy did. So we'd have to hit them with something pretty deadly, or it wouldn't be any worse than what they already live with.* She gave Anna a guarded look. *That almost puts us back into biological weapons territory.*

Crap. Anna took another bite from her vegetable skewer.

You're probably right. She chewed distractedly. *Let me think about this some more.*

Remember, this invasion is the Persians' and Greeks' fault, not ours. Indy took the last bit of frog leg from the skewer and crunched it down. *This situation sounds like it's been developing for decades.* She tossed her head. *There may just be nothing we can do.*

They walked the rest of the way in companionable silence. Once back at the Lebadeian camp they unloaded the food, gratefully handing off the cooking responsibility to Nephele and the others. Then they settled down in their own corner to listen to the meeting again as they watched the stage from a distance.

Up to this point, the delegates had mainly discussed the previous congress, and the happenings between then and now. A few months ago, the Greek allies had sent a force of ten thousand or so by ship to somewhere up north called the Vale of Tempe to try to intercept Xerxes' army. They'd been warned away by Alexander, king of Macedon, who basically told them the Persian army would squash them flat, since it outnumbered them and could come at them from two sides. Of course, this was the same Alexander who was supplying the Persians as they rolled through his land, so who knew which side he was really on?

The Greek army hadn't even seen a Persian yet at this point, but there was still some news to report. As Anna and Indy tuned back in, a grizzled representative from Sparta mounted the stage to speak. His time limit was measured by a jug of water on a squat pedestal, which slowly drained through a tiny spout into a lower jug.

Spartan delegate rhetorically reminds the congress that the Spartan queen Gorgo learned of the Persian invasion via encrypted communications from an informant in the Persian court, and says he has fresh news, Alixa said coolly over their link.

Oops. Anna spoke quickly via her earring. *Alixa, please switch off summary mode.*

"To those who would stand aside from this fight, or who think to placate the barbarians with money, consider my few words well." They couldn't see the Spartan delegate clearly at this distance, but to Anna it looked like he raked the assembled congress with his eyes. "We have already learned much that is bizarre and dismaying about our would-be conquerors. Now, from Sparta's own spies, we add another piece of infamy. The Persian emperor's delusions of godhood are such that he ordered the sea itself whipped after his first bridge across the Hellespont was blown away in a storm." This was met by general laughter, though it sounded more like a mixture of nerves and bravado than true amusement. The Spartan delegate waited for it to subside before resuming.

"And what is more! He is so hateful, even to his own subjects, that after the vastly rich Pythius of Lydia donated his entire fortune to aid Xerxes' army as they passed through—more than *four million* gold staters!—Xerxes would not even agree to spare the man's eldest son from military service to carry on his line." He paused dramatically. "Instead, Xerxes ordered Pythius' son split bodily in half, and he marched the entire Persian army between the pieces!"

A roar of voices arose, asking questions and shouting out insults to the Persians. The Spartan delegate waited for the noise to die down again. "So, do not think that Xerxes is merely another ruler, on whose mercy you might rely. He is a monster, and if allowed into Greece he will destroy us all!" He slapped the still-emptying water jug beside him. "You can pour out the rest! That's all I have to say, and it should be more than enough." He stood aside, and the chairman again took the stage.

The debate that followed was tortuous and frequently interrupted, so Anna turned Alixa's summary mode back on to make sense of it. Over the next hours, she and Indy heard expressions of outrage from the participants, estimates of the size of the Persian army and navy, rumors that the Persians had lost a great number of ships in a storm, and a motion from the Thebans that Athens had provoked Persia by encouraging the Ionian colonies to revolt, and so should be left to face the consequences alone. This last was shouted down, and the Theban delegation eventually withdrew the motion.

I wish we could tell them what we know, Anna said. *There must be something in all our drone video that would help.*

That's assuming we could make them believe us. Indy sighed. *And they're so outnumbered, it probably doesn't much matter what they do.*

Anna looked pained, but she couldn't think of a good answer to that.

Finally, after much back and forth among the delegates, a plan was agreed upon. The Greek allies would send a force to Thermopylae, a narrow seaside pass which would hopefully prove more defensible than Vale of Tempe had. Boeotia alone would send 400 Thebans and another 700 soldiers from Anna and Indy's region to join King Leonidas of Sparta and his men at the pass. There they would be joined by reinforcements, both by land and sea, and hopefully turn the Persians back.

If the Persians broke through at Thermopylae, then Boeotia would buckle down and hope to be merely invaded and pillaged, instead of destroyed outright. Athens, as a special target of Persian ire, would evacuate its citizens to Troezen to the south. And southern Greece would regroup and try to repel the invaders again at Corinth.

By the time Timais and the other Lebadeian delegates returned to their little camp and sat down to dinner, the sun was dipping low in the sky, and spirits were even lower.

"Personally, I don't see how we can hold back so many." Timais spoke between mouthfuls of hot grilled fish wrapped in bread. "After all that fine speechmaking, those idiot Spartans say they can't even send their full army because of the festival of Carneia and the Olympics!" He snorted. "I think we all know the truth. They're holding back so they can defend the isthmus here at Corinth if the Persians crush the rest of us." He took another bite. "At least King Leonidas has enough honor to join us at Thermopylae. He's only bringing 300 hoplites, but there should be a few thousand other Peloponnesians with them. Maybe that'll be enough to tip the scales."

"It's times like this when I'm glad we're only merchants and not nobles or generals." Nephele arched an eyebrow as she handed her husband a napkin. Timais wiped his greasy chin with a smile for his wife that mixed sheepishness and affection. "But merchants or not, we'd all feel an invasion's effects," she continued gravely. "Even if Xerxes passes us by, we'll be living on millet and acorns next winter after they strip us bare."

"What will you do?" Anna was nibbling on a piece of the bread, still full from her snack in Corinth earlier. Plus, the stressful situation had taken away her appetite.

Nephele stood and slapped her hands together, dusting the crumbs of her meal into the fire. "We'll do what we always do. Hide what we can. Run if we must. Stay alive."

"An invasion can't last forever," Timais said. "Xerxes must be overextended, even with help from that traitor Alexander. His men need to be back in Ionia before winter, or they'll starve right along with us." He dug with one fingernail for a fish bone caught between his teeth. "So we'll spend months placating Persian soldiers, then learn to deal with whatever puppet rulers they leave behind." Timais grimaced bitterly. "Not a pleasant thought, but we can probably survive it." He exhaled a long breath. "The Athenians, on the other hand, are doomed if we can't hold Thermopylae. They really poked the lion in the eye when they helped the Ionians burn Sardis!"

Nephele looked sorrowful. "When Xerxes' father died, it seemed like they had escaped their fate. But the son seems bent on his revenge. Even if it's only an excuse for conquest."

Timais put his hand on his wife's arm and squeezed it gently. "Don't worry, my dear. Enough of our holdings are in currency now that if things get truly dangerous, we can flee."

"But what about the people in Lebadeia? And Haliartos and all the rest?" Anna's dark eyes shone in the firelight. "We can't just abandon them!"

"What else can we do?" Timais said gently. "Nephele is right. For all my talk, we're still only merchants. And the Persians may be too much for anyone." He gazed into the fire. "You should join us, if it comes to that. I hate to think what might happen to you, and to a strange and wonderful creature like Indy, at the hands of those barbarians." He turned to include Indy as well. "Whatever happens, we'll keep our family safe."

The journey back to Lebadeia was a somber one for their little group. Initially the Boeotians all travelled together, but they split off as they approached their own cities, and eventually the Lebadeians were on their own for the final leg of their trip. Finally, after saying goodbye to Timais and Nephele in town, Anna and Indy trudged wearily up the hill toward their school, half an hour after the sun had set.

"Strange to see it with so many windows dark," Anna said.

"We can't very well start another term with a war coming." Indy's legs moved steadily, their feathering dusted by the week's hard travel. "If our students have any sense, they'll be somewhere far away from here."

"I know." Anna sighed. "I just wish things were different."

Indy's eyes softened. "Me too. But tonight, I'll be glad to sleep in my own den again."

The front door of the school unbolted and opened at their knock, revealing Phaia's slim figure illuminated by a lamp she held up in one hand. "Took your time getting back," she grumbled, but she couldn't hide the worry on her face. "Give me a minute to get the others. You can tell us the news all at once." She trotted off down the hallway toward the faculty quarters.

A moment later, a huge brown-and-black blur hurtled out of the darkness, barking joyously. "You're back! Back! Back!" Argos shout-barked, prancing in a circle around them.

"Yes, yes, we're back, no need to shout," Indy said. She laid her muzzle beside his in a long greeting, then broke the tender mood by shouldering him playfully aside.

Argos wagged his tail wildly for a few more moments, then remembered his dignity and turned to Anna. "You're back too! Good!" he said, still a little too loudly for the entrance hall. "Sorry." He lowered his volume with an effort. "Talking still hard." He turned another circle and nuzzled Indy again. "Back!"

Phaia reappeared with her lamp, this time with Themis and Melas in tow. Themis smiled and embraced Anna and then Indy, while Melas busied himself relieving them of their bags and gear, setting it all aside for the moment in the hallway.

The big former smith smiled tightly. "We will get you unpacked properly after some food and drink. The kitchen staff just sent word around about dinner a few minutes ago."

"Screw dinner, let's hear the news!" Themis said. "I've been bored cross-eyed here the last few days, with no one to teach and not much to do. And every time there's a knock on the door, I jump out of my skin, thinking it's the Persians here to start the pillaging early."

"Indeed." Melas' low voice was tense. "There is only so much study and preparation one can do when it sounds like war is imminent."

"You got that right, hoss." Themis thumped Melas in the ribs. "It's almost scary, when *we* finally agree on something."

"Let us feed our friends and hear their story," Melas said amicably. "Then we will know if we worried for good reason or not."

The six of them, two hybrid canines and four humans, walked down the hallway to the dining room, Phaia lighting the lamps inside from the one she carried. Anna could hear noises from the kitchen, and after a few minutes the door bumped open and their cook emerged, bearing a large platter of stuffed fig leaves. She set it on the table before them with a smile, then retreated slowly back toward the kitchen.

Indy saw this and called out to her. "Feel free to sit with us and hear the news. None of it will be a secret for long, and you deserve to know as much as anyone else. You can bring out your assistant too," she added.

"If I do that, who'll finish plating dinner?" The cook looked mildly scandalized. "But I'll stay for a minute, if you don't mind." She settled at the next closest table.

Indy took a deep breath and launched into the story, with Anna interjecting here and there to expand or clarify. The cook went back to the kitchen after the initial summary, but sat down with them again after she delivered the main dish, a lentil soup with chunks of yesterday's roasted goat, seasoned with salt and coriander.

They ate as they talked, with Anna and Indy each taking turns so the other could eat. Argos devoured his meal in moments, then curled up under the table and immediately fell asleep. Indy smiled and continued talking, but the tale didn't take that long to tell. When it was finished, the company ate quietly for a few more minutes, Melas wiping up the last of the soup with his bread. The cook took the empty dishes and returned to the kitchen with a nod of thanks.

"Sounds like that's it, then." Phaia regarded Anna and Indy, her gaze flat. "And of course, those rich bastards in Athens have a plan to evacuate themselves, while the rest of us get run over." She looked around at the others. "I don't know about you, but I'd say we should pack up and head south for a while. The Athenians brought this on themselves. No reason for us to suffer for their mistakes."

Themis leaned back, flicking her eyes toward Phaia. "My girl here probably wouldn't spit on Athens if it was on fire. But she's got the right idea." She pursed her lips in distaste, gesturing at the walls around them. "I'd hate to have to build all this again if the Persians wreck it while we're gone. But keeping all my organs on the inside is kind of a personal top priority."

"I am not disagreeing, precisely." Melas' voice was even slower and deeper than usual. "But I wish there were some other option." His heavy brow furrowed. "Think of all the suffering that is in store for the Greek people. With what we know, we could do much to help."

No one spoke, and a long silence crawled by as Anna struggled with her doubts. Then, hesitantly, she forced herself to stand up.

"I have a plan."

"A plan?" Phaia seemed more surprised than contrary. "A plan to do what?"

I'll explain later, I promise. Anna shot Indy a quick glance. *But I can't just stand by again, like we did at Krommyon.* She swallowed, her throat suddenly gone dry. *Back me up?*

All the way. Indy's words came back without hesitation, and Anna's heart swelled with gratitude.

"There might be a way to turn back this invasion," Anna said.

"How would *that* work?" Phaia asked.

"Anna and I have discussed some ideas." Indy spoke from where she sat, one haunch pressed against Argos' sleeping back. "None of them are certainties, and there's no predicting exactly what might happen as a result. But I think there is at least a chance of doing what she says."

Melas' face settled into skeptical lines. "Armies are dangerous things." He looked aside, voice bleak. "With strength enough, even a peaceful man may find himself a killer, in a moment of rage or grief." He nodded at a sympathetic look from Themis, opening hands which had clenched unbidden into fists. "And invasion is not the work of peaceful men."

Anna squirmed, thinking of what to say. "We were already doing what we could to make things better here, with your help." She looked across the table at the Greeks. "And we always figured that eventually, you guys would know everything we do."

"But we've been working toward that goal carefully," Indy broke in. "You're all good people. But it's dangerous to introduce too much knowledge too quickly, even to the best of people with the best of intentions." She looked an apology at Phaia. "We saw that first-hand back in Athens."

"This invasion changes everything, though," Anna said. "To do anything about it, we really need your help, so we're going to have to risk speeding up the timeline." She paused, looking uncomfortable. "I can't give you the full explanation quite yet. But the short version is, we need to travel somewhere close to the Persian army and navy, carrying probably a couple hundred pounds of stuff between us. We'll drop the stuff near the bad guys, stick around for a bit to make sure it's working, then run away quick if everything goes like we think it will."

Phaia stood up slowly from the table. "I spent ten *years* as a slave." She looked at Anna wearily. "It's not your fault. But you can't know what it was like. How many curse-tablets I buried, calling down the gods' vengeance on the people who… *wronged* me." Her eyes flashed. "Cursing them instead of suing them, because a slave's testimony is only valid under torture." She looked down. "I'm not risking my life to help them."

"I don't want anyone to risk their life." Anna spoke earnestly. "We'd be traveling *toward* danger, but not *into* it. We only need to get within a few miles of the Persians for this to work."

"The element of risk remains," Melas said. "Traveling on the eve of war, things happen. People and armies are not where you think they will be. Even with all due care, this plan could prove to be very dangerous."

"I've got no love for the elites here," Indy said. "Phaia's right. They're slavers and worse, in many cases. Anna and I have *met* one of those cases." Beside her, Anna shuddered at the memory of their encounters with Hylas in his compound north of Athens.

"But think about the rest of the people of Greece," Indy continued. "Or even just the towns and cities here in Boeotia. Thebes may be sympathetic to Persia, but that won't save them if a huge army occupies this area." She paused, considering how much to say. "We believe the Persian army is so large that it exceeds the capacity of the entire Greek land mass to feed it. They've only managed to travel this far by building up supplies for years in advance along their route. If they can't be turned back, they'll eat the land bare in weeks. Most of them would have to leave before winter one way or the other, but there will be famine behind them."

"I'm willing to listen." Themis' expression stayed neutral. "I can't promise anything more, though." She tapped a finger on the tabletop in thought. "My people are from Ephesos, originally, so the ones that stayed behind have lived under the Persians for a long time now. And yeah, it's not great sometimes, but they're surviving."

"I will need more convincing as well," Melas said. "My nephew and my shop are still in Athens, but people can be evacuated, and shops can be rebuilt."

"I'm sorry." Phaia stepped back from the table. "I know everything you two have done for me." Her voice shook with emotion when she continued. "I'll stay here and help guard our school, or I'll help move our things down south. I just can't—" She broke off. "I'll see you all in the morning." She turned and walked swiftly out of the room.

Melas slowly made to rise and follow her, but Themis put a hand on his shoulder. "Give her some time." She looked at the big smith. "I've worked with you for years now, on and off. And I may talk a lot of smack, but that's only for fun. I know you're a good man." Her eyes hardened. "That's why I'm sure you can't even imagine the things that happen to female slaves in this country. Every day."

Melas' face darkened at this, and he looked as though he would object, but then settled down with a sigh. "Who can blame her?"

Themis turned back to Anna and Indy. "And not to be mercenary, but what's in this for us?" She tilted her head toward Melas. "Prancing all over the countryside where I could get my rump roast carved off isn't exactly what I signed up for."

"Fair enough," Anna said. She shifted uncertainly, looking at Indy. "Let me work out a few details first. And we may need to leave before we can lay it all out for you."

Themis opened her mouth to object.

"But I promise you," Anna said quickly, "before we get near anything dangerous, we'll come clean. And then you can tell us if you're in or out."

70

The next morning, Anna woke up late. The sun was already well up in the sky, its rays slanting in through her window, which looked out over the school's back courtyard. She and Indy had stayed up long into the night, with Anna first explaining her latest plan to her skeptical friend, then the two of them working out details and starting fab orders before finally returning to their rooms at the school to fall exhausted into bed.

She stood up, body aching from the hard travel of the last week, then groaned when she saw the contents of her backpack still scattered where she'd dumped it out after dinner last night. She dug through the mess to find her toiletries, and a few minutes later she was out the door, hoping that there was still something left from breakfast.

When she got to the dining room, she saw Indy and Argos lying companionably side by side near one of the tables. When Argos saw her, he jumped up and began tapping his forefeet, drool gathering at his jowls as he rocked left and right.

"Don't mind him." Indy looked at Argos with amusement. "He's just been waiting for you to come down before I let him eat all the rest of the food." At this, Argos salivated even more, long strands wagging down toward the stone floor.

Anna laughed, then loaded up a plate from the remains on the serving platters. When she was done, she set the platters on the floor for Argos, who wasn't as dexterous as Indy yet, and the big sheepdog gobbled as if he hadn't already had breakfast.

Anna bit into a sausage. "What's up with him, by the way?" She waved the stub of her sausage at Argos. "Is Doros around here somewhere too?"

"Doros is due to visit tomorrow, but Argos is here most of the time now, apparently." Indy shook her head. "Themis told me that he showed up three days ago and insisted that he was staying right here until I got back." She looked at Argos fondly as he ate. "He's been keeping the cooks busy, too. Dogs grow a *lot* during uplift, so he's always starving. Doros caught up with him the day after he got here, and we arranged a room next to mine for Argos to sleep in, so he wouldn't run himself ragged traveling back and forth."

Anna grinned widely and elbowed Indy in the ribs as she took another bite of sausage.

"Don't even say it," Indy said.

"What? I didn't say anything." Anna grinned even wider.

Argos trotted over, having polished the serving platters with his tongue, and settled down on the floor beside Indy again. He glanced at Anna, but soon his eyes drooped closed, and seconds later his breathing was slow and even.

"Sleeping the sleep of the innocent." Indy's eyes softened, and she looked at Argos a moment longer before turning back to Anna. "His manners are improving, at least. Two weeks ago, he would have put his paws up on the table."

Anna finished the rest of her breakfast quickly. With a murmured reassurance from Indy, the two of them left Argos to his nap, and walked down the hall toward their secret tunnel entrance. After they slipped through the hidden door and started down the long hallway to their rooms, Indy updated Anna on their progress.

"Last night's fab orders are finishing with no problems, so it looks like we're going to make it. Assuming Xerxes' army doesn't do a sudden forced march, at least." Her heavy paws met the stone floor silently as she walked. "We'll end up with about one hundred and eighty pounds of equipment to carry, but it's in small pieces, so it should be manageable for the four of us. Though it will be heavier than I would prefer." She made a show of looking over Anna's sturdy but petite frame.

"Don't worry about me," Anna said. "I can carry my share."

"I know you can," Indy said. "All the same, I'm loading myself and Melas heavier. It's just common sense," she said to cut off Anna's objection. "We both outweigh you, and not by a little. Melas must be packing thirty pounds of biceps alone."

"I'll work on our food for the trip, then," Anna said. "If we carry dried food and get our water along the way, that'll help lighten us up. We can probably map out every little creek in this part of the country from all the drone flights we've been doing."

"Good idea. Summer's not too far along, so the streams should still have some water in them." Indy turned into the storage room where their helper-drones had been stacking their gear as it came out of the fab, surveying the new items there with a critical eye.

There were four leather backpacks: Anna's old one, which she'd brought over last night, plus three more in varied designs, suitably rustic-looking with hair left on the leather at the edges, along with Indy's stylish black-and-silver saddlebags, re-fabbed after they were burned up in Athens. Indy walked over to one of the new backpacks and flipped open the unlaced top, revealing a thin inner sack occupying the bottom half of the pack. It held what looked like many small wooden boxes with red lids, tapered slightly at their bottoms. Indy scooped one of the boxes out with a dexterous paw and tossed it to Anna, who caught it with a surprised grunt. "These are heavier than they look."

"Don't open it," Indy cautioned. "They can flex out of shape if you pop the lid. And try not to handle them too much. They're finished to look like wood, but they're made of very stiff paper. They won't stand close inspection if we get searched along the way, but we had to save weight somehow."

"What about these packs?" Anna tugged at the strap of one of the new ones. "No one's ever said anything about mine, but I don't recall seeing anyone else wearing one."

Indy shrugged, the gesture incongruous on her canine frame. "The ancient Greeks don't seem to have anything quite like a modern backpack, but hopefully these are not too unusual. If anyone asks, we'll blame the Iberians, the same as we do for the rest of your peculiarities." She opened her mouth and let her tongue hang slightly in a mocking smile. "I did take the liberty of padding the straps. There's no sense in the four of you chafing your shoulders raw."

Anna sighed and pulled one of the packs aside. "Just three of us now, remember? Might as well redistribute Phaia's share while we're here." She paused. "And hopefully the other two won't back out once we tell them what we're planning. If we have to carry all this ourselves, we won't make it five miles."

They spent a while sharing out the load, then looked over their original equipment, checking for wear and making sure their waterskins were still supple. Finally, there was no more to do, so Anna asked Alixa to tell one of their helper-drones to come by later and transfer everything into the school's storage room once everyone was at lunch.

She dusted her hands together and looked at Indy. "So, back to the school, grab lunch, then hand out packs to Themis and Melas and let them put their own supplies on top?"

"Perfect." Indy rose to leave the room. "Just remember to tell them not to open the boxes."

Anna grinned. "That's going to drive them crazy. Maybe they'll stick with us just so they get to see what comes out."

"Then dinner and a good sleep tonight," Indy said. "We leave at first light tomorrow."

77

Just before sunup the next morning, the air was still cool from the night before, but the clear sky promised a hot day of traveling. Anna was the first one to drop her bag in the school's entryway. A few minutes later Themis joined her, then Melas soon after that, looking bleary.

"I never did like getting up early." He rubbed at his eyes. "The best feature of smithy work is that it provides its own light source, so we can do it after dark, like civilized people." Themis snorted at this, but forbore to comment.

The three of them turned at the sound of paws on stone, and a moment later Indy and Argos rounded the corner, both fully kitted out for travel.

Anna looked at Argos, surprised. "He's got a harness and bags? Since when? I thought he was staying behind to help Phaia watch the school."

Indy looked abashed. "Once it sank in with him that we were going on a long journey, he wouldn't take no for an answer." Argos' tail waved slowly at this, and he looked very pleased with himself. "Plus, he'll help lighten all of our packs. Which is just as well, because he said he'd follow us anyway if we tried to leave him here."

Anna went to one knee in front of the big brown-and-black herder. He had grown considerably larger during his ongoing uplift treatments, and from this angle with all his gear strapped on, he looked formidable.

Anna looked Argos in the eye, and he met her gaze with very un-doglike directness. "Argos, we may be going into danger. We'll be careful, but there's always a chance something might go wrong. Do you understand?" She put a hand on his shoulder. "I don't know if you're ready for this yet. You're still developing, and there's no shame in being careful."

Argos looked back at Anna steadily, then nodded his head toward Indy. "Where she goes, I goes. Go." He planted all four paws solidly. "I'm ready!" he barked.

Melas smiled at Argos' determination, and Themis shrugged. "Splitting this load one more way is the best idea I've heard all morning." She shed her backpack and started pulling out the contents. "Come on over Argos, you can have some of mine. Damn straps're already giving me goose-neck, and we haven't even left the building."

The five of them milled about rearranging their packs, so nobody noticed at first when Phaia joined them in the entryway. She had cut her hair off just below the ears, closer to its old slave length than she'd worn it since leaving Athens. It was a bit ragged in places, but she was dressed for travel.

Anna looked at her blankly in surprise. "I thought you were going to stay behind. To take care of the school." She glanced at Argos. "Also."

Phaia smiled lopsidedly. "That's what I thought too." Her face grew more serious. "But I was up half the night tossing, thinking about you idiots out there traipsing across the country without anyone street-smart to keep an eye on you." She took in Argos' trail-ready appearance with a snort. "And I can't leave you alone for a whole day without you picking up strays."

Melas stepped forward and embraced Phaia solemnly. "Your help will be welcome."

Themis came up as well and the two women clasped forearms, Themis glancing at Phaia's uneven hair. "I can shape up the back for you on the trip. You decided to stop growing it out, then?"

"Just didn't feel right on me," Phaia said. "The real change was on the inside, anyway. Someone doesn't like short hair on a free woman, that's their problem." She backed up a step. "And let's be clear. I'm here to make sure you all don't get yourselves killed. We go, we drop your stuff, we come back, story over. If it doesn't work and Athens gets burned to the ground, I'm not going to cry."

"Understood," Anna said with a smile. "We're glad to have you. And I really like not being dead." She took in Phaia's gear with a critical eye. "Let me go get you a backpack. We've got some stuff for you to carry."

During the repacking, there was a sharp knock at the school's front doors. Anna looked around, but no one seemed to be expecting anyone else. She opened the doors to find Leitus and Helene, both breathing hard after rushing over from their cottage.

"We heard you'd be leaving this morning." Leitus' face was grave. "Going off to do who knows what."

"And there are a few formalities to take care of," Helene said. "When a man sets off on a long journey or goes off to war, usually it's his wife who's responsible for seeing him off properly." She looked around at their motley group of humans and canines. "But in this unusual case, I think the job falls to me." She held up a small jug and a flat dish. "Come on, we need to do this outside."

Once the party had assembled outside the school doors, Helene poured watered wine from the jug into the dish and held it up. "Hermes, god of travelers, bless their journey." She poured a few drops of the wine onto the path leading away from the school.

Leitus took the dish and continued the invocation. "Pan, the Arcadian, friend of Athens, enemy of Persia. And god of shepherds," he added, looking at Indy and Argos. "Bless their journey." He dribbled more of the wine onto the nearest tree trunk, then passed the dish around the party so each traveler could take a sip.

"And now that that's done, one last thing." Leitus pulled out a floppy, wide-brimmed traveler's hat, similar to the kind that Thrasius had always worn, and handed it to Anna. "For shade, on your journey," he said. "It's hot out there."

"Thank you both." Anna took the hat and gravely settled it on her head. "And don't worry. We'll be back before you know it."

"Heroes! We go!" Argos barked.

Anna looked at Indy. "Heroes?"

"Doros has been telling him stories like 'Jason and the Argonauts' to teach him more words." Indy dipped her head in embarrassment. "So now he thinks we're... going on a quest."

Anna laughed, bright and carefree. "Well, he's not wrong, I guess." She smiled and looked around their little group. "You heard the man. Er, dog." She pointed along the trail. "We go!"

The six friends waved their farewells to Helene, Leitus, and the staff who had come out to see them off, then started down the trail. The way was easy at first, the road down to Lebadeia familiar. They had to travel further to reach the shore of Lake Kopais, since it had already begun to recede for the summer. And instead of turning right as they always had, toward Haliartos and Thebes, they turned left and followed a narrow "summer road" that cut through the drying marsh in the other direction.

"Hard to believe the Mycenaeans drained this whole thing, way back in the Trojan Horse days." Themis gazed out over the lake on their right. "Maybe it's a little squishy and buggy, but it's not like Greece has water to burn."

Indy laughed. "Anna and I had the exact same thought, the first time we saw it." *Though in our case, it was the British who drained it,* she added over their link. *It sounds like history repeats itself.*

Melas spoke up. "They say Herakles and the Thebans filled it back up by plugging the outlets, to defeat the Minyan king Erginos of Orchomenos."

Themis laughed. "The big guy's always been like this," she said to Anna and Indy. "Brain-muscles even bulgier than the rest of them. Either that, or he just makes this stuff up to see if anyone notices."

"Well, this would have happened seven hundred years ago or

more, so the truth of that tale is uncertain." Melas looked sheepish. "But I remember reading it somewhere."

The travelers threaded through the marsh until they reached Orchomenos, at the lake's westernmost point. They crossed the Kephissos River and passed quickly through the sizeable town, pausing only a few moments here and there when Melas couldn't restrain himself from pointing out sights like the blunt masonry cone of the ancient tomb of King Minyas, or the gravestone of the poet Hesiod.

On the far side of town they crossed a bridge over the springs that fed the Melas River, stopping for a few minutes to rest and refill their waterskins. "Purely a coincidence," Melas said with some irony when Anna asked about the name. "My mother named me after Melas, the son of Poseidon. But in the name of this river, the word means simply 'dark,' for the color of the water." He gestured to where the river ran out toward the distant marsh. "Later in the summer, this river threads even farther out onto the plain, but in the winter its course is mostly submerged beneath the lake."

As they headed north, up into the low mountains of northern Boeotia, the going was difficult, but not impossible. There were narrow trails and paths, though the party only occasionally saw other travelers. Thanks to the excellent maps that Anna had fabbed before they left, they were able to find their way along narrow tracks through the hills, and to refill their water from tiny rills and hidden springs. As the sun at last began to set, they were just reaching the southern slopes of the Knemis Mountains, so they decided to make camp before the last climb. They could make their way over the pass and down to the shore of the Malian Gulf in the morning.

Melas traced a finger along the map, which he had been examining with great interest. "It looks like there is a sheltered place a little to the east of here." He looked at Anna with mild amusement. "I look forward to hearing how you were able to incorporate this level of detail."

Anna took a deep breath and looked over at Indy, who nodded back. "I think it's time to explain the rest of the plan, so you guys can make your choice about whether you want to go ahead with this." She kept walking, stepping off the trail and heading east into the brush. "It's gonna take a while, though. We'll have to explain… wow, a *lot* of stuff." She looked doubtful. "Or the plan won't even make sense." She paused, holding a branch aside until Phaia could catch it behind her. "The *whole* whole story may have to wait until we get back."

"Let's wait until we set up camp, at least," Phaia said. "A story like this wants some food and drink."

"Seconded." Melas squeezed his bulky form through the narrow gap in the trees. "I can wait a few more minutes, after this long."

They reached a clearing in a grove of tall trees, well-placed in the lee of a hill, and set about making camp. It didn't take much work, since the early summer evening was perfectly comfortable. A few minutes later they were gathered around a small fire, munching on their travel rations. Argos gobbled his down in moments, then curled up as usual with his back against Indy and fell instantly asleep. The rest of the Greeks tried not to look expectant as they ate.

Indy nodded to Anna again, who took a last sip from her water-skin and began to speak.

"Thank you guys again for coming with us before we explained everything." Her throat tightened with emotion. "Your faith in us really means a lot."

Themis lifted a wry eyebrow. "Not like it was *purely* on faith. It's pretty clear that you two have been holding back the really juicy stuff." Phaia smirked at this, and Melas nodded agreement.

"Still. And hopefully you'll… well, you can decide for yourselves after you hear everything." Anna paused to dig around in her pack. "First, we have presents for you." She brought out three thin, matte-black rectangles a little larger than her hand, each one a twin to her own phone. She passed one to each of the Greeks, and Themis immediately began turning hers this way and that, tapping it with a fingernail and rubbing at its surface to feel for hidden seams.

"Hold it up like this, in front of your face." Anna pulled her own phone out of its hidden inner pocket under her belt to demonstrate, and the three Greeks copied her. "Okay, now wait a moment." She tapped her own phone, and the three other screens came to life, Greek words and background imagery glowing bright against the darkening day.

Melas dropped his with an involuntary grunt, then prodded its glowing surface with a finger before picking it back up with an embarrassed expression. Themis laughed at him good-naturedly as she peered closely at her own screen.

"We call these things 'phones.' Try not to drop them." Anna smiled as she tapped her own phone lightly against a rock. "They're pretty tough, but no point taking chances."

Phaia snorted. "Are they going to talk?"

Anna looked surprised. "Well yeah, actually. But how did *you* know?"

"An accident of history," Indy said. "When they were first invented, they were used to talk to others at a long distance, so we called them 'telephones.'"

"Ah, 'far-voices'! That makes sense." Phaia looked up from her phone. "Though that still doesn't explain why so many of your outlandish things have Greek names, when you two are from Iberia."

"Getting off track here," Anna said quickly. "We're giving you these phones so we can communicate if something bad happens when we're separated. Phaia, put your finger close to your phone, like you're going to poke it."

Curious, Phaia complied. "It shows little pictures of us now!"

"Exactly," Anna said. "Tap the picture of me."

After a moment of searching the screen, Phaia tapped the picture. Anna's phone rang, and she held it up so the Greeks could see. "When someone calls you, tap this thing to talk to them." She demonstrated, then aimed her phone at her face and spoke. "Phaia, can you hear me?"

Phaia laughed with delight as Anna's small voice emerged from her phone. "I can see you too! It's a tiny picture, and you're at a strange angle, but it moves!" Melas and Themis crowded closer to see, then started to experiment with their own phones. Anna quickly demonstrated the other basic communication features and had the Greeks practice calling each other a few times until they'd gotten the hang of it. Melas tapped Indy's picture out of curiosity, and laughed in delight when Indy's collar lit up and her answering voice emerged directly from his phone instead of from her collar.

"You can also talk to the phones themselves," Anna said. "They're not self-aware, since it'd be wrong to build a thinking being into a phone. But their neural nets can answer questions and help you make sense of things. I call mine Alixa, but you can call yours whatever you want, or just say 'hey phone.' You'll have to talk to your phones out loud for now, since you don't have special implants like me and Indy." She paused. "Oh, and one last thing. You'll need to put your phones near mine every couple of days to recharge. Um, to feed them energy," she added at Melas' questioning look. "Sorry about that, but we can't make more of the power cells that are built into my phone and Indy's collar yet."

Indy spoke up. "There's another reason for you to have these phones now, in addition to communication." She looked at the group soberly. "They're for you to use in case both Anna and I are killed during this mission somehow." Indy paused. "If the worst happens, your phones will show you how to get to all of our secrets back in Lebadeia. And at that point, the future will be in your hands, not ours."

They all sat for a few moments digesting this possibility before Anna broke the silence again. "So, back to our super-secret origin story." She paused, considering how to continue. "We *do* come from a land far to the west of here, just like we said. We've really tried never to straight-up lie to you guys. And my ancestors *were* from Iberia, a long time ago. But we came here from a place that Greeks have never visited. It'd be more than 6000 miles west of here if you could fly." Anna tapped her phone, and a map appeared on the phones of the three Greeks. "Here's where we are now, in the north part of Boeotia."

"Look, you can see Euboea across the gulf to the north!" Themis traced a finger along her screen.

"I suppose this answers my map question," Melas said, amused.

"The black dot is where we are now." Anna manipulated her phone, zooming the map out to show a wider area. "The red stars are Xerxes' army and navy. But don't worry about them yet."

"Only a few dozen miles from here." Phaia glanced up. "Good thing we didn't go any further west."

Anna manipulated her phone again, zooming their maps out further. "This is the eastern half of the Inland Sea, what my and Indy's people called the Mediterranean. You can see Persia to the east, and Egypt down here to the south."

She zoomed out again. "This is the whole Inland Sea, with Iberia, what we called Spain, at the mouth where it connects to the ocean." She zoomed out still further. "Then, 3600 miles of ocean west of that, is the eastern shore of our continent." She zoomed out a little more, showing the curvature of the Earth. "Then finally, halfway across *that*, is a place called Texas. That's where we came from." She tapped her phone again, bringing up grid lines and measurements for the Greeks to read.

"Hmm." Melas rubbed his chin, face intent.

"Pretty cool, right?" Anna looked smug.

"Indeed, indeed," Melas said, distracted. He looked at the map more closely, moving his phone slowly from side to side, then tilting it.

"Huh." Anna looked nonplussed. "I figured you guys would be more surprised, finding out the shape of the earth and how big it really is."

"Woman, please." Themis rolled her eyes upward. "We're not barbarians! Even Pythagoras knew the Earth was round decades ago, and he was a crackpot cult leader who thought fava beans have dead peoples' souls in them."

"What was the question again?" Melas looked up. "Apologies, I was just realizing that this phone must be aware of my eyes' position somehow. This map is like looking through a window, not down at a flat page. Fascinating."

"Whoa." Anna looked at her own phone, shocked. "You're right! Somehow, I never thought about it. That's just how they always worked."

Themis burst into laughter. Melas chuckled a moment later, and even Phaia smiled.

"What's so funny?" Anna asked, self-conscious.

"Sorry, boss." Themis made an effort to compose herself. "But you should have seen the look on your face!"

"Nice to see that we can surprise you," Phaia put in. "That you and Indy don't know everything."

"Of course we don't," Indy said with some asperity. "That's what we're trying to explain to you, if you would ever let Anna get to it." This with a pointed look at Anna.

"Okay, so try this on for size." Anna spread her hands. "We came here from almost 2800 years in the future."

"That, I was not expecting," Phaia said. Themis shushed her and leaned forward to listen.

"Our time wasn't so different from here. Or at least the people weren't," Anna continued. "I guess people have probably been the same since we split off from our monkey-like ancestors. Maybe before." Melas raised a hand at this as if to ask a question, but he saw Themis' glare and lowered it again silently.

"So, quick history of the next 2600 years for you." Anna gestured to suggest something expanding. "We got smarter and smarter about nature and science, and built bigger and awesomer things. We almost screwed up the whole planet from sheer stupidness, but pulled ourselves back just in time." She took a sip of water. "That was about 200 years before I was born, so I'm a little sketchy on the details. You can read our history books yourselves on your phones, once we're done with this trip."

"So then one year ago, my time, I'm going to school like any normal person," Anna continued. "And one day I go to visit my father, and run into this one here for the second time." She nodded toward Indy.

Anna went on to give a highly condensed summary of how the two of them had gotten to ancient Greece and what they'd done since, with Indy filling in the occasional detail. Even with much abbreviation, it took the better part of an hour.

At the end of her recitation, Anna sat back, looking relieved. "It feels weirdly good to finally tell all of that to someone here."

"That was… quite a story, boss," Themis said slowly. "I completely believe you," she added quickly. "But still!"

Phaia nodded slowly. "Explains how they could be so clueless about daily life, and yet have all this strange knowledge."

"And why Anna's speech is slightly delayed!" Melas said. "You're hearing Greek in your head, then repeating it out loud!"

"Well, not as much anymore," Anna said. "I picked up a good bit of the language after all this time. But I still have to listen to my translator if I want to say something hard." She patted Indy on the shoulder. "Indy always talked this way, so all she had to do was change a setting, and it comes out in Greek."

"It still sounds strange to my ears, hearing Greek when I'm thinking in English," Indy said. "But at least I don't have to speak with my mouth, like some sort of animal." Her jaws gaped in a grin, and Anna smiled back.

Anna drew in a big breath and let it out. "So anyway, long story very short, we're here from the future, we can't go back because it doesn't exist anymore, and we want to improve things enough so that when people *do* get back to our time the hard way, 2800 years from now, they have some chance of fixing or fighting whatever happened to us." She looked around. "Any more questions?"

The Greeks looked back at her and Indy, mute for once. At Indy's back, Argos was snoring softly, paws twitching.

Melas considered for a moment longer. "It is a fascinating tale. And it will take me some time to digest well enough to ask any deep questions," he said. "But I think there is at least one obvious question I should ask at this point." He poked the fire with a stick, raking it back to life, and added another piece of the dead wood they'd collected. "Namely, what is our plan to somehow defeat the enormous army of Persians that is camped not more than twenty miles away from this little fire?"

"Oh yeah," Anna said. "I forgot about that last bit. But compared to the story before that, this next part should be easy."

The next morning dawned gray and drizzly. Anna awoke slowly, chilled with dread from a dream where she and the rest of their little group had been discovered and run down by faceless Persian soldiers. The Greeks had all agreed to go ahead with the plan last night, but far from feeling reassured by their support, Anna felt an extra burden of responsibility, since it was her idea that had led them all into this.

This is going to work, right? she thought over the link to Indy.

I think there's a good chance. Indy looked over at her as she nudged Argos awake. *But I also read somewhere that the first casualty of any battle is the battle plan.*

Anna pressed her lips together. *Not what I needed to hear.*

It took a few extra moments to rouse Themis. It turned out she had been up all night watching historical videos about manufacturing techniques on her phone. "I regret nothing," she said, red-eyed, as she handed it over to Anna for recharging. "But I had to go back about four hundred years before your time before I could understand a damn thing." She gave Anna an appraising look. "When Phaia first told me about you guys, I figured I'd roll up, hit the books for however long, and then head back to Athens to cash in once you were tapped." She smiled tiredly. "But I think you're gonna be stuck with me. This is more like the work of a lifetime."

They broke camp and set out, Anna angling the hat Leitus had given her to keep the rain out of her eyes, and after a few hours' uncomfortable hike over the pass and down out of the mountains, the six friends stood on the shore of the Malian Gulf, the northern shore of Boeotia.

They'd had to wait half an hour under cover before emerging onto the beach, as a company of Greek soldiers marched past along the road toward Thermopylae. It was the first time Anna had seen such a thing outside of a history video, and even though some of them were talking and laughing together as they walked, the sight of that many people, armed and armored to kill their fellow men, struck her with an unexpected fear and disgust. She shared a look with Indy, but kept her thoughts to herself.

Out across the rainy waters of the gulf, Anna could see the hills of the long island of Euboea through the fog. Dark storm clouds hovered in the distance, but where they stood only a light rain was falling, and since all of them were soaked through after the morning's hike, it made little difference. To their right, there was a fishing village not too far distant. To their left, where the Greek soldiers had gone, she could see nothing but rocky shoreline, but she knew from their drones that the closest parts of the Persian army were less than twenty miles away in that direction. The air smelled of sea salt, with undertones of wet dog and sodden wool cloaks.

"So." Water dripped from the fur of Indy's belly, and she stepped back and shook briefly before continuing. "As we discussed, Argos, Themis, and I will hire a boat in the village to take us across to Euboea. It's only two miles or so to the other side, and a herdswoman and her two dogs shouldn't surprise anyone." She shook again, ineffectually. "Though I'm sure it'll cost us a premium to get anyone out in this weather."

"And after we cross, it's still twenty miles over the island to Artemision," Themis said. "Good thing I have you two to carry most of the weight." She patted the two sets of canine saddlebags with a smug expression.

"Be safe," Melas said to Themis. "There is no shame in running from danger. We're teachers and artisans, not fighters."

"Damn right about that, hoss," Themis said. "And you." She gave him a significant look. "If things go sideways, don't hold back. Because you know the other guy won't." Melas looked resigned as they clasped hands and stepped back.

"We'll coordinate by phone," Anna said. "The three of us here on the mainland need to get closer to the Persians for this to work, but we'll stay out of sight up in the hills as much as we can." Phaia nodded at this, and Melas looked thoughtful.

Indy looked at Anna. "Remember, there's no instant communication between separated armies in this age. We don't have to synchronize our actions, or worry that other forces will hear of them immediately. So just strike when your circumstances are right."

"Good point," Anna said. "Hopefully they'll never know what hit them."

"From your mouth to the gods' ears," Phaia said.

"Let's set out, then." Indy stepped forward. "Argos, with us!"

"We go!" barked Argos excitedly, then he looked apologetic. "*We go*," he whispered, as he remembered the need to hide his speech outside their hometown. He wheeled his wet, shaggy bulk around, much larger now after months of uplift, and followed Indy. Themis waved and set off after them, striding down the shore toward the fishing village and its boats.

"Before we start, let's use some of our unfair advantage." Anna looked back to Phaia and Melas. "Phaia, once we get under cover, would you like to check the map?"

The three remaining travelers walked away from the beach and back up the way they had come until they were hidden by the low trees and shrubs that grew here along the seaward sides of the mountains. Then Phaia pulled out her phone and began fiddling with its screen, still looking unsure despite their brief training session earlier. But after a moment she smiled as the map came up, showing the latest update from their spy-drones. All three of their long-range drones had finally converged on the area, so they had constant coverage now except for when one was recharging, or when the terrain or foliage blocked the view. They could also relay commands and data from one to the other, so as long as they stayed nearby and didn't let the drones get badly spaced, they could see everything as it happened.

"Looks like the bulk of the Persian army is still some way out beyond Thermopylae." Phaia poked at the rain-slicked screen, moving from a real-time view of the area back into recordings the drones had made of the past. "How can I look closer? I want to find out if the Persians have sent any emissaries yet."

"Slide your finger on the left side of the image to move your eye closer in," Melas said, looking over her shoulder.

"Got it," Phaia said. "Hard to get a handle on this *technologia* stuff of theirs. Greek name or not, it wants to slip right out of my brain." She panned to the edge of the Greek forces, then moved further backward in time until she saw a group of Persians in elaborate clothing approaching. "Aha! Got them." She peered closer. "Looks like the Persians showed up two days ago and talked to that tall, handsome specimen who must be King Leonidas."

"What?" she said at Melas' mildly amused expression. "No offense Melas, but everyone knows the Spartans are as good-looking as they are fanatical." She zoomed the screen in even further. "Can this thing look any closer?" She smirked. "For reconnaissance purposes."

"Are they covered with olive oil or something?" Anna leaned in to see for herself. "They're all shiny and muscley."

Phaia laughed as Anna looked away in embarrassment, then laughed harder as Anna looked back at the screen again. "And wait, are some of them... naked? Well, except for weird strings tied around their..." Her face colored. "Why?"

Melas shook his head, unable to suppress a grin.

"So, it looks like the Persian and Greek sides first talked to each other two days ago." Anna pulled her eyes away from the mostly-naked Spartans. "And from the best historical guess our nets could piece together, we think the Persians waited until four days after that to attack." She looked thoughtful. "But who knows how accurate that is? Even if we had a real history book for this time period, it was probably all hearsay when it was written down, anyway. We just need to get in there quick." She looked at Phaia's screen again. "Where's the closest we can get to the Persians without running into the Greeks?"

Phaia zoomed out and panned around some more. "It looks like we can climb up into the hills, away from the sea, then up onto Mount Kallidromo to stay south of our Greek allied armies. They're mostly bunched up at Thermopylae along the coast, with some spread out along the road between here and there." She poked at the screen. "These flying 'drone' things that show us these images should be able to warn us before we come too near any scouts as we climb. We should be able to overlook Thermopylae from a couple of miles away, if we get to the right spot. It'll be rough going, though."

"We will not be the only ones there." Melas looked up from his own phone. "It looks like some of the local folk have already moved into hiding places in the mountains." He looked grim. "They are probably wise to flee. Nothing good will happen to the villages here if Xerxes' armies punch through." He looked at his phone with a smile. "How could anyone ever plan a military campaign without one of these?"

"Think about it the other way around," Anna said. "What would Xerxes do to you to get hold of that phone?"

Melas' smile became brittle. "Or what favor could I gain from the emperor of Persia, if I sold him its advice?" He shook his head. "Assuming I could even keep possession of it. That would be a very dangerous game." He wiped the rain from his forehead with one hand.

Anna nodded. "We've been sleeping with that worry since we got here."

"So far, you've been pretty damn lucky." Phaia nodded her head upslope, and the three of them began walking as they talked, weaving here and there to avoid rivulets of water, as well as ripe figs that had fallen from a few trees growing wild among the scrubby oaks and bushes. "You started way out in the boondocks, among the poor and credulous." She smiled to take away the sting of her words. "Don't get me wrong, the Lebadeians are the salt of the earth. They're happy to take any blessing that falls on them, without trying to stab you in the back to get more. At least not right away."

Walking beside her, Melas nodded in agreement. "If you had arrived in Athens, well…" He gave Anna a sympathetic look. "We should just be glad that did not happen."

The land before them steepened, and the three of them saved their breath for climbing as the trees closed in around them. They checked their phones occasionally to find the best path, the Greeks still handling their new toys uncertainly, but with growing skill.

Finally, around midday they crested the shoulder of the low mountain, finding an overlook that let them gaze left and right along a mountainous valley. The Spercheios River ran down the wide valley floor from their left, its marshy delta emptying into the narrow Malian Gulf in front of them. Far beyond their view on the right, that same gulf led past the island of Euboea where the rest of their party should be hiking even now, and then out into the Aegean Sea. The rocky headland of Thessaly formed the other side of the valley, across the narrow gulf. Down below them, on their side of the gulf but hidden from this angle, was the narrow seaside pass of Thermopylae where the Greek army waited. And spread out everywhere in the distance, as far as they could see in the slackening rain and farther, was the Persian army.

The three friends stopped involuntarily at the sight. "By Zeus!" breathed Phaia.

"And Hephaistos too." Even stoic Melas seemed awed. "It's one thing to see it on a tiny screen. But I have never seen such a thing with my own eyes."

The smoke of thousands of campfires threaded up into the gray sky, some of the fires close enough to see, others just distant sparks or hidden behind hills and mountains. What must have been hundreds of supply dumps and campsites dotted the landscape, covering both sides of the marshy riverbed as far up the valley on the left as they could see, and extending all the way around the coast of the Thessalian headland across the gulf on their right. Distance and fog made it impossible to discern individual soldiers, but their drones' images, transmitted via their phones, made it all too clear how many Persians the Greek allies faced. The Greeks themselves were bunched up behind Thermopylae down below them and to the right, but couldn't be seen from their vantage point, since the pass was tucked so tightly against the steep slope down where their mountain met the sea.

"It's not looking good for our heroes, is it?" Anna looked around, then checked her phone and pointed upslope, back away from the overlook. "There should be a bit of shelter back there. It looks like it's time to see if this crazy idea works."

The three walked a short way to a copse of trees, then doffed their packs gratefully, Phaia setting hers down with a thump. "No matter how this turns out, I'll be glad not to carry all this back to Lebadeia."

Anna opened the top flap of her pack, then removed the small boxes inside and arrayed them on the ground nearby. Their tops were marked in red, to make it easy to orient them upward. Phaia and Melas followed her example, and soon the burden they had carried for so many miles was set out all around them.

Anna checked her phone one last time. "Well, we're definitely close enough." She frowned as she inspected the display. "The wind's not ideal, though." After a moment's consideration, she picked two of the boxes up again, replacing them in her pack. "I'll keep a couple in reserve, in case the weather improves later. But it could just as easily get worse, so we'll have to take our chances with the rest." She looked at Melas and Phaia. "Would one of you like to do the honors?"

"To make sure this is fairly done," Melas said, "the one who knows the most of its reasons and likely results should be the one to set it in motion. Not to deny my own responsibility," he added quickly. "I have thrown in my lot with you, and I trust your motives. But let it not be said that you were afraid to face the gods' judgement for your actions."

Beside him, Phaia nodded respectfully. "Well said."

Anna sighed. "I was afraid you'd say that." Her smile was rueful behind the water dripping off the brim of her hat. "Indy and I have done the best we can to make sure this will work. But at some point, we've got to roll the dice." She swallowed. "And if this all goes horribly wrong somehow, it's on us."

She raised her phone, took one final look at the display, and pressed a button.

The red paper lids of all the boxes popped open with a quiet noise. Inside were what looked like tightly packed black beans. But after few seconds, the beans began to move, revealing themselves as what looked like ordinary houseflies. Each one slowly wriggled free of its neighbors, unfolding its legs from under its body and spreading its wings. They took flight quickly, streaming away into the gray sky and disappearing.

Each box was solidly packed with the tiny fly-drones, and they had to take off one layer at a time, starting from one corner of the box and working toward the other, or there wouldn't be room to open their wings. Phaia crouched close to the nearest box to watch the little drones take flight, eyes wide. After a moment, Melas abandoned his dignity and did the same, getting down on all fours on the wet ground for a better view.

"Close in, you can tell they aren't really flies," Phaia said.

"They do have a bit of a metallic sheen." Melas looked closer. "Though I am not sure I would notice if I was not paying attention." He tapped his box lightly. "They are heavier than real flies too, even accounting for how tightly they are packed."

Anna paced nervously, watching the fly-drones stream up into the sky. As she looked on, a small blue-green bird took flight from a nearby dead tree, swooping through the fly-drones and emerging with one held in its beak. Moments later, more birds emerged from holes in the tree to join the hunt.

"You little savages!" Anna glared at the birds, then waved her arms at them and jumped. "Shoo!"

Melas looked at the foraging birds with concern. "Will enough of these flies survive for this to work?"

"I hope so," Anna said. In front of her, a fly-drone fell to the ground, crushed by a beak and discarded as inedible. "This has been a problem for us since we got here. We're always having to tweak our drones so critters don't go after them. But in this case, they had to look like real flies or the plan wouldn't work." She held up the crushed drone for a closer look. "Once they reach the Persian army, they have to crawl all over their weapons and equipment, and if they looked too strange, people might swat them all, or shoo them away until they run out of power."

Anna watched and worried as the boxes emptied out. But it didn't take long. Within fifteen minutes, the last fly-drone had left, and even so great a number of them were all but invisible against the fog and drizzle. A few that had been crippled by bird strikes buzzed drunkenly along the ground, unable to fly.

Melas waited a moment after the last drone had departed. Then he shrugged and began collecting the leftover boxes, scooping up the disabled fly-drones as he did. "No point wasting them," he said to Phaia's questioning look. "Besides, the boxes all stack inside each other." He fitted the dozens of boxes into a nested stack, dumped out a bit of rainwater, and had it back inside his pack within moments. He hefted the depleted pack with one hand, but didn't put it back on.

"How long will this take?" Phaia asked.

"Well, if the winds are favorable, it should only take a few hours for these little guys to reach most of the Persian army," Anna said. "Even natural flies can go pretty fast. Then another hour to deliver their payload as they crawl around." She lifted her wide-brimmed hat and raked her hair back with her fingers, letting the humid breeze cool her neck. "Even in the rain, Greece is really hot in the summer!"

"Just noticing that, are you?" Phaia laughed. "This midsummer season of Sirius is always our hottest time."

"I guess Texas is probably hotter," Anna said. "But I wasn't crazy enough to climb any mountains there." She looked around. "We might as well get comfortable here for a bit. The drones'll warn us if anyone comes our way, and I want to keep an eye on the weather to see when I should let out the last of the drones. We can hide until it's dark, then do a cold camp and head back toward our meeting point in the morning." She huffed out a breath. "We'll find out soon enough if this is going to work."

73

Forty miles further down the Malian Gulf, having crossed over the island of Euboea to reach its northwest corner, one slight woman and two huge dogs stood near Cape Artemision, looking out over the gray afternoon sea.

"They're out there, all right." Themis looked up from her phone. "Most of the Persian fleet is right here in the gulf, over on the Thessalian side."

"Our drones say it's been stormy here the last few days." Indy sniffed the air thoughtfully. "They were probably sheltering there, riding out the weather."

Themis checked the clouds and looked down at her phone again. "Looks like a few of them are casting off now that the rain's finally let up." She looked up. "So what now, chief?"

By now Indy's translator handled Themis' idiosyncratic speech patterns smoothly, translating her words to their nearest English equivalents. It was still strange but mostly understandable, though Indy wondered how Themis sounded to other Greeks. She made a mental note to ask Melas later.

"Their scouts have probably told them that the Greek fleet is somewhere close by." Indy paced back and forth, looking frustrated.

"Hold on a moment." She reached into a pocket on the outside of her pack with an unnaturally dexterous paw and fished out her own small screen, grinning at Themis with ear tips spread wide as she lifted it to view the drone footage.

"Finally, I can do this in front of you." Themis was trying not to look surprised as Indy worked. "My collar *tells* me information, but it can't *show* me." She scrolled around her map with deft strokes of a toenail, then gestured at the screen. "The Greeks beached for the night a bit further along the coast and are rowing this way now, though they're taking their time. They want to be fresh in case they run into the Persians, I suppose. But it looks like we have no time to spare. There's not much wind right now, so if we act quickly we can catch the Persians before they can row out of range." She reached back to pop the fasteners on her saddlebags, Argos watching with interest.

"You can do that too," Indy said to him.

"Yes." Argos' voice was becoming better modulated now, more like his calm persona before the uplift. "I still forget. What I can do now." He sat and reached back, brow furrowing as he felt for his own saddlebags' fasteners. It took him a few seconds, but Indy waited patiently, and shortly both sets of bags were spread out on the ground. Indy rummaged through them, pulling the little fly-drone boxes out and standing them upright.

"Don't just stand there," Indy said to Themis. "Get your boxes out! Red sides up, please." Themis belatedly dropped her own pack and pulled out the boxes that she hadn't transferred to Argos at the start of their journey.

"Stand back." Indy's collar lights flashed as Argos and Themis backed away. The lids of all the boxes popped in unison, and tiny fly-drones began streaming out, making a rough line northwest across the strait.

Argos crept forward and poked his muzzle into one of the boxes, then snorted as a fly-drone buzzed across his nose. "Tickles!"

"Don't do that," Indy said tolerantly. "You don't need a drone up your nose. Though it would probably find its way out soon enough." Her ears swiveled as she looked around suddenly.

"Themis!" Indy spoke low and urgently. "Someone's coming from downwind! Put away your phone and help us get our packs on. Quickly!"

Themis looked from side to side along the shoreline, speaking in a whisper. "I don't see anything!" But she hurried to help the two big canines, nevertheless. In a few moments she had their packs clipped back on, the dozen boxes on the ground continuing to disgorge their buzzing occupants all around them. "This doesn't exactly look innocent, though."

Indy put her head close to Themis'. "We'll go that way, along the shore, to meet whoever it is away from the boxes. Argos, no talking now." Argos nodded agreement, his heavy ruff rising as he stood taller and looked around for a threat.

Themis set off, and it was only a few seconds before she heard voices ahead. "Coming up, boss," she said very quietly. "I guess I'll do the talking," she added with a tense smile.

Two Greek soldiers came into view around the rocky coast, just a few yards away from Themis. They were lightly armed, and looking out to sea, but spotted Themis and the big hybrid dogs quickly.

"Girl!" one of them called out. "Come here!"

Themis gritted her teeth at the overly familiar address but walked closer, with Indy and Argos coming up behind.

The two men smelled like they hadn't bathed in a few days, but looked tall, strong, and dangerous. The one who had called out to Themis eyed her with a sour expression behind his full beard. "I need you to answer some questions," he said brusquely.

"Athena's sake," the second, larger man said. "Would it kill you to treat our own people with a little more respect?"

Sourpuss glared at his companion. "Can't believe I got stuck with you again." He spat noisily. "Always finding some way to chap my ass." He turned back to Themis. "So, girl. You see any Persian ships off this shore?" The second soldier sighed, but gestured for her to answer.

"Not that I noticed," Themis said. "But I've mostly been humping it over land, headed for my father's place." She gestured to the two dogs, now sitting neatly behind her. "Been loaning these two out down south, but it's time to get them back home."

"Useless!" Sourpuss exhaled noisily. "Get on your way, then."

"And look out for yourselves," the second soldier added more gently. "I'm from Troezen, originally. One of our ships was captured near here by the barbarians. They picked out the handsomest man among the rowers and sacrificed him at the prow to their pagan gods. Like you would a sheep!" He gave them a dark look. "So there's no telling what they'd do to you." The two Greeks started to walk on.

"Wait!" Sourpuss turned back to them as they stopped short. "You got any food in those packs?"

"Some," Themis said, surprised. "But it's a short trip."

Sourpuss eyed them. "So why are you and two big dogs all carrying packs that are mostly empty?"

"Okay sport, you got us." Themis laughed, trying not to look nervous. "We do a little trading around the island too." She doffed her pack and reached inside. "I think I've still got some nice cheese in here. Let me give you a sample, on the house."

Sourpuss snatched the pack from her hands. "You look like a smuggler, if I ever saw one. You pay your taxes on this?" He fumbled with the top flap of the pack and reached inside.

Argos snaked his head in between the soldier and Themis and snatched the pack with his teeth, yanking it from the soldier's grip. He backed up and bowed playfully, his barks muffled by the leather. Then he turned and ran away from the beach up into the brush, tail high.

"Dammit, Argos! Come back here with that!" Themis said. "Sorry," she said to Sourpuss, thinking fast. "He saw I was going for the food, and couldn't let anyone else have a bite. Argos!" she called again. From a dozen yards away, Argos emerged, play-bowed with a sneeze, and vanished into the trees again.

Themis backed away from Sourpuss and the other soldier, hands raised. "I've got to chase him! He's my father's best herder. If he runs away, I'll get a whipping!" Behind her, Indy added her own bark to the cacophony, looking back and forth between Themis and the forest where Argos had disappeared. "I'm coming!" Themis said to Indy.

"You're not going anywhere." Sourpuss reached out to grab Themis' chiton, but she dodged back out of reach.

"Give it a rest, Korax. Save it for the Persians." The second, larger soldier's voice was thick with disgust. "Go on, get your dog," he said to Themis. "Korax is too slow to catch you anyway, and we've got an actual job to do here. In case you've forgotten." He glared at his comrade.

Korax's hand fell to the hilt of his sword, but he swore and released his grip when he saw the other soldier's eyes turn flat with challenge. He turned and gestured at Themis dismissively instead. "Get out of here, then. But I see you again, I'll make you'll regret it."

Themis instantly turned away and ran up the hill into the trees where Argos had gone. Indy followed closely, with one last look behind to make sure the soldiers weren't following. The two pelted along for a full minute, Indy taking the lead now, nose low to follow Argos' scent.

They came upon the big brown and black herding dog sitting in a clearing a few hundred yards uphill, with Themis' pack sitting by his side, and a self-satisfied look on his face.

Indy ran up to him and barked, quiet but furious. "What was that about? You could have gotten us killed!"

Argos remained unperturbed. "Themis left phone in pack. Soldier would find it." He grinned a doggy grin. "I act bad, give you an excuse to run and follow. Tricky, like Jason in the Argonauts stories." His grin faded. "Then we don't have to bite anyone."

Indy chuffed in surprise, but looked thoughtful.

"Your boy here is right," Themis said. "I wouldn't want to try explaining my phone to that pair of dangerous idiots." She walked over and reclaimed her pack, wiping a smear of saliva off the leather with her tunic. "And people expect dogs to wild out like that sometimes. It was a clever bit of misdirection."

Argos puffed up with the praise, looking at Indy expectantly.

Indy snorted, but then softened her expression. "You were right, you big dummy." She laid her muzzle beside Argos'. "You just scared me. I thought you had gone berserk!"

Argos panted with laughter. "I got you good." His eyes sparkled.

"You got me," Indy agreed. She tried to shoulder-check him affectionately, but he dodged back, play-bowed and tore off around the clearing, Indy in hot pursuit. They chased each other back and forth for a few moments before circling back to face Themis, panting lightly.

"We should get some more distance between us and those two soldiers." Indy's collar voice sounded as if it was slightly out of breath, matching her facial expression. "And we left all the fly-drone boxes behind. They'll be empty by now, but it's still suspicious."

"Good thing they're only thick paper," Themis said. "Unusual, but nothing otherworldly like this." She pulled her phone out of her pack and checked the map quickly. "I can't see our buddies Korax and Niceguy. They're probably walking inshore among the trees to hide from the Persians. That must be why your drones didn't warn us about them."

Indy pulled out her own screen and took a long look. "There's nothing more we can do here, in any case. We may as well head back while we wait to see what happens. We can control these fly-drones from a fair distance if we relay our commands through the spy-drones. They just couldn't fly all the way here on their own."

Indy, Argos, and Themis picked their way through the trees, splashing across rain-swollen streams occasionally as they headed southwest, back the way they had come. They tried to stick to the little valleys that threaded through the low mountains of this part of Euboea, since there were sometimes military lookouts with signal fires laid at the peaks, watching for Persian invaders. They took special care to avoid any areas of high foot traffic recorded by their spy-drones, and swung wide around the lowlands where a few locals tended fields and sheep. At last, the early evening saw them camped in the foothills in the southwestern toe of the island.

Themis sank to the ground at their campsite with a groan. "You four-legs set a fast pace," she grumbled. "The distance was bad enough, but that up-and-down was killing me. Said the flute-girl to the farmer." She doffed her pack and unlaced her sandals, massaging the balls of her feet.

Indy shed her own bags, then checked her screen. "Looks like both fleets are beached for the night again. No battle today." She switched to fly-drone status. "A reasonable number of fly-drones intercepted the Persian fleet. Hopefully they'll have enough time to work before they find the Greeks." She scrolled further down. "I had a few fly-drones land on the Greek ships too, just to watch what happens. Our spy-drones don't have the range to follow ships out to sea, but we can pull video from the fly-drones later once they come back to shore."

Indy put away her screen. "I'm landing the spy-drones for the night to save power," she told Themis. "It's been overcast, so they're running low." Argos had unclipped his pack on his own and was rolling unashamedly on his back in the damp leaf litter. "We might as well have some dinner and get a good night's sleep. I'll set my collar to keep watch, and we'll try to catch another fishing boat back to the mainland tomorrow."

"Fishermen wake up *early*," Themis said unhappily. "But I'm not arguing. Some of that sausage and cheese, and I'll bet I'm sacked in half an hour anyway. No more videos for this girl tonight." She stretched out her bare feet experimentally, then decided to leave her sandals off for the night. "At least the ground here is pretty cushy." She pulled some food from her pack, followed by her rectangular cloak, and started munching away.

Fifteen minutes later, Themis was sprawled on her back, sound asleep, only partially under her cloak, with a last piece of half-eaten cheese in her outstretched hand. Argos sniffed the bit of cheese, then looked to Indy. "Okay to eat?" He licked his lips and glanced back toward Themis' sleeping face.

"I don't think she'd mind." Indy looked fondly at Argos' expression of naked hunger. "We can buy food on the way back, if need be."

Argos gently pulled the cheese from Themis' fingers and gulped it down, then walked back over to Indy and settled with his back to hers. He relaxed with a sigh.

Indy looked over at Themis. "I could pull the cloak over her," she said softly to Argos, "but I don't know if she'll notice one way or the other."

"So worried, earlier." Argos smacked his lips. "Maybe not smart enough yet to trick humans. Maybe not a hero like Jason." His voice was soft in the darkening forest. "Not used to worrying. Before, I'm always sure, always right. Now is more confusing." His lips curved into a self-satisfied expression. "Worked well, though. Questing with heroes. Happy."

"You did well." Indy spoke into the darkness.

Argos settled in for a moment, then lifted his head again.

"What is it?" Indy turned toward him, but couldn't see his eyes since they lay back to back.

"Nothing." Argos looked around a moment more, then laid his head down again.

Then he rubbed his face against his right wrist and sat back up. "Not nothing." He twisted around enough where he could look back at Indy. "Have I said yet? That I love you?" There was no fire, because Themis had fallen asleep before she could light one, but Argos' dark eyes gleamed in the dusk.

Indy's breath caught. "No. I don't think you mentioned that yet."

"Oh. I should have. You're the best thing." Argos smacked his lips again, sleepily. "Better than sheep. Even better than father's barbeque."

Indy swallowed around a lump in her throat. "I could say the same about you."

"Good." Argos's face relaxed, and he lay back down again, pushing his back up against hers. "Good. To know for sure." His eyes sagged closed, but he kept talking softly through his collar. "Tell me tomorrow. We'll mate. Better in the morning, anyway. So tired and..." His words trailed off.

Indy waited, but soon she could tell that Argos was fast asleep, his snores blending with Themis'. "We'll mate?" She huffed in amusement. "I re-started my cycle just for you, when you first got your collar. And you just now notice?" She got up and tugged Themis' cloak into place over the sleeping woman before curling up once more against Argos' broad back.

"Goodnight," she whispered, and settled down to sleep.

74

The more Anna looked at her phone, the more worried she got.

Alixa, show me the latest predictions of our fly-drone coverage.

It was the middle of the night, and she was lying awake, looking at the reports relayed back from the fly-drones they'd released earlier. The winds had turned against them as the sun went down, and many of the fly-drones had had to land short of the Persian army, to conserve their energy.

A map flashed up onto her screen. *Coverage of the nearer Persian forces stands at ninety-five percent,* Alixa said. *However, fly-drone range has been significantly reduced by prevailing winds. The second half of the Persian forces across the river may retain sizeable uncovered areas after all fly-drones are exhausted.*

Anna forced down the dread she felt rising in her chest. *Can we still win like this?*

Alixa replaced the map with a list of various outcomes, each bearing a probability. The top three lit up. *There is currently more than a seventy percent chance that the outcome of the battle in this timeline will match that of the original timeline.*

You mean we'll lose. Anna could feel the whole plan coming apart around her.

Yes, Alixa said. *We will likely lose.*

What about our last two boxes of drones? Anna still clung to the hope that she could make this work somehow. *If I get closer and then release them, can that make a difference?*

The optimal release point for the remaining drones is from inside the enemy formation, Alixa said. *Confirm that this is not an option?*

Anna snorted. *No, that's not an option.* She took a deep breath. *But what if I just get as close as I can? I might be able to get down the side of the mountain without anyone noticing.*

Overall success probability increases nonlinearly with proximity to the enemy, Alixa said. *Due to uncertain conditions, it is impossible to know exactly how close is close enough.* Her dispassionate voice paused. *But every extra bit helps.*

Anna looked toward Phaia and Melas to see if they might still be awake and willing to talk this out. But the night sky was overcast, too dark to make anything out more than a couple of yards away.

But I don't want them awake, anyway. Anna stilled as a terrible resolve flowed through her. *I promised them we'd stay away from danger. I can't wake them up and ask them to walk right up to the edge of the Persian army with me.*

Chances of detection increase with the number of personnel involved, Alixa said.

Sorry, Alixa. I didn't mean to think that out loud. Anna rolled to her feet as quietly as she could, then eased her cloak over her shoulders. She lifted her pack, reassured by the weight of the drone boxes inside. *Time to get moving. Before I get too scared to go through with this.*

She walked carefully out of their cold camp, stepping lightly. The ground was still damp from the rain of the day before, dulling the sound of her footsteps, and in a few minutes she was far enough away to move more quickly. She brought her phone up in front of her and switched it to night vision mode, using it to step around and over rocks and fallen trees.

Alixa, plot me the safest path down in the dark. Anna winced at the noise as her foot cracked a branch.

It is approximately six miles, and negative 4000 feet of elevation, to the edge of the enemy formation from here, Alixa said. *Walking safely under these conditions will be slow.*

Safely. Anna snorted at the absurdity of it, and hitched up her pack as she walked into the darkness. *I'm walking toward the biggest army anyone here's ever seen. Just make sure I don't accidently fall off a cliff before I get there.*

75

It was still quite early the next morning when a fishing boat pushed up against the southern shore of the Malian Gulf, carrying two huge hybrid canines, one tired Greek woman, and one grumpy fisherman.

"Get a move on!" The fisherman used one oar to push against the shallow bottom and hold them ashore as Themis stirred sluggishly. "There's still fish out there for me to catch, once you get your ass out of my boat!"

Argos and Indy jumped over the side smartly, trotting ashore in the low, lapping waves. Themis was slower, first fumbling in her purse, but then she produced a few pieces of silver that mollified their boatman. She stepped over the gunwale, wincing as she put her sandaled foot in the cold water.

"Ah! Poseidon's oysters, that's cold." She reluctantly put her other foot in and slogged ashore. Behind her, the fisherman was already under way, rowing back out into the gulf to try to add some fish to the day's profits.

Indy watched as Themis struggled up the beach. "Are you ready?"

"Ask me again when my feet aren't freezing." Themis pulled her cloak tighter around her. "I'll be glad when this stupid war is over, so I can sleep in again like a civilized person."

Argos huffed a laugh, and set out to the left along the shore, heading southeast to where his collar said Anna and the others should be waiting for them.

"He's really prancing this morning." Themis nodded toward Argos's retreating form as she and Indy trailed behind. "I'm glad someone's full of energy." She yawned. "Some kind of yowling noise out in the forest woke me up out of a dead sleep when it was still dark." She darted a knowing look at Indy. "I don't suppose you'd know anything about that? Both of you were gone, too."

Indy yawned widely. "Argos went off early this morning to sniff around." She shook out her coat with elaborate casualness. "I went to check on him. Thought he might be ready for the next step in his… hero's journey." She struggled to hide a self-satisfied expression. "I didn't hear anything unexpected, though." She changed the subject. "We should see Anna and the others in just a few minutes." She nodded ahead. "Right over that low hill there."

The two dogs and one woman crested the hill shortly, and followed their phones' guidance to a dell, hidden from the shore by low trees. As they entered, they saw Phaia and Melas waiting for them.

Themis clasped hands with Melas in greeting. "Glad to see you with all your bits still attached, big man."

"And you as well," Melas said. "Your telegraphic communication said you had a dangerous encounter." He smiled. "I'm glad you were able to escape unharmed."

"Things got wobbly there for a few moments." Themis smiled. "But we pulled it off. It was a long day of walking, though. I barely remembered to text you before I fell asleep."

Phaia walked forward and shook paws with Indy, then clapped Argos on the shoulder. "Out of our hands now," she said. "And it's past time to clear out. Things are about to get ugly."

Indy looked around. "Where's Anna? She messaged us late last night that she would be here."

"She was gone when we awakened this morning." The big man

looked worried. "She left a telegraphic communication—a message, that is, saying that she had gone to release the remaining fly-drones closer to the Persian army."

"That message also said she'd be done and here by now." Phaia looked up from her phone. "I tried calling her a few minutes ago, when we showed up and she wasn't here, but she's not answering."

"What does she think she's..." Indy's collar lights flashed. "She's not answering my call either. And she's blocked her location." Indy's lips pulled back tight in fear.

Phaia's phone pinged with an incoming message. "It's from her!"

"I got it too," Themis said.

Melas' look of concern deepened as his own phone buzzed, followed by the lights on Indy's collar. "We all did."

Indy played the message out loud for Argos' benefit, Anna's voice sounding strange coming from Indy's collar. "Hey guys, I'm setting it up so you'll get this message once you're back together. Sorry for sneaking off like this, but this mission is already way too risky, and I didn't want to drag everyone in even deeper when the whole thing was my idea." She sounded out of breath, as if she'd recorded the message while hiking over rough terrain. "Alixa and I gamed out the probabilities, and if I don't release these last two boxes of drones super-close to the Persians, it looks like the Greeks will still lose the battle, and this whole trip will have been for nothing."

Indy began stress-panting as she relayed the end of Anna's message. "I'm turning off incoming messages and tracking for a while, because I know you'd try to talk me out of this or come find me, and then we'd all be in danger. Don't worry, I'm just going to sneak down there, drop the rest of these drones, and I'll be on the way back by the time you get this. I'll turn messages and location back on then. See you all soon, and stay safe."

"What was she *thinking!*" Indy paced tensely back and forth.

"Did she really have to do this?" Themis eyed the rest of them skeptically. "I thought the drone releases went fine on our side."

"The weather turned against us here on the mainland." Indy's collar lights twinkled as she reviewed the data. "And getting a few miles closer *would* increase the chances of success." She shook her head, scared and exasperated together. "But she's got no stealth or wilderness training. She should've gotten out of there!"

"What do we do now?" Phaia said. "Can we figure out where she is?"

"She blocked her phone's location beacon," Indy said. "But if one of our spy drones spots her, we'll be able to trace her after that."

"It pains me to say it, but perhaps we should proceed." Melas looked uncomfortable as he spoke. "Anna's course of action is a worrying one, but her choice was freely made."

"And there's damn little we can do to change it now," Themis said.

"I need to—if I run, I can get there in just a few—" Indy started to walk north, toward Thermopylae. Then she stopped and looked back at Argos. "But it'll be dangerous. You'll need to stay here with the others."

"Where you go, I go." Argos set his jaw, eyes flashing determination.

Indy drew herself up to argue, worry and anger clashing on her face. But then she sagged, defeated. "All right. We'll get to a safer distance while we wait to hear from Anna. But we need to stay close enough to have line of sight to at least one drone, or we can't see what's going on and respond to events if we need to." She looked into space as she consulted her collar's net. "We should be able to keep a couple of miles away from danger if we cut across this way."

Their diminished party turned inland at the next stream, winding their way up into the low mountains as the day warmed up around them. Phaia glanced at her phone from time to time, but always put it away again afterward with a frown.

After seeing this for the third or fourth time, Indy called out to her. "I'm worried about Anna too. But I've put all our spy-drones on alert. They'll tell us the moment they spot her."

"I'm right there with you, P." Themis pulled her own phone from her pack and thumbed it to life. "It can't hurt to keep an extra eye out."

"It's not just that," Phaia said. "I'm trying to see if—"

All five of them stopped, simultaneously feeling their phones' alarm vibration. Themis scrolled around looking for the source of the alarm as Phaia and Melas pulled their own phones out to do the same. Indy brought her screen out and held it where Argos could see, since his fine motor skills were not up to that yet.

"The Persians are definitely up to something." Themis eyed the view from one of their spy-drones hovering invisibly far above Thermopylae. "What are they doing?"

Indy frowned at her screen, the corners of her thin black lips pulling back a little. "It looks like they're massing for an attack." She shifted on her haunches. "Hold on a minute, let me give us a better display. We've got spy-drones at three different angles now, and plenty of compute power, so… there, that's got it." The view on their phones changed, zooming down close to ground level where they were almost face to face with the Persian front line.

"Whoa!" Themis jerked back reflexively.

Indy glanced over. "You can each move your virtual viewpoints anywhere on the battlefield now. Yours just all came along with me to start with." She dragged a claw across her screen, sending the viewpoint flying along the Persian columns. "They're forming up for a frontal assault on the Greeks, here where they're blocking the pass between the mountain and the gulf." She let her screen dip. "That doesn't make any sense, though. Our fly-drones definitely landed and crawled all over this closest part of the Persian army. Someone should have noticed the effects on their equipment by now. They should be retreating, not advancing!"

"Hold on." Phaia tapped at her phone's screen with unpracticed gestures. "Look at this." She held her phone out for the others to see.

Themis peered at the screen, then recoiled at the image of officers wielding heavy whips against stragglers at the rear of a formation, drops of blood catching the light as they flew. "Why are the Persians whipping their own soldiers?"

Melas spoke up. "This is not an army of free men such as we have in Greece. Many of the Persians will have been forced to march on this mad venture for months, perhaps years. They are far from home, and understandably reluctant to run head-on into a fortified position."

"I would be too, hoss," Themis said. "But check this out." She held out her own phone, which she had zoomed in on a column of Persian spearmen in the rear. Iron scales sewn to their multicolored long-sleeved tunics glinted dully in the sun as they waited for their turn to advance.

"I am not sure I…" Melas frowned, looking closer. "Wait. There is something odd about their spears."

Phaia zoomed her own phone in to the same view. "Why are some of them carrying spears with no heads? Or are those just staffs?"

"So our plan *is* working." Indy stood motionless. "But Xerxes is attacking anyway. He's going to risk it all. He'll try to beat the Greeks in one huge assault, through sheer weight of numbers, before they realize what's happened."

Themis' face went still. "Those idiots are going to get massacred."

"But such a strategy does fit what we know of Xerxes' character." Melas looked up from his phone. "He was crowned only six years ago, but news travels quickly. All Greece has heard how mercilessly he put down the rebellions in Babylonia and Egypt, and how freely he spent his soldiers' lives to do so. In this campaign, the majority of his army will probably die of disease or privation before they can return home, even if they conquer our land." He looked at the others soberly. "Such an emperor would not hesitate to send thousands to their deaths, even tens of thousands."

"That's got to be the most insane thing I've—" Phaia broke off, looking back at her phone as it buzzed anew. She crowed as she saw the display. "It's him! I knew it!"

"Knew what?" Themis asked. But then her own phone vibrated in her hands as a skull-and-crossbones icon appeared on the battle-field. "Wait, what the hell is *that?*"

"I *knew* Hylas would be down there somewhere." Phaia's voice held grim vindication. "Rich guys like him have plenty of hoplites outfitted, and I saw what their equipment looks like when I was locked up in his compound. So I asked my phone to show me people who were leading groups like that, and I've been voting them up or down based on how much they looked like Hylas." Her face showed disgust. "And of course, he shows up on the Persian side. Though it's not surprising, I guess. His father's been exiled to Persia for a while now. He's probably that old guy standing right beside him."

Indy's collar lights shimmered and she froze. "No." She cocked her head, listening to a message the rest of them couldn't hear. "No, no!" She zoomed her screen in on the skull-and-crossbones icon, rolling the view back in time to resolve the other figures around Hylas. One of them was a short, dark-haired young woman wearing a dirty chiton, closely escorted by two of Hylas' soldiers. As Indy watched, an icon of Anna's face appeared beside Hylas' skull-and-crossbones.

"He's got her." Indy looked up at the three Greeks in horror. "Hylas has got her. And they're right in the middle of a war."

76

By the time the sky began to lighten with the dawn, Anna was tired, her hands scraped and bruised from catching herself as she'd slipped and stumbled down steep mountain slopes in the darkest part of the night. But now she was almost at the bottom, as close to the Persian army as she could get without coming out from under cover. She couldn't quite see the nearest soldiers through the trees, but she knew they were out there, courtesy of the video feed from their spy-drones.

Alixa, let me know if any of them head this way, okay?

Tree cover in your area greatly reduces the likelihood of early warning, Alixa said. Her normally dispassionate voice almost sounded tense. *It is recommended that you leave immediately.*

Anna was on her knees by then, digging into her pack for the two boxes of fly-drones she'd held back earlier. She set them out quickly, red lids upward, then put her pack back on over her cloak, clumsy with haste.

Just a few more seconds and I'm out. She checked her phone's display one last time. *What's our probability now?*

Releasing the remaining drones from here will give a cumulative success probability of fifty percent.

Still that low? Anna frowned. *You're sure we can't do any better?*

It is recommended that you leave immediately.

Yeah, yeah, I heard you. Anna raised her phone, preparing to release the fly-drones.

Lie down slowly and do not move, Alixa said. *Enemy proximity detected.*

Anna fought back her instinct to drop instantly to the ground. Instead, she crouched and then lay down, mind racing. *Alixa, can I launch the drones now?*

Do not take any action.

Fear clutched at Anna's heart then. Alixa had never flat-out ordered her not to do something before. She looked around, then stopped as a plan formed in her mind.

I can't believe I'm even thinking this. She grabbed the hem of her cloak and ripped it, stitches purring apart as she opened a seam, leaving a gap a few inches long.

Do not take any action.

Sorry, Alixa. Anna tapped at her phone's screen, entering a quick sequence of commands.

The lids of the drone boxes popped with a quiet but clearly unnatural noise. But the fly-drones, instead of taking to the sky, crawled over the rims of their boxes, streaming along the ground toward Anna.

Do not take any action.

Anna lay still as two thick lines of fly-drones heaved and twisted their way in through the newly opened gap in her cloak hem. Her cloak twitched and wriggled oddly, growing heavier across her back and legs as the tiny drones distributed themselves evenly inside.

Do not take any action!

Anna jerked at a sudden noise. One of the fly-drone boxes had fallen over now that it was almost empty, the weight of the last evacuating drones on the rim tipping it out of balance. The other box followed a moment later.

Prepare to flee. Shield activated.

No. Turn off my shield, Alixa. Anna shoved a few straggling fly-drones into the hole in her cloak. Then she stood up and slowly raised her hands. The first Persian scouts appeared between the trees a few moments later, bows raised and arrows nocked.

Anna raised her hands higher. "I surrender."

77

One of the scouts searched Anna quickly and efficiently while three others stood guard, arrows trained on her heart. He took her pack first, tossing it to one of his men when it proved to contain only food and water. Then he stripped off her cloak and patted her down roughly.

She had hoped he would miss her equipment somehow, but that hope was quickly crushed as he relieved her of her phone and stun prod. He turned the unfamiliar items over in his hands for a few moments, then dumped them on her cloak and resumed the pat-down. His hands found the shield projector hidden at the small of her back.

"What's this?" His voice was bored.

"Well, I—"

"Just hand it over." He nodded at his comrades, who backed up a couple of steps but didn't avert their eyes. "Or I'll have to take it off you, whatever it is."

Anna flushed, but loosened her broad belt enough so that she could drop the shield projector down inside her chiton and let it fall to the ground between her feet. She kicked it over to the man who had searched her, then tightened her belt again. "Satisfied?"

The scout searching her glanced at the unadorned metal box for a few moments, then tossed it onto her cloak with the rest of her equipment. He prodded the two empty drone boxes with a toe, but abandoned them when he saw they were empty. "Don't know what the hell kind of spy doesn't even carry a knife," he mumbled to himself. He rolled her cloak around the confiscated items and stood.

"Right. Back to the captain, and we let him figure this out." He glowered at Anna. "Follow me close, and stay in front of my men. Try anything, and we'll tie you up and drag you." He addressed his men. "Straight back. I've got a feeling we're about to be in it, and I want her off my hands before then."

They set out, and in just a few minutes were through the trees and out onto the narrow strip of land that lay between the mountains and the Malian Gulf. The rocky coastline was teeming with soldiers, most clustered in place with their units, awaiting orders, but some marching to the right in long files, taking up positions closer to the Greek forces a mile further up the coast. The scouts guided Anna in a winding path through the chaos, and soon they approached a group of men circled up in an impromptu conference. Many appeared to be aides or messengers, but a few wore more elaborate armor, with rich cloaks draped from their shoulders.

"Cap. Cap!" One of the men turned as the scout who had searched Anna called out. "Caught a spy for you."

The man beside the captain turned to look as well, and Anna found herself staring, horrified.

Hylas.

Her steps faltered, and one of the scouts behind her shoved her forward.

"Ah." Hylas' voice held a deep satisfaction, and he smiled widely as Anna was forced closer to him. "I had hoped that we would meet again, though I did not think it would happen quite like this." He tapped the shoulder of an older man standing beside him. "Father, this is the young lady I spoke to you of."

"Really?" Hylas' father turned away from his aides and looked at Anna. The resemblance to his son was clear, though his hair and beard were streaked with gray, and his limbs less corded with muscle. "She looks perfectly ordinary." He took a step closer, looking Anna up and down.

"Allow me to demonstrate." Hylas stepped forward without warning and punched Anna in the gut, putting his whole body behind it.

Anna folded up around the blow with a gasp, then fell to her knees, retching. The pain was bad enough, but the shock of being hit with full strength by an adult man for the first time in her life was even worse. Her mouth worked, but she couldn't make any words come out.

"Well." Hylas looked at his fist, nonplussed. "She was much more formidable, before." He regarded Anna speculatively. "Something must have changed, or she would not have been captured by ordinary men such as these."

The scout who had searched Anna handed over her rolled cloak containing her equipment. "She was carrying these, sir. Just metal and glass boxes though, no weapons."

"Hmm." Hylas nodded to the scouts and their captain. "Excellent work, men. You will be amply rewarded when we return home. You may return to your duties."

The scouts took their leave, closing in to talk to their captain as they walked away. One of them still had Anna's pack over his shoulder, and she watched it go from where she wheezed on the ground.

Hylas unwrapped Anna's cloak and prodded through its contents. Then he re-wrapped them and addressed Anna, who had regained her feet but was still bent over, panting with pain.

"I will have you taken behind the lines. And then, when we've dealt with these—"

A Persian soldier ran up to the group, dark-haired and bearded, wearing a felt cap and brightly colored tunic. "Lord Peisistratos," he said to Hylas' father. "You will attend the emperor now." He ran off without awaiting a reply.

Anna rubbed her bruised stomach with one hand, the pain slowly beginning to dull. *At least my earring is still working.* The messenger seemed to have spoken in Persian, but it had been repeated in her mind in English without any problem, so their nets must be able to translate Persian as well as Greek, at least to some degree. She tried not to look at her rolled cloak in Hylas' hands. *At least as long as he keeps my phone in range.*

"Let's go," Peisistratos said to his son. He gestured to two nearby Greek guards, who fell in behind Anna. "The emperor does not like to be kept waiting. Keep your prisoner quiet, and we'll deal with her afterward."

Hylas tucked the rolled cloak containing Anna's belongings negligently under one arm, then set off beside his father. Anna hastened behind them despite the pain in her stomach, not wanting to be shoved along again.

Anna reached out via her link. *Alixa, please unblock my messaging and location.*

—you hear me, Anna? What are you doing down there? Indy's frantic voice came through the moment the link opened.

I'm so sorry. Anna tried to keep her face still as she talked. *The drones couldn't make it all the way to the far side of the Persians on their own. I needed to get closer, and I didn't want Phaia and Melas to risk their lives for my dumb plan.*

You should have just left! Indy's mental voice was furious. *It was good enough!*

It wasn't. Even at the edge of the army, it still wasn't. Anna sounded calmer than she felt. *And then when I realized I was about to get captured, I figured I might as well go all in.* She paused. *I'm sorry I blocked you guys. But I was afraid if you saw where I was going, you'd come after me, and then we'd all be in danger.*

What's your plan? Indy asked. *Tell me you have a plan.*

Well… I think I do. Looking between Hylas and his father, Anna saw they were approaching a large wooden framework of some kind. *Hold on a minute, something's about to happen.*

Their group was challenged at the edge of a formation of heavily armed Persian soldiers, then allowed to pass through. Once inside the line, they joined a group of a few dozen Greek and Persian commanders and their guards, assembled in front of a raised platform, upon which sat a heavy throne.

On that throne sat Xerxes, absolute ruler of the Persian Empire.

Anna didn't know what she had expected such a man to look like, but Xerxes seemed ordinary enough. He was perhaps forty years old, neither handsome nor ugly, with dark hair and a full, square beard. Everything else about him was extravagant, though. He wore gold-plated ceremonial armor over richly embroidered clothing, and a tall, cylindrical crown of gold.

"Greetings upon the occasion of our greatest victory." Xerxes' voice was deep and unhurried, the voice of someone who was used to being the sole focus of attention. "You will have already received your final orders. They will not be changed, regardless of recent events I have been made aware of." He looked out over his audience. "All of you should know by now that mighty Persia does not bend itself to circumstances. We *are* the circumstances."

There was no hubbub of protest among the assembled commanders, but the utter stillness among them telegraphed their shock and surprise as well as a shout would have.

"Each of you will maintain his forces in good order." Xerxes fixed one man after another with his eyes, and each one cast his gaze down, either in fear or deference. "No one will retire from this field until we have broken through, and the Greek forces are in rout."

Anna must have gasped audibly at this, because suddenly faces were turned toward her from all around. Hylas gripped her arm tightly in warning.

"Well, my vassal?" Xerxes addressed Hylas' father with deadly amusement. "Is there some objection to this strategy among our Attic contingent?"

The color drained from Peisistratos' face. "Of course not, my lord. Forgive us. We came straightaway in response to your summons, and there was no time to—"

"Our prisoner knows something of these 'recent events,' my lord." Hylas cut in before his father had finished speaking. "She is a foreign witch of great power, who our scouts discovered near our forces this morning. Her presence here, on this day of all days, is surely no coincidence."

"A witch?" Xerxes' earlier amusement shaded toward something more predatory. "I had heard that you Greeks were a suspicious bunch." He swept his eyes over the rest of his commanders. "The rest of you are dismissed. Any further directives will be relayed to you as our victory progresses. But you—" Xerxes looked back to Hylas, tone peremptory. "Join us." He motioned to his guards, one of whom stepped forward to usher Hylas and Anna up onto the platform. "We have a few moments before the action begins, and this could be diverting."

"My lord, I—" Peisistratos looked truly afraid now, seeing his only son called forward by such a man.

Xerxes' lazy smile faded. "You have men to command. Leave us." He gestured with one hand. "If your son has something useful to tell me, he will rejoin you at my pleasure."

Peisistratos swallowed, then bowed and backed away, trailed by his two guards.

Anna hesitantly mounted the stairs to the high platform, hemmed in on every side by Persian guards in peaked caps, Hylas close behind her. As she stepped up, she saw that the whole platform was actually a kind of giant palanquin, meant to be carried on poles by dozens of bearers, but now supported by sturdy folding legs while the bearers rested in its shade. In a few moments, she faced Xerxes where he sat on his high throne, his head still above hers as he lounged at his ease.

"So. A *witch*." As Xerxes spoke, Hylas went to one knee beside Anna, then stood again at his negligent wave. "Do witches not know how to greet emperors?"

Two flanking guards made as if to seize Anna and force her obeisance, but they left off at a glance from Xerxes. "Well?" he asked.

"Your attack can't possibly work now." Anna finally found her voice, though she stumbled over the unfamiliar syllables of the Persian language. "It sounds like you've already found out why." She stiffened her spine. "If you don't turn back soon, it'll be too late."

"How do you know she is a witch?" Xerxes asked Hylas, as though he hadn't heard Anna's words.

"My lord, she possesses great strength." Hylas' voice was as smooth as ever, even though he might be only words away from death, or worse. "I watched with my own eyes as she overcame five strong men, myself among them, and snapped a heavy staff between her hands as you would a stick of kindling. She also consorts with a familiar, a giant talking hound." Hylas' neck reddened at Xerxes' expression of tolerant ridicule, though his face didn't change. "And she introduced into Athens a new form of medicine, one with great efficacy in healing the sick. I have been searching for her for some time now. Then suddenly she appears, just as we hear of uncanny goings-on within our ranks. I am certain that she holds knowledge that would help turn the tide of battle in our favor."

"We need no hidden knowledge for that." A giant of a man in gold-chased armor spoke up from beside Xerxes. "Given my lord's command, his Immortals and I would easily smash through this pitiable force we see huddling before us."

"I have no doubt of it, Hydarnes." Xerxes laughed, at ease. "The Medes and the Kissians will take a turn at the enemy first, but there will be glory enough for all of you. With one stroke, I will avenge my father's defeat, and make the empire greater than it has ever been." He looked at Anna, finally seeming to fully register her presence. "Watch and learn, little witch. It is not weapons which win battles, but will." He nodded to Hydarnes, who bowed and left the platform, issuing terse commands as he joined the rest of the military men on the ground. Then Xerxes spread his arms before him mockingly, indicating that Anna should look for herself.

She turned warily away from the emperor and looked over the railing of the platform, over the heads of thousands of soldiers holding a forest of spears. Half a mile or so to the east along the narrow, rocky shore was the front line of the Persian army. Then, across another few hundred yards of no-man's land, tiny with distance, stood the armored Greek defenders at Thermopylae.

As Anna watched, the Greek army roared its defiance, clashing sword hilts against shields and stamping their feet. But at this distance the sound came only faintly to her ears, almost masked by the ambient noises of so many Persian soldiers packed so closely together.

The Persians roared back in response, tens of thousands of men bellowing all around her, jabbing spears and swords up at the sky. The noise was overpowering, an ocean of sound that raised the hairs on her neck and forearms before it finally subsided.

For agonizing seconds, the tension rose. Then, at some unseen signal far ahead in the Persian forces, the first volley of arrows arced up toward the Greeks, and the battle began.

78

"Anna's back in contact." Indy quickly summarized their conversation for the rest of the party. "She says she has a plan, but we haven't had a chance to discuss it yet."

"She appears to be safe for the moment." Melas looked up from his phone, shaking his head. "But I still wish she had not taken this upon herself."

"Let's get under cover." Indy looked into the distance as she consulted her collar. "I'll try to figure something out." Her ears lay back with worry. "We could still move a little farther away from the battle without losing contact with our drones. But then if Anna... there must be something we can do besides just running away."

There was an anxious silence among the company as they moved off the trail and back into the trees, where they could lay down their packs and watch events unfold with less chance of discovery. Indy propped her screen against the trunk of a tree where she could watch it comfortably while lying down. Argos curled up at her side, keeping an eye back toward the trail. The Greeks sat or rested against their packs, watching on their phones as the huge Persian army advanced.

The Greek defenders had reinforced an ancient wall at Thermopylae that stretched from the shore of the gulf across to where the steep foothills of Mount Kallidromo arose perhaps a hundred yards inland. It had a few gates in it, wide enough for carts to get through, which the Greeks had piled with rubble. The wall was perhaps eight feet tall from the front side, with rock and earth stepped up behind it so the Greeks could climb up to half its height. The ground further out in front of the wall was marshy, threaded through with small streams that ran from hot springs at the base of the mountain out across the beach and into the sea, making poor ground for attackers to advance across.

Rows of Greek archers crouched behind the wall, with armored foot soldiers behind them. The Greek forces stretched back for hundreds of yards along the coast, but their number was tiny compared to the enormous mass of men approaching from the Persian side.

Just out of bowshot, the Persians stopped. Commanders walked back and forth across the front lines, exhorting and directing their troops, and setting the final order of battle. Afterward, they retreated back into the mass of soldiers, and all was quiet for a moment.

The Greek army shouted their anger and defiance toward the Persians, who replied in kind. Indy could only hear a distant echo of that sound through her screen, conveyed through their spy-drones' long-range microphones.

Long seconds later, the first arrows flew.

Thousands of Persian bowmen in the front ranks ran forward, knelt, and quickly loosed their shafts, sending a black river of arrows whistling toward the Greek army. Many of the Persians fell to Greek arrows shot from behind the wall, but more ran forward to take their places, and in a few moments the Greek archers had to take cover themselves or risk an arrow in the eye. At the same time, the front ranks of the Persian infantry broke into a fast trot toward the wall, their archers firing over their heads as they ran.

"Smart," Themis said. "Try to close as much distance as they can under an arrow storm."

And it was working. The Greek archers immediately behind the wall kept low and fired blindly over it at a high angle, trying to blunt the Persians' charge, but without much effect. The Greeks further back raised their large shields to protect vulnerable flesh as arrows thudded into the ground around them.

Themis cringed as she saw a Greek soldier fall with an arrow through the eye-slit of his helmet. But most of the Greeks stood firm. Arrows were even bouncing off their armor here and there, which drew puzzled looks from some of the Greek soldiers.

A signal horn sounded from the Greek side, and just as the Persian soldiers broke into a run to close the last distance to the wall, the Greek archers rose from behind it and fired directly into their ranks.

The Persians charged desperately onward, but all throughout the masses of running men, hundreds of them fell in moments. Some tumbled limply, instantly struck dead by steel-tipped arrows fired at close range, and others lagged back behind the charge, grasping at arrows that had pierced their flesh, often directly through their armor.

"It's working." Argos' ears twitched as Indy whispered, half-disbelieving.

Miles away, the first wave of Persians crashed into the wall, scrabbling for purchase. Greek spearmen stood up from behind the wall, stabbing down into the mass of climbing men with deadly results. And now the full effect of Anna and Indy's plan was finally apparent.

Their thousands of tiny fly-drones had spent the previous day touching down lightly all over the Persian army's equipment, sparsely dusting any bronze or steel they could find with tiny nano-motes. Each mote could only penetrate a short distance before running out of energy, but they weakened the metal's crystalline structure, working their way into existing flaws, deepening and widening them. And now, under heavy blows from undamaged Greek weapons, that weakened metal was crumbling and flaking away.

Indy saw Greek spear thrusts punch directly through shields and armor, which cracked and fell aside under the onslaught, leaving luckless Persian soldiers clad only in blood-soaked leather or cloth.

And Persian blows dealt against the Greeks had the opposite result. Persian spearheads exploded into shards when rammed into bronze shields, and sometimes blunted harmlessly or cracked even when they found cloth or flesh. In moments, the Persian front line was fighting with sticks against fully armored enemies with iron-tipped spears and arrows.

The slaughter was terrible. The Persians used their headless spear shafts like long staves, occasionally catching a Greek soldier a blow to the head and tumbling him from the wall to be trampled into the rocky ground. And some of the Persians still held intact weapons that had escaped the fly-drones' attentions. But for the most part, the Persians were defenseless, and they fell by the hundreds.

Phaia looked up after a few queasy minutes of watching this carnage. "Say one thing for the Persians, those poor idiots aren't backing down. Rather take my chances with the whips behind me."

"But if they keep piling on, they can still run right over us," Themis said.

It was true. The Persian dead were mounding up in front of the Greek wall, but the ranks behind them advanced over the bodies of their comrades like ants, keeping the pressure on the Greek defenders.

"Indy was right." Melas held up his screen and pointed. "Xerxes is risking it all, right here. Look!"

Far back in the mass of the Persian army, a giant palanquin was pushing forward, borne by dozens of men and surrounded by Xerxes' Immortals, an elite force of ten thousand heavily armed soldiers.

Indy belatedly noticed that Anna's icon was right there on the palanquin beside those of Hylas and Xerxes. "Anna, are you all right?"

"Still good," Anna's reply came back immediately, translated from thought into speech by Indy's collar net so the Greeks could hear it. "They just picked up this giant platform thing that we were all standing on, and they're carrying us in the middle of the army."

Her voice sounded nervous, even in facsimile. "I think Xerxes wanted to get a closer look."

The palanquin stopped well back from the fighting front, but still acted as a plug in the narrow stretch of land, stiffening the back of the Persian lines and pressing their men forward. The Greeks, even though they had been steadily rotating in fresh men to replace those who had tired or fallen, were wearing out. They didn't have the endurance to grind up against a force so much larger than their own, even if they did have a huge advantage in weaponry.

"So where the hell are Leonidas and the Spartans?" Phaia scrolled around her screen. "I thought they might have been hanging back in reserve for a while, but I can't see them anywhere."

"Good question." Indy's collar lights flashed, and the viewpoint on her screen changed. The video shifted backward in time, tracking back to find when they had last seen Leonidas a few hours before. "Here they were at the beginning of battle," she said. "Then it looks like they rotated further back during the fighting. Here's where they are now." She zoomed the viewpoint in, and Phaia leaned in to look at the bearded figure at their head.

"That's not him." Then Phaia looked closer. "He *is* wearing Leonidas' armor and helmet. But that's not his... face." She smiled crookedly. "Definitely not."

"So where is he?" Indy furiously thought commands into her collar's net, trying to trace Leonidas' location forward from the first time they had seen him.

Horns sounded from the Greek forces, and the Spartans, including the fake Leonidas, rose up and began to move to the front, tightening up into formation as they went. They clasped hands and slapped shoulders with the other Greeks as they went to join the fighting at the wall. Once formed up behind the wall, they waited until the horns sounded again.

This time, they were answered by the same horns, but from somewhere up in the hills, back past Xerxes' palanquin.

The Spartans behind the wall charged forward in a tight wedge. Their comrades stepped aside, letting them climb up the low side of the wall and leap out onto the mounded bodies of the Persians on the other side. They ripped into the Persian forces, their steel swords taking a terrible toll on the all-but-defenseless Persians, whose long spear-poles were no protection against a close-in attack.

At the same time, in the rear of Xerxes' elite guard, Persian heads were turning back toward the horn blasts, trying to figure out where they had come from.

"What are those horns behind us?" Anna's synthesized voice asked. "Alixa says she can't see what's going on."

"Hold on," Indy said. "I'm moving one of the drones to get a better view."

Gray areas on her screen filled in with detail, sweeping past Xerxes' palanquin and back along the steep hills on the inland side of the narrow pass. There, out of a narrow gap in the hills, more Spartans streamed, quickly forming into a narrow wedge as they came. In moments, a force of perhaps three hundred men, looking desperately small compared to the huge mass of Persians, was running toward the enemy flank, aimed like a spear directly at Xerxes' Immortals and the palanquin they surrounded.

"Leonidas located." Alixa's voice sounded from everyone's phones, relayed the same way Anna's was. All their screens changed to show the same view as Indy's, and a little crown icon appeared above the head of the Spartan king at the point of the wedge.

"*That's* where Leonidas got to," Phaia said with satisfaction. "He must have swapped out his armor with some other Spartan."

"And led a few soldiers up through the hill trails for a sneak attack, to try to take out Xerxes," finished Themis. "That's borderline suicidal, though. You'd get crushed by the bigger force, or shoved right back up the trail."

"But with the Persians at such a disadvantage now..." Melas' voice trailed off thoughtfully. He dialed his phone viewpoint in to observe the mass of the Persian military. "It will all depend on how the soldiers react."

At first, the Persian ranks showed only mild confusion as they looked back and forth between the two Spartan horn signals. But then, as Leonidas' men began cutting into the Persian flank, the screams of mortally wounded men filling the air, the Persians became restless, pushing one way and another, trying unsuccessfully to see what was going on.

A few moments later, the first Persian soldiers broke and ran.

Many of the spearmen retreating from the wall shoved back toward Xerxes' elite force, trying fruitlessly to push them aside before splashing out across the marshy shore of the gulf to slog around them. Those under attack by Leonidas' Spartans fled back toward the main mass of the Persian army, leaving fewer and fewer defenders between the oncoming Spartans and the Persian emperor.

In the space of a few minutes, a hard-fought battle had turned into a chaotic rout, with demoralized Persians streaming back from the wall and bypassing both Xerxes and Leonidas on their way to escape. Leonidas' oncoming wedge of heavily armed warriors ignored the fleeing Persian soldiers, merely knocking them aside when necessary to advance toward the emperor.

But Xerxes was still surrounded by thousands of elite Immortals who showed no signs of panic. A huge man in elaborate gold-chased armor ran to the head of his men, gesturing powerfully toward them with a heavy staff and shouting something that their drones couldn't pick up from this distance. Whatever he said, it rippled quickly through the Immortals, who began a deliberate advance directly toward Leonidas' oncoming wedge.

"On the move." Anna spoke tersely, as if she'd forgotten her friends were still listening. "Might have to go any second."

"If Xerxes can break out," Melas said, "he can withdraw behind the mass of his troops, and even with their weapons ineffective, we will never get to him."

"I think Leonidas has something to say about that." Phaia sounded pleased. "He's aiming the Spartan wedge right at them. There's not enough room for Xerxes to go around them on solid ground, and his elites' armor is too heavy to go running through the mud out on the shore. Xerxes—" Her voice turned fearful as she remembered where Anna was. "Xerxes and Anna have to go right through them."

Horns sounded again from behind the Greek wall, and the Boeotians and remaining Spartans began climbing over it, advancing quickly to engage the rear of the retreating Immortals. Greek weapons sheared through weakened Persian armor like brittle clay, cutting down dozens of men in moments. But with each Immortal that fell, another stepped forward to take his place and prevent Xerxes' rear from being overrun.

At the new front of Xerxes' formation, Leonidas' men had been forced to spread out into a reinforced line, to keep the Persians from simply streaming around and enveloping them on their way to escape. The two sides met in straining, face-to-face combat, with the immense weight of the Persian force slowly pressing the Spartans back. The Persians were losing dozens of men for every Spartan who fell, but even so, the Spartans were being inexorably pushed aside.

But then the entire remaining Greek force came streaming over the wall, leaving nothing behind. Even heavily armed horsemen in elaborate armor charged right up to the wall before dismounting to climb slowly over it and attack the Persians on foot. And instead of joining the fight at Xerxes' rear, the more lightly armed foot-soldiers skirted though the boggy marsh, out past the reach of Xerxes' forces, and around to join and reinforce Leonidas' line.

"Guys? It's not looking good here." Even synthesized, Anna's voice sounded tense. "I'm about to do something really stupid. Just follow my lead."

n Xerxes' huge palanquin, none of the generals or advisers surrounding the emperor spoke in anything but measured tones, or in any way implied that a Persian victory was less than inevitable. But from their fixed expressions and rigid postures, Anna could tell that they knew exactly how much trouble they were in.

Hylas was looking around the battlefield, no doubt trying to locate his family's troops. He was distracted, but he still held Anna's rolled cloak under one arm.

No point in trying to hide anymore. Anna steeled herself. *Alixa, please activate my fly-drones and send them off to the uncovered parts of the army. No matter how this comes out, at least that'll be done.*

Her cloak began to buzz and writhe, and Hylas dropped it with a startled curse. It twisted about on the wooden floor of the palanquin until the ripped corner flopped free. Then a steady stream of fly-drones began to pour out, heading for the skies.

Anna squatted down and reached for the cloak to retrieve her equipment, but a recovered Hylas kicked the bundle back behind him, away from her grasp. It slid across the floor, still buzzing with escaping fly-drones, and stopped in front of Xerxes' throne. The emperor leaned back instinctively, hands going up to swat the tiny drones away from his face.

"Keep it out of her hands!" Hylas called back over his shoulder to the emperor's guards, then turned back to Anna. "I have your game figured out now. As soon as we break free of this melee, we will see how——"

Alixa, call my shield to me!

Behind Hylas, Anna's cloak rose from the floor like a ghost, draped over the shield generator underneath. The generator shook its way free of the heavy fabric, tumbling Anna's phone and stunner out onto the floor of the platform. Then it zoomed around Hylas and into Anna's outstretched hands.

Yes! Anna hurriedly shoved the flat metal box under the back of her belt, barely dodging Hylas as he dove for her. She raised her hands, engaging her shield directly now, and her phone and stunner smacked into her palms an instant later. She tucked them into the front of her belt and dove over the palanquin's railing into the sea of soldiers below, just inches in front of Hylas' grasping hands.

Alixa, engage slippery mode.

Anna had been thinking about this and a few other tricks since their encounter with the pirates a few weeks ago. But obviously there had been no way to test anything out in anger. As she dropped to the ground, she mentally crossed her fingers. She landed with a jolt, her bruised stomach throbbing with renewed pain, and started running.

"Get her!" Hylas called out from the edge of the palanquin.

The nearest Persian soldiers turned in her direction, reaching out to lay hands on her. But their fingers slid off the smooth, invisible surface of her shield as she jinked this way and that, never running into anyone head-on, always at an oblique angle. She slid through their ranks like an eel, taking advantage of the noise and confusion of battle to outrun the cries for her capture.

In moments, her field of view had narrowed to a shifting sea of armored backs and surprised faces as she darted along. The soldiers were all taller than her, so she couldn't see more than a few feet ahead no matter which way she turned. Her only hope was to keep moving fast.

Alixa, guide me out! Which way to hit the fewest soldiers?

She accelerated, Alixa's voice calling out directions in her mind, and suddenly she was diving through the Persian front line, sliding out from between the legs of a surprised infantryman and into the sandals of Leonidas' Spartans. The first one drew back reflexively at her unexpected appearance. Then he jabbed his sword down at her chest.

Her shield slid the point of the sword aside without resistance, and it sank into the ground beside her. She rose to her hands and knees and scuttled forward, soldiers' clawing hands slipping fruitlessly away from her as she dodged deeper into the Spartan line, then through it and out the back. In a few more breathless moments, she was running along the tree line at the base of the hills, the Spartan ambush left behind her and streams of fleeing Persians off to her right, between her and the shore.

Guys, I'm out! But I'm gonna be coming in hot, Anna said over the open link. *Alixa's guiding me to you, but it sounds like it's a couple of miles along some back trails once I turn off.* She was panting heavily already, but fought to maintain her pace. A few of the Persian soldiers watched her pass from just a dozen yards away, but she wasn't armed or armored, and they looked too preoccupied with their own flight to worry about one lone girl fleeing along with them.

Anna, look out! Indy shouted over the link. *He's right—*

"Got you!" Hylas and a small group of his Greek turncoats burst out from among the Persian deserters, so close that she had to swerve uphill into the bushes to avoid them. They must have cut through the Persian side of the battle line to get around the front of the Spartan phalanx and intercept her.

She put on another burst of speed, looking back over one shoulder at the men chasing her. They were all armored, but some of them lightly, and they all looked distressingly fit and healthy. Anna put her head down, running faster than she ever had in her life. Then, as she turned left up into a narrow canyon, she played her final card.

Alixa! Kangaroo mode!

Anna wobbled as her shield put a spring into her step, boosting her speed. The clanking of men running in armor receded behind her, but it didn't disappear, even though each of her uphill bounds was launching her forward six feet or more.

Three minutes remaining at this velocity. Alixa didn't sound at all terrified at Anna's dire situation. Maybe her threat assessment algorithm was confused, now that she'd run straight through a battlefield.

Anna snatched another look behind her. The fastest of the men was still in sight, but the rest had strung out further back. Hylas, in his heavier armor, was nowhere to be seen. She slowed as much as she dared, but kept pushing herself, turning down her kangaroo assist and working her legs harder to conserve energy. Her lungs burned as she climbed into the steep hills.

Anna, you need to get out of there. Indy's voice was no longer a shout, but still sounded worried.

"I'm! Trying!" she said out loud, too distracted by running to remember to use her link.

I mean it. There was a pause, where Indy must have consulted her collar. *The whole Persian army's breaking up behind you. Xerxes and his heavy infantry are cut off and surrounded by the Greeks, but everyone else is either running back the way they came, or taking to the hills.* Her voice paused again. *That canyon you're in is too narrow for our drone to be totally sure, but it looks like Hylas is a good ways behind you now. You can probably lose him if you just keep running.*

Easy for you to say. Anna felt her shield heating up at her back, and dialed down the kangaroo assist still further. Her run had slowed to barely more than a jog. Even mortal danger wasn't enough to enable her to sprint this far uphill at top speed, shield assist or no.

It's only a few more minutes until you hit the crest of the pass, Indy said. *We'll head your way and meet you on the other side.*

No! I don't want anyone running into danger. Anna's head swam with exertion, but the thought gave her another jolt of adrenaline. *I'll catch up. You guys need to start moving.*

There was a long silence from Indy's side. *Just hurry.*

Anna finally felt the path begin to slope down in front of her, and turned back for one last look toward Thermopylae. From this height and distance, soldiers from both sides blended into tiny milling figures, like an enormous kicked anthill, and Xerxes' palanquin was lost amid the seething confusion of the battlefield. But from somewhere closer, she could hear men's voices calling out. Whether in search or in flight, she couldn't tell.

She worked her dry mouth and kept running.

80

A few exhausted minutes later, Anna rounded one last bend in the narrowing canyon and could finally see Indy and the rest of the party waiting for her. Argos ran out to her and circled, barking in welcome until she shushed him with parched lips. Indy trotted out more slowly, but her lazily wagging tail gave her away. She stood up briefly on her hind legs to put both paws on Anna's shoulders.

"I'm so glad you made it out of there safely." Then Indy shoved off hard enough to make Anna take a step back. "But don't ever do that again! I was about to have a heart attack, watching you slither your way through a battle, then bound off like a jackrabbit."

"Pretty cool, eh?" Anna looked unrepentant. "I worked that out—" She paused, panting heavily. "I worked that out with Alixa after what happened with those pirates near Corinth. It just doesn't last long." She pulled her shield projector from under her belt and pressed it against her phone to recharge, her hands shaking with fatigue and adrenaline. "My shield's about tapped." She looked back over her shoulder. "And we need to keep moving. I left Hylas' men some way back, but who knows how fast they can run."

The party started off at a quick walk, which was about all Anna could handle after running so far already. She gratefully swigged from Melas' proffered waterskin as they went, catching her breath between swallows as Indy and Argos took the lead.

"I wish you had not gone off on your own." The big man looked at her gravely as she handed him back the waterskin. "Our goal here is a worthy one, but not worth your life. You could easily have been killed down there."

"You're right." Anna looked down. "And I'm sorry for blocking you guys earlier. I just couldn't stand the thought of any of you getting yourselves killed coming after me."

"Some of us have enough sense not to go for a joyride on freaking Xerxes' own party platform." Themis smiled sardonically, giving Anna a brief side-hug as they tried to keep up their pace. "Did it at least work?"

"As far as I know." Anna worked her phone where it lay on top of her shield projector, holding the two together like a sandwich as the shield slowly recharged. "Alixa says that most of the fly-drones made it out of my cloak, so they should be hitting the far sides of the army pretty soon."

Phaia held up her phone from Anna's other side. "I know you had other things to worry about while you were getting out of there. But take a look. You made it just in time."

She wound the video back to before Anna's escape, then advanced it quickly. In jerky double-time the Persian vanguard was surrounded. Their retreat slowed, then halted entirely. The Immortals fought with suicidal bravery, but now they were cut off, hemmed in by sharp swords and spears that their armor couldn't turn aside, and they died by the hundreds. Blood soaked the ground and ran out between the feet of the oncoming Greeks to stream down the marshy shore as the fight wore on, oozing more slowly now as the video caught back up to the present.

"Aren't the Persians going to surrender?" Anna swallowed uneasily as she pushed herself to walk faster. "They're never going to get out of there."

"There is too much history behind this conflict," Melas said, his longer legs making their brisk pace look easy. "When one side gets an advantage, they are unlikely to give it up, even if the other side sues for mercy." His big shoulders drooped. "Remember, in your history, the Persians killed every Greek defender and burned Athens to the ground." He paused. "Today, we may see the opposite happen."

Anna scrolled around frantically on her own phone, looking for she didn't know what. "There must be something we—"

"I'm sorry, little sister." Indy didn't look back, but her voice brimmed with regret. "The die is cast. There's nothing we can do now but bear witness."

On the screen of Anna's phone, the distant armies continued their clash, the noises of battle tinny with distance, and dull since only one side fought with hard metal. She let the phone and shield projector sandwich drop to her side, stumbling as she tried to keep pace with the others.

"This will be hard to watch." Indy cast a quick glance behind her to make sure everyone was staying close. "I believe we did the right thing, throwing in with the Greeks to prevent this invasion. But many men will die today. Men whose only crime was being drafted into Xerxes' army."

"I know." Anna felt sick. "I know we made the best decision we could. It's just…" She stopped walking for a moment, her exhausted body briefly shutting down. "It's just hard knowing that all these people are dying because of *us*." A tear tracked its way slowly down her cheek as she fought her way back into motion.

"We've got trouble." Themis' voice was tense, her eyes still locked to her phone as she walked. "Look at what's happening back here." She held up her phone to show a view of the bulk of the Persian army, back past where Xerxes' guards were locked in their doomed last stand against the Greeks.

Red icons marked where the Persian forces, formerly concentrated, had burst apart in a disorganized rout. Many small groups had flung aside their useless, crumbling armor and were fleeing with desperate speed in all directions, crowding into every hidden pass and canyon, including the one they were fleeing along.

"Uh oh." Anna scrolled around her map, fingers trembling with tension and weariness. "But the way we're going already leads pretty straight inland. If we turn off of it, we might even end up behind the bad guys."

"I agree." Indy nodded after looking at the map. "Staying ahead of them looks like our only chance." She gave Anna a worried look. "But you're already tired."

"You guys need to go ahead." Anna guiltily sped her walk again, but she was almost done in. "If I hear someone coming, I'll just hide in the trees or something."

"Not going to happen," Indy said. "Lean against me, I can take some of your weight."

The six of them moved on for several more minutes. The humans in the party were sweating in the warm midday air, but Indy moved easily even while supporting Anna, and Argos spent most of his time waiting for the rest of them to catch up.

"Losing our lead." Phaia frowned at her phone, gauging the distances involved. "Desperate men run fast."

"Sorry Anna, but we need to pick up speed." Indy was looking back up the canyon, toward Thermopylae. "And I'm pulling one of the drones in to shadow us more closely. We're tracking dozens of little fleeing groups, but we've still got far too many blind spots back there."

Anna gritted her teeth for one final effort as the humans broke into a trot, Themis tightening the straps of her pack so it didn't slap against her back. Indy and Argos loped along, easily keeping pace.

Persian group 6-A will overtake our party in five minutes at current speed. Alixa's voice sounded loud in Anna's head, not masked at all by her strenuous breathing. She looked over at Indy, whose eyes showed that her collar net had just told her the same thing.

"These guys aren't turning off." Themis looked up from her phone, panting as she trotted. "And they're gaining on us."

"To stay ahead of running men, we would need to run ourselves." Melas didn't sound out of breath at all, despite his bulk.

"If we do, and they catch us anyway, we'll be too tired to even put up a fight." Phaia looked grim. "And Anna can't make it much further."

"You're right." Indy stopped abruptly, Argos pulling up beside her. "New plan."

Anna looked as though she wanted to object, but was too winded to speak. She stood bent over, hands on her knees, trying to catch her breath.

Indy pulled her stunner from its holster with her mouth, flipped it in the air, and offered it to Phaia butt-first. "This is a weapon. Touch the metal end to someone, and they'll be knocked unconscious." She looked over at Anna. "Anna, give yours to Themis, so the weakest of us will have some defense if this goes wrong."

"Hey, I'm not *that* weak." But Themis took the proffered stunner despite her objection. She looked it over closely, taking care not to touch the business end.

"It knows… not to stun any of us." Anna straightened up, still breathing heavily, and touched the end of the stunner in Themis' hands to demonstrate. "It fires based on your body language. So make sure to… give it a good poke when you use it." Themis nodded her understanding.

Indy pointed down the canyon a few yards, where a small stand of trees eked out a living in the rocky soil. "We'll cower over there and let this group of Persians go past before we start running again. The drone says there are only eight or so of them, and they're running for their lives without any metal weapons. They've got better things to do than stop and engage with Greek civilians."

"What if they *do* decide to 'engage'?" Melas might have been posing a geometry question back at their school for the lack of fear in his voice.

"They can't stop for long, or they risk getting caught themselves by the Greeks that are chasing them. And Anna and I have hidden defenses that should be able to keep them away from us." Indy paced over to the trees as she talked. "Just stay close and they won't be able to touch us."

Themis looked skeptically at Anna. "How the hell does *that* work?"

"This little box here." Anna separated her shield projector from her phone and showed it to Themis before dropping it down the back of her sweaty chiton and awkwardly working it into its normal place above her belt. "It's how I slipped through all those soldiers before. It can push things away from us." Her brows knit with concern. "For a while. I used up most of its power getting away, and it's only had a few minutes to charge."

"One minute until Persian group 6-A overtakes this position." Alixa's voice came from Anna's phone now, where she'd directed it so the Greeks could hear.

"We're out of time." Indy walked a few feet through the trees to stand against the canyon wall. "Anna, don't waste your shield power holding anyone in place, just deflect them if they try to touch us. Everyone else, stay close."

"One moment." Melas stepped over to a dead tree, gripped a huge branch in his powerful hands, and wrenched it free, pulling down with all his considerable weight. He broke the narrow end off under one sandaled foot to shorten it, then smashed it against the canyon wall a few times to test its strength, muscles bunching under his chiton as he swung the formidable weapon. "Just in case." Themis tapped her stunner against his makeshift club in a grim salute.

Indy planted her shoulder firmly against Argos' as they looked back up the canyon with feral intensity. Her ears rotated forward, followed by his an instant later. Then a motley group of fleeing soldiers, Persian mixed with a few Greek supporters, came around the bend in the canyon only a few yards distant, running hard.

Most were archers, wearing wicker armor sewn over thick cotton. A few were spearmen, their armor mostly broken off or hanging in pieces, carrying only the heavy shafts of their spears now that their heads had shattered in the fighting or their subsequent flight. There were about twelve men in all, a few more than their spy-drone had seen from overhead.

One archer drew an arrow from his hip quiver and fired on the run in one smooth motion. The arrow struck Melas squarely in the chest, but bounced off the shield which Indy and Anna had extended to protect their party. Melas rubbed his chest in surprise as the arrow ricocheted away with a *thunk*, the metal arrowhead broken and crumbling in flight. "Very effective."

Another two archers loosed arrows at them, with similar results. The running men seemed puzzled, and slowed in their headlong flight, but there wasn't much time for them to think about it. In moments, they were streaming past, glancing sidelong at their party, but apparently willing to leave them be in favor of a quick escape. Anna released her fists, which she had unconsciously clenched at her sides, and started to relax. *It's working!*

Two stragglers came around the bend, a little behind the others, out of breath and red-faced. The first one must have discarded his embroidered cape and helmet for speed, though he was still weighed down by the remnants of his elaborate metal armor, and he carried a silver-plated sword hilt uselessly in one hand. When he raised one hand to pull off his skewed arming cap, Anna recognized him instantly.

"Hylas has joined Persian group 6-A, along with a retainer." Alixa's voice sounded from Anna's phone where she'd forgotten to silence it.

"Of *course* he has," Anna groaned in despair.

Indy's lips skinned back from her teeth, and Argos stared hard at Hylas and his man in challenge, picking up on her hostility.

Hylas' eyes lit in triumph as he saw Anna and Indy's party, and he slowed his flight. "Back here!" His voice carried the crack of command, and the rearmost of the fleeing Persians and Greeks turned obediently to rejoin him, calling out to the others as they did so. He pointed at Anna, speaking to the most senior of the Persian soldiers. "She doesn't look like much, but she's worth a king's ransom back in the empire. Enough to erase the shame of desertion, and more."

"Long way to drag a prisoner, with only the two of you." The head Persian's skepticism shaded into calculation as he looked over the rest of Anna's party, most of them seemingly weaponless and carrying large packs that he didn't know were nearly empty.

"But we will need supplies if we're going to survive long enough to escape this cursed land."

Argos growled low at that, hungry as he was from his accelerated growth.

"Move on." Indy's voice boomed from her collar in Persian. "There's nothing for you here, and the Greeks are closing in on you."

The head Persian soldier didn't show any surprise at a talking dog. *Maybe he didn't realize who was talking,* Anna thought.

"Strip their packs quickly and continue our retreat," the head Persian said to the rest of the men who had come back to rejoin him. He cocked a thumb at Hylas and his man. "Hand over the girl to our allies here, and leave the rest of them. Sorry about this," he said to Melas, apparently assuming the largest of them was in charge. "But you'll probably survive if you drop that club."

One of the Persian spearmen approached Argos and Indy, who bared their huge canines in challenge, but remained in place. The man thought better of it and reached for Phaia instead. She instinctively jabbed him in the hand with her stunner, and he fell to the ground with a strangled cry and lay still, tongue protruding slightly between his teeth.

"The hell?" A second Persian swung at Phaia with his spear shaft, but it bounced harmlessly off their shared shield. He swung again, harder, and cursed this time as the rebound stung his hands. "Captain?"

"This is why she's worth so much," Hylas said. "But there are limits to her power. She barely managed to outrun me here. She can't have much left."

"We'll attack all together." The Persian captain cast a shrewd eye at the stunners Phaia and Themis held. "Whatever they're doing, it can't hold us all off. And watch those cudgels of theirs, they must be poisoned." He stared hard at Phaia. "You'll regret killing that man."

"I didn't poison him, you idiot! He's just stunned." But Phaia spoke in Greek, which the captain apparently didn't understand.

In moments, their party was surrounded. The spearmen swung

their heavy shafts at Indy and Argos, who snarled and barked their defiance but held their positions, while the archers pelted the rest of them with arrows. The air filled with curses and flying fragments of arrowheads. One Persian's hand came away from his face bloody after a spinning chunk of metal hit him, and another barely missed being punched in the throat by a rebounding arrow shaft. But they redoubled their attack, screaming indecipherable battle cries now that their blood was up.

"Shield projector failure imminent," Alixa announced.

Anna silenced her with an inward curse. They'd never had the chance to fully re-fab Anna's shield after their encounter with Hylas, and even at their best, two personal shields couldn't withstand a sustained assault from a dozen strong men for long. Plus, Anna's shield had been mostly depleted before the first shot was fired, since it would have taken hours more to fully recharge after her earlier escape from Thermopylae.

Themis and Phaia traded worried looks, and Melas lifted his club to one shoulder. One of the Persians, who must have understood some Greek, ran to their leader and spoke in his ear. They redoubled their attack, and now Anna could feel the shield at her back heating up again, worse than it ever had before. Hylas stood behind the Persians with his man, a look of glee on his face.

Thermal runaway. Remove shield projector immediately. As Alixa spoke, Anna could feel one side of the projector flare red-hot. She loosened her belt frantically, trying to drop the projector out of the clinging folds of her chiton before it burned the skin off her back. The sounds of the spear and arrow impacts on their shield dropped in pitch as Indy's projector took on the entire load by itself. But it couldn't last for much longer.

"Everyone!" Indy's voice rang out, amplified by the collar to sound over the din of battle. "Ready to attack! In three! Two! One!"

Anna scurried behind Melas, tightening her belt again, her shield projector charring the fabric of her chiton where it hung, tangled, near her feet. She shook it smoking out onto the ground and faced the Persians, weaponless.

In front of her, Melas voiced a gravelly scream, an incongruous sound from the quiet smith, and charged the nearest Persian spearman. One mighty swing of Melas' makeshift club smashed the man from his feet, his spear shaft falling from nerveless fingers as his head hit the ground with a sickening crunch. Melas dropped the broken club and snatched up the Persian's spear shaft, reversing it so he swung the heavy silver-clad butt of the weapon, and laid about him with terrifying force, the thick spear shaft bending with the strain.

Themis and Phaia kept their backs to the canyon wall, menacing the Persians with their stunners, but not venturing out where they could be surrounded. Phaia cursed as an arrow punched into her gut, but by now these were recovered arrows with the heads crumbled off, so they couldn't bite deeply. She pulled it bloody from her midsection and cast it aside.

Indy lunged forward and wrested the spear from another Persian, throwing it back near Themis and Phaia where it couldn't be reached without braving their stunners, and shrugged off arrow impacts as she pounded the unlucky spearman to the ground with her heavy paws. But it was only a matter of time until the Persians overcame them all by main force, and then, outnumbered two to one, the fight would be quickly over.

Argos *roared*, his voice as deep and menacing as a lion's, and ran suddenly toward the canyon wall at full speed. He leapt as high up on the wall as he could, claws scrabbling for more height, then bunched his hind paws against it and jumped off, stretching to his full length as he sailed over the heads of the startled Persians. He landed, legs bent, behind the Persians and directly in front of Hylas, who fetched him a blow on the muzzle with his heavy sword hilt.

Argos shook off the hit, drops of blood flying from his mouth. He shot forward, trying to catch Hylas' sword arm in his teeth. Hylas swiftly pulled his arm back to deliver another blow with the hilt, but Argos had only feinted at the sword arm, and as Hylas swung, Argos seized the other forearm in his mighty jaws, teeth sinking deep into flesh.

Hylas pounded Argos in the side with his free hand, the heavy sword hilt thudding into unprotected ribs, but Argos held on, snarling, and a moment later Hylas gasped in pain as his left hand dangled limply, tendons severed by Argos' teeth. He tried for another swing with the sword hilt, but now Argos released the left arm and grabbed the right one, breaking it with a twist of his thick neck that had his whole body weight behind it. Argos released the broken arm, and Hylas staggered to his knees.

Then Argos lunged for the kill.

"Remember! Break the arms, but leave the legs for them to run!" Indy's voice rang out. But Argos didn't hear, and in any case he was going for the throat.

Beside them, Hylas' retainer had finally overcome his surprise and horror at Argos' charge, and drawn his own sword. Unlike Hylas', this sword still had its steel blade, and the man swung it hard overhand, desperate to save his master's life.

The blade smashed into Argos' skull, shattering into dozens of crumbly chunks of nano-degraded metal. But despite that, it was a heavy blow. Argos slumped to all fours, then to the ground, blood drooling from his muzzle.

"*Argos!*" Indy's voice came as a deafening shout from her collar, paired with an anguished howl from her deep chest. She charged through the archers who had witnessed the brief conflict between Argos and Hylas, scattering them like chickens, and bowled Hylas right off his knees, sending him skidding across the rocky ground, useless arms flailing and bloody. She stood protectively over Argos' unmoving form, facing down Hylas' retainer as the archers quickly re-formed, firing their headless shafts which eventually would find a vulnerable eye or throat.

Then there came the bright ring of undamaged metal swords leaving their scabbards, as a half-dozen Greek soldiers charged down the canyon from the north and laid into the Persians with triumphant shouts. Wicker and cloth armor were no match for sharp steel, and blood fountained as the Persians were cut down without mercy. Hylas tried to stagger to his feet from where Indy had pushed him, eyes glazed with pain from his savaged arms, but he was stabbed in the back by a Greek short spear and trampled in the pursuit of his comrades.

One Greek soldier ran over to the man Phaia had stunned, quickly checked his pulse, then efficiently cut his throat with a dagger. Phaia and Themis stared, horrified, as the Greek soldier spoke to them.

"What the hell are you idiots doing so close to a battle?" He wiped the dagger on the dead man's clothes and sheathed it. "You need to get out of here, now!" He rose and joined the pursuit of the fleeing Persians, leaving Anna, Indy, and their party stunned and wounded.

"Argos!" Indy desperately pushed at Argos' face with her muzzle, but his head lolled bonelessly on his neck. "Don't you dare leave me!" She leaned close, trying to hear if he was still breathing. Anna ran over, feeling under Argos' thick ruff for a pulse at his throat.

For a long, tense moment, she couldn't find it. But then there it was, strong under her fingers. Anna looked up at Indy. "He's alive."

"Still alive!" Argos' voice sounded small and dazed from his collar.

Indy licked him all over the face, fear and hope mixed in her voice. "If you die, I swear I'll bite you so hard your dam will feel it!"

Argos groaned, then opened his eyes. He stretched, then winced and lay still again. "Just need a minute," he said to Indy's worried look.

"Argos, look at my hand." Anna moved it back and forth in front of his eyes. "Both his eyes are moving together, at least. And the pupils are the same size." She looked worried. "But I'm not a doctor."

Argos groaned again, then slowly rolled upright. He panted, but held steady. "Head hurts."

"Of course it hurts, dummy. You might have a concussion." Indy examined his broad skull. "At least your head's still the right shape, and it's not bleeding. Rest for a moment." She looked around at the rest of their party. "How's everyone else?"

"Big guy's okay." Themis looked up from her examination of

Melas' back, where he'd taken a hit protecting her after her stunner failed to drop one of the archers through his thick cotton armor. "Or at least not leaking vital juices."

Melas grimaced as he rotated the arm on that side. "Nothing seems to be grinding. I call that good enough, after a fight like that." He exhaled, and his features paled for a moment before he steadied himself.

Themis gave the big man a sympathetic smile. "I know this probably brought back some memories you'd rather forget." She clapped him on the other shoulder. "But thanks. If you hadn't been here…" Her smile faded. "Well, I'm just glad you were."

Anna looked over at Hylas' body, lying facedown a few feet away. "What about him?" Sprawled ungracefully in death, he looked nothing like the murderous nemesis who'd almost succeeded in snuffing out both their lives.

"He chose this path." Indy walked forward and shook the dust of battle out of her coat. "He chased you all the way out here to try to recapture you and sell you to the Persians." Her voice was hard as stone. "He's lucky Argos or I didn't finish him first."

"Not pretty seeing anyone die like that," Phaia said. "But I'm glad he's gone."

Anna looked at Hylas again, then at the bodies of the other soldiers who'd attacked them. She nodded tightly, but said nothing.

"Time to leave." Indy looked around, then back at Anna. "There could easily be another group of Persians coming that the drones can't spot under these trees. And the rest of Hylas' men are probably still looking for you, scouting all the side canyons you passed on the way here." She checked her collar net. "Our spy-drone says the way is clear in front of us for the moment." Argos levered himself to his paws beside her with a grunt, drooling blood from one side of his muzzle, but standing tall. "We'll have to move slowly, but we need to get out of here while we can."

"What she said." Phaia pressed a hand to the bloody wound in her midsection. "Next arrow might have a head on it."

87

ounded and bleeding, they fled at a walk.

Occasionally the spy-drone that Indy had overflying them would give an alert, and they'd wait in place for a while, or move off one path and onto another, avoiding pursuing Greeks and fleeing Persians alike. Steady updates about the battle at Thermopylae came to them via the other two spy-drones in relay.

Anna glanced at her phone. Xerxes' surrounded Immortals were still fighting hard, miles to the north of them on the narrow, marshy ground of their last stand. Elsewhere on the battlefield, Greek soldiers had pushed the rest of the Persian forces back across the Spercheios River and were harrying them mercilessly. The bulk of the Persian army was struggling to retreat back along the coast the way they had come, but there were too many of them to move quickly, and the rear of their army was being shredded by the victorious Greeks.

Anna switched Alixa to summary mode and tucked her phone away under her belt, feeling sick and unwilling to witness more slaughter. "Summary mode activated," came Alixa's voice. Indy moved closer to listen, since she couldn't hold her own screen as she walked. The Greeks did likewise, though Themis continued watching events on her phone at the same time. Argos just concentrated on putting one paw in front of the other, holding his injured head stiffly as he walked as quickly as he could, which wasn't very.

"Primary marker 'Xerxes' surrounded by Greek forces," Alixa said. "Secondary marker 'Peisistratos' fleeing the battlefield at the rear of the Persian army."

"I really don't want to hear any more." Anna swallowed uneasily at the reminder of Hylas' father. "But I feel like I need to."

"We both made this decision." Indy looked over as she walked. "It's not just on you."

"Plenty of blame to go around." Phaia grimaced as she pressed a folded cloth against the arrow wound in her midsection. "And we're not out of danger yet. Let's not beat ourselves up too hard until we've survived this."

They all walked a little faster after that.

A few more minutes passed before Alixa spoke again. "Xerxes' defensive circle broken," her dispassionate voice narrated. "Xerxes mortally wounded." A few tense seconds passed. "Xerxes dead. Shifting drone focus to secondary marker."

"I did *not* need to see that." Themis put her phone away, looking green. "Golden armor may be good against fly-drones, but it can't stop a half-dozen iron spearheads through the brisket. Sorry, boss," she added at Anna's stricken look. "He went down fighting, I'll give him that."

"The empire will survive him, as it did his father." Melas was holding one arm still as he walked, trying not to flex the side of his back where he'd been struck by a heavy spear-shaft earlier. "Xerxes' older half-brother Artobazan will likely claim the throne when word of Xerxes' death reaches them." He looked thoughtful. "Perhaps he will not be as vengeful as his brother was."

The party continued in silence for a while, but their injuries and the fatigue from their brief but intense skirmish were taking a toll. Argos' head drooped lower and lower as they walked, and after a few more miles, Indy couldn't bear to push him any further.

"Argos needs to stop and rest." She looked at his panting face with concern.

Argos struggled to raise his head higher. "Plenty strong." Bloody saliva drooled from his open mouth. "Keep going. Finish. Quest."

"No, dummy." Indy's voice was tight with fear. "You're still in the middle of uplift. You could kill yourself if you push too hard." Her collar lights twinkled briefly. "There's a bit of shelter over this way. And our drones can't see any more Persian stragglers. If any are still out there, they've probably circled west and north by now to try to get out of Greece."

"I could use a rest as well," Melas said.

"And some food," Themis added.

"Food?" Argos perked up briefly, then hung his head again, panting with pain.

"We'll get you some food. Just a few more minutes." Indy led the party off the trail they'd been following, and shortly they entered a sheltering grove of trees. Argos slumped gratefully to the ground in the shade, and Indy hovered anxiously as Anna unclipped his harness and made him comfortable. She poured water from a bottle in her pack into his collapsible bowl, and he drank it all steadily, then lay down again, still panting.

Melas sank down with a groan, supporting himself with the arm on his uninjured side. "One of my ribs may have been fractured in the back." He eased out of his pack and pulled out his own water bottle. "It seems to be swelling up, but I do not think it is broken."

Anna dug into her pack and came out with two pills. "Fast-healing pills." She handed one to Melas. "Wash it down with water. It wouldn't be enough for something life-threatening, but it should help you feel a little better." She handed the other pill to Phaia. "Take this, and I'll check your wound over."

"It's not that deep." Phaia held up the cloth she'd had pressed against it. It wasn't soaked with blood, which seemed like a good sign.

Anna looked at the puncture in the other woman's lower belly, which was puckered closed but bruised from the impact of the blunt arrow shaft. "The pill should keep it from getting infected, at least. We'll check for internal injury once we're home tomorrow."

She couldn't meet Phaia's eyes. "I'm so sorry this happened. You warned us how risky this plan was."

"I'll survive." Phaia's voice was gruff. "I owed you, for saving me before. And I chose to be here, you didn't make me come along." She looked around. "How's Argos doing? Does he need one of these pills? He got it the worst."

Indy looked up from where she was licking Argos' muzzle clean. "His lips are cut up on the inside, from that first hit with Hylas' sword hilt. But nothing seems to be broken." She looked him over critically. "His uplift treatment will naturally accelerate healing better than our pills would, but we need to get a lot of food into him for it to work."

"So let's do that, then." Anna stood, legs aching in the aftermath of their long flight, and walked over to Argos' saddlebags to hunt through them for something for him to eat.

"Secondary marker 'Peisistratos' re-acquired." Alixa's voice was loud in the quiet of their grove. "Peisistratos captured by victorious Greek forces while attempting to flee the battlefield."

"Serves that traitor right." Phaia smiled without joy. "But they'll probably just ransom him back to Persia." She looked thoughtful. "Though they might confiscate his estates, now that Hylas is gone."

Anna finished laying out food for Argos, her movements slowed by exhaustion, then pulled out her phone as he began to eat. The viewpoint of the spy-drone image was immovable now, since there was only one drone left close enough to the battle to see it. But Anna could clearly see Hylas' father Peisistratos the Younger, battered now after his capture, and missing his helmet and weapons, but still defiant.

"Peisistratos argues that he should be allowed to go into exile," Alixa said.

"Alixa, why can't we hear them?" Anna asked.

"Distance exceeds audio pickup range," Alixa said. "Event reconstruction by facial and postural analysis. Unknown Greek general denies exile request," she continued.

On the screen, Peisistratos was forced to his knees by their captors. He yelled something they couldn't hear as the nameless Greek general drew his short sword, stepped forward, and stabbed him in the chest. Anna turned away, horrified.

"Peisistratos executed by Greek general," Alixa said. "Tracking of secondary marker ended. Summary mode concluded."

Anna put her phone away, numb and dizzy. Even Phaia looked shaken, her jaded expectation of his ransom erased by the shock of seeing him die. Argos, oblivious to what had been happening around him, finished the last of his food and laid his head down, instantly asleep.

"Greek generals have the power of capital punishment during war." Melas spoke quietly into the silence. "Even against citizens. Peisistratos was just unlucky. If he had been captured by a greedier man, he could very well have been sent back into exile again."

"He damn well deserved it." Phaia's expression was grim. "But that was hard to see."

"He made the choice to come in on the Persian side," Indy said from where she sat beside Argos' sleeping form. "If they had won, he probably would've lobbied to make Hylas the local Persian overlord here. Then we would've been on the run from the government as well as the Persian army."

"Remember what Hylas said to me?" Anna looked down, shamefaced. "That if I killed him, I'd be making his wife a widow, his daughters orphans?" Her relief that Hylas was finally gone mixed uneasily with her guilt over the consequences to his family. "I was so proud of myself for sparing him, after that. You helped me do the right thing." She rubbed at her face with one hand. "And now..."

Indy stood up and walked over to Anna, leaning against her to lend her comfort. "We did the best we could." The big canine looked around sadly at their wounded party. "We probably will have saved many lives here. In the long run." She looked aside. "But I wish we hadn't had to make those choices. What gives us the right?"

After that, there wasn't much to say. Anna, Indy and the three Greeks ate a cold dinner and lay down early to bed, but none of them found sleep easily.

82

The next day dawned, unaware of the thousands who had died the day before.

Anna awoke beside Indy's warm bulk and lay there for a moment, spirits sinking as the events of the previous day rushed back into her mind. Forcing down dread, she sat up and pulled out her phone to check the aftermath of the battle. She deliberately avoided zooming in too closely, but it was clear that thousands of Persians and not a few Greeks lay dead on the field. Especially heartbreaking were the horses and pack animals which had been caught in the fighting, now staring sightless into the cloudy sky.

Indy shifted beside her and opened her eyes. They shared a look.

We did what we thought we had to, Anna said over their link. *What we thought was right. But this still feels awful.*

It does, Indy thought back. *I truly believe it would have been much worse if we'd let the Persians invade, or used some terrible weapon from the old days on them. We probably saved tens of thousands of lives, preventing the sacking of Athens. Hundreds of thousands, maybe. But we'll never know for sure.*

I'm glad you were here with me, Anna said. *There's no way I could've got through this by myself.*

We're in this together, Indy said. *All the way.*

Anna breathed deeply, trying to get her equilibrium back. Then she swiped the battlefield images away and checked their spy-drone's summary report of the events since the previous afternoon. After killing Xerxes and pursuing the remnants of his army for some distance around the gulf, the exhausted Greeks had withdrawn behind their wall at Thermopylae and rested, while their auxiliary forces hunted through the hills to the north looking for Persian forces that had fled the field.

A good portion of the Greek fleet had hauled out nearby after defeating or driving off the Persian fleet near Artemision. Video pulled from the few fly-drones left onboard showed that they hadn't been quite as decisive a factor in the sea battle, since many of the tiny drones had been blown away by the sea winds before they could find their targets. But their nano-motes had destroyed the bronze rams of several of the Persian ships along with the metal weapons of some of their occupants, and that had swung the battle in favor of the Greek navy. Now, marines from the beached ships helped stiffen the Greek lines against a possible counterattack by the still-vast remnants of the Persian army. But after Xerxes' death and the defeat of the Immortals, the Persian forces seemed to have no more taste for combat, and were in continued retreat as the sun rose.

"They must have got word of the sea battle, so they know we can land troops behind them at will. I can't blame them for wanting to get out of here." Themis looked back to her phone's screen, which showed a few opportunistic Greek captains coming ashore amid the Persian army, relying on their superior arms and armor to strike quickly and withdraw without being encircled.

"I wonder what those ships are thinking." Indy sounded subdued as she munched at her breakfast of hard travel bread and sausage, offering any extra bits to Argos, who'd already finished his. "They've won. Why risk these new attacks?"

"Spoils of war." Phaia's face was grim. "Looks like they figured out that your magical metal-destroying bugs don't affect precious metals." She zoomed her phone in and pointed. "They're looting the gold and silver pomegranates from the Immortals' spear-butts, and anything else that looks worth stealing."

Anna gritted her teeth, feeling a surge of guilt and anger well up in her. "We did this to save Greece from getting invaded, not so a few jerks could get rich!" She poked at her phone. "There are still fly-drones out there with a bit of power left. Maybe we should see how those Greeks like being defenseless!" Her finger hovered over her phone's surface.

"As much as I hate to say it, that's probably not wise." Indy spoke sadly but calmly. "The Persians still outnumber the Greeks by a huge margin. If we take away some of the Greek advantage, it could have an unpredictable effect."

Anna seethed. "It burns me to see those pirates running in and killing defenseless people, just so they can grab some loot."

"Me too, boss," Themis said. "Dirty deeds like that are how we get into all these damn wars in the first place." She thought for a moment. "Can we tell the fly-drones to drop off of the Persians and onto the Greeks if they go beyond the battlefield? Then if any Greeks pursue that far, they'll see some of their own weapons getting eaten. Maybe that'd scare them out of chasing further."

Anna sighed. "That sounds like a safer idea." After looking around for assent, she punched the relevant commands into her phone. "I just wish we could have done something where not so many people got killed." She looked heartsick. "The Persians were supposed to retreat!"

"You spoke to Xerxes yourself. He would never have left without a stinging defeat." Melas said gently. "And defeats cost lives."

"Unfortunately, we don't have the power to simply keep two armies apart." Indy leaned protectively against Argos, where he lay in his usual post-meal slumber. She hadn't left his side since he'd been injured the day before.

"Even if you did have that power," Melas said, "you would be fighting against human nature. Wars happen for a reason! One man covets the land or belongings of another, so he kills the other man and takes them." He looked at his own mighty forearms as he spread his burn-scarred hands before him, pain from his injury flickering across his face. "There will always be those who ask themselves, 'Why shouldn't I?'" He looked haunted. "And, 'Who can stop me?'"

Phaia stood and dusted her hands. "The doctors I know say to treat the disease, not the symptoms. But if war is just a symptom, then the disease must be more than anyone can cure." She bent to pick up her pack, light now that all their fly-drones were gone, and winced as her belly wound was compressed. "We did well. I'm no friend of Athens, but seeing the size of that Persian army, I'm glad they won't be ending up on our doorstep."

Their subdued little group took almost the same path back to Lebadeia as they had traveled before, though more slowly in deference to their injuries and Anna's exhaustion. As they passed back through Orchomenos on the western shore of Lake Kopais they could see that the news of the Persian defeat had beaten them there. The sun was beginning to set as they arrived, but Anna could still see the odd Boeotian soldier showing off a piece of looted Persian gear, or telling the tale of the Greek victory with much excitement and waving of hands.

"Look at that." Themis pointed discreetly to where a man with the look of a smith stood talking with one of the returned soldiers. The soldier was showing off small pieces of Persian metal armor. As they passed, the soldier crumbled a part of it off in his fingers, to the smith's intense interest.

"In a couple of weeks, every metal-head in the whole country will be puzzling over this," Themis said once they were well past the pair. She shot Indy an inquiring look. "Can they suss out any of your secret knowledge from those shards?"

"No." Indy sounded certain. "Our nano-motes weaken metal by joining and extending the microscopic flaws in its crystalline structure. But if you were to melt down the shards and re-forge them, they'd be as good as new."

"I still want the full story on how that works, by the way," Themis added.

"You'll have it," Indy said.

Phaia eyed the setting sun. "You all want to press on, or find a place to camp? It's about eight more miles if we bypass Lebadeia on the way back home."

Anna looked around at the others. "My feet are killing me, but I'd rather sleep in my own bed tonight."

"Agreed." Argos spoke unexpectedly from beside Indy. "My paws are strong, always," he said proudly. "But my head hurts. Tired of sleeping in mud."

Indy laughed. "Take a dog out of the sheepfold for a few months, and now he's too good to sleep on the ground." She butted Argos affectionately with her shoulder, then cringed as he winced with pain. "Sorry!" But in truth, Argos had barely wobbled with the impact. He'd grown visibly larger during their trip, though their travel rations had left him lean as a wolf under his heavy fur.

"I vote to move on." Themis plucked at her chiton. "I'd smooch a Gorgon right in her snaky chops for a bath right now. I don't even want to think what I smell like."

The group continued their weary walk, pressing on into the hills past Lebadeia until finally, long after sunset, they stood on their school's front doorstep again. A small lantern shone reassuringly in the window, and after a few knocks, one of the assistant cooks unbolted the door and greeted them warmly.

"You got here just in time." The girl helped Melas remove his pack after seeing him struggle due to his bruised back, while the rest of them set aside their own gear and stretched exhausted limbs. "Some of us were having a late dinner, talking over the news." She laid Melas' pack against the wall with the others. "You look tired. Come and have some hot food, then get to bed." Her eyes sparkled. "We've got some good news, too. You'll never believe what happened at Thermopylae!"

83

The next day, Anna awoke with a smile—no school! That meant she could sleep in a little. Her smile faded as she remembered the events of the last few days. But it didn't disappear altogether. She was home, and she was alive, and so were her friends.

Okay, so I slept in more than a little. The sun was high outside, and a quick look at her phone revealed that it was almost eleven o'clock. Apparently, run-walking across half of northern Greece could tire you out.

She had slept on damp hair after a late-night shower in their hidden quarters, so she spent a few minutes trying to brush it into shape. At last, she just gave up and pulled it into a ponytail. Then she went out to face the day.

She found the others, except for Indy and Argos, already at lunch. She waved hello, then went back to the kitchen to see what was left to eat. After a minute, she emerged with some warm bread and sausage, and joined Phaia, Themis, and Melas at the table. All three looked rested, though a bandage showed at Phaia's midsection under her chiton, and all of them were covered with arrow-scrapes and odd bruises.

"So. How you feeling there, chief?" Themis spoke with a bit too much nonchalance.

"Pretty good, considering." Anna folded some bread around a piece of sausage. "I'm surprised I managed to get through our trip without blistering something, or growing mold in all that rain. Or getting killed, I guess." She took a bite of her sausage wrap. The three Greeks watched her chew.

She swallowed her food. "Okay, something's on your minds. What's up? Next semester won't start for at least a few weeks! We should all be relaxing and healing up." She took another bite, enjoying the taste of soft bread not meant for travel.

Phaia spoke first. "On our trip, you said you'd explain *everything* once it was over." She smiled. "Now it's over."

Melas' mouth quirked up in a smile. "It is a good thing you are a pharmacist and not a diplomat."

"She's just saying what we're all thinking." Themis measured Anna's uneaten breakfast with her eyes. "I'm about to pop a brain-vessel over here. She's been asleep *all morning*."

Anna smiled. "Don't worry. Indy and I haven't changed our minds." Anna looked back toward the hallway. "But Her Highness is apparently sleeping in too."

Just then Indy came through the doorway, followed closely by Argos, who looked inordinately pleased with himself. The two went back to the kitchen, Argos still padding softly to avoid jarring his sore head, and returned with bread and sausage carried in wooden bowls that they could grip easily with their mouths.

"Good morning, everyone." Indy set her bowl carefully on the tabletop, delicately plucking out a sausage and crunching it down.

Argos opened his mouth in a doggy smile, dropping his bowl on the floor in the process. Then he started eating like he hadn't seen food in a month, his injured muzzle not slowing him to any noticeable degree.

"The guys were just telling me how they're ready for some more explanations." Anna's voice was wry.

"I imagine so." Indy licked her lips. "Give us a few more minutes, though. Poor Argos here is starving." Argos had already finished his first bowl and was carrying it back to the kitchen for seconds. "It takes a lot of energy to grow like he's doing, and he didn't get to eat as much on our trip as he should have. And now he has to heal, too." She frowned. "Hopefully it won't affect the uplift process." Indy finished her breakfast, then groomed her muzzle against her forelegs as she waited for Argos to return.

Argos returned and dropped his second bowl. "After quest done. Food even more delicious!" he said through his collar as he gobbled.

Once he finished, Indy got to her feet and looked a question at Anna. Anna rose too, and the Greeks all stood up eagerly.

"Follow me!" Anna turned and led the way down the hall.

After a few moments, they arrived at the small storeroom that hid the entrance to their secret lair. It was tight, but all six of them could fit in the room at once, and after they closed the door behind them, Anna thumbed her phone to open the secret door in the blank wall in front of them. The lights in the tunnel ahead faded up, revealing the smooth stone walls and floor stretching off under the hillside.

"I wish I could say I'm surprised about this." Themis rubbed at the seam between the walls and the door, trying to figure out how they were joined. "But I've already seen so many things from you two, that secret doors and tunnels don't even rate."

Phaia snorted a laugh at that, and Melas smiled.

"All of you have the permissions to open this door now." Anna held up her phone to show the door control. "Just check here and you'll see it." She paused. "Don't let anyone see you come and go, though. Your phone will show you if anyone's outside the room, and the door won't open if anyone's too close."

Anna led the way into the tunnel, followed by the Greeks, with Indy and Argos last. Phaia brushed her fingers against the stone as they walked, but there wasn't really much to see beyond the diffuse lighting coming from the ceiling panels. After a few minutes' walk, they emerged into the living area, a cozy common room with two couches, a large screen in the wall, and a door opening into the kitchen.

"We'll come back here shortly." Indy looked around. "Though now that our little cabal has grown, we may need some more couches."

Anna smiled in response, and led the group on down the main hallway to the lab.

"Here's our lab—our workshop." Anna waved an arm. "That door over there connects to a little cave in the mountainside that we first tunneled in from. We'll explain the equipment here as you need it, or you can read about it on your phones whenever. We've got a medical scanner here too, so we'll do a quick check of everyone, to make sure nobody's hurt worse than they seem. We've set up your phones so you can read absolutely everything we have, but you can't change anything or create any dangerous stuff yet." She looked serious. "We still have to work out a system where there can be some sort of checks and balances between us when we make decisions. Just so there's some protection against one of us doing something dumb, or turning bad. Not that we think that's going to happen," Anna added quickly. "But we can do a lot of damage to people's lives if we're not careful." She looked somber. "Or even if we are careful."

Anna left the lab and walked back out into the hallway. "There's one more bit to show you, then we'll do the explanations."

As she led the Greeks further down the main hallway, it broadened out into a gallery held up by pillars, set closer and closer together as they extended off into the underground gloom. To one side, a steady stream of mining drones came and went from a gleaming structure that now surrounded the original fab they'd carried with them from the future. Thick cables snaked out of it, disappearing into the sub-ceiling of the main hallway to supply power to the rest of their rooms. Their larger and newer fab sat nearby, with beetle-drones tirelessly filling its intake hopper.

"This is the heart of our current operation." Indy walked to the front of the group and pointed her muzzle around the gallery. Argos sniffed at the line of beetle-drones on the floor, eyes darting from one drone to another as she talked. "Our economy is based on the transmutation of one kind of matter to another, and the conversion of matter to energy. These mining drones feed in raw material that they've carried back here from far under the ground, and these two boxes here take it in and covert it to whatever we need."

The big fab dinged. "Right on time." Indy's tail waved high and slow. "This one's been in the works for weeks." In front of her, the fab door opened, and a medium-sized spy-drone floated out, about the size of a melon. Themis walked forward and reached out to touch it, but then yanked her hand back. "Is it safe?"

"Totally. We wouldn't have something dangerous flying around where you could touch it." Anna pointed at the bottom of the drone, where dozens of small holes were visible. "This is like the spy-drones that we've been looking through for the past few days, but bigger. The eyes are on the bottom."

"How does it float?" Melas tapped the shell of the drone with a blunt finger. "It feels like solid metal, but it's floating like a leaf on the water."

"Indy's the expert on that stuff." Anna laughed. "But it'll probably take a while to explain it all."

Indy nodded. "I'll teach you everything you want to know about it. You have access to all our knowledge on your phones now, but it's hard to learn something so complex simply by reading and watching on your own. Where we come from, a student would have a full understanding of this technology after about fifteen years of secondary and tertiary education."

Melas looked daunted at this, but Themis just rubbed the drone's surface, pressing down to feel how strong its repellers were. She looked up and smiled with uncharacteristic glee. "Almost getting killed is finally paying off! I can't wait to get started."

"Okay, tour concluded!" Anna sent the drone off to its hangar with a double-slap to its side, then walked back down the gallery toward the living room. "We already told you the outline of the story on our trip. Now we'll fill in the details and answer more questions. And from then on, we'll be in this together."

She ushered the group into the living room and gestured for the three Greeks to seat themselves on the couches. They looked bemused for a moment at the unfamiliarly high backs of the furniture, compared to their own reclining couches, but then settled in expectantly. Melas sat back with a grimace as the couch pressed against his bruises, then leaned forward in his seat instead. Indy and Argos lounged on the soft carpet.

Anna thumbed her phone from where she stood, and the big screen on the wall came to life. "Here's a quick history of the world, starting from right now, through all the years up to our time, and then back to here." She considered a moment. "Alixa, could you summarize that first part out loud, and throw in some pictures and video? I'll take over once you get to my last trip to Austin."

Two hours and many questions later, Anna finished the story, then tapped her phone to darken the big screen. Her eyes burned, but after all they had seen and done, it felt like she had no tears left to shed. It had been hard to relive the final days of the old world again, especially her father's last words to her. But despite all they'd been through, she felt more hope now than sorrow, even though there'd been far more negative consequences to their actions than they'd ever expected.

The Greeks looked like they'd been worn out by the long stream of revelations. Even Melas looked like he was out of questions. He just sat, slowly shaking his head.

Phaia recovered first. "Still can't wrap my brain around this, even after hearing it twice now. Twenty-five hundred years in the future, something bad happens, the whole world is destroyed—"

"It is hard to imagine," Melas cut in. "What could possibly destroy an entire *world?*"

"—And now we have to decide what we want to do about it," Phaia continued. "You two already decided what *you* want to do," Phaia said at Anna's surprised look. "But now *we* have to decide too. It's our future just as much as yours. We've got thousands of years to go until your time, so we're only planting seeds at this point. None of us will live to see what happens." She paused. "But I saw things in your quick history that scared the hell out of me. Things *before* the world was destroyed." Phaia looked at the other

Greeks. "Do we really want to go down that path? It turned out well for them eventually—"

"Except for that world-destruction bit at the end," Themis put in.

"Except for that," Melas said. "But to Phaia's point, it seemed there was plenty of suffering before then. The Greece of the future was barely recognizable. Dried-up and rocky like a worked-out mine." He looked at Anna soberly. "I would like to steer away from that, if we can."

Anna exhaled, recovering from seeing her father's face again. "That's why we need you guys. No matter how good Indy and I are as people, we can't be the only ones deciding things this big."

"We need to *democratize* it, as the ancient Greeks might say." Indy raised an eyebrow expectantly, but the Greeks didn't get the joke, not realizing that much of their future fame was based on their role as democracy's creators. Argos twitched in his sleep beside her, where he'd dozed off during Anna's presentation.

"There'll be plenty of time to talk about voting and stuff later on." Anna put a hand on her friend's furry shoulder. "If you guys have any more questions right now, we can answer those. And we should do our quick medical check on everyone too, just in case." She paused. "But first, I vote that we get some snacks and drinks." She stood up and started toward the kitchen. "Let me introduce you to some of the traditional foods of my homeland. Starting with queso, tortilla chips, and margaritas."

ACKNOWLEDGEMENTS

used to think that this section of a book was a little weird, or even self-indulgent. Does it *really* take that many people to write a book? And who cares, anyway?

Well, now that I've written a book, I know. Yes, it does take that many people. And *I* care. Sure, it's possible to write a book completely on your own. But it's not a good idea. At least, not if you want the book to be any good. And many of the people involved get nothing but thanks in return. So a bit of gratitude can make a big difference.

I put everything I had into this book. Nobody's going to read your second book if you don't hook them with the first one, so there's no point holding anything back for the sequel. But as any real author probably could have told me, wringing every last drop of juice from your brain is only the first step. After that, you have to pound your book into a shape that someone might actually enjoy reading. And to whatever extent I've managed to do that, I owe a lot of thanks to a lot of people.

My first and last reader was, of course, my wife Su. She knows all my weaknesses and strengths better than I do, so she could tell me what I didn't want to hear but needed to hear about the story. And she knew the real Indy, in addition to being an expert in animal behavior and canine agility. She read this whole thing, twice, and covered it with great advice both times.

Next, there were my three author friends. All of whom read this gigantic manuscript, for free, during long hours that they could have spent with their families, friends, and pets. Then they spent even more hours giving me detailed notes to make it better. Robin Todd filled her printed copy with distinctive block lettering in blazing red ink, and then we spent countless evenings hashing out the philosophy of sci-fi in between watching anime, eating pizza, and drinking margaritas. Nick Pausback reminded me that actions should have unintended consequences, and that technological solutions rarely work out right the first time. And R. Zane Rutledge asked me the invaluable question, "How can you write this character so an actor would be excited to play him?"

Raquel Barela, a colleague from work, read the manuscript on her Kindle, and taught me that if you're going to make your book available on an e-reader, you'd better make sure that every obscure fact checks out, since Google is only a click away.

My moms read an early draft too, of course. It turns out that moms can only summon up the most gentle criticism of their offspring. But the book was still better for them having read it, since they gave me the confidence to keep churning away through eleven long drafts.

At last, there comes a time when you and everyone you know and love have done their utmost to create a good book. Then it's time to bring in the professionals to let you know, in the most tactful way possible, that your book still could be and must be even better. Rebecca Brewer of brewereditorialservices.com drew on her experience at Ace/Roc under the Berkley imprint at Penguin, and gave me the freedom to redo a lot of things that weren't working as well as they should have been. Apparently, first-time authors write their worst stuff at the beginning of a book, and then get attached to it, and then need someone who's seen it all before to make them aware of this. And Victoria Miller of victoriamillerartist.com proofread the whole thing, in the process demonstrating that even the most compulsive writer-engineers can still get hundreds of details of the English language wrong.

Even if it's got the best words in the world, nobody's going to buy a book that doesn't catch their eye. Fernanda Suarez came up with the cover concept, then illustrated it masterfully, turning my mish-mash of references and vague suggestions into something that looks like the great books I grew up reading. You can see more of her work at fernandasuarez.net.

And finally, Alan Dino Hebel and Ian Koviak of *the*BookDesigners did everything else that turns a Photoshop file plus a Word file into a real book. I have them to thank for the cover lettering and design, and the interior design of the book, and I can't think of enough great things to say about their work. You can find them at bookdesigners.com.

Okay, maybe that wasn't quite the end: here's to anyone I might have forgotten, as well. Your contributions are much appreciated, I just spaced on writing them down somehow. Remind me next time I see you, and I'll apologize properly over a beer!